slant of his lips over hers.

The shock of his action threw her off stride. She placed her hands on his chest, intending to push him away. Then he softened the kiss, stealing her ability to think. She sank against him, opening her mouth under his.

In the next instant she was teetering on her own feet while he strode to lean against the mantel.

Not trusting her legs to hold her, she perched on the bench of his weight equipment. She glared at him. "That was unprofessional. We're in a professional relationship. It would complicate things unnecessarily to inject a personal element into the situation."

She blinked up into his silver gaze…

HER BOSS BY ARRANGEMENT

BY
TERESA CARPENTER

MILLS & BOON

Published in Great Britain 2014
by Mills & Boon, an imprint of Harlequin (UK) Limited,
Eton House, 18-24 Paradise Road, Richmond, Surrey, TW9 1SR

© 2014 Teresa Carpenter

ISBN: 978-0-263-91316-3

23-0914

Harlequin (UK) Limited's policy is to use papers that are natural, renewable and recyclable products and made from wood grown in sustainable forests. The logging and manufacturing processes conform to the legal environmental regulations of the country of origin.

Printed and bound in Spain
by Blackprint CPI, Barcelona

Teresa Carpenter believes in the power of unconditional love, and that there's no better place to find it than between the pages of a romance novel. Reading is a passion for Teresa—a passion that led to a calling. She began writing more than twenty years ago, and marks the sale of her first book as one of her happiest memories. Teresa gives back to her craft by volunteering her time to Romance Writers of America on a local and national level.

A fifth generation Californian, she lives in San Diego, within miles of her extensive family, and knows that with their help she can accomplish anything. She takes particular joy and pride in her nieces and nephews, who are all bright, fit, shining stars of the future. If she's not at a family event you'll usually find her at home—reading, writing, or playing with her adopted Chihuahua, Jefe.

Dedicated to my twin nieces, Michelle and Gabrielle.
They call themselves wombmates
and they turn twenty-one this year.
Thanks for the inspiration. I love you both.
And may the world beware.

CHAPTER ONE

"Parking, code blue." Tori Randall heard the request for assistance from the valet station through her headset. They usually had three valets for an event of this size but one of their regulars had called in sick at the last minute, leaving them shorthanded. They were one short in the kitchen, as well. The darn flu was killing them.

"EN ROUTE," SHE RESPONDED and caught her twin sister's gaze across the open expanse of the living room from where she stood just outside on the top level of the terraced patio. Lauren nodded subtly, indicating she'd heard.

"Hey, do you see the spark between those two?" Tori gestured to a stunt coordinator and a production assistant seated on the patio, chairs pulled close so their heads nearly touched. "Love is blossoming."

Lauren's gaze touched the couple and Tori knew her twin felt it, too, the sense of knowing when two people were meant to be. It was a talent they shared.

"No meddling," Lauren cautioned, though her eyes softened. She was a sucker for true love. For everyone but herself. "We agreed to focus on the business."

"We don't meddle," Tori protested. "We introduce. I don't think we're needed in any case."

"No," Lauren agreed. "They've found each other all on their own."

"The buffet has been refreshed and new appetizers are circulating." Tori gave Lauren an update on the food. This was their first event for one of Hollywood's top directors, Ray Donovan. Everything needed to be perfect. "We're past the witching hour, so desserts are coming out in a half hour. I can use a bit of fresh air."

"Keep an eye out for Garrett Black," Lauren said.

"Are you still expecting him to show? Give it up, Lauren, he's not coming. As usual." The new head of Obsidian Studios was the newest "it" guy everyone wanted at their event. But the man was refusing to play. No surprise. He had a rep for being antisocial as a director and producer. Why should running the show make any difference?

Their company, By Arrangement, had landed a coveted contract with Obsidian Studios to organize their events at the Hollywood Hills Film Festival starting in six weeks. Lauren hoped for an opportunity for them to introduce themselves to the top dog.

"Midnight is young by Hollywood standards. My source said he was planning to attend. He and Donovan go back."

"Right." Tori rolled her eyes. But the truth was Lauren's infamous sources were uncannily correct. "I'll keep a lookout."

She still doubted they'd see the elusive Black tonight. Injured in the car accident that killed his father eleven months ago and left him as head of the fifth biggest studio in Hollywood, Garrett had been conducting business from his Santa Barbara home. Until a month ago. Gossip now had him appearing at the studio daily.

She stepped outside and breathed in the salt-tinged air. Malibu was one of her favorite places in the world. She scanned the driveway filled with world-class vehicles. All was quiet. She continued down the front steps to the valet station.

"Hey, Matt, what's the problem?" She rubbed her bare arms. The fresh ocean air was heavenly but a bit crisp in early November and the black dress she'd chosen for tonight had a halter neck, leaving her arms bare to the elements.

"Sorry, Boss, I need a quick restroom break and John is taking a car down to the church." The driveway and garage held a good number of vehicles, but for the overflow they'd made arrangements to use a church parking lot down the hill.

Matt had been out with the flu last week and looked a little pale. "Are you feeling okay?"

"Yeah, just not pushing my luck right now."

Shivering, she nodded. "No problem. I'll cover. Go ahead."

"Thanks. It's slowed down a lot so maybe no one will come along." He shrugged out of his jacket and handed it to her. "Here. I'll try to be quick." And he ran up the drive and around back to the service entrance.

She shrugged into the jacket, which was oversize but not too bad, Matt being on the smaller side. Crossing her arms, she rocked on her three-inch heels, deciding in that moment to allow the valets to use stools. What she wouldn't give to sit for a minute.

With no one around she slipped out of her black pumps. What Lauren didn't know wouldn't hurt her. Against Tori's protests, Lauren demanded they wear the punishing shoes for evening events. Of course Lauren wore the spiked torture devices for hours without flinching.

Tori flexed her sore toes. She preferred no shoes at all. The cold of the stone step felt good.

The rumble of a powerful engine filled the night and a Maserati Spider turned into the drive. Tori forgot all about shoes as the beautiful machine pulled to a stop in front of her. She clasped her hands behind her back to keep from rubbing them together at the prospect of driving the Italian muscle car.

"Thank you, sir." Focused on the car, she paid little attention to the driver until he refused to release the keys, and then she looked up into pale gray eyes ripe with irritation.

He looked familiar but she couldn't quite place him. When he'd stepped out of the car, he'd turned so his features were shadowed. He wore an ill-fitting black suit over a black sweater. And from the little she saw, he didn't look in the mood to party. His square jaw was clenched, his fine features drawn into harsh lines.

One thing for certain, this guy was no wannabe, not with this car, and it bothered her that she couldn't bring a name to mind.

He towered over her, a belated reminder she'd forgotten to put her shoes back on. When she wore the thee-inch heels, it made her five-seven, but even at that height, he'd top her by several inches.

She smiled all the brighter, hoping he wouldn't notice. She tugged on the keys. "I'll take good care of your vehicle, sir."

The brooding gaze he ran over her disabused her of that notion. She had the feeling he missed little. "What do you drive?" he demanded in a gruff voice.

Now that was just rude. "A Mustang 500GT."

"Huh," he grunted but still held possession of the keys. "Is there a male attendant?"

"In the restroom." She took delight in informing him.

"Be polite," Lauren warned in her ear.

His thin lips took a downward turn. "Park it close by," he ordered as if he knew of her longing to put the car through its paces on the downhill trip to the church. "I won't be long."

The keys dropped into her palm and she nearly danced on her pink-tipped toes. She half expected him to inspect the car so he'd know if she added any dings to his beauty. But then he probably didn't have to.

She moved into the V of the open door.

"Miss." She glanced up at him. He'd stopped halfway up the steps to pick up her shoes. "I prefer you to use these."

"Of course." Skipping up the wide steps, she reached his side and accepted the black pumps shoved at her. She bent and placed them on the ground, putting her headset on Mute as she did so. "Thank you. Let's just keep this part between the two of us."

"Worried for your job?" he mocked, his lack of sympathy obvious. Up close he took her breath away. Well-defined features and shadowed eyes were framed by a square jaw and broad brow. Too masculine to be pretty, he was a beautiful man.

"Worse, a lecture." She teetered a bit and a suit-clad elbow was thrust at her. She shot him an appreciative glance that did nothing to soften his stern demeanor and used his arm to steady her as she slipped into the heels.

Hard muscles flexed under her fingers, triggering a feminine response, which flat-out annoyed her. She refused to be attracted to a jerk. Ignoring her protesting toes, she released him as soon as she had her feet encased in leather. Flipping her blond ponytail over her shoulder, she reengaged her headset.

"Enjoy your party, sir." She gave him another bright smile and turned back to the car, tugging Matt's jacket down around her hips as she went.

In the car she adjusted the seat. The interior smelled delicious, of rich leather, linseed oil and a hint of spicy cologne that must belong to Mr. Rude. She turned over the motor and it purred like a lion. She bit her lip, half tempted to take the beast down the hill after all. But she reigned in her impulsive side and pulled the lovely car into an open slot in the garage. Penance for being seen without her shoes.

Not that Lauren would see it that way.

When Tori reached the front of the house, both Matt and John were there. She gave Matt his jacket and the keys to the Maserati, told him where it was parked and made her way inside.

Lauren was waiting for her. "You went off-line. What was the problem?"

"Really?" Tori tapped her headset. "It must be a short." She gave a quick look around but her brooding combatant was nowhere to be seen. "Did you see a big guy in an oversize suit come in?" She'd hoped for a better view of him in the light to help her place him.

At least that was her story and she was sticking to it.

"No. You shouldn't lie, Tori. You're not good at it. What did he want you to use?" Lauren's honey-brown eyes, identical to her own, narrowed. "Tell me you didn't take off your shoes."

"I didn't take off my shoes."

Her sister's hands went to her hips. "We talked about this."

"And as long as you require me to wear these stilts, we'll be talking about it again."

"It's unprofessional."

"No one was around," she protested.

"Except for the big guy in the oversize suit."

"Who drives a Maserati." She couldn't hide her awe. "OMG, Lauren, it's the sweetest thing I've ever driven. I lost my head for a few minutes." She confessed.

Lauren drew her down the hall toward the kitchen and away from the crowded front room. "I suppose you already tagged Dad."

"I may have texted him a picture."

"Tori, this is an important event. We can't afford for anything to go wrong."

"Relax, Lauren. The event is already a success." Two waitresses passed them carrying trays of delectable sweets. "There go the desserts. After I put out the candy table, it's all smooth sailing." Hoping to avoid further lecturing, she swung toward the kitchen.

"Black drives a Maserati."

Surprise spun Tori back around. "What?"

"Garrett Black. Drives. A. Maserati."

"Well, fudge sticks." With the name, the familiarity fell into place. Garrett Black. She'd been thrown off because he'd cut his hair and lost weight, which explained the oversized suit. Of course the shadows hadn't helped. "We may want to put off the introductions to another time."

"Garrett, my friend, you made it." Ray Donovan broke away from a small group near the terrace and met Garrett halfway across the room. They shook hands and Ray pulled Garrett into a full body hug.

"You threatened to pull your next movie if I didn't." Resigned, he squeezed back and then stepped away, creating the distance he preferred. "I'm no fool."

Ray laughed. "You're all kinds of a fool, but you're not stupid."

Garrett shrugged. There was no arguing with the truth.

"Let's get you some food." Ray led him to the dining room and the table spread with a diverse array of dishes, pretty, elegant dishes that probably appealed to the many starlets drifting about.

"I'm not really hungry."

"My friend, you've got to eat, you're wasting away. Get your nose out of the air. Just because food is beautiful doesn't mean it should be dismissed. This is the best food I've ever had at a party. Try the bacon-wrapped meatballs and the chipped beef poofs. I particularly like the spaghetti stuffed garlic bites." He tossed a bite-size nugget into his mouth.

"So I lost some weight. I had a broken jaw if you'll remember." Along with a crushed left leg and shattered collarbone. All compliments of an SUV crashing broadside into the car he was traveling in. He'd lived through it. His father hadn't.

Garrett felt a pinch at his lack of grief.

"Some? That suit is hanging on you, buddy."

Garrett glanced down. "So?"

"So, you're the head of the studio now. You need to dress the part. Here—" Ray picked up the plate of spaghetti bites, tossed on a few mushroom caps and assorted other items "—let's take this upstairs and you can tell me how you're doing. Oh, whoa." An attendant walked by with a plate of chocolate cupcakes. "Diane, be a doll and give that plate to my friend, would you."

"Yes, sir, Mr. Donovan." The attendant handed Garrett the plate with a smile.

Ray took his booty and walked around the corner to a spiral staircase that took them to a loft overlooking the living area below. A wall of windows offered a spectacular vista of the ocean during the day. Tonight the view consisted of the dancing on the patio below. A four-foot-high glass balcony wall ran the length of the loft.

Garrett sat down in a cream leather armchair and set the plate down on a black glass table. Ray set the food on the ottoman and Garrett took a chipped beef poof. Kudos to Ray. The food was the best he'd had since the accident. He reached for another.

"How's the leg?" Ray asked.

"Better. Therapist says it's at 90 percent."

"Wow, that's great." Ray went to the bar. "You were

pretty messed up when I visited you in the hospital. So they put a pin in?"

"Several. Total reconstruction of my thigh and knee." Four surgeries kept him in and out of the hospital for eight months. It's only during the past two months he'd felt like he got his feet under him again. "Just call me Robo Director."

"Robo CEO. You're head of the studio now."

"There's something I never expected." He accepted a Scotch, took a small sip, and set the cup down. He was driving and on meds. He'd come too far in physical rehabilitation to risk a setback now. "I have to admit I'm still wrapping my mind around the fact."

"Really? You used to have a lot of ideas of what you'd do when you got the reins." Ray dropped into the ivory bucket chair next to him.

"Not since Dad and I had a falling-out. I told you about that."

"Sure, he insisted you take on director of creativity for the studio and then overturned most of your decisions."

"I warned him to stop, but he did it once too often and I quit. He retaliated by blackballing me from the studio."

"Ah. You didn't tell me that."

"Sorry. It wasn't something I wanted to get around." Just as he didn't tell his friend about the studio's damaged reputation. "Needless to say, I figured I was out of the will."

But he'd been wrong. Or more likely Dad hadn't gotten around to changing his will in the past six years. He still didn't know what prompted the invitation to Thanksgiving dinner. Either way Garrett had his work cut out for him if he wanted to bring the studio back to its former glory. Gossip traveled fast and far in the movie business, which accounted for the loss of contracts. He didn't want anyone knowing a continuing decline could put Obsidian Studios in financial distress.

"You're an only child," Ray pointed out. "The studio has been family owned for ninety years. Obviously in the end blood was stronger thangrudges."

"I suppose." Whatever the reason, the studio was now his, and Garrett refused to let it fail on his watch.

Looking for a diversion, he swung the chair around to overlook the crowd below. Absently he reached for another meatball. Immediately he spied the sleek ponytail of his bothersome valet. She stood in a hall just off the entry talking to another woman.

She'd lost her jacket and under it she wore a halter sheath dress square at the neck and ending a few inches above her knees. The little black dress at its classic best. It didn't cling but draped her lithe figure, hinting at more than it revealed unlike so many of the other dresses shrink-wrapped on the women roaming the room.

His gaze returned to the women in black. He frowned and blinked. Then blinked again, wondering if the one sip of alcohol was enough to have him seeing double. No, there were two of them. The second woman's dress was scoop-necked and she wore her hair in a lower tail clipped back rather than banded.

"Who are the dynamic duo?" He lifted his chin in the direction of the girls and Ray shifted in his chair to see who he referenced.

"Ah." His friend's blue eyes lighted on the women with unerring precision. "They are Lauren and Tori Randall, my event coordinators. They handled the premiere of *Pretty Little Witches* a few months ago."

A dark brow lifted at that. Even cooped up convalescing, he'd heard of the successful event.

"The movie flopped," Ray went on. "But people are still talking about the premiere. When I decided to throw a party, I had my assistant call them. The name of their company is By Arrangement."

Garrett's mouth quirked up at the clever name, a nice play on their being twins. Actually the name sounded familiar. Probably in connection with the premiere. The women broke up, his valet heading to the kitchen, the other moving off in the other direction. Garrett turned away. The woman had already taken up too much of his time.

He nailed Ray with a pointed stare. "When are you going to be finished with my house?" He'd rented his place to Ray for his current film project *Gates of Peril* while he stayed at the family manor adjacent to the studio. The drive was easier on his leg, but he'd like to get away from it on the weekends. "I'm getting tired of the dusty old manor."

"Not much longer. Maybe a month."

"A month? What the hell, Ray? I happen to know you're also over budget."

"Yeah, but the special effects are sick. Another month and two million should see a wrap." The director shook his head. "The set is a circus. All kinds of people underfoot. Jenna Vick is stellar, but she just got engaged and she's distracted by her fiancé. And the effects coordinator has his kids on-site because his sitter was in a fender bender."

"Those are not the studio's problems. You're supposed to be finished with my place and shooting on the West Lot. Another movie is scheduled for that lot in two weeks. The studio takes a hit if they can't start production."

Ray shrugged. "Add it to the budget."

Garrett shook his head. That's exactly the attitude that led to the studio's teetering reputation. "Ray, I love you like a brother, but the days of open budgets died with my dad. You have two weeks and one million. I'm closing your set to all nonessential personnel. Get your people under control, and get it done."

Tori popped a candy-coated peanut in her mouth and surveyed the candy table. Perfect. Sticking to the colors red, black, silver and white, she'd used martini-shaped glasses large and small to create her design. Drops, gummies and foil-wrapped candies filled the dishes. White letters filled with dark chocolate-covered mints spelled out *RAY*. A black satin table cover and silver and red ribbons pulled the whole look together.

No sooner did she step back than guests converged on the treats. Oohs and aahs followed her retreat. In spite of her less than fortuitous encounter with Black, Tori counted tonight as a success. She'd received lots of compliments on the food and given their card to three prospective clients.

Reminded of Black, she moved to the entry and lingered near the living room where she had a view of the front door. Matt had found the claim ticket for the Maserati in his jacket pocket and brought it to her to pass on to the owner. She grimaced, as if she needed another run-in with Black.

As if her thoughts had conjured the man, he suddenly appeared from the crowd. And he was headed directly for her.

She summoned a smile. "Mr. Black, is there anything I can get for you?"

He lifted a dark brow at the use of his name. He glanced to the left where the food filled the table and a crowd surrounded the candy display, and then dropped to the martini glass she'd filled for herself.

"This will do." Taking the glass from her, he dumped half the contents into his hand. "Thanks."

Surprised by his sweet tooth and offended by his rudeness, she warned him, "Careful, I'm a peanut fiend, so I hope you aren't allergic."

"Nope. Did you enjoy driving my car, Ms. Randall?"

"It was the highlight of my night." She stifled any reaction to the use of her name, unable to determine if it was a good thing or bad.

"Which reminds me." With a sheepish smile she dug into her cleavage and retrieved his claim ticket. "I forgot to give you this."

He accepted the paper, looked from it to her bust. Heat flared in his gray eyes before they lifted to meet her gaze.

"Sorry," she murmured, shrugging, "no pockets."

"No need to apologize." He flicked the ticket with his thumb. "I may have to keep this as a memento of the evening."

Okay, what did that mean? Good gracious. Was he hitting on her? Wouldn't Lauren love that? As for Tori, sure he tipped the studometer, but his aloof, brooding attitude triggered one of her hot buttons, putting him off-limits even more than the fact he was a client.

Of course there was that gorgeous car. "If you need a designated driver, I'm happy to be of assistance."

"Do I appear drunk to you, Ms. Randall?" The gravel in his voice took on a gruffness.

Oops, she'd upset him again. "No, but a girl can hope."

"Very amusing."

She shrugged and was rewarded by him taking the last of her candy.

"You don't mind, do you?" he challenged her.

"Of course not." Jerk. "I can get you one of your own if you'd like."

"No, yours is good enough."

Was he trying to outdo himself in boorish behavior or was it simply his default mode? Whichever, charming he was not. Then again she didn't remember ever hearing the word attached to his name. *Hardworking, brilliant* and *brooding* were the words used to describe him. Usually as a director. Looking into his pale eyes she didn't doubt the truth of them.

As a guest, he could use a lesson in playing nice with others.

"Good night, Ms. Randall." He stepped past her toward the door.

"Drive safely, Mr. Black," she said to his back. She wouldn't want anything to happen to his beautiful car.

CHAPTER TWO

LATE MONDAY AFTERNOON Tori worked on a spreadsheet displaying the menu for a fiftieth wedding anniversary scheduled for Thursday. She was making the final notes to the grocery list when the bell over the front door sounded.

"Be right there," she called out as she took a moment to save her file. A quick glance through the glass wall of her office revealed the visitor was a man, but he had his back to her. By Arrangement rarely got drop by traffic. The nature of their business generally took them to their clients. In fact Lauren was out with a prospective client now, which left Tori to handle the man haunting their showroom.

Her toes searched under her desk for her shoes. She ended up kicking them farther back and bent to retrieve the ballerina flats. Happy she chose to wear black jeans today, which were slightly dressier than regular jeans, she walked out of her office, tugging at the hem of her olive sweater as she greeted the visitor.

"Welcome— You." She stopped short at the sight of Garrett Black. He stood tall and broad in the middle of the showroom in another ill-fitting suit. "What are you doing here?" Hearing the strident tone, she cringed. "I mean, Mr. Black, how can I help you?"

"Ms. Randall." He glanced around the converted restaurant, taking in the glass offices, the tables dressed in different styles for special occasions, the well-stocked bar. He lifted a brow at her.

"We occasionally host events here," she explained. "Or we used to." She and Lauren bought the restaurant four years ago for the kitchen because they'd outgrown her apartment kitchen for food prep. Business continued to bloom, and after six months, the front was converted to offices, storage and the current showroom.

He nodded and continued to wander. At one of the tables he picked up a fork, set it back down. His presence confused her. She and Lauren had great ideas outlined for the film festival, but the next series of meetings with Obsidian weren't scheduled until the first part of December.

"Would you like to sit?" she asked him.

"No." He faced her, shoved his hands in his coat pockets. "I've come about the toe prints."

She blinked at him. "Toe prints?"

"Yes. Upon inspection of my vehicle this morning I found toe prints on the carpet of the driver's side. I wanted to let you know I'll be forwarding the cleaning bill."

Tori listened with growing outrage. He had to be kidding. "No," she corrected, keeping her tone easy. "Remember, I was barefoot when we met, but you stopped me before I got in the car." His precious oh-so-fabulous car.

Aggravating man. How petty of him to try to get a car cleaning out of her, especially when money wasn't the issue. He was upset because she'd made him feel. Anger, arousal, humor, she'd seen flashes of each emotion in the brief conversations they'd had.

Whatever had happened to him, and it went way further back than his accident, he'd cut himself off from emotion. She imagined the accident and losing his dad only added to the pain he hid behind a brooding facade.

All too familiar with the destructive force of repressed feelings, she easily recognized the anguish simmering in his silver eyes. She felt for him, but not even his manly beauty tempted her to go there again.

Caring for an emotional recluse was equivalent to treading through a mental minefield.

"You were the only one near the car barefoot. I assume you will want to take care of this matter promptly as it would be awkward working together on the film festival with this issue unresolved."

She gritted her teeth. He was right. Having this issue hanging over By Arrangement while she worked the film festival was unacceptable. Arguing with him didn't make sense, either. Not while Black was a client.

Plus, no way did Tori want Lauren knowing about this. She would never let Tori forget the need to wear appropriate shoes if she learned Tori was being billed for footprints. Yet she still protested.

"Between the two of us I'm sure we can figure this out." Much as she disliked confrontation, Tori didn't care to be pushed around or taken advantage of, either. "Let me see the prints." She headed for the door and the parking lot beyond.

Hey, she had a right to challenge the totally bogus accusation. Innocent until proven guilty, she wanted to see the evidence, to defend her good name. The truth was she admired the beautiful machinery of the Maserati too much to mar it and she found the accusation insulting.

"You honestly believe I'd make up footprints?" The caustic question came from behind her. "For what reason? Some half-witted excuse to see you again?"

She froze with her hand on the car handle, struck by the concept. For all the derision in his words, she knew he found her attractive. Perhaps that was the answer. He was punishing them both for the chemistry between them.

And perhaps she was overthinking it. He was a jerk, reason enough for his contrary behavior.

She tried opening the door of the red Maserati Spider convertible and about pulled her shoulder from the socket when it refused to give. Locked. She turned to him, forced a smile. "Open, please."

She met stoic resistance.

What now? Then it hit her, she hadn't answered his question.

"Look, I'm not vain enough to figure you manufactured an excuse and went out of your way to pursue me. Since I didn't step barefoot into the car, I want to help you determine what it is."

"I know toe prints when I see them." But he clicked the locks, allowing her to open the door.

Bending over, she stuck her head inside. The scent of well-tended leather filled her senses. Such a sexy aroma. It made her think of smart cars, long drives and hard men. None of which were appropriate to the moment. Discounting the hardheaded male looming over her.

She ran her hand over the soft buttercream upholstery, eyed the matching carpet. Three small smudges were grouped close together. She supposed they could be toe prints, but she didn't think so.

"They look like paw prints," she said, glancing over her shoulder in time to catch him eyeing her butt. Her blood heated at the appreciation in his pale gaze. But she tamped it down as she stood and faced him, reminding herself of the complications he presented—client, tortured soul.

"Absolutely not." He denied her explanation. He stepped back and seemed to wobble a bit on the uneven asphalt. He glared at the ground before turning the look on her. "Impossible. Unless you left a window open when you parked the car."

"No. I adjusted the seat." A necessity considering, at six feet, he stood a good eight inches taller than her. "But I just pulled it into the garage. There was no need to adjust the mirrors."

"Then the only explanation is toe prints."

"Unless the marks were there before you reached the party," she offered in what she felt was a reasonable tone. "Do you inspect all areas of the car before driving it each time?"

"Of course not." He scowled, his annoyance over the discussion more than clear. "But they weren't there before."

"How do you know?"

"Because I didn't drive it barefoot. And I live alone. Not even a cat. No one else to leave toe prints or paw prints."

"Okay." She moved toward him so she could close the car door.

He took a hasty step backward, his heel landed in a small hole and his leg buckled, sending him sprawling on his butt. A grunt of pain was cut off by a string of vile curses.

It was one of those fast-forward, slow-motion moments. Tori saw the fall unfolding and reached out to grab him, but his momentum pulled his hand right through hers. She had to catch herself from falling on top of him.

"Are you okay?" Stupid question. His complexion had gone white and his jaw was clenched against the pain. She crouched next to him. "How can I help?"

"Back the hell up." He shooed her away. "Give me some room."

Respecting his wish, she stood back but watched him carefully. In high school she worked two years as a life-guard at her dad's golf club. From his paleness and the clamminess of his skin, he looked about to pass out. If that happened, she'd have to call an ambulance because there'd be no handling his deadweight.

"Garrett, are you light-headed?" She knelt next to him.

"A little," he admitted, which said a lot.

"We don't want you passing out. I would have to call an ambulance…" Mention of an ambulance got his attention.

"No hospital. I just need a moment." He supported himself on one arm, leaning sideways. The other hand clutched at his right leg, the obvious point of his pain. He tried to rise but slumped back. "My head is spinning."

"Okay, you need to sit up. And put your head in your lap." He no doubt saw spots before his eyes. She helped him into position and rubbed a hand over his back. It was supposed to be your head between your knees. She hoped this would be enough to stop the dots from merging into total darkness.

After a moment, he lifted his head. "It's better. Thanks. Sorry to snap at you."

Dark tendrils fell over his eyes. Brushing them back, she felt the dampness of his skin. It had been a close call. "Okay, let's get you on your feet."

Without asking this time, she tucked an arm under his right shoulder and lifted. He managed to get his left leg under himself, and between the two of them, he reached his feet.

He brushed off his clothes, teetering, but unwilling to ask for help.

"I'll send you a bill for the carpet cleaning." It would be a great exit line, except his right leg wouldn't hold his weight. He almost went down again when he tried.

"Enough of this." She invaded his space, cupped his face in her hands, feeling the prickle of an approaching five o'clock shadow, and met his pain-filled gaze. "Either you accept my help or I call for that ambulance. It's your choice."

Just for a moment he hooded his eyes, leaned into her touch. In the next instant, he jerked away. Squaring his shoulders, irritation stamped his features, eradicating any flash of vulnerability she may have imagined.

"No hospital." He repeated his earlier decree. "I strained

an old injury. I just need to get home and put some ice on it."

"It's your right leg. You aren't driving anywhere."

His jaw clenched as he struggled between desire and reality. "Fine." He gritted the word through his teeth. "You can drive me home."

Lucky her. As if hauling his injured rear was a highly sought after reward. She rolled her eyes, pretended her heart hadn't leaped at the notion of driving the Maserati and tucked her shoulder under his arm to help him around the car. This close he smelled of a spicy cologne touched with lavender and citrus, raw male and, oh, Lord, leather.

The sexy combination nearly knocked her on *her* tush.

Unfortunately, once they reached the passenger side, it became obvious the car was too low-slung for him to comfortably lower himself into it.

"This isn't going to work," she declared, raw with frustration.

"For once, I agree." He shifted on his good leg, and suddenly she was in his arms, her hands clutching his waist. "I need to keep my leg straight." His breath caressed her cheek, sending a shiver down her spine.

"We can use the company SUV. It's higher and has more legroom. Wait here." Relieved, she ducked out from under his arm. She blamed her near sprint inside on the need to get rid of him. She wasn't running scared.

"Liar," she muttered while snagging the keys to the fuel-friendly Ford and locking up the showroom. Wanting him gone had everything to do with running scared. And a strong sense of self-preservation. So she'd drive him home, pay to clean his blasted carpet and put him firmly from her mind.

Garrett clicked the locks on his prized Maserati, a gift to himself from the profits of his first successful film. He rued the impulse that brought him to West Hollywood and the offices of By Arrangement.

When he found the toe prints in his car this morning, he'd been annoyed.

Tori Randal's barefooted impersonation of a valet fell short of professionalism in his opinion. He'd come here today in the hopes she could redeem that impression before he put his company's reputation in her hands at the upcoming international film festival.

Of course the insolent blonde couldn't simply admit her mistake and agree to right the wrong. No, she questioned his motives and his eyesight. Whatever.

What really needed questioning was his sanity.

He should have remembered how he'd reacted to her. She glowed as only a true optimist could, lush lips too ready to smile, amber eyes sparkling, demanding everyone she came in contact with join her in the dance of life. And the long line of her ivory neck displayed by her sophisticated ponytail at the party and a serviceable braid today just made him want to take a bite.

Exactly when had he become part vampire?

During the long, lonely, pain-ridden nights since the accident came the ready answer. Better to be exhausted from physical therapy and reviewing studio business than to lay awake raked by pain and regrets.

Now he'd let the perky blonde with no sense of boundaries get to him again. And the result was a pulled muscle in his bad leg. His own damned fault, tripping over an inch-deep hole and twisting his foot. Pain had streaked up his weak leg and it gave. He'd done it before, pushing himself too far, too fast, but it still hurt like a bitch.

A white SUV pulled up next to him, and Tori hopped out and came trotting around to his side. He didn't wait for her. He opened the door, plunked his butt down and pulled his leg in.

"Oh, yeah, much better." Tori arrived in time to help lift his leg in.

"I can do it." He scowled at her, both for the interference and the cheerful optimism. "Let's just get going."

"Aye-aye." She saluted him and made the reverse trip around to the driver's seat.

He might appreciate the impertinence if he weren't in pain. And mortified. He closed his eyes, as it was he just wanted to get home.

"Here." She thrust a water bottle at him after climbing in next to him. "Do you have any pain pills with you?"

"I don't like taking pain meds." The usual protest sprang automatically to his tongue.

She gave him a schoolteacher glare, the kind that made you question your own intelligence. "That's not what I asked. If you have something with you, take it."

He glared back, not caring in the least that it screamed petulant rebellion. He may have tripped up like a little boy, but he was a grown man capable of knowing the needs of his own body.

"I can always take you to the hospital. I'm sure they'll give you something."

"Why do you care if I'm in pain?"

She looked truly confused by the question. "I care whenever anyone is in pain."

"The painkillers don't help the injury. They just mask the pain, making it possible for you to hurt yourself even more."

"The pain medicine helps you to relax. If it's a pulled muscle like you seem to think, a lessening of the tension in the muscles actually will assist in the healing process."

"They make me sleepy." It wasn't quite a whine but too close for his pride. So he dug out the pills, popped one in his mouth and chased it with a long sip of water. "You seem to know a lot about physical ailments for an event coordinator."

"I got into first aid when I was doing my lifeguard stint. Where are we going?" She'd been driving as they argued but had reached the freeway. "Do I go north or south?"

He directed her north and gave her the address, which she put in her GPS.

"I know that address. You're living at Obsidian Studios?"

"Sometimes it feels like it, but no, I'm staying at The Old Manor House."

Her head whipped his way. "How can you be living at The Old Manor House?"

He cocked a brow at her surprise. "My family does own the house."

"Of course." Eyes back on the road, she shrugged. "But I thought it was closed up."

"It was, most of it still is, but after his last divorce, my father moved back into a wing on the bottom floor." Why was he explaining anything to her? But what the heck, he preferred to be alert. Talking helped. "I'd rather go to my place on the coast in Santa Barbara, but I moved into the Hollywood mansion when I started working at the studio. It's closer, more convenient when I have to be there every day."

No need to admit driving still bothered his leg. In fact, no need to talk about himself.

"From lifeguard to event coordinator. That's quite a change. How'd that happen?"

Her luscious lips pursed. "Well, after high school we went to UCLA." Her gaze touched him for a second. "You're an alum, too."

"Yes." He agreed. "A few years before you I'm guessing."

"Four," she answered promptly.

"Very precise." Why would she know that?

A grin flashed his way. "I searched for you online. Standard research prior to putting in the bid to Obsidian Studios."

"What was your major?" He lobbed the focus back to her. Smothering a yawn, he convinced himself it was drowsiness and not disappointment he felt. Of course her research had been business related not personal.

"Communications, but I switched to business when By Arrangement came to be."

"You started your business in college?"

She laughed. "Sometimes I think we started our business in the womb. My mom is big on celebrations. Birthdays, holidays, accomplishments were all good reasons to have a party. So we grew up entertaining. When we hit the sorority at UCLA, we naturally stepped up whenever there was an event. Our reputation grew and we started doing other events around school. It started as a way to make extra money. But as people graduated, they still called us and we started doing events outside the school. Our junior year, we named our business By Arrangement, changed our majors to business and never looked back."

The love for her job rang loud in her animated chatter. The pride in her accomplishments, which she clearly shared with her sister, indicated a bond of trust and affection. From what she'd said of her mother, it sounded as if she'd had a happy childhood.

Too much cheer for him.

"I must say By Arrangement came highly recommended. Your previous clients must have missed out on the toe print experience."

In profile he watched the joy in her switch off.

He heard a sigh and then a very polite, "I'm sorry. Please send me the cleaning bill and I'll see it's paid."

Blessed silence filled the vehicle.

He turned to look unseeing out the window, feeling as if

he'd spanked a puppy. She was the one in need of a spanking. If she'd gracefully accepted the blame when he'd first arrived, he would have left immediately and been sitting down to a nice meal at Antonio's right now.

On cue his stomach rumbled.

Ignoring it, ignoring her, he closed his eyes and pretended to sleep.

Tori kept her eyes on the road. In another ten minutes she'd drop his ungrateful hide off at the curb. She couldn't wait.

Thank heavens the meds finally kicked in and he fell asleep, lifting the need for conversation. If you counted grunts and sarcasm as conversation. She got it. He'd had a bad year. But there was no reason to take it out on her.

She took the off-ramp that led to Obsidian Studios and The Old Manor House. He deserved to live alone in a spooky old place. The house got its name shortly after it was built because the house and grounds were used in an old black-and-white movie of the same name. The movie became a Gothic horror classic. It scared her spitless as a kid.

Only a few more blocks.

Then she heard it again, the rumble of his stomach. Her brow puckered as she tried to recall if he'd mentioned staff. He probably had a cook and a housekeeper, right? She had no doubt whatsoever that his father would have had a staff. But Garrett spent several months in the hospital. It was totally possible the staff had been let go. Especially as Garrett had his own home.

Dang it. Sometimes she was too nice for her own good, but she couldn't leave him at the curb both hurt and hungry.

Dark had fallen and she panned the street in front of her and then in the rearview mirror. Spotting the pink neon sign of a fast-food Chinese restaurant, she whipped a U-turn and zipped into the parking lot. Perfect.

She glanced at Garrett, who didn't move. Good. She may be willing to feed him, but she was done talking to the man. Grabbing her purse, she went inside. The savory scents of East Asia immediately enveloped the senses. The smell of garlic, ginger, onions and chicken made her mouth water.

Yes, this would do nicely for dinner. Having no idea what Garrett liked, she requested both beef and chicken items. He didn't strike her as a vegetarian. Too much the predator.

Back in the car she tucked the bags behind the passenger seat and reengaged the GPS. A few minutes later she turned into a gated drive. Of course it would have security.

Man, she'd really been anticipating the curb.

"Mr. Black," she called, hoping to rouse him. He didn't move, so she said his name again, louder. Then she shook his arm. "Garrett!"

His pale eyes opened, appearing silver in the glare of the spotlight aimed at the SUV. The light triggered when she pulled up to the security display situated just short of the ten-foot-high brick wall. Garrett blinked at her and then the house.

"We're here." His voice was thick with sleep.

"Yes. I need the code."

He rattled off a number, the gate began to open and she inched forward. A groan sounded next to her as Garrett shifted in his seat. Out of the corner of her eyes she saw him scrub his hands over his face.

Once she cleared the gate, streetlights came on showing the way to the house in the distance. She drove a quarter mile curving around to the front of the house, where the drive circled a large fountain. Six steps led up to an extensive porch. That presented a problem.

"Is there a better spot to drop you?" she asked. "An entrance without steps?"

"Yeah, pull around to the back. There are only two steps up to the back porch."

She followed his directions and stopped so her lights shined on the steps. A gray cat sprang up and darted away.

"No cat, huh?"

"I've never seen it before."

"Of course not." As if she believed that.

"And it hasn't been in my car." He opened his door and slid out. "Thanks for the ride."

"Wait." She hurried around the front of the SUV to reach his side.

"I don't need your help." He advised her, the short nap unfortunately not improving his disposition.

"Probably not." She agreed and took his arm. "You're getting it anyway. It's dark and the ground is uneven. I prefer not to take any chances."

A put-upon sigh filled the chill November evening. Once they reached the porch, he made a point of climbing them unassisted. Irritating man!

But good. She didn't need to worry about leaving him. At the bottom of the stairs she waited until he opened the door and turned on the light.

"Good night, Ms. Randall."

"Good night, Mr. Black." Good riddance, more like.

"Oh, wait." She ran to the SUV and came back with the white bag of food. Climbing to the porch she crossed to him and pushed the package into his arms. "Bon appétit. You probably shouldn't feed the cat."

CHAPTER THREE

Lauren walked around Tori's Mustang and slid into the passenger seat as her sister made her way to the back door of The Old Manor House. She heard Tori's knock just before she closed the door.

Lauren wasn't sure she bought Tori's explanation that Black had been driving by and decided to stop by their showroom to introduce himself. But there had to be some truth to the part where he hurt his leg and couldn't drive or he never would have left his Maserati.

The light over the back door came on and Garrett Black opened the door. He stepped outside wearing only a pair of low hanging gray sweatpants and nothing more. Oh, my. She found his muscular physique impressive even as far away as the vehicle where she sat. The two exchanged words and for a moment she envied Tori her closer view.

But then she felt the warmth growing in her chest. Her eyes went wide as the feeling grew. It dimmed as Tori moved away from Black, stomped down the steps and got back in Garret's car. Across the way a garage door opened. Tori drove the Maserati inside.

She reappeared, returned to the back porch and dropped the keys into Black's outstretched hand with more force than necessary. The closer Tori drew to Black, the stronger the warmth bloomed in Lauren's chest. Distracted by the discovery, she jumped when Tori suddenly opened the driver's door and slid inside.

"Ungrateful beast." Tori slammed the Mustang in Reverse.

"He wasn't happy to have his car returned?"

"Not in the least." Gravel sprayed as she headed for the gate. "Nobody drives his car but him."

"You drove it the other night." Lauren pointed out.

"That's what I said. It appears valets are an exception."

She laughed at Tori's outrage and decided to test her. "You like him."

"Are you insane?" Tori exclaimed, sending Lauren a sideways glare. "The man has the manners of a mule."

"And the body of a stud."

Her twin remained silent until they cleared the gate and turned toward the freeway.

"Come on, Tori. You're not blind."

She rolled her eyes, but Lauren saw the corner of her sister's mouth twitch.

"OMG, he's hot." Tori fanned herself. "He had to repeat himself because I was staring. It was mortifying."

Oh, yeah. There was no doubt in Lauren's mind. Tori had met her match.

"I'm ready to take out a contract on Garrett Black," Jenna Vick announced and took a sip of her margarita. "Mark has been banned from the set. Work has become such a drudge."

Thinking of her encounters with Black, of his unsmiling facade and his penchant for being a bit of a jerk, Tori wasn't totally shocked by the redhead's reaction to the man. What a shame such a gorgeous car belonged to such a dysfunctional individual.

"Count me in." Cindy Tate tucked a wisp of blond hair behind her ear before tapping her glass to Jenna's. "My mother came to town to see me work. She'd really been looking forward to being on the set. But the guards refused to let her join me. I asked for a few days off to spend with her and was told no because the film is behind schedule."

"I'll pitch in," Olivia Fox chimed, not moving an inch as she basked, tanned and toned, in the sunshine, her jet-black hair flowing over her bright yellow bikini.

"Did you have someone banned, too?" Jenna asked. The three actresses were rising stars working together on a futuristic action film, kind of a *Charlie's Angels* in space.

"No." Olivia adjusted her sunglasses, then resumed her boneless position. "But the set has become a morgue. Everyone is so serious and intent on their job, no one laughs anymore."

Remembering the threat of a cleaning bill for nonexistent toe prints, Tori controlled the urge to offer her own funds. Obviously the man was making friends wherever he went.

"Why do you blame Black?" Tori asked as she met Lauren's gaze across the deck, where they were all gathered at Jenna's Venice Beach home. They'd taken care of the plans for Jenna's engagement party, and were now relaxing poolside, enjoying the ocean view.

By Arrangement would be working with Black on several events when the Hollywood Hills Film Festival started in a month. Actually make that working *for* Black, which suited Tori much better. It meant she'd be less likely to run into the man.

Either way Tori knew Lauren had her ears perked, she inhaled information and used it like a weapon.

"Because it's Black's decree." Cindy rolled her eyes and touched her tongue to the salt rimming her glass. "Visitors have been limited on all sets. But if a film is over budget or over schedule, he closes the set down altogether."

"Lucky me," Jenna groused. "I'm going from one Obsidian production to another, so I get no break." She sank onto a lounger next to Olivia. "It was really nice having Mark on the set. Now I hardly get to see him." Gesturing to Tori and Lauren, she implored them to understand. "You two introduced us. You must know how much I miss him."

"Not to mention it's going to be much harder planning the wedding now," Cindy pointed out helpfully. "Tori and Lauren are great." She flashed a grin at them. "They introduced me to my hubby, too, and they gave me a spectacular wedding. Still they did need occasional input."

Lauren choked on a sip of iced tea. Probably remembering the fit Cindy threw when they went off-line for a Saturday wedding three months before her event. She wanted to tell them about a wine she tasted at a local winery she just had to have at her reception. When Lauren checked her voice mail, they had over fifty messages and had been fired. Twice. All this was after they'd advised her they had a wedding and would be unavailable. Never had Tori been happier that Lauren was the voice of By Arrangement.

Tori didn't do confrontation.

Lauren thrived on it, in a calm, controlled manner, of course.

She let Cindy vent for a couple of minutes, made noises of sympathy for her distress, showed regret for losing the contract and then hit her with the fact By Arrangement would be billing her for the work already done. Lauren wrapped it up in a pretty little bow, reminding Cindy they had told her they would be unavailable and of the clause in the contract stating on the day of a wedding By Arrangement gave the bride and her event our exclusive attention. It was a courtesy we extended to our brides and it wasn't something we were willing to compromise on. The clincher was our disappointment as we introduced Cindy to her fiancé.

Cindy apologized for her snit, which wasn't her first or her last, and By Arrangement went on to give her a "spectacular" wedding.

"We do need input," Lauren agreed, calm as always. "But you needn't worry. It's our job to make the whole process easy for you."

"But I'm getting married in March," Jenna said, pouting, "I planned to take a couple of weeks for a honeymoon, but it's in the middle of my next film. Now I'll be lucky to get a few days off."

Tori sympathized with her friend and client. She genuinely liked these women, but seriously, Jenna did sign a contract. It was a tad unrealistic to expect an entire production to halt filming so she could honeymoon. Not that Tori could voice her opinion to these three. They weren't used to being thwarted. They were in demand, which pretty much meant they got whatever they asked for. Tori supposed they could be forgiven for being a bit full of themselves.

"Obviously Garrett Black has no life or he'd understand our plight." Cindy sighed.

"From what I hear, Black is spending all his time in his office. Probably reviewing all the production contracts so he can collect on deadline penalties." Jenna scowled into her drink, absently running a finger around the rim of her glass, knocking off all the salt. "My last three projects ran over. Doesn't he realize delays are the nature of this business?"

"Were all the films Obsidian productions?" Lauren asked.

Jenna shook her head, ginger curls flowing over her bare shoulders. "Just this one, but we used Obsidian Studio's lots for the other two. And we were delayed because the lots weren't available when we were supposed to shoot. Which proves my point."

"Black is new to the job," Tori pointed out, though she had no idea why she felt compelled to defend him. "Maybe he's just trying to fix a problem he sees."

"Do not defend the man." Cindy shook a finger at Tori. "He's a coldhearted bastard."

Yeah, no argument there.

"What he needs is a woman." Olivia sat forward and wrapped her arms around her knees. "He's all work and no play. And he wants the rest of the world to be the same. If he had a woman in his life, he'd have less time to mess with ours."

"Yes." Jenna hopped up and began to pace excitedly. "A woman would distract him, soften him. He'd be more understanding of other people's relationships. He definitely needs a woman."

Uh-oh. Tori saw where this headed. She glanced at Lauren and knew her twin had come to the same conclusion. But the ball was rolling. There was no stopping it now.

"It's the perfect solution," Cindy agreed, blue eyes alight as she shifted her gaze between Lauren and Tori. "And we know the perfect pair to find her for him."

"Oh, no, he did not." A few days later, Tori clicked on an email to open it because the preview couldn't be right. Garrett Black hadn't actually sent her a bill for the cleaning of his car's carpet. But, oh yeah, he had. The attachment confirmed it: two hundred dollars for an interior cleaning.

TO: trandall@byarrangement.com
FROM: garrett.black@obsidianstudios.com
SUBJECT: Cleaning bill

Ms. Randall, please forgive my delay in providing the bill for the carpet cleaning of my Maserati. I appreciate your willingness to take responsibility for your actions. It gives me hope By Arrangement will conduct themselves in a professional manner while representing Obsidian Studios at the upcoming film festival. You may send a check to me care of the studio.

Why was she even surprised? If she looked up his birth certificate, she'd see the *A* in Garrett A. Black stood for *arrogant*. He had some nerve talking about professionalism while blaming her for toe prints that were clearly paw prints.

Obviously her gesture in returning his car to him had counted for nothing. So okay, her motive had been purely selfish. She wanted the car gone so she didn't have to deal with him again.

By taking the car to him, she controlled the where, when and how long.

What she hadn't planned on was finding him half-naked. The man was seriously built, broad shoulders, muscular arms and oh, those abs. He'd been ill, okay laid up with a broken leg. He had no right to look so good. Flustered, she'd embarrassed herself by staring.

He'd thanked her at the same time he made his annoyance clear; declaring he never left the car out at night. It wasn't enough she went out of her way to return his car; he had to guilt her into moving the car into the garage for him.

She managed to keep her cool by remembering they would be working together very soon. Something she kept in mind as she replied to his email.

TO: garrett.black@obsidianstudios.com
FROM: trandall@byarrangement.com
SUBJECT: Re: Cleaning bill

Mr. Black, it distresses me to think of your lovely vehicle being marred in any way. Payment will be forwarded promptly.
PS: How is the cat?

"I knew this matchmaking thing was going to bite us in the butt someday," Lauren announced in the car on the way to an impromptu meeting with Obsidian Studios.

"Yes," Tori agreed. "But I always thought it would be a failed relationship that caused the problem. I mean, really, we have a 100 percent success rate. You'd think one of the couples would experience troubles."

"True. Even Kate and Brad from high school are still going strong. I was talking to Mom the other day and she mentioned they're expecting their third child."

"That's so cool." She pleated her skirt and thought about her gift. "How does it feel for you?" She glanced at Lauren. "When you know two people belong together?"

For a full heartbeat, her twin met her gaze before turning back to the road. "It's a warm glow, like a surge of happiness, when I see them together."

"Me, too." Tori nodded. "It's a total sense of rightness. But I have to see them together. I never get a sense someone would be good with anyone else."

"No, me, neither," Lauren confirmed. "And we're stronger when we're together."

"I've noticed that, too. And only with people who are open."

"What do you mean?" Lauren frowned at her.

"Some people are more open than others." Tori tried to explain what she'd always felt but never expressed. "Sometimes I can actually pick up on moods if they're strong enough—happiness, sadness, fear, anger, guilt."

"Sorry to tell you this, sis, but those emotions are pretty easy to read."

"Ha-ha." Her sister completely missed the chiding glance Tori sent her. "I mean from across the room. People I don't even know. Do you ever get that?"

Lauren lifted the shoulder closest to Tori and let it drop. "Yeah, I guess. If I concentrate. I choose not to concentrate."

"I know, me, too." It was uncomfortable picking up on other people's emotions. Made her feel intrusive. "But if they're close I get blips of emotion. I think that's what we're cluing into when we feel the connection."

"Okay, that makes sense. Why all the psychoanalysis?" A touch of irritation crept into Lauren's voice.

"Because Black is as closed up as a teenage girl's locked diary. Standing or sitting right next to him, I got nothing."

"Really?" Lauren sounded surprised, drawing Tori's gaze to her profile. "You get no feeling from him at all?"

"No. Why? Did you?" Tori turned as much as the seat belt would allow. "You didn't mention you saw Black at the party."

"There was no reason to since you'd already advised me it was best not to introduce ourselves. But I saw you chatting with him before he left."

"Did you see him steal my candy?" Jerk. Lauren gave her "the look," the one that said "focus." "Okay, not relevant. Still, it wasn't nice."

"Tori."

"Right. So did you get a read on him with anyone? It would really help if you did, because the starlet trio is counting on us."

Quiet filled the car for a moment and then she muttered, "I'm not sure."

Tori started to ask what she meant but they'd reached the studio. Lauren turned into the drive and up to the guard station. She gave their names and was directed to a building two down and one over, top floor.

Once they were in the elevator, Tori demanded her sister explain her comment.

"I just meant we told Jenna, Cindy and Olivia we'd try to find someone for Black. We didn't make any promises. They don't know how it works for us."

"No, but they're going to be looking for results. And there's no dodging them, either. We're working with them on the engagement party, the bridal shower and the wedding. We need to keep them happy or life will be miserable."

"I hear you. But we aren't responsible if we don't have access to the man. They think we will because we're handling the events for Obsidian at the film festival, but the likelihood of us actually interacting with Black is very slim."

Tori liked the way her sister thought. It was the perfect out. For the matchmaking and for her. She wasn't looking forward to encountering Garrett Black again. He bothered her in a curious way. It was the brooding. She never did well with brooding.

Her chest constricted as memories rose up. The slow pulling back, the moodiness, that tragic final call.

Shane. She hadn't purposely tried to tune into anyone since she tried to read him at the height of his withdrawal. The pain and anger had overwhelmed her to the point she never tried again. And she really had no interest in putting any feelers out to Garrett Black. She'd learned her lesson there.

Thankfully the elevator opened into a reception area. From sheer force of will, she pushed the past back where it belonged and followed Lauren to a wide glass desk. Lauren gave the thirty-something blonde manning the desk their names.

"Welcome." The woman immediately bounced to her feet. "Mr. Black is expecting you." The woman came around the desk to lead them toward an inner door.

Behind her back Lauren mouthed, "Black?"

Tori shrugged, no happier than her sister at the prospect of a meeting with Black. Mystified, Tori followed Lauren toward the inner sanctum. What was this all about? They received a call at By Arrangement yesterday requesting this meeting regarding the film festival. There had been no mention of Black's involvement.

She stutter-stepped, dread filling her. Had he called them here to fire By Arrangement? Had she not been fast enough, humble enough in her acquiescence to his demand for payment? She suddenly regretted the jab about the cat.

If it were just her, she'd suck it up, take the loss and move on. But there was Lauren. The contract with Obsidian Studios was the biggest and most prestigious By Arrangement had earned. It was the first true step on the road to their goal of staging the ultimate Hollywood party, the Governors Ball after the Academy Awards.

Plus they'd already put a lot of time and effort into the plans for the film festival. She hated confrontation, but for Lauren she would fight.

She wouldn't let Black blow them off over a set of toe prints.

"Ms. Randall, Tori." Garrett stood up as she entered the room behind Lauren. Gone were the ill-fitting suits. He looked imposing in an impeccable black suit custom-made to fit the broad stretch of his shoulders. He waved them to a conversation area near windows overlooking the back lots. "Please have a seat. I'm expecting Kira, who you've been working with, but I've also asked the head of the PR department to join us."

"I don't understand, Mr. Black." Lauren gracefully sank into the corner of a black leather couch. "Do you have a problem with the plans we sent over? We received notice they'd been approved."

Tori felt the weight of Garrett's pale gaze as she sat down. She released the button on her navy blazer and crossed one bare leg over the other, meeting him stare for stare.

"I've seen the plans," he said, turning his attention to Lauren. "They are quite ambitious, but I want Obsidian to make an impression at the film festival, so yes, I approve.

I've asked you here because I want to add an event to those already contracted."

Another event? Tori was already anticipating the end of the film festival and putting Black behind them and he wanted to add another event?

Tori met Lauren's gaze. As he'd stated, their schedule was already ambitious. Lauren gave a slight nod. Tori sighed. What the heck, go big or go home. It was a lesson they learned at their father's knee.

"Of course," Lauren stated with confidence. "What did you want to add?"

"A ninetieth anniversary celebration."

CHAPTER FOUR

"Wow." Tori fought to control her expression. "How many people were you thinking of for this event?"

"I don't know." He shrugged. "Maybe three hundred."

She met Lauren's gaze, saw the figures were already running through her head. Really? A small, intimate affair would be one thing, but an anniversary party? That sounded huge.

Time for a dose of reality.

"It's going to be really difficult to find a venue for a party that size. Between the film festival and the holidays everything is booked up."

A knock sounded and the door swung open. A plump redhead with amazing skin and a slender African-American woman with a mass of braids drawn up in a high ponytail entered the room. Garrett stood and introduced the public relations manager, Irene Allan, and Kira respectively, and then caught them up on the details discussed.

"I don't understand, sir." Kira sat braced on the edge of her seat as if ready to hop into action or flee at a moment's notice. "We have a yearlong campaign planned for the ninetieth anniversary ready to launch in January."

"Yes, and the film festival gets a lot of national coverage. The anniversary is actually in December. I want to take advantage of the celebrities and exposure already provided by the event." He focused his silver eyes on Tori. "Surely something is available."

"Possibly," She tried for optimism. "If you're willing to go outside of Hollywood Hills—"

"No." Black gave an emphatic shake of his head. "It has to be in Hollywood Hills. I want there to be no doubt the party is part of the film festival. And we have to find a place quickly. I talked to the head of the film festival. We have a week to provide the venue information for it to be included in the program."

"Garrett." Pale eyes narrowed. She cleared her throat. "Ah, Mr. Black, nothing is available in Hollywood Hills. I received two calls this week asking if our plans were finalized because they were looking to take over our space."

"I got the same calls," Kira confirmed.

"Mr. Black," Lauren began in her conciliatory tone, "considering our time constraints, perhaps we can compromise. There are some very nice hotels in Beverly Hills within ten miles—"

"The Old Manor House," Tori blurted.

"—of the film festival." Lauren turned an inquiring glance Tori's way. "Excuse me?"

"Sorry." She sent her sister an apologetic smile. "I just thought of the perfect place. The Old Manor House."

"Absolutely not." Black cut her off. "That's not an option."

"Thanksgiving is this week, which means we really only have four days. The Old Manor House is perfect," she repeated. "It's in Hollywood Hills. It's iconic Obsidian Studios. And people will flock to the event to see it."

"I said no. The place is in no shape for a party."

"We have three weeks. If we start now—"

"You have my answer." He stood and buttoned his jacket. "Find me a venue close to the film festival."

* * *

"Mom and Dad will be here in an hour." Lauren propped a shoulder against the door of Tori's office. "We should head home. Any luck with the venue?"

"Two. One that exceeds our approved budget and one that's below our usual standards. I have a third but it's outside the perimeter Black set. The man is beyond stubborn."

"Look, I agree The Old Manor House is no-brainer the best option for the party. But Black is living in the house now and according to you his father was living there at the time he died. I can understand why he might not want to have a party there."

"I suppose." Okay, Tori grudgingly acknowledged she hadn't considered the father angle. Hard to when Garrett appeared so closed off emotionally. "That doesn't change the fact he's set an impossible task."

"He's the client." Lauren crossed her arms over her chest. "Have you gone over the pros and cons of the venues with Kira?"

"Yes. She's as frustrated as I am. This has been a colossal waste of time."

"Tell me about it. Forget the need to know for the program, we need to know what we'll be working with."

"You're right." Tori turned to her computer, picked up the email she sent to Kira with the venue links, made a couple of changes and hit Send. "It's in his hands now."

Lauren rolled her eyes. "Tell me you didn't do something rash."

"Just gave our client his options. Besides tomorrow is Thanksgiving. Time was up." She closed down her computer and felt around for her shoes. She refused to think of Garrett Black and his impossible demands any longer. "Let's go home. I'm anxious to see Mom and Dad. I'm really looking forward to a family Thanksgiving. I thought we were going to miss it this year."

"Me, too." Lauren linked her arm through Tori's and drew her over to Lauren's office, where she grabbed her purse from the corner of her desk before they headed for the door. "Are you sure you're up to cooking? I can still call in a favor and put in an order for turkey and all the trimmings, but tomorrow it will be too late."

"No." Tori locked up. "I miss cooking. Plus I did a bunch of prep work here today. It's already packed in the car. And I plan to put you to work to give Mom a break." She laughed as Lauren cringed. "Relax, I'm keeping it simple."

"Good. Because I plan to be on the couch watching football with Dad and Nick."

Tori's turn to send her eyes rolling. Her thing with Dad was cars, Lauren's was football. "You can peel potatoes while sitting on the couch."

"Oh. You're too kind."

"Remember that when it comes to cleanup."

"Mom put that knife down." Tori took a paring knife from her mother on the way to removing the turkey from the oven. "You're a guest this year. Oh, this smells great." She set the roasting pan on a wooden cutting board on the granite island.

"I want to help," Liz Randall protested. "I'm family, not a guest. What a beautiful bird." Mom squeezed Tori's shoulders.

"We need to let this rest. You always cook." Tori turned and gave Mom a real hug. The kitchen light bounced off the golden highlights in her new short bob. Tori thought her mother was beautiful. Young and vital, she took good care of herself and Dad. "I want you to enjoy yourself today."

"Hug fest!" Lauren suddenly threw her arms around them and the love multiplied by three. "This is better than an extra point."

"Wow, praise indeed." Mom stepped back and tweaked

both her and Lauren's hair. "My babies all grown up. So tell me, any new men in your lives?"

"Mom!" she and Lauren chorused.

"Well I'd like to hold some babies." Mom was unapologetic as she reclaimed the knife Tori had taken from her. She went to work on the chives for the mashed potatoes. "So spill."

"Tori has a nemesis," Lauren volunteered.

"Right, throw me under the bus." Tori wondered briefly how Garrett would spend the day. Did he have extended family or was he now alone in the world?

"I have nothing to share." Lauren plucked a carrot from the veggie tray. "And don't try to pretend you're not obsessed with Black."

"Now this sounds promising." Mom stole the carrot from Lauren. "You'll spoil your appetite." She pointed the carrot at Tori before popping it in her mouth. "I want all the details."

"Forget it." Tori chopped her hand through the air. "I refuse to let that man ruin my Thanksgiving."

"Spoilsport," Lauren teased and then groaned when her phone rang. "It's Ray Donovan."

"Don't answer." The words flew from Tori's mouth. "It's Thanksgiving. He has no right to expect us to be working."

"Ray Donovan the director?" Mom demanded. "Of course you have to answer. He's an important man."

"He's a client."

"You called him an arrogant jerk." Not that he'd ever been less than charming to Tori, but this was their only day off.

"I know." Lauren bit her lip, clearly torn. "I have to take this. Hello." She carried the phone out the back door, her greeting cut off as it closed.

"Ray Donovan is a jerk?" Mom's disappointment made Tori feel guilty.

"Not really. But he and Lauren have had a couple of altercations."

"I didn't think I'd have to worry about holidays being interrupted by emergencies when I married a dentist, but it's happened a few times. And, of course, it happens to your brother, the doctor, all the time." Mom stirred the gravy. "But never in a million years would I have guessed you girls got emergency calls."

"We're in the service industry." A taste of the sweet potatoes confirmed they were ready. "You'd be surprised at what people believe our availability should be. And the more VIP they get, the worse they are."

"So your success is your own downfall?" As usual Mom's perception cut to the heart of the matter.

"Yep." Tori glanced at Lauren's back, wondering why she'd even had her phone on. "But we love the work, so mostly it's okay. What's up?" she asked as Lauren stepped back inside.

"He has an unexpected guest for the holiday. He was hoping we could pull off a miracle for him."

"At three o'clock on the holiday? That would be a miracle. They'd be better off going out to dinner."

"I suggested that or that he try ordering in."

"Ha," Tori scoffed. "Pizza maybe."

"Well…"

Tori got a bad feeling. Very carefully she set the stirring spoon on a trivet. "Lauren, what did you do?"

"Don't worry. I told him our family was in town and we were about to sit down to our own meal."

Knowing her sister too well to relax, Tori propped her hands on her hips. "And?"

Lauren sighed. "And he invited us all to his place."

"Eee!" Mom slapped a hand over her mouth. "Sorry."

Tori narrowed her eyes at Lauren.

"What's up?" Dad and Nick loomed large on the family room side of the island, drawn by Mom's scream.

"Ray Donovan has invited us to his house for Thanksgiving dinner." Mom's excitement showed in the flap of her hands.

"The director of *Bots and Cops* Ray Donovan?" Dad demanded. "You know Donovan?"

"Good flick." Nick chomped a celery stick.

"He's a client," Lauren informed them and slid closer to Mom, dodging Tori's glare.

"He wants our turkey," she stated baldly. "Not us."

"Yes." At least Lauren made no attempt to sugarcoat the truth. "But he said he and his friend would appreciate the company. I guess the friend has had a tough year."

"I think we should go," Nick said.

"Seriously?" Tori looked at the meal ready to be plated. What was Nick thinking?

"It's a day of thanks and of giving. We're very lucky in what we have." Nick clapped Dad on the shoulder as he included the rest of them in a sweeping glance. "We can show our thanks by sharing with those less fortunate than us."

"You know we'd be eating in a Malibu mansion?" Tori clarified.

"Money is not what's important today." Mom added her support. She kissed Tori's cheek. "I'll help you pack this up."

"Okay." She sighed. "But it's all going to have to be reheated. I don't want to hear a single word about dry turkey."

An hour later Nick pulled to a stop behind a red Maserati in Donovan's driveway.

Dad whistled from his seat in the front. "Now there's a sweet ride."

Tori exchanged looks with Lauren.

"You owe me so big for this," she warned her sister.

"What is it?" Mom gazed back and forth between them.

"Who," Lauren corrected. "Her nemesis."

Garrett sipped a beer and pretended interest in the football game Ray had on the big screen TV. His buddy demanded Garrett come over when he heard Garrett intended to spend the holiday alone.

It sounded like a good idea at the time, but he should have stayed at the manor. Or gone home to Santa Barbara, now that the film had wrapped up. He was poor company. The accident that killed his father happened a year ago.

Lonely, between wives, good old dad had shown up at Garrett's asking if he wanted to get a meal together. They usually spoke once or twice a year, but it had been a while so he agreed. They talked about a whole lot of nothing. And at the end of the night his dad was dead.

Who knew he'd actually care.

The doorbell sounded. Ray hopped up.

"More company?"

"Dinner." Ray rubbed his hands together.

"Pizza?" Garrett guessed. The meal of champions suited him fine. He wasn't real hungry. Much better than the lobster Thermidor his father had ordered for them at his club last year.

"We can do better than that." Ray headed for the door. "I invited the Randall twins and their family to join us."

The beer bottle froze halfway to Garrett's mouth and he stared unseeing at the eighty yard runback on the screen. Tori Randall was here? Definitely should have stayed home.

"Come on." Ray slapped him on the back. "You can help bring in the turkey."

Oh, joy. Garrett finished the beer he'd been nursing. Suddenly a bit of a buzz seemed like a good idea.

He arrived outside to find everyone surrounding his car and introductions being made. There were worse ways to spend a few minutes, so he popped the hood. Talk of cars and motors relaxed him some. Having a common interest eased the awkwardness of strangers thrown together.

Ray wandered off with Lauren and Mrs. Randall. The Randall men were affable and intelligent, and best of all, wanted nothing more from him than to talk cars. They had no idea to pitch, no complaint to lodge. Garrett relaxed even more.

Until he glanced up to see Tori petting the slick red paint. He felt every stroke as if she touched flesh instead of metal. She'd been present but quiet, observing rather than participating, allowing him to ignore her.

No more. His body stirred. He needed a distraction now.

"So I heard you brought turkey," he said when she lifted her gaze to his.

"Yes." She shifted her weight from one foot to the other and his eyes followed the sway of her hips in skintight jeans. Her deep rust top, lower in the back than the front, brought out the honey-brown of her eyes. "We brought the full deal."

"I can't wait. I'm starved." Nick clapped a hand down on Garrett's shoulder. "Don't get me wrong. The women in my family can cook. But Tori's idea of snacks is a few veggie sticks. A man needs substance on Thanksgiving."

"You're a doctor." Tori's hands landed on her hips, highlighting the sweet curves of her body. "You should be touting the value of vegetables as a snack. I swear, it's a wonder you aren't three hundred pounds."

"Hey, it takes a lot of calories to put in ten-hour days."

"Time on the golf course doesn't count."

"Ha-ha. At least I exercise."

Nick led the way to the back of the SUV and opened the hatch door. Heavenly scents hit Garrett's nostrils. That quickly, his appetite flared and he was as hungry as Nick professed to be.

"I exercise."

"Right, you shake your butt to music twice a week."

"Zumba is not for the weak. We'll put it on later and see who outlasts whom."

Obviously a well-worn argument between the siblings. Garrett hoped they moved off topic soon. Images of Tori wiggling her behind until sweat glistened on her skin felt like punches to his gut. And did nothing to cool down his libido.

"Children, no arguing in front of company."

Her father's playful chiding brought a rosy glow to Tori's cheeks.

Garrett sighed and reached for a box, resolving to ignore the woman at all costs. What had Ray been thinking to invite the Randall family to dinner? Of course Garrett knew. His well-intentioned friend meant to take Garrett's mind off memories of last year.

Hefting his box, he followed Tori's tight backside up the front steps. Damned if Ray hadn't succeeded.

Heating up the meal barely took any time at all. Unfortunately. At least she was safe in the kitchen. Tori didn't have to fear where she looked in case she happened to link gazes with the head of Obsidian Studios.

Safe? Fear? Strange words.

Why did Garrett disconcert her so much? She wasn't afraid of him. She'd experienced his bark and lived through it. She didn't fear him physically. No, she wasn't afraid of his bite. But the thought of his touch? That disturbed her.

Because she wanted it too much.

Sweet sunflowers but she wanted his hands on her. He felt it, too. He liked to pretend he didn't. Right. As if the chemistry between them didn't sizzle like an electrical current.

But Garrett had issues. She saw them clearly in his eyes—when he allowed anything to show. More often he kept his feelings locked carefully away. That, too, was a clue to his lack of emotional availability.

Tori didn't do issues.

Sure, everyone carried baggage. But some felt things more deeply than others. Some brooded, which allowed the pain to continually rise to the surface no matter how hard they tried to bury it. The problem was if they never dealt with the issue, if they never got to the other side of anger or denial, they didn't heal, and they became a powder keg of emotion.

She knew from personal experience if he blew when he was in a bad place, the result could be fatal.

She didn't want to go there again.

So she, too, avoided the sizzle.

"Your dad likes your young man." Mom strolled in from setting the table.

The plate of asparagus landed on the counter with more force than Tori intended, causing a clatter and one of the spears to roll off. She scooped it up and threw it away.

"What are you talking about, Mom?" She wiped her hands down the front of her black apron.

"Don't play dumb, dear. Garrett Black. You're smitten."

"No, I'm not." Refusing to give her mother any encouragement, Tori moved the asparagus to a tray along with the potatoes and gravy. They'd be eating family style at the dining room table.

"There's something there." Mom grabbed the butter and corn pudding and followed Tori through to the dining room. "I've seen the way you look at each other."

"Shh. He'll hear you." But a peek at the group in front of the TV showed Garrett occupied in the game. Obviously sides had been chosen and the lead depended on the field goal about to be kicked.

She returned to the kitchen for the turkey. Thrusting the broccoli salad into her mother's hands, she declared, "He's a client, Mom. I don't get personally involved with clients."

"No?" Mom lifted the salad bowl and arched a finely plucked brow.

"Today is an exception," she insisted. "And Lauren's fault."

"True, but I'm not sorry we came. Ray Donovan is charming. Your father and Nick are having a great time and I'll have something to tell all my friends when we return to Palm Springs." She set the dish down to hug Tori. "And I'm glad you're getting a chance to spend time with Garrett. You're an event coordinator, kiddo, not a doctor. There's no reason once the film festival is over that you can't see where the attraction between the two of you leads."

"Mom." Love and exasperation filled the word.

"Tori." Stubbornness and affection came back at her.

"It smells delicious in here." A male voice broke into the standoff. "Can I help with anything?"

"Garrett." Surprise added a bit of a squeak to his name. Lord, had he heard her conversation with Mom? His stoic expression gave nothing away. She cleared her throat. "Dinner is ready."

"You're just in time to carry in the turkey." Mom handed Tori the broccoli salad and, hooking her arm through Garrett's, led him to the platter holding the holiday bird. "It's quite heavy."

"Sure," Garrett said.

"Excellent." Mom released him and moved away. "Tori will help you. I'll go rally the troops."

Tori glared at her mother's disappearing back. Subtle, much?

"This looks wonderful." Garrett leaned over the turkey and took a big whiff before lifting his gaze to Tori. "It's been a long time since I actually had a traditional Thanksgiving meal."

Something in his tone made her think there was more to his statement than the surface meaning.

"Many families have traditions besides turkey." Tori sought to ease any awkwardness. "What does your family do?"

"Nothing."

She laughed. "Kind of like us, huh?" She waved in the direction of the living room. "Football and turkey is it for us. But it's all about getting together, isn't it?"

"When I said 'nothing,' I meant nothing. It was only my dad and me. Last year was the first time we'd gotten together in years. It was the last time I saw him. I'll take this through." He picked up the heavy platter and carried it to the adjoining dining room.

Oh, God. No wonder Ray called them. Tori rubbed at a pain over her left eye, extracted her foot from her mouth and followed Garrett.

Surprisingly, she thoroughly enjoyed dinner. The TV was muted at Mom's insistence, which allowed for discussion. Dad said grace and then the food began to flow around the table. As host, Ray cut the turkey. Garrett ribbed him some, but it was all in fun.

Nick asked Ray about his last megahit and he entertained them with stories from the set of that movie and several others. He drew Garrett into the conversation and he lit up as he recalled some outrageous incidences from his films. For the first time she saw his passion for his work.

Thank goodness. After his revelation in the kitchen, she'd worried he might brood through the meal. She actually caught herself staring when he laughed. Had she never heard him laugh before? Now she thought about it, no. He was always so somber.

Dad and Nick threw in a few humorous stories from the dentist office and hospital. She shared a glance with Lauren, and they silently agreed not to join the trend. Yeah they had funny and outrageous stories about events they'd handled. Still, it wouldn't be smart to share with clients at the table.

"I made pumpkin pie for dessert," Mom announced. A round of groans flowed around the table followed by a flood of compliments aimed at Tori for the meal just consumed.

"Thanks," she responded, pleased by the appreciation. "I seriously want some pie, Mom, but I have to wait for a while."

The others wholeheartedly agreed. Ray and Garrett both showed interest when Lauren mentioned the annual poker game.

"Okay." Nick rubbed his hands together. "Let's get the table cleared and get started."

"Don't worry about the dishes. My staff will clean up tomorrow." Ray picked up his plate and headed for the kitchen. "I have a game table upstairs in the loft. I'll go get it set up."

"I'll help." Lauren dropped off her plate and joined Ray.

A warm feeling swelled behind Tori's heart, bringing her to a dead stop as the two of them walked by. Hmm. There was definitely more than antagonism between the two of them. She'd have to tag Lauren for more information tomorrow.

She continued to the sink, began to run hot water.

A large hand reached past her and turned it off. "Ray said his staff would take care of the cleanup."

Garrett. Who knew he spent so much time in the kitchen?

"Yes, but I have to clean my containers." Forget leftovers, two extra male appetites took care of those. "Plus I should rinse the dishes. It'll only take a few minutes."

"I can't let you do that." He took the sponge from her hand. "You cooked. You shouldn't have to do dishes, too."

"Well, if you insist." She stepped aside and waved him into place. "I'll stack the dishwasher."

Dark brows lifted, but he accepted the challenge by rolling up his sleeves and stepping up to the sink. He brandished the rinse wand like a pro.

"Garrett, how sweet of you to help." Mom came in with the last of the serving dishes. "I'll scrape and we'll have these done in no time."

"Mom, you don't have to help." Tori tried to protest, but her mother waved her off much as Tori had tried to wave off Garrett. Once Mom finished her self-imposed chore, she went in search of dirty dishes in the living room, brought her collection into them and bustled off again.

"She's a bit of a dynamo, isn't she?" Garrett muttered. "I can see where you girls get your energy."

Girls? "You say that like it's a bad thing."

"No, but it can be unnerving." He handed her the last container, leaned back against the counter and reached for a dishrag to dry his hands. "It's also easy to see where you get your looks. Your father is a lucky man."

Oh. She smiled slightly. So he did find her attractive. Not that it mattered. Too many strikes against them. She dried the last of her containers and tucked it in a box. Looking down she realized she still wore her apron. With a grimace she pulled it off and tucked it in the box, too. No wonder he thought she looked like her mother.

"Thanks for the help. I'm going to run this stuff out to the car." She lifted one of the two boxes she'd brought the food in and set it on the rolling cooler.

"Let me." He set the other box on top and began rolling. He took it out the back door and they walked down the drive.

Tori shivered. Salt and smoke from a fireplace scented

the air. Dark hid the ocean view. And a low marine layer obscured the stars.

"It looks like we'll have fog tonight. We probably shouldn't stay too late."

"Yeah, I feel the damp in my leg."

Oh, man, she couldn't catch a break. He'd actually been decent today, participating in the conversation, helping with the chores. And she kept reminding him of all he'd lost. She watched while he packed the boxes and cooler in the back of the SUV.

"Listen, I'm sorry for your loss. Today must have been difficult for you."

He shut the hatch. "Yes and no. Your family made today easier. My father and I weren't close."

"I kind of got that, still he was your only family. You must miss him."

For a moment she didn't think he'd answer. He turned and headed up the steps to the front door, his slight limp now evident. She slowly trailed him, wishing she'd learn to keep her mouth shut.

He stopped with his hand on the door handle. "I miss knowing he was there. We weren't close, but there was a sense of connection that's gone."

He was all alone in the world. How sad. Without thinking about it she took his hand.

"I'm sorry," she said again. Impulsively she kissed his cheek.

His fingers threaded into her hair and he turned her mouth to his. "Don't be sorry for me," he said against her lips and kissed her.

CHAPTER FIVE

GARRETT'S LIPS SEDUCED Tori, starting out soft and growing firmer. He ran his tongue alone the seam of her mouth, seeking entrance, which she granted on a sigh. His heat drew her closer as the world disappeared.

The man knew how to kiss. One hand held her head captive to his mouth while the other started between her shoulder blades and slowly wandered down her spine to the small of her back, where his thumb caressed her sensitive flesh and his fingers teased the first swell of her derriere.

She melted under his expertise, arching into his hold, wanting his hands on more of her, all of her.

All thoughts of complications and incompatibility fled her mind. All that mattered was his mouth on hers. His body sheltering hers. Hands caught between them, she thrilled to the feel of the hard muscles under her fingers. There was no give to him as she ran her hands up his chest to loop her arms around his neck. She leaned into him, giving everything he demanded. And seeking a response of her own.

He pulled his lips free to tease the corner of her mouth and begin a trail of kisses that led to the curve of her neck. He bit her just short of the point of pain and she almost fell apart in his arms. But he pushed her back, held her until she gained her own balance, then released her.

She blinked up at him. Why did he stop?

"I appreciate the sacrifice you and your family made today. But never make the mistake of pitying me again, Ms. Randall." He opened the door and disappeared inside.

Still shaking with desire, she eyed the empty doorway. Feeling cheated and chastised, she folded her arms around herself. And boom. Just like that the brooding recluse was back.

Oh, yeah, no way would she ever make that mistake again.

Hands clasped behind his back, Garrett paced his office. He'd read Tori's report on the available venues for the anniversary party and he was unhappy with the results. Unfortunately Kira confirmed the information, leaving him with the choice of going substandard, over budget or out of the area. None of which was acceptable.

He walked to the window overlooking the north lot, which included the western panorama. Of the three, the only one he'd consider was the high-end hotel, but he found it hard to reconcile that decision when he was asking all his directors and departments to watch their spending.

In the distance he spotted the top gable on The Old Manor House. Tori had not repeated her suggestion of using the house for the event. She didn't have to—once mentioned it lingered out there as an option. Of course he saw the appeal of the house as a draw for the event. Seeing inside the iconic old house would ensure participation by press and industry professionals alike.

But it would be like opening a vein and exposing the wound to the world.

He'd spent many lonely years in the house that was more museum than home. Both as a child and in recent months. He'd love nothing more than to get rid of the house, but it was entitled. As if he'd ever want to thrust the albatross onto his child.

Hell, as if he'd ever have a child. That would require letting a woman close again. He'd decided the pain wasn't worth the risk.

He turned away from the view, strolled back to his desk, where he stared blindly at Tori's email.

He obviously lacked whatever was necessary to sustain a long-term relationship. His mother left. His father wanted him near but couldn't be bothered to spend time with him. Stepmothers barely acknowledged his existence. And his fiancée dumped him when he left the studio, proving she'd cared more for his status than him.

A man could only take so much rejection before he determined it wasn't worth the effort. These days he preferred short-term, no involvement associations. And he'd been too busy, too scarred up over the past year to even bother with that.

Which explained the madness of kissing Tori Randall.

It had been too long since he'd touched a woman. Or had a woman, besides a physical therapist, touch him. For a moment he'd forgotten Tori was an employee, or the next best thing. He preferred to keep professional relationships just that, regardless of how beautiful the woman.

And if he were honest with himself, surgery had given him back the use of his leg, but the Frankenstein results were an ugly reminder of what he'd been through. Not something he wanted to show off. The doctors said cosmetic surgery could clean it up, but the thought of more time under the knife turned his stomach.

Back to business, the decision on the anniversary venue finally came down to expedience. He disliked having his space invaded, but it would be the biggest draw, reach the biggest audience to turn around Obsidian's failing reputation. Yes, it would require cleaning and repairs, but it was updating that needed to be done.

With his decision made, Garrett picked up the phone to

call Lauren Randall. All things considered, he felt it best to keep his interactions with Tori to a minimum.

Looking crisp in a red skirt suit, Lauren strolled into Tori's office and sank gracefully into a visitor chair. "I heard from Garrett on the venue."

Tori sat back in her chair, arms crossed over her chest, brows reaching for her hairline.

"He contacted *you?*"

"Yes."

"Why?"

Lauren crossed her legs. "Don't you want to know what he chose?"

"We'll get to that." Tori leaned forward on her desk, pinned her sister with a narrow-eyed stare. "Did you know Garrett was Ray's guest yesterday?"

"No."

"Because it would have been helpful to have the information ahead of time."

Lauren held up both hands in a sign of surrender. "I promise I didn't know. Ray didn't say."

"Ray." Tori tapped her fingers on her desk as she contemplated her wombmate. She was hiding something. Which reminded Tori of the feeling she'd had when she saw Lauren with their host. "You two were pretty chummy yesterday. Anything you want to share?"

"About me and Ray? There's nothing to tell."

Uh-huh. She appeared her usual poised self, except for the rocking of her high heel, a tell Tori had never clued her sister into. Oh, yeah, something was there. Exactly what was hard to say. Tori thought she picked up on a romantic vibe, but it could be the same type of thing she was going through with Garrett, an attraction she had no intention of acting on.

Especially after the way he left her hanging yesterday.

Today she wondered what she'd found so attractive. A beautiful profile and godlike body were no excuse for a shadowed soul.

"So what venue did Black choose?"

"He's decided to hold the event at The Old Manor House."

"Really?" She plopped back in her chair. "It truly is the best choice."

"Agreed. Unfortunately it's going to be a lot of work. Most of the place has been closed down for years."

"He mentioned that when I drove him home last month." Tori pulled a pad toward her and started to make a list. "How bad is it?"

"Hopefully not too bad." Lauren hesitated, causing Tori to look up from her list. "I have an appointment with him tomorrow to assess what needs to be done."

She carefully set down her pen. "You have an appointment?"

"Yes."

"And Black contacted you?"

"Yes."

"What's going on, Lauren? You handle the clients, subcontractors and vendors so I understand him contacting you about his decision even though I was the one who provided the information. But I handle the site and food service. I should be the one doing the walk-through."

"When he called, he asked that I be the point of contact."

Tori blinked, her first and totally unprofessional and inappropriate reaction was hurt feelings. He found their kiss so offensive he had to disassociate himself from her? Fine. She understood completely.

After spending the remainder of Thanksgiving pretending nothing happened between them, she wasn't particularly looking forward to a repeat performance.

Except she had a job to do. And his little tantrum was getting in the way of that.

"Did you explain to him how we work?" she demanded.

"Of course I did. He didn't care. He prefers I relay information to you."

Another pinch she determinedly pushed away. She didn't have the luxury of giving in to hurt feelings. "But after the initial walk-through, I'll have access?"

Lauren shook her head. "He wants to keep the intrusion into his private quarters as minimal as possible."

"That's not going to work."

"No. It's not. What happened between you two?"

"Nothing." Lauren dodged the question about Ray; Tori figured she deserved the same privilege.

"There has to be some reason he doesn't want to work with you," Lauren pointed out.

Yeah, message received. And she'd be happy to give him his way, but she couldn't effectively do what needed to be done from a distance. And they were way too busy to play games.

"You heard Jenna and the others. He's temperamental. Who knows why the man does anything? I'm totally stumped on how we're ever going to find a match for him. What I do know is we can't let the man dictate how we conduct our business."

"True enough." Lauren lifted one fine brow at Tori. "You know what we're going to have to do."

"Oh, no." The denial came out as instinctively as the hand that flew up in a halting gesture. "It's been years since we attempted that."

"It'll be fine. We never failed to fool our target."

Tori threw up her hands. "I can't believe you're the one suggesting we trade places. You always argued against it."

"Because we were only ever fooling around and the risk was not worth the reward."

"Right, we were having fun. This is business. Black will be furious if he finds out."

"So he can't find out." Lauren leaned forward, her golden gaze earnest. "You said it, we can't let him dictate how we do our business, but we can't afford to antagonize him, either. Desperate circumstances require desperate measures."

Tori smoothed her hands down the sides of Lauren's plum business suit and followed Garrett from the front parlor to a large drawing room with attached conservatory.

So far, so good. Tori paired the pencil skirt suit with a black turtleneck sweater and black pumps, which were a good two inches shorter than anything Lauren owned. She'd swept her longer hair into a French twist and used a heavier hand with her makeup to complete the transformation.

She'd tested her impersonation by stopping at the showroom before heading to The Old Manor House. None of the kitchen staff noticed anything off. Eyeing Garrett's broad back, she continued to channel her sister. It amazed her how easy it was to know how Lauren would act in any given situation.

Tori made a mental note to remember this the next time she had to confront someone. She tended to duck and dodge. Projecting Lauren might save her from a bad haircut.

"The lines of this room are wonderful. And I love the way it opens to both the conservatory and the terrace. Having the event here will be a huge draw. We can anticipate at least three hundred people."

She continued to stroll the room. About twenty-by-forty, it would hold a good number of people, once they removed the gym equipment and some of the dated furnishings. She pushed open the terrace doors, stepped outside. The large outdoor space had been designed for entertaining. Doors also opened onto it from the conservatory.

"Nice cat." A large gray cat, very like the one she'd seen when she drove Garrett home, sunned itself on the stone balustrade. But no, Black didn't own a cat.

He joined her outside and scowled at the sleeping cat. "It's not mine."

Right.

She retraced her steps inside. "The carpet is faded here by the terrace doors. How long have the rooms been carpeted?"

"That would be stepmother number two, so about twenty years ago. Stepmother number three kept the carpet but changed everything else. That makes the drapes and furnishings about fifteen years old."

He spoke so casually, she wondered how he could be so unaffected by such drastic changes in his childhood.

"How many times did your father marry?"

"Five. His fourth and fifth wives didn't care to live in the manor, so he bought them their own homes."

"Wow. Any half or stepsiblings?" He'd said he had no other family but perhaps there was someone out there he could claim.

"No. My father didn't care for children. Will the carpet need to be replaced?"

Four stepmothers. No siblings. And a father who didn't care for children. No wonder he was so impassive. Had he known any love in his life? Hearing his history explained some of the angst lurking in his eyes.

She felt for him, but she couldn't let her feelings go beyond sympathy. Trying to reach someone who repressed his emotions was a lesson in futility. And if you did manage to get close, it just blew up in your face. Like the kiss on Thanksgiving.

Best to stay on task.

"It wouldn't be an issue if the carpeting was a paler color, but with this deep burgundy it really shows. Tori's better at these things than I am." She couldn't resist the dig. "I'll talk to her and see what can be done."

Already her mind flowed with ideas. For the party she could get a nice rug and lay it across the threshold. Or a better fix would be to cut out the faded sections and lay down tile.

"If the weather is nice, the downstairs rooms, except for the study—" where he slept "—should be all that's needed for the party. But we're talking December so there's no telling. Do you have rooms upstairs that could be used?"

A scowl lowered his brows. "The library and media room. However, I really don't want people traipsing throughout the house."

"That won't be a problem," she said in her best Lauren voice. "Security will be on hand to protect your privacy. We'll post them at the top of the staircases to help direct traffic, and we'll have one patrolling the rooms to make sure no one wanders where they don't belong."

"Staircases? There's no need for anyone to go to the third floor."

"Three hundred people," she reminded him. "We're going to need access to every bathroom in the house."

The corner of his firm mouth turned down. "Oh."

From the look on his face she knew he was rethinking his decision to have the party at the manor. His next words confirmed it.

"Maybe this is more trouble than it's worth."

"Garrett, you're out of options." Tori's gut clenched as she realized she must take a stand. *Think, Lauren,* she breathed deeply to keep the shakiness out of her voice. "The film festival starts in less than three weeks. By Arrangement has four other events we're handling for Obsidian Studios. If you want to have an anniversary party, then this is where it will be and we need to get the cleanup crews in immediately."

His shoulders went rigid. "I'm the client. I'm the one to say how it's going to be."

"No." She swallowed hard, squared her shoulders. "We contracted for the first four events. We agreed to take on the party, too, but it's not in the contract. If we can't move forward with the party starting today, then we can't continue with it. Otherwise we put your other events at risk."

Her heart pounded and her hands found the sides of her skirt again, yet she stood her ground. Lauren would have a fit at disappointing a client, but she'd support Tori's decision.

"I— We can do this, Garrett. We just need your cooperation."

"Funny you should mention cooperation."

The silky quality of his voice sent goose bumps rippling over her skin. Uh-oh. Edging away, she half turned, giving him a view of her profile.

"Shall we take a look at the upstairs room?" she suggested, deliberately cheerful. "I'd also like to see the kitchen." Putting action to words, she headed off, half hoping he wouldn't follow.

"Hold on." The hard rasp of his demand sounded right behind her. He grabbed her arm, swinging her to face him. "Tori."

Fudge sticks. Caught.

She cocked her head and raised her eyebrows in feigned confusion, hoping to brazen it out. "I'm Lauren." She pretended to wave off his error with a small laugh. "Don't worry, people make that mistake all the time.

He crossed his arms and stared down at her. "You're Tori. And I'm waiting for an explanation."

"You're mistaken—"

His mouth cut her off, his kiss a hard slant of his lips

over hers. The shock of his action threw her off stride. She placed her hands on his chest intending to push him away. Then he softened the kiss, stealing her ability to think. She sank against him, opening her mouth under his.

In the next instant she was teetering on her own feet while he strode to lean against the mantel.

"Now, Tori, tell me why I shouldn't fire By Arrangement right now."

Not trusting her legs to hold her, she perched on the bench of his weight equipment. Once seated, she glared at him. "That was unprofessional."

He arched a dark brow. "Don't get me started on unprofessional. Lauren was to meet with me today."

"You're right." Indignation fueled her recovery. "The gig is up, and I'm glad. We would never have done it if you hadn't hog-tied us."

"You're seriously blaming your lying on me."

"Yes. I can't believe you, kissing on my sister. We may look alike but we are not interchangeable." He just tapped into a twin's worst nightmare, that the guy you liked might like your sister better. Well, her worst nightmare. Lauren was a hard act to live up to.

"I didn't kiss your sister. I kissed you. Stop stalling."

Legs sturdier now, she surged to her feet. "And why do you keep doing that? You obviously have no affection for me."

His eyes blazed. "What can I say? You bring out the worst in me."

"I mean we're having a serious conversation about a difficult time in your life. I show some simple compassion. And boom you're kissing me and yelping about pity." She paced to the terrace door and back again, cautiously keeping to her end of the room. "As if anyone in their right mind would pity you."

"Are you done? Perhaps ready to talk about the real issue?"

"No." His very stillness irked her. "Because that wasn't a quick get-my-attention-I-won't-be-pitied kiss. There was tongue involved and passion. You don't kiss someone like that, then walk away and pretend it never happened."

"Ms. Randall." A touch of menace echoed in her name. "Do you want me to kiss you again?"

"Uh, no." She retreated a few steps, the backs of her knees hit the exercise bench and she abruptly sat. Darn, that could have come out stronger. She lifted her chin. "We're in a professional relationship. It would complicate things unnecessarily to inject a personal element into the situation."

"My feelings exactly. If you need to hear me admit I like kissing you, the answer is yes. It's the reason I asked Lauren to be my point of contact with By Arrangement."

"Oh."

"And as we both agree a personal relationship is not an option, we've managed to spend a lot of time accomplishing nothing. Perhaps we can now get down to business."

Still reeling from his admission, it took a moment to catch up. She stood and straightened her jacket with a tug.

"I wouldn't say nothing. We understand each other better now."

"You think so?" That dark eyebrow took another trip up his forehead.

"Of course. Communication is important in any relationship, personal or professional. We'll be better equipped to deal with each other moving forward."

"If we move forward. I still don't know why you were masquerading as your sister."

"We're small at By Arrangement. My sister and I each have a role to play." Okay it wouldn't do to remind him Lauren had already explained the way they worked. How did she put this so he'd understand and still keep By Arrangement under contract? "Would you ask one of your accountants to edit a film, or vice versa?"

"Of course not." He rubbed a hand across the back of his neck. "They're different skill sets."

"Exactly, but that's what you're asking of Lauren and I. We can cover for each other short-term, but to be our most effective, we each need to stick to our strengths. Especially when we're as busy as we're going to be over the next few weeks. Besides the film festival, we have three other events in December. Lauren has vendor meetings all day going over the logistics for all of the events. It was important she take those meetings."

"Why didn't she just schedule me for another day?"

"Because we can't afford to lose another day." She drew in a deep breath, let it out slowly. "Sorry. We didn't want to blow off your request, but we couldn't honor it, either."

"So you became Lauren so she could be in two places at once."

"And because this is what I do. I needed to see what we're working with here. I oversee the site and the food. It's my job to evaluate the site, conceive the design and calculate what's needed to pull off the event."

She blinked up into his silver gaze. Her passion had driven her across the room until she stood right in front of him.

He contemplated her for a moment, then moved to the open terrace doors and stood, hands clasped behind him as he stared outside. She held her position, allowing him time.

"So in your professional opinion you feel the manor would work for the anniversary party?"

"I think it would be freaking fabulous." She walked over until she faced his profile. "It would be the event not to miss. But I meant what I said, if you choose not to have it here, By Arrangement can't handle the event. We can't afford to spend any more time spinning our wheels."

"But you believe you can whip the manor into shape in the time we have?"

"What I've seen is mostly cosmetic. The house has been kept up, the structure is sound. So yes. If we get started today, I can get it done."

He turned his unreadable gray eyes on her and gave a brief nod. "Do it."

"Yeah." Relief and excitement lit her up inside. She threw her arms around him in a big hug. "You won't be sorry." Ideas rolled off her tongue as she searched for her notebook. She found it on the exercise bench, retrieved it and kicked off her shoes before heading for the stairs. "I want to see the upstairs and the kitchen. Then we'll go through each room again and go over the specifics."

Behind her, his muttered "I'm already sorry" barely registered.

CHAPTER SIX

"This is not working, Ms. Randall," Garrett stated, the cell connection bringing his irritation up close and personal. "There are too many interruptions. I need you on-site."

"That's not going to happen. Our schedule is insane right now." She keyed her screensaver up in order to give Garrett her full attention. "What's the problem? The dust will settle down once they get through all the rooms." Saints have mercy, it had only been two days.

"So you said." Exasperation echoed down the line. "The carpet people came out today and there's hardwood under the wall-to-wall carpet."

"Really?" That could be good news for their schedule. "What shape is it in? Are you going to be able to use it?"

"Possibly. I'm told it may take longer to resurface than to lay the new tile you suggested, which brings me to my point. You need to be on-site. We lost half a day's work while the carpeting staff waited for me to arrive home and direct them. We can't afford that kind of delay."

"I'll come by tomorrow and talk to the contractor."

"Yes, and ten minutes after you leave they'll be calling me again. I, too, have a busy schedule."

"Maybe you could work from the house for a few days?"

Silence met her suggestion, then a grinding noise.

"I am not a designer, Ms. Randall. This was your suggestion. I expect you to handle it." This time the silence was followed by a trill announcing the call ended.

Aggravating, demanding man. Nothing was easy with him. She activated her computer and scanned her schedule. She wedged the promised trip to the Old Manor into an already packed day. Then she turned her attention to the preview event scheduled in a few hours.

She'd probably be having the same conversation in person. Garrett was nothing if not tenacious. Strangely, she looked forward to it.

"Red carpet is active." Lauren's voice came through the headset. It meant they had three hours until the *Tattoo Murders* postpremiere party.

Tori passed the information on to her kitchen staff. They were working off-site. The beautiful old theater had the seats to accommodate a large audience, including the balcony section where the postparty would be held, but there was no kitchen to speak of, so the food would arrive thirty minutes prior to the end of the screening.

Until then, she and Lauren were on-site supervising the setup of the balcony into an ultrasuave lounge. Black leather sofas and chairs created conversation groups while chrome cocktail tables added a reflection of light. Three bar stations provided easy access to liquid refreshments. Waiters and waitresses would carry trays of food.

Large banners showing a portion of the skull tattoo featured in the movie spanned the length of the theater. Two cupcake displays were already in place and picked up on the skull theme. Temporary tattoos matching the movie were available throughout.

For the preevent waitresses wearing the tattoos were ready to serve iced water and freshly popped corn. A candy table featured all kinds of theater delights.

Tori stole a pack of Sweet Tarts as Lauren strolled up.

"We should see the first guests in a few minutes." Her sister shook her head when Tori offered a Sweet Tarts candy. "The space looks spectacular. The way the banners curve with the theater really make the tattoo come alive."

"We're ready here," Tori assured her. "I'd like someone from security to keep an eye on the bar stations in case anyone decides to help themselves."

"I'll take care of it." Lauren selected a red Cherry Vines candy, took a bite. "Garrett will be here tonight."

"Probably. He didn't mention it when he called to complain about the cleaners. They only started two days ago and I've already gotten three calls from him. Today it was the carpet. Yesterday the dust. Tomorrow it'll probably be the sun is shining too brightly through the clean windows."

Lauren laughed. "He's not that bad."

"Nearly." Tori shook her head. "He's nervous about this project, so he's twitchy."

"Or he likes talking to you," Lauren suggested.

Tori placed her palm on Lauren's forehead. "Are you sure you're feeling okay?"

"Ha-ha. If we're going to do the matchmaking thing, we should take advantage of tonight. Try to observe him as he interacts with the women attending."

"If? Do we have a choice?"

"We could tell Jenna and the others that we've decided we can't put one client's needs before another's."

"I vote for that option." For some reason Tori found the idea of matchmaking for Garrett more and more distasteful. "Do you think they'll accept that?"

"I'm not saying they'll like it." Lauren straightened a dish on the table. "But what can they do?"

"Make our lives miserable until after the wedding. Cancel their contracts. Bad-mouth our business." Tori outlined the worst-case scenarios. She liked the three women, they'd become friendly, but bottom line they were clients, not friends.

"The last is what concerns me. We can't count on friendship when it comes to our business." Lauren voiced Tori's thoughts. "We've reached a new plateau. We can't risk what we've achieved."

"Obsidian is the bigger contract." Tori swept a hand out, encompassing the current venue. "We don't want to antagonize Garrett."

"You've already done that, with the whole trading places thing."

"Me?" Tori planted her hands on her hips. "It was your idea."

"Yeah, but you got caught," Lauren taunted. "How did he know?"

Tori wondered about that, too, but hadn't thought it very smart to ask. "We were talking about whether we were going to match him up or not. I vote we don't."

"Really?" Lauren surveyed her, an odd look in her eyes. "I vote we do. I'm not happy about it, but it's not like we'd be hurting him, just helping him find love. And hopefully he'll be none the wiser."

"I suppose," Tori conceded. She felt cheated, as if she'd had a treat dangled in front of her then yanked away. "I'll keep a look out tonight, but it won't be easy while we're working."

"What are you talking about? We were working when we paired up both Jenna and Cindy."

"Here come our first guests," Tori noted with relief. "Let's rock this event."

The postpremiere party for *Tattoo Murders* was in full swing when Garrett sprung free of the theater. A reporter from one of the entertainment magazines had waylaid him.

Word traveled fast in the film industry, and he'd heard of the changes Garrett mandated on current productions.

Garrett shrugged it off as the normal tightening of the reins with the takeover of new leadership. Which was true as far as it went. No need to advertise the fact his father had gotten too lax in his policies.

A waiter offered him an option of appetizers. He chose a stuffed mushroom and headed for one of the bars. Glass in hand, he made a circuit of the room. People hailed him from all sides. He nodded, shook hands and exchanged quips.

The venue was perfect. Everyone raved about being able to walk right into the party. Tori's idea. Garrett must admit he appreciated the convenience.

Overall By Arrangement had done a great job. The food was tasty, the bars were well-placed, the seating comfortable while allowing for flow of movement and the movie graphics were tasteful and fun. Many people sported the temporary tattoos.

It all seemed effortless, but he spotted Tori directing a waiter to collect empty glasses from a table. His gaze swept over her. She wore a black sheath dress with interesting cutouts in the asymmetrical neckline. Her long blond hair fell over one shoulder in a river of molten gold, drawing attention to the ivory perfection of her neck.

She probably thought she faded into the background. Not so. The black fabric faithfully hugged every subtle curve. He noted more than one male head turn in her direction as she wandered the length of the room.

He continued to move, following in her wake only because he'd already been headed in the same direction. He made a point of congratulating the director and stars of the movie but avoided any in-depth conversations. Once he spoke with Olivia Fox, the female lead, he'd consider his duty met.

He spied her standing at a cocktail table with Jenna, Vick and Tori. He stopped for another drink, then strolled up behind them.

"I was hoping we'd see Black with someone tonight," Vick was saying.

"Me, too." Fox sounded disappointed. "I now know what you were talking about. Getting through security on the lot is worse than the airport. It's a pain."

"Sorry," Tori said. "We're really busy, and we don't actually have a lot of access to him."

What was this about? Why would Tori apologize?

"Maybe there's someone here tonight?" Vick suggested. The two actresses moved to flank Tori while they all looked down the length of the room. "What type does he like?"

Type? His gaze followed theirs, perusing the beautiful people of Hollywood. A bad feeling brewed in his gut.

"It doesn't work like that," Tori advised her companions. "It's not like there's a questionnaire or anything. It's more instinctive."

"Well, whatever it is—" Olivia turned a pleading moue on Tori "—do something. Black seriously needs a woman to mellow him out."

"Before Christmas would be good," Vick added. Tori and Olivia both glanced at her. She shrugged. "Just saying. It would make a nicer holiday for everyone."

He took that as his cue. "Good evening, ladies."

The three women jumped and swung to face him.

"I hope you enjoyed the movie," he said pleasantly. "Ms. Fox, you were particularly moving in the role of Grace."

"Thank you, Mr. Black." Olivia Fox quickly recovered. "I hear there's a lot of award buzz for the movie."

"I've heard whispers, as well. We'll keep our fingers crossed, shall we?"

"Fingers and toes, as my mama would say." Olivia's smile proved her sultry role drew from true life.

"You'll have to invite her to the Academy Awards," he proposed. "Perhaps she'll bring us luck."

"Oh, so family is allowed at the awards show," Vick mused in an odd tone. "Good to know."

He ignored that. "Ms. Randall, if I can have a word."

"I should really get back to work." Tori began backing away.

"No." Garrett caught her arm. "You really should talk to me."

"We'll let you two chat." Vick waved as she walked away.

"Bye, Tori." Olivia strolled away with Vick. "Good luck with that project."

He drew Tori to an alcove half-hidden by the long flow of curtains and one of the tattoo banners.

"Garrett, I've already taken a break to chat with Jenna and Olivia," Tori protested. "If this is about the house, I put it on my calendar to stop by tomorrow morning at ten. I really should go. Lauren will be looking for me."

"It's your little chat with the girls that I wish to talk about." He crossed his arms over his chest and eyed her expectantly.

She closed her eyes on a pained expression. "You heard."

"About the woman intended to mellow me out? Yes." He lifted both eyebrows in inquiry. "I'm waiting for an explanation."

"I can explain. But before I do, let me make it clear it's all your fault."

"My fault?" He couldn't help it, the corner of his mouth twitched. He pressed his lips together to quell the inappropriate humor. "How is that possible?"

"You're the one who's made life on the set tough for everyone."

His brows slammed together. "What are you talking about? What do you have to do with my film sets?"

"Nothing!" she exclaimed as if he'd proven her point. "And I don't appreciate being put in this position."

"Enough with the two-step," he demanded. "I want to know what the hell is going on."

"Tori." Lauren appeared around the tattoo banner. "The kitchen is looking for you." She turned to him, flinching slightly as she recognized him. She pasted on a smile as she greeted him. "Hello, Garrett, I'm sorry to interrupt. Perhaps I can help you while Tori takes care of business?"

"That's okay." Oh, these two were good, their choreography nearly flawless. "Tori will be stopping by the house tomorrow morning." He snagged Tori's amber gaze and sent a clear message. "I'll get my answers then."

Tori arrived at The Old Manor House earlier than planned. She didn't want Garrett to think she was running scared. She'd decided to be completely honest with him about the matchmaking situation.

It may well surprise Garrett to know, but she preferred to be truthful. Which probably explained why she was off her game with him. Circumstances had forced her into playing games she generally avoided.

Best to just come clean and ask for his cooperation. After all, it would benefit him and his studio to be friendlier to the industry professionals using his services.

Right. He owned the studio. It wasn't as if he needed Jenna's and Olivia's goodwill.

Tori refused to let the dynamics deter her. Instead she focused on the house. As she walked through the downstairs rooms, she understood how the chaos could be daunting to Garrett. The necessary destruction before re-construction tended to be quite messy. And loud.

She spoke to the cleaning and construction supervisors. Gave both a stack of her cards, and instructed all calls be directed to her. She would determine if Garrett needed to be consulted. The men nodded their agreement.

"What do you want to do with the flooring?" The cleaning specialist drew her attention to the hardwood floors unearthed near the terrace doors.

The three of them examined the area. The flooring specialist had polished up a section to give an indication of how the finished flooring would look. The grain in the wood gleamed in the late morning sunshine.

"This is expensive wood, meant to endure," the specialist said. "It was a crime to cover it up. I advise pulling up the carpeting and refinishing the floors."

She agreed with his assessment, but the construction supervisor pointed out the time constraints and the possibility of complications. "The floor appears sound, but you never know what you'll find. With your deadline I suggest going with the tile you originally wanted or polishing this section. The problem is all other work has to stop when you're laying down the varnish or you risk a messy finish."

"Let's go with the hardwood in this section, and I'll talk to Mr. Black about completing the job after the party."

The men nodded and went back to work.

There'd been no sign of the man himself, so she knocked on the door of the room he'd been staying in downstairs. There was no answer, so she peeked inside. The room was empty. A twin-size bed was made and everything appeared neat and tidy, except for the dust on every surface. A garment rack full of clothes stood in the corner and a lovely mahogany desk had been pushed against the wall. No personal effects graced the space.

Tori backed out and headed upstairs, looking for the

master suite. She'd managed only a glimpse on her previous tours. Maybe if she gave Garrett a nice oasis away
from the construction zone, he'd deal better with the work
being done. She had plenty of money to work with. He'd
given her a generous allowance for the transformation,
financed from his personal account. She had a separate
budget from the studio for the party.

She checked out some of the other rooms, seeing what
furnishings she might switch up and a plan began to form.
Garrett found her at the kitchen table making notes for
the crew.

He came in the back door, hesitated upon spying her,
then continued into the room to set his briefcase on the
big butcher-block table.

"Tori, thanks for waiting for me."

She glanced at the clock over the stove. Ten-thirty. Excellent. She loved checking items off her to-do list. Today
she felt very productive. And if he saw himself as late, that
only worked to her advantage.

"No problem." She rose to get him a cup of coffee from
the pot she'd brewed. A teaspoon of sugar and a splash of
cream later, she set the mug in front of him and resumed
her seat. "Congratulations. Great reviews on *Tattoo Murders*."

He looked from her to the coffee and back again before
pulling out a chair and sitting across from her. She'd obviously thrown him with the pleasantries.

"Yes. It looks like your friend Olivia has a good chance
at the accolades she covets." He sipped and settled back in
his chair. "Now tell me what the hell is going on."

Oh, yeah, his patience was at an end. She drew in a
deep breath, blew it out over her coffee.

"Lauren and I are matchmakers." She stated it baldly,
not trying to soften the news.

He rubbed his temple. "I thought you were event planners."

"As it turns out, we're both." She calmly detailed the events that led up to last night. "So you see, By Arrangement is just trying to make everyone happy."

"By pimping me out?" It was the softness of his words that told her of his feelings more than the coarseness of them.

Her chin went up. "There's no need to be crude. Their motives may be selfish, but all anyone wants is your happiness. Is that so bad?"

He shoved the coffee aside so hard liquid spilled over the edge. "I don't need anyone to find me a woman."

The vehemence of his response spoke volumes. She asked softly, "Don't need or don't want?"

"Both. Neither." Blunt fingers plowed through dark hair, mussing his neat appearance. He pushed away from the table, paced to the counter.

The uncharacteristic display revealed a depth of emotion beyond annoyance at simple matchmaking. It sparked a memory of something she read when she researched him.

"I read on the internet you were engaged at one time."

He tore off some paper towels and returned to the table to clean up the spilled coffee, all without answering.

"Obviously you don't have a problem committing." She chipped away at his reserve.

"Please desist. Your friends are wrong. I have no need of a woman in my life at the moment." He moved to throw the paper towels away. "You can consider any request to the contrary as unnecessary."

"Sorry, it doesn't work that way," she informed him. "As you saw last night, the girls are looking for results."

"Too bad—" he shot back "—because I'm not giving you any information to help find this paragon of a woman."

"We don't need it." Gathering her composure, she settled back in her chair and reached for her mug. "That's not how Lauren and I work. We feel it."

"Feel it? Like an electrical buzz?" He dropped back in his chair. "That must hurt."

"Very funny." She leaned forward on her elbows. "Tell me what happened with your fiancée."

"No." His arms crossed over his chest, a firm barrier against further intrusion. "Tell me what you're going to do about the house."

"Already taken care of." This was proving more difficult than she anticipated. And the fiancée was the key. She just needed him to open up a little. "Did you break it off or did she?"

"None of your business." He failed to relent. "What arrangements did you make for the house?"

"I spoke to the crew supervisors. They know to call me with all questions. I told them to leave the carpet and go with the hardwood floor over the tile. There's no time to varnish the whole room before the party, but you should consider finishing the job after the event."

"I'll think about it," he said.

"Good. I asked them to bring in a second cleaning crew, so the dust issue should be resolved soon."

He nodded and relaxed enough to drop his arms and lean on the table. "Obviously being on-site was helpful. I told you, you're needed here."

Bingo. He needed something and so did she. She smiled and planted her forearms on the butcher-block surface so only a few inches separated her from his pale gray gaze.

"I'll try to come by every couple of days if you agree to go on a few dates."

His eyes narrowed. "Absolutely not. You're lucky I'm not canceling our contract. First you pretend to be your twin and now you've gone behind my back to play matchmaker. I don't care for liars. Tell me why I don't fire you right now."

"Because you're too honorable to blame By Arrangement for something beyond our control." She responded honestly and without hesitation. Garrett may grouse but he was fair. In fact, he seemed more grim than usual. She glanced at her watch, after eleven. "And because it's too late to get someone to replace us. Face it, we're stuck with each other."

"Maybe." He bit out the concession. "But this project was your idea. I expect you to hold up your end of the agreement."

"Are you hungry?" She rose and checked out the refrigerator, saw the makings for sandwiches. "I am handling the renovations." She carried her cache to the table, went to the drawers for a knife. "I'll deal with the calls. But you know how heavy our schedule is. I can't promise to get by more than every few days."

"That's blackmail."

"Unfortunately it's reality. I know as a director and as president of Obsidian Studios you prefer order and control in your business dealings, but coordinating events is a matter of planning and damage control. We have to be on top of every detail to offset the inevitable disaster.

"Come on," she urged, layering meat and cheese onto wheat bread, "just five dates. It will do wonders for your reputation. You know Jenna and Olivia aren't just complaining to Lauren and me."

"Damn it," he muttered, recognizing the truth of her statement.

"It's only a few hours of your time." She pressed her advantage. "And who knows, you may actually meet someone." She slid a sandwich in front of him, started making one for herself.

"Highly unlikely." He eyed her as he took a bite.

"Can't you give it a chance?" A bit of mustard smudged her finger and she licked it off. His gaze followed the movement of her tongue. The blaze of heat in his eyes when they lifted to hers sent a wave of awareness shivering down her spine.

Ignoring her inappropriate reaction, she turned her attention to her sandwich, carefully cutting it into quarters, a habit left over from childhood. She kept half and put the other two pieces on his empty plate.

"You can set your own terms," she offered.

"Now you're suggesting fake dates?" His tone dropped several degrees.

"No." The word reflected her shredding patience. "It may surprise you, but I prefer honesty, as well. But you can have a say in the where and when."

He finished off another quarter sandwich while he thought about it. "Two dates and you come by twice a day."

She gnawed her lower lip. This was going to play havoc with her schedule. But she really had no option. She practically felt Lauren prodding her along. A good thing because her twin would have to do her part to help.

"Three dates and once a day," she countered, crossing her fingers for good luck.

His jaw clenched but he gave a brief nod. "I get to set the terms."

"Of course." Thank goodness. She reached for her electronic pad. "What are your terms?"

"No wannabes. Only established women."

"Okay." She nodded as she noted it down. "That makes sense. What else?"

"Public events only, no one-on-one dates."

"But—" Her protest cut off midsentence when she met his implacable gaze. "Public events only," she confirmed.

"And you have to be somewhere nearby to save me if things get unbearable."

Her fingers stilled. The thought of witnessing Garrett on his dates held little appeal. In fact everything in her objected to the very notion.

"Is that really necessary?"

He pinned her with granite-hard eyes. "It's a deal breaker."

She gritted her teeth and finished the notation. "Is that all?"

"For now. Except I want this done by the end of the year. I don't want it hanging over me."

"Agreed." The sooner the better suited her just fine. The chore of finding him a woman got more distasteful by the minute.

Two days later Tori completely understood Garrett's frustration with the renovations. Once she arrived at the house, she got sucked in and found it difficult to get away. With so much to be done in such a short amount of time, hundreds of details needed to be dealt with or approved. Her schedule was completely disrupted.

She glanced out the library window at the light rain currently delaying the outdoor work. With any luck it would end soon, allowing the landscapers an opportunity to make up for lost time. The gardens were in need of pruning, then a few small repairs, cleaning, sanding and painting. Last came the lights and decorations. For now she put them to work in the conservatory.

A light knock came at the open door. Maria, a lovely Latina woman in her early thirties and lead on the bedroom crew, stood framed in the doorway. "Ms. Randall, the master suite is ready for your walk-through."

"Thanks, Maria." Tori followed the woman from the room. "I'm anxious to see how the changes look."

"The room is *muy bien,*" Maria advised. "Cleaning

helped a lot, but your suggestions make it more current and masculine. Señor Black will be happy, I think."

"Let's hope so." Tori really needed a win with Garrett, especially as she had news on his first date.

The room didn't disappoint. Garrett was a bit of a minimalist so she'd kept the furnishings and knickknacks to the basics. A tufted screen in dove-gray velvet outlined in black with asymmetrical points on the ends, lending it an Art Deco feel, stood as headboard to a pedestal bed. A large black area rug with gray swirls covered the floor. Warmth came into the room via the dark wood dresser and matching bedside tables she'd found in a spare room. Touches of royal-blue added a bit of color. The art was understated and soothing.

Best of all, the bed, heaped with a down comforter in steel-gray and plump pillows in black coverings, made you want to dive headfirst into slumber. The retro elements along with the modern art and bedding made the room both relevant and comfortable.

"It turned out as you wanted, *sí?*" Maria inquired.

"Yes, it's perfect." Tori looked into the bathroom, saw that it sparkled. "Mr. Black will be very pleased. Thank you." She moved into the hall. "And the other rooms?"

"Cleaned, as you requested," Maria replied. "Including the study downstairs. It has been converted back to an office."

"Excellent." Tori made a quick tour. Satisfied with the results, she sent Maria and her crew upstairs to continue with the cleaning and polishing. Tori collected her laptop. She had an appointment and then she wanted to swing by her place before coming back here to talk with Garrett. Turned out he was right after all.

Garrett entered The Old Manor House through the kitchen. He set his briefcase on the table, tossed his jacket over the back of a chair and went in search of Tori. Her car in the drive indicated she was here somewhere.

He found her in the study.

"What are you doing in here? Where are my things?"

He'd put up with a lot from this woman. For some reason her quirkiness appealed to him. He never knew what to expect next. It was like a good movie, right when he thought he had things figured out, there was a new twist. But this was going too far.

Not even the play of the late afternoon sun in her blond hair offset his anger.

"Garrett." She sprang up. "Good, you're home."

"I asked you a question," he stated.

"Come with me." She walked around the desk, his ire blipped as he admired the swell of her breasts in a bright red sweater. "I have a surprise for you."

"I don't like surprises," he said for the sheer principle of it. He preferred order and discipline. Tori lacked both. How she managed to pull off the spectacular events she did baffled him. As did his irrational fascination with her dimples.

She laughed and tugged him along. "Oh, boo. Everyone enjoys a good surprise. Trust me, you're going to like this."

"I already don't like it." Okay, he did like the way her hips gently swayed in tight black jeans as he followed her up the stairs. "These rooms are closed up. The dust downstairs may be bad, but these rooms are worse."

"Not anymore." With a dimpled smile, she pushed open the double doors to the master suite. "I had all the rooms cleaned. We'll be using the bathrooms up here. It seemed smart to just clean everything." She waved him inside. "For you. Up here you'll be out of the chaos of the renovations, have your own personal bathroom and won't be squeezed into a twin bed. Your leg hasn't seemed to bother you lately, so I hope the stairs won't be a problem."

"I can handle the stairs," he asserted, pleased she didn't feel the need to coddle him. Self-conscious of his weak leg, he'd been afraid his fall would cause her to treat him as an invalid. She never did.

Perhaps that's what appealed to him, beyond the dimples and heart-shaped derriere.

"Excellent."

He took in the inviting bed, noted the Art Deco feel. He enjoyed the black and grays, the touch of blue. "You made changes."

"A few. To freshen it up." She stayed by the door while he toured the room. "I hope you like it."

Freshen? He supposed that was a nice way of saying "purge memories." He appreciated the gesture. "I might be able to live with this surprise."

"Good. Because I have another one." She dazzled him with a smile, flashing that alluring dimple.

"Another what?" He wandered to the window, pretended interest in the view to avoid temptation.

"Another surprise," she clarified. "It turns out you were right. Someone is needed on-site during the work."

"Finally. I believe that's the first sensible thing I've heard you say."

"Very funny."

He thought so. The corner of his mouth tugged up. "So does this mean you'll be stopping by more often?"

"No, it means I'm moving in."

CHAPTER SEVEN

GARRETT LAUGHED. A rare occurrence, one she'd enjoy if it weren't at her expense. She crossed her arms and sent him a disgruntled glare.

The laughter faded to be replaced with an appalled expression. "Oh, come on. You aren't serious."

"It makes perfect sense." She defended her decision. "If I work from here, I can actually accomplish something."

"So work from here," he agreed, advancing on her. "It doesn't mean you have to move in."

"I've spent the last two days working here and I've got nothing done."

He spread his arms out, gesturing to the room where they stood. "You got more done in two days than I did in twice the time."

"But I got nothing else done. Juggling home, the showroom, the manor and appointments has been impossible. If I make this my base, I can get things going in the morning and I'll be here to check on the progress between trips to the workshop and appointments."

"It's inappropriate."

"How sweet of you to worry about my reputation. But this is the twenty-first century, Garrett. No one will care."

"I care."

For a split second her heart bloomed at his words, but

she quickly corrected herself. His concern was for his own comfort, which was much easier to ignore. "Since you're office is in the library, I've set up in the study. You'll never know I'm here."

"That's highly doubtful."

Okay, no missing the scorn there.

"We'll be on two different floors," she pointed out. "We don't even have to see each other."

"You got rid of the bed in the study." He tossed the words at her.

"The new sofa can be converted to face either direction or go flat into a bed. It's really quite cool. And if you do have a bad spell, you'll have a bed downstairs." She held up a hand. "After I leave, of course."

He shook his head. "Tori, you can't stay here."

"Garrett, I really have no choice if we're going to make this work. Now, you need to change your clothes. Something warm and casual. I'll meet you in the kitchen in ten minutes." She twirled and headed for the stairs.

"Where are we going?" floated after her, and then, "I need a shower."

"Fifteen minutes," she called.

And hoped it was enough time to get her calm back. The look in his eyes when he said she couldn't stay almost singed her eyelashes. She'd wanted to throw herself into his arms and prove they'd do all too well together.

Common sense came to her rescue. Because the flash of delight she'd seen on his face when she revealed her surprise exposed a vulnerability she couldn't ignore and wouldn't exploit. Too easily memories of despair and betrayal surged to the surface, reminding her of what happened when she reached out to a wounded soul.

No. Singed eyelashes or not she needed to keep her cool and her distance while she pulled off the makeover of the year.

* * *

"You brought me out to shop for a Christmas tree?" Garrett sent her a skeptical glance.

"Christmas trees," she corrected. Hooking her arm through his to keep him from escaping, she strolled into the festive lot. The spicy sent of pine filled the chilly air. "Smells wonderful, doesn't it? We'll need at least three."

"Why so many?" Little puffs of steam appeared with each word.

"Everyone loves Christmas trees." Two young boys raced right for them, Tori sidestepped out of their way right into Garrett. "Ugh. Sorry."

"No problem." But he untangled his arm to place a hand at the small of her back and direct her through the slick lot. "Be careful." He moved her around a puddle. "Everything is wet from the rain earlier. I'm surprised to see so many people here."

"Hey, nothing stands in the way of Christmas."

"So it seems." He actually appeared surprised, which made her wonder about his childhood. From what she'd read, his mother left his father and Garrett when he was three, a very young age to lose a mother. And it was probably more confusing than comforting to gain a stepmother within a few months. "Now explain why we need three."

"Each tree will create a cheerful focal point, helping to set the tone for the party. We get big impact for little effort."

"Fa la la la."

She grinned. "That's the spirit. Now we need a big tree for the foyer."

"This way." He drew her to the left. "The larger trees are at the back."

"Great." She eyed his chiseled profile. At least he hadn't bolted. "Does your family have any special ornaments you'd like me to incorporate into the decorating?"

He shrugged. "Hell, I don't know. I can't tell you the last time I had a Christmas tree."

"Surely when you were a child there were trees?" Tori couldn't conceive of a Christmas without a fully decorated tree. Her mother, the queen of holidays, always made sure they had a big, beautiful, live tree. It was one of Tori's favorite parts of the season.

"I remember some in the servants' quarters, but none in the main house." The lack of inflection in his voice told her he really had no expectations for the season.

"Oh. Was it a religious preference?" She could think of no other reason a child would be deprived of the magic of the holiday.

"No." He frowned. "My father didn't like the fuss."

"Wow, that's sad." She patted his arm. "We'll make up for a few of those years tonight."

"No need." Appalled, he sent her a quelling glance. "I'm fine."

"I don't believe that. Everyone deserves a merry Christmas. Ah, here we are, eight feet and up." She rubbed her gloved hands together as she contemplated the huge trees all lying on their sides. "Here is where we need your muscles. I need you to hold them up so I can check out their shapes."

Her request earned her another glance from piercing gray eyes, but he manfully stepped forward and hauled up the first tree, a beauty easily nine feet tall.

"We're never going to get this in the SUV," he advised her.

"No, we'll have it and the one for the terrace delivered." Circling to the left, she spotted a sparse section and gestured him to the next tree. "We'll bring home the one for the parlor."

"Why not have all the trees delivered?" He patiently held a twelve-foot Noble fir for her inspection.

The majestic tree was tall and full and beautiful. Beads of water glimmered in the overhead light. Perfect.

She clapped her hands. "This is the one."

Garrett nodded and waved an attendant over. The freckle-faced teen tagged the tree and took over Garrett's place holding the trees for their next pick.

"We need another one for the terrace, maybe not so big." She shook her head at the first one. "Too skinny."

The next was too squat. Garrett moved along with her, but stood hands in pockets, a look of disinterest on his face. She continued on task. Business first, pleasure second. She couldn't take too long or he'd lose patience. Luckily the next pick met her exacting criteria and the teen tagged it and gave them a delivery receipt.

"I love Christmas." She rubbed her hands to together. "This is really putting me in the mood. Hey, I had a great idea today. What do you think about having snow at the party? We can set up a machine so it falls onto the terrace."

"No."

She couldn't prevent a small pout. "You're not even going to think about it? Just a light snowfall, for show. We're putting heaters out there and there's the fire pit. It'll be fanciful but toasty."

"I've lived in New York. I can tell you it'll be wet, damp and mushy."

"Southern Californians will love it," she promised. "I've always wished for a white Christmas."

"It's pretty." He wasn't moved. "Until you're sitting in a puddle."

"Oh." Disappointment was sharp at the visual. "That wouldn't be good. Okay, no snow."

"Excellent decision." He verbally applauded. "Does that mean we can go home?"

"Nope. Now we look for the family tree, which will go

in the parlor." She hooked her arm in Garrett's again and headed back to the smaller trees.

"Family?" he mocked. "There's just me."

"You count." She took it as a victory when he didn't pull away. "This time I'll hold the tree and you choose. Do you prefer a Douglas fir," she asked, pointing to a bushy tree with longer needles, "or the Noble fir like the others we got?"

"I like the Noble."

"Me, too. Here we go. Six feet, that's what we're looking for." She trudged down a narrow alley of trees, reached down and grabbed one by the spine and pulled it up for Garrett's appraisal.

"That one's good," he declared.

"Nice try," she chided. "There's a big hole on this side. Remember you're looking to impress three hundred of your closest friends."

He scowled at her and shook his head. She set it down and bent for the next. After the fourth tree and catching him looking at her backside, she demanded, "What's wrong with this one?"

"It's bottom heavy."

"Bottom heavy my—"

"Wow, Mommy, that one is booiful," a young voice said with awe.

Tori looked behind her and down, way down, to a little boy with a blue knit cap on his head. He stood hands on hips staring up at the tree she held.

"You like this one?" she asked him.

His small head bobbed up and down. "It's booiful."

"Sam!" A young woman with dark hair and a baby in her arms struggled up to them. "Sam, I've told you to not run off like that."

"But, Mom, I founded the perfectest tree." Sam held his arms wide as if he'd personally conjured the tree.

The joy on his face reflected the true magic of the season. Tori's heart melted at his innocent delight.

"Oh, baby, it is pretty, but these people have already chosen it." She stood and faced Tori and Garrett. "I'm sorry."

"No need." Tori smiled, happy to inform her, "In fact, we aren't taking this tree if you want it."

The woman's pale skin pinked as she shook her head. "No. It's out of my budget. Come on, Sammy."

"But, Mom!" the boy protested loudly. "They said we could have it."

Tori met Garrett's gaze over the kid's head. He hunkered down to talk to the boy. "Sam, you need to listen to you mother. She need's you to be a good boy and help with your little sister. Can you do that?"

"But this is our tree." His mouth trembled. "Mommy wants to leave it."

"Sometimes mommy's need to make hard decisions," Garrett explained. "Getting a smaller tree might allow her to get you and your sister a nice present."

"A present?" Sam blinked.

Garrett nodded.

"I'm sorry, Mommy." Sam moved over and tucked his little hand into his mother's. "We can get another tree."

"Thank you." Sam's mother bobbed her head in appreciation at Tori and Garrett, then started to turn away.

"Actually—" Garrett's voice stopped her "—since Sam is being so good, we'd like to give him a present. If you don't mind?"

Clearly uncertain, the woman gently bounced the baby while she made up her mind. She glanced down at Sam, who stood silently at her side. Finally she shrugged. "He is being good, so okay."

"Excellent." Garrett waved the freckle-faced teen over. "We'd like to give him this tree."

"Yipee!" Sam hopped up and down.

"Oh, but," the mom protested, "it's too much."

"Please accept it." Tori handed the tree off to the teen and dusted her hands together. "Believe me, he needs to make points with Santa."

The woman gave Garrett an odd look, but a tug on her hand pulled her gaze down to her son. At his pleading expression, she gave in. "Thank you both. You're going to make great parents someday."

"Oh, no," Tori objected. "We're not—"

"Ready?" the woman supplied. "I understand. You have that newlywed glow. Enjoy your time alone. But believe me kids truly are a blessing. You made Sam very happy. For that I wish you both a merry Christmas."

Careful not to glance at Garrett, Tori decided to let it go rather than embarrass everyone with awkward explanations. "Happy holidays to you, too."

Once the small family wandered off to collect their tree, Tori confronted Garrett. "That was incredibly sweet."

He lifted one shoulder in a half shrug, his expression as stoic as ever. "He's a good kid."

"Yeah." She nodded, continuing to pin him with an inquiring gaze. Finally a hint of red appeared in his cheeks.

"And apparently I need Santa points."

She grinned. "Considering you could give the Grinch a run for his money, yes, you do. Helping to decorate your family tree will gain you more points. Now, which of these trees did you really like?"

He reached down, wrapped a large hand around the trunk of the second tree she'd held up and brought it to a stand. "This one will do."

"Garrett." She propped her hands on her hips. She didn't want just any tree. It had to be prefect.

"You said my choice." He took off for the cashier.

"Wait." She trudged after him, careful of the ground

slick with puddles and pine needles. "You said it was thin on one side."

"I'm sure your Christmas magic will hide any flaws."

"Yes, but—"

He stopped, cupped her head in his free hand and kissed her quiet.

Without conscious thought she pushed to her toes, angling closer to him as she opened her mouth under his. He sipped from her, tantalizing her with the need for more, before pulling his head back.

"Enough, darling. It's time for the newlyweds to go home."

The next morning Tori woke to a strange room awash in sunshine. She squeezed her eyes closed. Ugh. The study had east-facing windows and she'd forgotten to close the heavy drapes.

A peek at her travel clock showed the time of 6:10. Work crews would arrive at seven. She wanted to be up and dressed by the time they arrived. According to her cleaning supervisor, Garrett generally left the house just after seven.

Remembering how things got a little carried away last night, she figured if she timed things right, she could miss Garrett by giving the crews their directions for the day first. Then she'd make herself breakfast before starting on her to-do list.

Cursing the fact she'd forgotten her slippers, she shivered as she tiptoed to the bathroom across the hall.

In the parlor she spotted their purchase from the night before standing bare in the middle of the room. She'd planned on completing the decorating, but Garrett's kiss had changed her mind.

He may be aggravating, but the truth was she found his touch all too addicting. So she chose to retreat instead.

She circled the tree, still feeling the need to draw him into the holiday festivities. Sometimes the sadness in him was so strong she sensed it coming off him. No one deserved to be sad and lonely at Christmas. He may not have happy holiday memories, but that didn't mean he couldn't make some.

Tonight they'd decorate the tree.

"Ms. Randall, there's a nursery truck out front with a delivery of poinsettias," the construction supervisor advised Tori when she answered the kitchen door.

"Excellent. Please direct them to put them on the porch." While he went off to deliver her instructions, she moved to the counter. Thankfully there was fresh coffee in the pot but the cupboards were bare and the refrigerator nearly empty. She dropped a stale piece of bread in the toaster and added grocery shopping to her to-do list.

Coffee in hand, she did a walk-through with the crew bosses. The cleaning was done except where the construction needed to be completed, so Tori moved the cleaning crew to decorating. There were hundreds of white lights to go up inside, and outdoors she wanted spotlights to showcase The Old Manor House. The creepy old place was what people expected to see, so she'd leave the exterior alone, cleaned up but otherwise unadorned. Inside would be warm, welcoming, festive and elegant.

Hmm, maybe she would have the house framed with white lights for when people left the party. It would provide lighting and leave people with a jovial impression.

The large trees would be delivered today and she'd bought some pine boughs from the Christmas tree lot last night. Enough to get them started. Then she directed Maria to join her in a hunt through the attic to see if any family ornaments could be found.

Thirty minutes of dust and spiderwebs later, she gave up. There was little in the attic beyond old furnishings and a few paintings. The Blacks were not big on storing family keepsakes.

"There is nothing here." Maria finally stated the obvious.

"No." Tori dusted her hands. "That means we add it to our shopping list." She reached for her smartphone and pulled up her schedule. "I'll meet you in the kitchen in ten minutes, and we'll get started." She had the next couple of hours flagged for shopping but then she had to be at the showroom to go over the menu for tomorrow's event. "You drive, and I'll see what I can get done on the phone." She had the brilliant notion of sending the household grocery list to her head chef and sent off a text.

Garrett pulled the Spyder into the garage and cut the ignition. He ran a hand over the tight muscles in his neck. He'd been holed up in meetings with his executives all day. He was determined to have a solid strategy going into the new year.

Weary to the bone, he climbed from the car and made for the house, a house shining bright with welcome. It gave him a sense of homecoming unlike any he'd ever known.

"Don't be a fool," he muttered under his breath. "Nothing special going on here. It just means your temporary roommate is home." Yet he felt lighter as he bound up the back steps.

Inside the savory scent of meat cooking bombarded his senses, making his mouth water and adding to his odd feeling of…belonging. There was no other word for it. And repeating his little pep talk did nothing to kick-start his common sense.

Instead, he dropped his briefcase on the table and went to investigate the contents of the pot on the stove.

"Stew," Tori announced, causing him to jump as if caught with his hand in the cookie jar. The humor in her eyes told him she'd noticed the movement, but she chose not to call him on it. "I hope you're hungry."

"Smells good," he acknowledged.

"It is," she assured him as she took his place at the stove.

She stirred the pot. Leaning forward, she breathed deep and gave a soft hum of approval. The sound sent a surge of lust through his blood. Suddenly he was hungry for more than food.

"My mother's recipe," she shared, and then she winked, "with a few tweaks of my own."

He barely heard the words, so focused was he on her mouth, her soft, slightly moist lips. Her cheeky wink lured him closer until he loomed over her, his gaze locked on her plump, rosy-red mouth.

She glanced at him through thick lashes. Licking her lips, she shifted slightly to the left. "Ah, why don't you go freshen up while I dish this up? I'll give you an update on the house while we eat."

"Sounds like a plan." He backed away, realizing the luscious aroma had momentarily clouded his reasoning. The true plan was to avoid each other, but on this chilly night, after a long day, the draw of the stew overrode the annoyance of Tori's company. His last home-cooked meal had been Thanksgiving and for one crazy moment his hunger had transferred from the meal to the chef.

Garrett showered and changed in record time.

The woman talked too much. And was too damned cheerful. How did she stay so optimistic? She really did care about people. He'd seen the way she talked to the workers. She treated them as equals, listening to all opinions, making everyone feel valued while going about her own plans.

She even got to him. He preferred a steady, low-key existence yet he'd enjoyed the trip to the Christmas tree lot, took satisfaction in giving Sam a special holiday moment. The truth was Tori challenged him. She made him think, made him laugh, made him live. Too bad all he really craved was to be left alone.

He headed downstairs, rolling up his sleeves as he went. In the kitchen Tori had set the table with two servings of stew and a plate full of golden-brown biscuits.

"You didn't have to cook." As he took his seat, Garrett's stomach rumbled. Cringing a little, he met her gaze with a sheepish smile. "But I'm glad you did. This looks great."

"Tastes good, too. If I do say so myself." She boasted with a wrinkle of her nose as she reached for a biscuit. "I love a hearty stew on a cold night."

"Me, too." Though he couldn't remember the last time he had stew. No need to go into that. He dug into the food while she poured them each a glass of red wine. Silence fell as they ate.

After a few bites, she gave the report she'd promised on the ongoing projects. She talked about the progress made over the past couple of days, some of which he'd seen on his trip upstairs. The newly gleaming bannisters were decorated with greenery, crystals and lights. And the biggest of the trees now stood in the entry hall waiting to be decked out.

"It's good to see it coming along. I knew your being here would help."

"I'm glad you're happy. You'll be able to add to the progress tonight." She clicked her glass to his. "We're going to decorate the family tree after dinner."

"Oh, no." He shook his head. "I told you there aren't any family ornaments."

"I know. I scouted out the attic today. Not much up there."

"My father was never very sentimental."

"Which is why I went out and bought a slew of ornaments." Her amber eyes glittered with her excitement.

"Tonight we're going to dress the tree and next year you'll have them to use again."

She was so pleased he didn't have the heart to tell her he had no need of them. Next year he'd be back in his Santa Barbara house, back to his solitude, where a Christmas tree and happy memories would only serve to remind him of all he'd lost.

"I don't have much experience decorating," he warned her.

"Don't worry, I have lots." She rolled her eyes, then poked at the remains of her meal. "I told you my mom loved to celebrate, well she really does Christmas up big. She chooses a theme and decorates the whole house."

"Themes?"

"Yes, Santa's workshop, winter wonderland, Dickens, angels, anything Christmas related. Don't get me wrong, they're all beautiful trees. And special because we worked on them together, but my favorite ornaments were the homemade ones she kept from us kids. She pretended to grouse if they didn't fit the theme, but she let me tuck them in somewhere."

Full after two servings, he pushed his bowl aside and wiped his mouth. Her happy family memories baffled him. Her roughest recollection was having to tuck the home-made ornaments to the back of the tree?

"We had very different childhoods."

"I realize I'm lucky." She gathered the dirty bowls and carried them to the sink. "I'll do these later." Back at the table she grabbed the wine and their glasses. "Come on, we'll finish this while we work on the tree."

She sashayed out of the kitchen. He slowly followed, trailing her to the parlor, where the tree he'd chosen stood majestically in the corner between two windows. Tori set her bounty down on the coffee table and went to the wall to flip a switch.

The tree bloomed to life with hundreds of tiny lights. He stuffed his hands in his pockets, admiring the vision with just the lights. "It's beautiful just as it is."

"I agree." She came back and stood beside him to share in the admiration of the tree. "It'll look even better when we're done. You have a creative side, let it loose."

A click of a remote button had a Christmas carol singing brightly of silver bells. Tori drew him to a table laid out with gold bows, crystal icicles, glittery white snowflakes and shiny bulbs in many complimentary colors and shapes.

"Quite a collection you have here, everything but the kitchen sink."

"We don't have to use it all. Just pick what you like." She plucked up several of the melon-size gold bows. "I prefer ribbon bows to garland. I think it gives a more symmetrical balance to the tree." Suiting action to words, she stuffed the bows into the tree, then repeated the process several times. "Can you get the higher branches?"

He did as requested and quickly saw the results of her plan. Between the lights and the bows the tree seemed to glow. Next she did the same with the icicles and the snowflakes, bringing even more light into play.

Inspired by a sip of wine, he decided red would be his theme. He sorted through all the ornaments, pulling out all shades of red from the deepest claret to the brightness of Santa's cap. It didn't matter what shape it took, bird or harp, round, diamond or star, he mixed it all up and let the color make sense of it all. Occasionally she directed his hand into the depths of the tree with an ornament, adding dimension.

When she got done with the snowflakes, Tori took over putting the hooks on the ornaments and handed them to him to place in the tree.

"The red is a lovely touch. It's eclectic but traditional at the same time."

"I decided to go with theme, like your mother."

She grinned. "It's a good place to start." She curled into a corner of the couch within reach of the table so she could continue her self-appointed task. "Tell me about your mother."

The question didn't surprise him. The woman constantly had her nose in his business. Plus she'd shared family stories; she'd expect him to do the same. She'd be disappointed. On this subject he had little to say.

"Which one?" He kept his back to her as he tucked a deep red rose next to a glittering red apple.

"Let's start with your real mother." She sounded truly interested.

More evidence she cared for people. Which didn't explain why he answered, but he heard the words spilling from his mouth.

"I didn't know her very well. She left when I was three and died when I was ten."

"So young," she noted softly. "Did you see her much after she left?"

"Not a lot. Maybe once or twice a year." He said it without emotion now, but for the first time in a long time he remembered the sense of loss and betrayal he'd felt at the time. "At first all I wanted was my mother, not a stranger, be it nanny or stepmother. But it didn't take me long to realize my worth to her. I don't know if she ever loved me, but it didn't stop her using me as a bargaining chip against my father, who hated giving me into her care."

"I'm sorry," she said, reacting to the raw pain of his disclosure. "At least that shows he loved you."

There was the eternal optimist. "My father never loved anyone but himself."

"What about your stepmothers?"

"All young, beautiful actresses looking for the fast track

to stardom. He gave them that then traded them in for a newer, younger model."

"So cynical," she chastised him. "Was there no affection in your life?"

"I was well cared for. The staff saw I had everything I needed. I went to the best schools, had every advantage. My father even supported my request to go to UCLA. They have one of the best film schools in the United States."

"Your father must have been happy you wanted to follow in the family business."

"Not particularly." She kept giving his father credit for emotions he hadn't been capable of feeling. And he made sure Garrett followed his example. "He wanted me to be a mini-me of him, something I refused to do, so he didn't care what I did."

"But he made you his head of creative projects several years ago."

The article she'd read hadn't left much out.

"It didn't take."

"Why not?"

"We had creative differences."

She turned liquid gold eyes on him. "What does that mean?"

"I like projects with a good story. He wanted special effects—the bigger, the brighter, the better."

"He overrode your decisions," she guessed.

"Not for long. I quit. And got an Academy Award for my next picture. It had story as well as special effects."

She grinned. "You showed him."

He scowled and pretended to assess the tree. She read him too easily. Time to change the subject or he'd be blabbing away about how his fiancée deserted him when he left the studio.

"Do you think that's enough ornaments? I don't want to overdo it."

"You can't overdecorate a tree." She leaned forward to count the remaining red items.

In her new position the scooped neck of her sweater fell forward, providing him with the delectable view of her cleavage. He should step back out of politeness. Instead he lingered, enjoying the vision of plump breasts encased in ivory lace. His body stirred and he remembered the taste of her sweet mouth.

In the yellow sweater, with her pale skin and flowing blond hair, she absorbed the soft light of the tree so it appeared to halo her.

She resumed her former position and he stepped back, taking a moment to lecture himself on flights of fantasy and employee relations. Maybe he needed a woman more than he thought. He definitely needed something to take his mind off this woman.

"There are only six more," she stated, none the wiser of his sensual side trip. "Put them all on. Then we'll decide what to put on top."

"What did your mom use?"

"Lots of things. We had angels, Santas, bows, feathers, flowers. She always likes to make a statement, so it's big or plentiful. This is your tree, your choice."

"Hmm." He tapped his cheek with a couple of fingers while he contemplated the tree. He liked what they'd done together, the layers of light, the depth, the balance, the beauty. His tree. The satisfaction surprised him. Tonight surprised him. He actually enjoyed himself. Using his creative side felt good.

"I bet it did," Tori responded, cluing him in to the fact he'd spoken his last thought aloud. "How long has it been since your last movie?"

"More than a year. We wrapped in August. I'd started casting my next film, but the accident put it on hold."

"Because most of this year was spent in surgery and

physical therapy." She rose and came to him. He braced for her touch, and still it rocked him to his toes when she threaded her fingers through his and squeezed. Her big eyes reflected her sympathy. "And for the past few months you've been stuck on administrative duty. You've had a tough year."

"Once the studio is in shape—" it took all his control not to steal a kiss and claim all that delicate concern "—I'll be able to get back to making movies."

"So you don't intend to run the studio long-term?"

"I'll probably put in a chief executive officer. I still have to deal with some issues to redeem our reputation." Damn, he wasn't ready to discuss his plans for the studio. She got under his skin all too easily. "Forget I said that."

"Of course," she readily agreed. "I hope the studio isn't in jeopardy."

"Nothing that drastic. Tightening the reigns should solve the issue. Once it's resolved, I'll reassess my options"

"Very wise." Lifting onto her toes, she kissed his cheek. "In the meantime, try to enjoy the holidays. It's not too late to make happy memories."

Her words too closely echoed his earlier sentiment for his comfort. Christmas trees and happy memories weren't for him. Retreating a few steps, he pointed to the tree-top. "Go with a big gold bow. I like things tied up nice and neat."

CHAPTER EIGHT

TORI STRODE SOCK-SHOD into the kitchen just after seven and went straight for the coffeepot. Cup in hand, she leaned against the sink. Inhaling deeply, she closed her eyes as the rich aroma fired her salivary glands, making her mouth water. She sipped and moaned softly.

"I can leave if you prefer to be alone with your morning cup of coffee."

She whipped around. Garrett sat at the table with his own cup and a plate of dry toast. "Good morning." She slid into a seat across from him and set a file folder on the table. "Sorry, my first cup and I have a very special relationship. It's not wise to get between us."

"I'll try to remember that." He toasted her with his cup. "What's on your schedule today?"

"I'll get things started here, but I have to leave by ten to do a site inspection with Lauren." She tore off a piece of his toast, buttered it lightly. "Then it's over to the hotel to set up for your head of departments' holiday dinner. Which reminds me, what time do you want to say your remarks?"

"Remarks?" Raised brows reflected his bafflement.

"Yeah." She waved the toast about. "It's traditional for the head of the company to give some accolades or awards. What do they usually do?"

"I have no idea. There are no awards that I'm aware of.

As for accolades, there wasn't much structure this year with Dad gone and me laid up."

"Right." His comments about the studio's reputation last night explained a lot. He wasn't closing sets and tightening schedules out of a sense of mean-spiritedness, but out of necessity. "Well, your remarks should be positive, so you might want to concentrate on the studio's accomplishments through the years and finish with a statement about your vision for the future."

His chiseled lips twitched at the corner. "Sage advice. I'll take it under consideration."

"Whatever you decide, I'll give you twenty minutes just before dinner service." The need for a second cup of coffee drew her back to the pot. "That's after the cocktail hour so you should have a receptive audience. Oh, and I forgot to tell you last night, but tonight is your first date."

"What? No."

"It'll be fine. I've arranged for a car service. They'll pick up you and then Gwen and take you both to the dinner."

"It's not a good idea." He sounded slightly panicked. "This is a company event, hardly conducive to getting to know each other."

"I didn't think you wanted to get to know your dates." The reminder was for him, not her. Or so she told herself. "And it's the perfect occasion. You'll be at a table with several department heads and their spouses. You don't want to be the odd man out."

He scowled as he thought about that, and then slowly nodded. "Okay, but stay close as we agreed."

"I'm sure you'll be fine." Why was this suddenly so hard? "But in case you need rescuing, just signal Lauren or me." She pushed away from the table, wiggled her toes in her warm socks. "I have to finish getting ready. The crews should be here any minute." Using two fingers she slid the file folder toward him. "The info on Gwen is in here. You might be surprised how well you like her."

"Can't you just give me the highlights? What do your spidey senses tell you?"

She scowled while topping off her coffee mug. She ignored the reference to her matchmaking skills. Men always wanted things handed to them. As if a woman could be defined in a few words. And then she thought of Gwen and realized for a man it really was that simple. "I have two words for you, *international supermodel*."

"How much longer are you going to be at the Old Manor?" Lauren tagged Tori as soon as she sat down at her desk.

"A few more days." She kicked off her shoes and powered up her computer at the same time. Only then did she turn her gaze on her sister. "Some of the repairs need the weather to warm up, including varnishing the hardwood."

"Well, we miss you around here. Hannah—" their executive chef "—is freaking out."

"Yeah, she's my first stop. I plan to go over the menus and shopping schedule for the next three events. Tonight we're working with the hotel catering staff. I've already called and confirmed the time, space and food choices."

Lauren checked a couple of items on her clipboard. "Great. I've talked to the meeting coordinator, too. We can start bringing in our props after three."

Tori double-checked her tablet. "That's what I have on my itinerary." She loved when a plan fell into place.

"So you'll be there at three?" Lauren asked.

"Yep."

"And everything is a go with Garrett and Gwen?"

Some of Tori's satisfaction dimmed. She shook it off. "I gave Garrett the file on Gwen at breakfast. He wasn't happy about the short notice, but he's on board."

"It was your decision to wait," Lauren reminded her.

"That's because he's never going to be happy about the dates. And if we gave him more lead time, he'd find a way to wiggle out of it."

"You know him so well?" A sparkle lit Lauren's eyes.

Tori refused to let the teasing get to her. "Sad, isn't it? If we're lucky, Gwen may be The One and we can put the matchmaking aside and concentrate on work."

"That would be lucky." There was something odd in Lauren's voice, drawing Tori's attention. She eyed Lauren curiously, but her sister gave nothing away. Which only made Tori more nervous.

"Time will tell." She dismissed Garrett and his date. It had already taken up too much of her morning. She opened the diagram of tonight's event and turned her screen toward Lauren. Tori relaxed as the conversation focused on work, completely missing the gleam of speculation in her twin's identical golden gaze.

Applause greeted Garrett's final comments. He breathed a sigh of relief, silently thanked Tori for the heads-up and the inspiration for his speech, and returned to his seat.

"Well done, Garrett." Irene Allan, manager of public relations, patted his hand on the table. "Your father would be proud."

Several other guests added their accolades. Garrett nodded his acceptance, feeling like a fraud. As Tori suggested, he'd kept his comments upbeat and brief. He and his father may have had artistic differences, but that didn't mean the studio lacked accomplishments over the past year. By focusing on the good, he comforted himself with the reminder he'd been truthful if somewhat optimistic.

"I'm sorry for the loss of your father." His date leaned toward him to offer her condolences, giving him a prime vantage point of her décolletage. Ample breasts swelled against the midnight-blue of her low-cut dress. Her lush curves only added to the total package of black hair, ivory skin and vivid blue eyes. She was a stunning beauty, and he'd received more than one envious glance with her on his arm.

"Thank you. It's been over a year now." He admired the view even as he acknowledged her appearance had more to do with her profession than with any desire to impress him. He supposed he could live with that.

"It was nice of him to give you a job at the studio."

The fact that her beauty exceeded her IQ, not so much, a fact he'd determined before they ever arrived at the event.

"My family owns the studio," he explained. "I inherited upon my father's passing." Obviously she hadn't read her portfolio. He looked around for Tori, frowned when he spotted her huddled with a slim man in a suit. The man seemed more interested in her blond hair as it flowed in a liquid ribbon of gold over her shoulder than in the clipboard she held.

"Wow," Gwen exclaimed. "You should do a movie about me," she said while twirling a raven tendril around her finger. "Everyone says my life would make a good story."

Good grief. It was going to be a long night.

Tori discretely followed the last of the diners as they wandered toward the dancing next door. Once the couple crossed the threshold, she closed the doors to prevent any of the guests from returning to the dining room.

"Dinner is a wrap," she advised Lauren.

"Great. I'll make a sweep through the room in a few minutes, collect any forgotten items." It was a service they always performed. Any items found would be placed on a table for people to claim on their way out of the event. "Any complaints?"

"The usual grumbles." Tori always asked for feedback

from the hotel. "Nothing serious," she muttered, her attention more on Garrett and Gwen than on her conversation.

"Getting any vibes off those two?"

The words were whispered directly into her ear. Tori jumped to find her sister so close. No use pretending she wasn't staring at their host. But then she had good reason.

"No. What about you? They seem to be getting along okay."

Garrett stood on the edge of the dance floor talking to his chief financial officer. Gwen clung to his right side, her arm linked with his, her head resting on his shoulder. He glanced down at the woman draped over him, but he faced away from her, and Tori couldn't see his expression.

"Do you think so? He looks restless to me."

"Really?" The corner of Tori's mouth ticked up. "So you're not getting any vibes, either?"

"Nope," Lauren confirmed. "No vibes for Garrett and Gwen."

Tori released a breath she hadn't known she'd been holding. And suddenly she was looking into her mirror image. Lauren stood in front of her, arms crossed over her chest.

"You seem pretty happy there's no attraction between them. Anything you want to share?"

"No!" The denial was instinctive and gut-wrenching.

Okay, yes, she'd come to think of Garrett as a friend. The Lord knew he could use a few. From what she saw besides Ray, he had no one. But any notion of a romantic link between her and Garrett was idiotic.

And yeah, the unexpected joy he'd shown in the simple task of decorating a Christmas tree and the vulnerability revealed by the few memories he shared got to her. Watching him retreat behind his facade also reminded her why he was off-limits.

If he didn't learn how to deal with his internal demons, he'd eventually implode, bringing down anyone foolish

enough to care for him in the process. She knew the dev-
astation that came with the fallout, and she couldn't—
wouldn't—go through the pain of that again.

"No," she repeated more calmly. "It's just a relief to
check matchmaking off tonight's itinerary so we can concentrate on the event."

"Uh-huh." Though she let it drop, the skepticism on
Lauren's face warned Tori the topic wasn't forgotten.
"Well, he's still the client, so we need to keep tabs on him."

As prompted, Tori kept her eye on Garrett throughout the
night. She wandered through the club. Low lighting offset with spotlights of violet and gold gave the room atmosphere while flowing walls of chiffon created interesting
seating alcoves. Larger couches in white leather ringed
the dance floor, offering comfort between songs. The live
band skillfully mixed beats between fast and slow to keep
the energy high.

Garrett and Gwen twirled around the floor to a sultry
melody. Turning away from the sight, Tori stepped outside.

On the terrace a tent transformed into a cigar room offered black leather seating and a black studded bar. Plants
and dark wood screens made up the walls. The space was
popular, in her estimation, more for the air than the cigars,
but a few gentlemen puffed away.

"We could use another server in the cigar room," she
said into her headset.

"On it," Lauren responded. "Sending two that way."

Lured by the beckoning hand of cool, fresh air, Tori
slipped past the screen and strolled across the terrazzo
decking to a poolside lounger. The fabric cushion was
damp to the touch, but a headache pounded behind her
eyes and the cold felt good. Kicking off her shoes, she sat
down and put her feet up.

Well-placed lampposts lit the area with yellow light.

Cabanas and palm trees cast interesting shadows and steam wafted just above the surface of the water. The music from the party sounded behind her.

"I'm taking ten on the patio," she informed her sister. "Wake me if you don't see me in a few."

"Ha-ha. The servers are setting up the coffee tables. I've started closing down the alcohol stations inside. The cigar room will be last."

"Sounds good."

"I don't see Garrett anywhere. Did he leave?"

"I don't think so. He was on the dance floor a few minutes ago."

"He's not there now. Maybe the date went better than we thought, and he's taken off."

Tori's heart kicked in her chest. Setting aside her initial reaction, she tried to think logically. "Doubtful. He told me he'd be at the door at midnight to bid his guests goodbye." Tori rubbed a throbbing temple and breathed deeply of the cool night air. Juggling an event and matchmaking had never been so hard. "I'm sure he'd tell us if he changed his mind."

"Okay. Enjoy your ten."

Unable to relax with Garrett's whereabouts in question, Tori called his driver and learned he was currently driving Gwen home. Alone. Once he dropped off his passenger, he was dismissed for the night.

So much for Lauren's theory of the date.

Tori relaxed back into the cushion and closed her eyes. The fresh air worked wonders on her headache.

"Star gazing, Ms. Randall?" Garrett's deep voice came from the darkness.

She smiled but didn't open her eyes. "Reenergizing, Mr. Black."

Lauren chirped in her ear, acknowledging Garrett had

been located. Tori hummed in response and reached behind her ear to disconnect her link.

"Another successful event for By Arrangement." His voice had shifted to above her. Unnerved by the thought of him looking down on her, she opened her eyes and looked right into his silver gaze.

"I'm glad you think so." She swung around so her feet touched the terrazzo. Being grounded helped as she moved into dangerous territory. "I understand you sent Gwen home."

"Yes. She had an early appointment."

Tori bit the inside of her lip. His lack of inflection gave her no clue to how the date went. She braved a direct question. "Will you be seeing her again?"

"What do your spidey senses tell you?"

"Stop calling them that." She pushed to her feet on the protest. And still he towered over her.

He tilted his head. "What would you call it?"

Actually it was as good a way to describe her talent as any. It was his mockery she found unacceptable. "We don't call it anything. In fact, we don't generally talk about our talents at all."

"Then how come I'm in this mess?"

"Please. As if it's a hardship to spend a few hours with a beautiful supermodel."

A flash of annoyance crossed his features. He crowded her a bit. "Are you purposely not answering or is there something you're not telling me?" Intimidated but unwilling to show it, she squared her shoulders. "We get a vibe, okay. And no, we didn't feel anything between you and Gwen."

That backed him up. Not much, but he lifted his head and stared down at her. At this angle the yellow pool lights turned his eyes an interesting shade of gold. He leaned over her until she inhaled the spicy scent of his cologne and stated softly, "In that case, I'll admit it wasn't a hardship, more a waste of time."

"Gee, thanks." Faint praise, but she'd take it. Heck, high on the scent of man and spice, she'd agree to almost anything.

"Would you like to dance?"

"What?" Startled by his request, she instinctively stepped back.

"Careful." He grabbed her arm and pulled her to him.

"Goodness." A glance down showed she'd retreated to the pool edge. He'd saved her from a nasty fall into the water. "Thank you."

"I'll take that as a *yes*." Wrapping a hard arm around her waist, he drew her against him and began to move to the music.

Oh, my.

Keep your head, girl.

Unfortunately the little pep talk did little good as his warmth surrounded her. Contrarily she shivered as his heat chased the chill away. Sighing, she melted into him. Her head found the comfort of his shoulder, her breasts cushioned his chest, her body swayed to the rhythm of his.

He smelled good, felt good, moved good. She snuggled close wanting more, more, more.

The rumble in his chest and the soft rush of laughter over her ear alerted her to the danger she faced. The fact she just wanted to smile and bury her nose against him proved how far gone her inhibitions were.

The feel of his lips in her hair did the trick.

She jerked upright, stiffened her posture. Dialogue, she pulled the word from a mind gone to mush. Conversation, chitchat, something to occupy the silence between them, anything to dispel the lingering intimacy. She completely dismissed the tiny voice in the back of her head urging her to just walk away.

"Let's talk about your date." Oh, man, she cringed internally. That was the last thing she wanted to think about.

"Let's not."

"It could be helpful as I start looking for your next companion." Stupid. Why was she pursuing this?

His sigh bridged the distance she'd created, bringing his chest in contact with her breasts for a tantalizing second. "A gentleman doesn't kiss and tell."

"So you kissed her?" Okay, it was official. Aliens had taken over her brain.

"I didn't say that." His breath heated the sensitive flesh behind her ear as he leaned forward. "Why? Does it bother you to think of me kissing her?"

"What? No. Of course not." Lord, she could hear the inanity of her response. She cleared her throat. "I want you to find someone to be happy with."

"And if I'm happier alone?"

"No one is happier alone." She repeated what Shane had shared with her so many summers ago. "They just pretend to be."

He gave a harsh half laugh. "Why would anyone pretend such a thing?"

"Because it's easier. Because it's predictable and controllable. And because self-imposed loneliness hurts less than being rejected or caring for someone more than they care for you."

His whole body went stiff and he stepped away.

Her arms dropped to her sides as she stared up at him. A tick or two passed before she realized the music had stopped.

He lifted a hand, brushed his thumb over her cheek. "Thank you for the dance." Then his eyes cooled and he turned to the side. "For the entire evening, actually. The club element worked well, even if you did dial it down for the geezer crowd."

Right, back to employer-employee mode. She should be glad, but was curiously saddened instead.

"*Geezer* is a bit harsh, don't you think?" She began a search for her shoes only to have them handed to her. "Thanks." She used his arm for balance to put them on. The hard flex of muscles under her fingers reminded her how close she'd come to letting hormones overrule professionalism tonight.

"Not by Hollywood's standards. You know what they say." He placed a hand in the small of her back and aimed her toward the patio door.

"Hollywood is a young man's field?" She waved the old saying away. "I think that's less true than it used to be. Digital has been a great equalizer. And with cable and internet shows the market is wide-open. Great directors and actors only get better with time."

"Maybe I should hire you for our PR."

"Not interested. But on that note, I need to get back to work." She paused just inside the door, pondered the wisdom of her next action, but it really only made sense. "Would you like a ride home? It'll be late," she warned. "I have to stay to the end, make sure everything is wrapped up with the hotel."

He hesitated, then nodded. "Sure. I'd appreciate a ride."

The next morning Tori waited until Garrett left the house before slipping into the kitchen. Call her a coward, but walking into the house together last night had been too surreal, like a couple coming home after date night. So much so she'd almost followed him upstairs.

Obviously she needed to do a better job of avoiding him.

She poured a mug of coffee, dropped a piece of bread in the toaster and sipped while it browned. When it popped up, she buttered the toast and spread on a dollop of raspberry jam. She crunched a bite on her way to the table.

And almost choked when she saw the cover of the tabloid sitting in the middle of the table.

Lauren wrapped in the arms of Ray Donovan.

The caption read: Elusive Donovan Romances Mystery Bombshell.

OMG! Her no-nonsense sister and the bad boy director? When had that happened?

Tori recognized Lauren's dress as the one she wore at last night's event, which answered when the picture was taken. Funny, Tori didn't remember Ray being at the party.

She was so shocked it took her a minute to identify the warm sensation Garrett called her spidey sense. She remembered feeling it on Thanksgiving, too. Dim but definitely there. Wow, wherever, whenever it came to be, it was the real thing. Her mind reeled. Should she say something to Lauren or just let nature take its course?

Barely had the thought formed when her phone rang. No surprise Lauren's picture showed on the display.

"Good morning," Tori said sweetly. "I see we made the tabloids this morning."

"That's why I'm calling," Lauren said more calmly than Tori expected. "I just got off the line with Jenna. She saw the pictures of Garrett and Gwen in the tabloids and she was thrilled."

"Garrett and Gwen?" Tori flipped frantically through the magazine until she found a photo of Garrett escorting Gwen into the hotel where the party was held. The two of them made a stunning couple. Had Garrett kissed her? And why did the very notion turn her stomach?

"I cautioned her we had no control on how well the date went or whether there would be a second date."

Tori closed the magazine, which left Lauren's steamy photo front and center. "According to Garrett there won't be a second date."

"Well, we figured." Lauren sounded resigned. "In the

meantime we've made the girls happy so we've bought some time."

"Great." Tori waited a beat. When her twin didn't bring up her own notoriety, Tori prompted. "Anything else you want to discuss about last night?"

"Like what?"

"Like you and Ray Donovan in a lip-lock on the front page of *Hollywood Live*."

Silence greeted her statement. Then she heard the click of keys on the other end of the line, followed by a sharply indrawn breath.

"Lauren?" Tori demanded. "You okay?"

"Umm. No." There was a clatter on the other end. "I've gotta go. Bye."

Tori blinked at the call-ended message on her cell.

What just happened? Clearly her sister wasn't ready to talk to Tori about her relationship with Donovan. A little hurt, she munched on her cold toast. It wasn't like Lauren to keep things from her. Then again she hadn't been too up-front with Lauren about everything that transpired at the mansion, either.

Because a few intimate moments meant nothing. No need to involve her sister over a few stolen kisses.

CHAPTER NINE

RAIN POUNDED ON the eaves of the old house. High winds whipped the moisture against the windows. Branches scrapped across exterior walls. Tori smothered a yawn. Tucked up in the parlor with a fire in the grate, lights twinkling in the tree and Christmas carols playing, she updated her files and created her to-do list for the next day.

Garrett had a late meeting, so she had the place to herself. She loved her cozy duplex and having Lauren right next door, but it was nice here in front of the fire and having a big, warm house surrounding her on such a nasty night.

Cross-legged on the couch with a mug of tea within reach on the coffee table, she fought off another yawn. Maybe she should have gone with coffee instead of tea.

She marked off most of the repairs for the Old Manor. Rain came with nightfall, but sunshine and warm temperatures over the past two days allowed the crew to complete the outdoor work and varnish the hardwood. A couple of days to finalize the decorating and they'd be ready for the party.

She sipped her tea, smiled over the mug, enjoying the mellow brew, definitely the right choice.

Boom! Crash! Darkness.

"Eee!" Tori shrieked and started. Then gasped as tea poured over her. "Sh—sugar cubes." The rumble of thunder faded while she realized a loss of electricity was what pitched the room into darkness.

She jumped up, tugging at her sweater to shake off the tea, thankfully it had cooled considerably. The flames flickering in the fireplace lent her little help. Wait, she could use her phone.

She sat and felt around. She found the mug and plate she'd used and set them on the coffee table. But no phone. Oh, dope, her computer. She felt around again, hoping desperately that she hadn't dowsed the laptop with tea. She found it on the couch, breathed easier when she encountered only a few drops on the keys.

"Thank goodness." It probably toppled off her lap when she jumped. She used the light from the screen to find her cell. Unfortunately, it read "No Service." There went the idea of calling Garrett to see when he'd be home.

Boo. She didn't want to make that call anyway. Too unprofessional, worse, too wimpy. She could do this. The danger was outside not inside. She had shelter, light and heat. Supplies if she needed them. She had it good.

"Now, to find flashlights and candles." Carrying the computer was awkward and the battery wouldn't last.

Her first step soaked her sock in tea. "Ugh." She hated wet socks.

"Pull it together," she chided. Somehow it helped to talk out loud. "You saw a flashlight in this place. Where was it?"

Kitchen, she decided. She tossed a log on the fire before making her way in that direction. Her faint hope the electricity would return by the time she reached her destination fizzled a sad death.

Lightning flashed, followed immediately by a boom of thunder. Rain pummeled the house.

Tori flinched.

Geez, she couldn't remember the last storm this bad. In

the next flash she saw the utility closet and remembered the flashlight on the top shelf. She set the computer on the counter facing the cupboard.

She didn't realize how badly she was shaking until she turned the flashlight on and the beam shook wildly over the table. Taking a deep breath, she managed to steady her grip. She shone the light around the room. Everything was neat and tidy. Steam still wafted from the spout of the tea kettle.

The normalcy steadied her nerves enough to look for candles, additional flashlights, batteries. No telling how long the outage might last. The gas stove worked in her favor if it went through the morning.

A search of the cupboards and drawers turned up nothing. Another crash against the windows drew her attention to the glass panes. She hoped they held. Time to check the mudroom.

She tried for a stiff upper lip, managed a few puckers and a bit lip. Giving up, she walked in her damp socks to the back door. The mudroom held the washer and dryer. A long folding counter with cupboards underneath ran two thirds of the room on the opposite side.

Tori found a box of candles, wooden matches and batteries. Unfortunately the wrong size for her flashlight. She carried her cache to the kitchen table.

She lit two of the stubby candles and set them on either end of the long butcher-block table in cereal bowls. The flickering glow gave light and a faux sense of warmth to the room. She shut down the computer to conserve the battery and contemplated her next move. Suddenly the big house felt cold and lonely.

The very real heat of the fireplace drew her back to the parlor. The fire and the candles made it cozy. If she discounted the oppressive darkness surrounding her.

Wrapped in the throw from the back of the couch, she

took off her damp socks and tucked her feet into the fleecy softness, prepared to wait for Garrett.

She stared into the fire, watching the flames. In perpetual motion, the brilliant oranges, yellows and reds flowed in a wild dance of beauty and destruction. The mesmerizing show almost distracted her from the unnerving creeks and groans of the old house, the unrelenting sounds of the storm.

Rain pounded the roof and lashed the glass while branches continued to buffet the house. Growing antsy with nothing except the storm keeping her company, she dug up her iPod put in her earphones and zoned to a country mix.

The unexpected feel of a hand on her shoulder spooked a shriek from her. She jumped to her feet, brandishing the flashlight, ready to fight off any specter. The big black shape looming behind the couch fit the description.

"Tori, stop," a gravelly rasp directed. "It's me, Garrett."

"Garrett?" She aimed the light at him. "Thank God." She launched herself into his arms, climbed right over the couch and threw her arms around his waist. "I'm so happy to see you."

"Hey." He drew her close so her head rested under his chin. She heard the reassuring thump of his heart under her ear. A large hand ran over her hair in a soothing motion. "Are you okay?"

"I am now that you're here." She breathed in his scent, comforted by his presence.

"It's a hell of a storm." He continued to pet her, his fingers feathering through the ends of her hair before starting at the top again. "Lightning hit a power pole. Half of Hollywood Hills is out."

"Do they know when it'll be back up?"

"No word yet."

The time to let him go had come. She knew it, yet she

clung to him. He was alive and warm, strong and steady, everything she'd craved while struggling alone. She needed a few minutes to let the tension of the past couple of hours fade away.

"I'm sorry you were afraid." His breath blew over her temple, lifting stray strands of hair.

His nearness made her feel safe, cherished. His demand for perfection may occasionally be annoying but tonight he was her rock. Still, his words jerked at her pride. And a drop of water hit her cheek. Reluctantly she pushed away from him, her fingers sliding over firm abs. Very reluctantly.

She cleared her throat, lifted her chin. "Unnerved maybe, but I handled myself."

"I can see that." He ran a large hand through his hair and it came away wet. "The candles were a welcome sight in the kitchen."

"Goodness, you're soaked." She circled the couch, grabbed up the dish towel she'd used as a teapot cozy and tossed it to him. "This should help."

"Thanks." He rubbed the cloth over his head, leaving his hair spiked and tousled. He draped the towel around his neck, held an end in each hand and gave her a half smile. "Better."

This was the most unkempt she'd ever seen him. It was rather endearing.

"You need a shower and dry clothes." She lit two candles, offered them to him. "Did you eat?"

"No. I just wanted to get home."

Thunder boomed overhead. Lightning flashed, then flashed again.

Tori shivered. "If you promise to hurry, I'll heat something up for you while you shower."

The offer earned her a full grin, the smile that tugged

at something deep in her. The grin along with the disheveled hair made him appear younger, more approachable.

"Best offer I've had all day." He raised a cereal bowl as if toasting her with the candle. "Be right back."

The house felt different with Garrett in residence. The storm still raged, but the darkness no longer oppressed. In front of the open refrigerator she surveyed her choices. She pulled out the leftover stew and a tube of prebaked biscuits and went to work.

"Smells good." Garrett came into the kitchen dressed in a sweatshirt and jeans.

"Almost ready." Tori closed the oven door and set the pan of biscuits on the stove top. "Take a seat at the table."

She placed the food in front of him and curled into a chair across the table to watch him eat. A companionable silence fell between them.

After a few minutes, she fought off a yawn and decided to give him a progress report. "The crews finished—"

He held up a hand to stop her. "Not tonight. I've had all the meetings I can handle today."

"It's good news," she tempted him.

He shook his head. "I don't care." He shoved in another bite of stew.

"Okay." Snatching a hot biscuit, she smeared it with butter and grape jelly. "Mmm," she moaned.

He froze with a biscuit halfway to his mouth. "None of that, either."

She frowned. "I can't have a biscuit?"

"You can't make those lovey-dovey noises."

She blinked at him. "What are you talking about?"

He pinned her with an intense stare. "Those little moans you make when you eat. I'm too tired to ward them off tonight."

"Oh." His comment gave her a lot to process. She hadn't realized she made lovey-dovey sounds when she ate. More important was the attraction he'd revealed with his admission. Sure there'd been a couple of kisses and the dance the other night, but his stoic professionalism discouraged any fraternization between them.

A policy she respected and agreed with. A policy she'd be smart to heed tonight.

Because of the party nature of what she did, it was important to be ever mindful of mixing pleasure with clients. With Garrett, she needed to take extra care.

He hid a lost soul behind his all-business facade.

For good reason. Abandoned by his mother, raised by an emotionally stunted father, later rejected by him. His fiancée left him over a career choice. Any one of these things was enough to damage a person's confidence. Add them together and it was no wonder he wanted to protect himself.

His vulnerability called to her.

But she couldn't heal his pain. She'd reached out to Shane, tried to fix their bruised friendship. But ultimately she couldn't give him what he needed. They'd been so close, and she'd failed. She still reeled from the loss she'd suffered so long ago.

No, she couldn't heal Garrett's pain. Only he could do that, either by forgiving the wounds of the past or by being strong enough to open himself to the possibilities of the future, of new relationships.

But tonight, none of that seemed to matter. They were two people holding off a storm raining havoc around them. Cocooned by the flicker of candlelight, they'd become reliant on each other, drawn together by the intimate circumstances.

She didn't need to touch his soul. His broad shoulders, those hard abs, were enough to get her through the night.

Holding his desire-darkened gaze, she deliberately lifted the other half of her biscuit and took a bite.

"Mmm," she moaned. A dollop of jelly fell on her finger. She made a sensual display of removing the sweetness from her skin with slow licks of her tongue.

An actual growl rumbled from his throat. "I only give one warning."

She wrapped her lips around her finger then slowly drew it out. "Are you done with your meal?"

"I'm finished." He stood and placed his bowl and the nearest candle on the counter. Then he came to her, passion burning in his eyes. He lifted her to him, claimed her mouth in a breath-stealing caress.

"But I'm still hungry." He swept everything else on the table aside with one swipe of his arm and laid her on the wooden surface. A biscuit flew through the air. The second candle almost toppled.

He didn't care. He buried his face in her neck, nibbling and kissing a trail to the tip of her chin. Her skin tingled with every little nip, her blood heated. He stopped for a kiss, a wild tangling of tongues, before beginning a downward descent.

OMG. She needed to halt him now, or they'd set the house on fire. Literally.

"Garrett." His name came out as more of a groan than a bid for attention. His fault. How was she supposed to think with his talented hands stroking over sensitive flesh? She tried again. "Garrett."

"Don't stop me." His teeth sank into the curve of her shoulder in sensual warning. "You chose this."

"I'm not." She arched into him, her blood humming from the pleasurable sting of his bite. "Bedroom," she said desperately.

"Here," he decreed and licked a path up her neck to the tender spot behind her ear. She shivered as need built in her.

"The candle will fall."

"Let it."

She laughed, moaned. "Your house."

"Mine," he agreed and stripped her sweater over her head.

She cradled his head, threading her fingers into the silky thickness of his hair to hold his mouth where she wanted it most. He gave her the attention she craved, laving her through the lace of her bra. The heat of his breath seared her skin, ignited her senses, sent her mind spinning.

Hunger for more of him had her tugging at his sweatshirt as she fought to get to his skin, all that yummy flesh stretched over hard muscles. "Mmm." Suddenly his mouth was on hers, cutting off the ardent whimper. His erotic penalty coaxed more lovey-dovey sounds from her throat, from her soul.

"Off." She dug her fingers into the thick fabric and yanked. "Now."

He stood, grabbed a handful of sweatshirt and pulled it over his head. In those few seconds the chill in the room wafted over her heated form. Losing his weight, his warmth revealed just how icy the room had grown. When he lowered to her, she planted her hands in the middle of his chest.

"It's freezing in here. And the table is hard." She cupped his cheek. "Can we please move to the bedroom? Mine is just across the hall."

He leaned his forehead on hers. "If it's comfort you want, mine is better."

"You win."

"Oh, I know." He helped her to her feet, tucked her under his arm and started out of the room.

"Wait." She tried to pull away to grab the candle at the end of the table.

"Oh, no you don't. Things I want have a way of slipping through my fingers. I'm not letting you go until I have you in my bed."

Her heart wrenched at his revealing comment. She looped her arms around his neck. "I'm not going anywhere," she promised. "Not until morning."

"That works for me."

Garrett let Tori get the candle, then took her hand and led her to his bed. Savage satisfaction roared through every cell at the sight of her golden hair flowing across his pillow in the soft glow of the candlelight.

He took the candle she carried and set it on the bedside table. He'd left another burning on his dresser across the room. The dimness allowed him to see her but wrapped them in intimacy.

Tori loved the sunshine and her lightly tanned skin blended with the soft beige of her lacy bra. Her lovely breasts rose and fell with each breath and her pulse raced under his fingers at her wrist, all signs of the desire in her molten gaze.

Beautiful.

He stood back, admiring the look of her in his bed. But need beat at him, poured through his blood like the liquid gold staring up at him, driving lust through every extremity. He craved the feel of her, longed to touch, to taste. Not any woman, but her.

He couldn't remember the last time he'd felt such all-consuming, primitive lust.

Holding her gaze, he reached for the button of her jeans. She lifted her hips, making it easy for him to remove her pants and thong. She sat up, giving him access to her bra clasp as her fingers went to work at his waistband.

"Let me." His hands shook slightly as he accomplished the task, but were steady when he lowered himself to her, pulling her in for a deep kiss. She tasted of honey and spice, intoxicating.

Her hands fisted in his hair and she arched into his embrace, a plea—no, a demand—for him to hurry. The small noises he found so irresistible whispered into his ear.

He gave into her insistent entreaty, stroking and soothing, nibbling and kissing every inch of her, and she matched him caress for caress, kneading, licking, sinking her fingers into his muscles.

"Garrett," she gasped his name, made it an endearment.

Her responsiveness torched his restraint and he took them higher, faster, reaching for the sky, touching the stars as fulfillment sent their senses spinning and their bodies shuddered harder than the house at the apex of the storm.

CHAPTER TEN

THERE WAS A MAN in Tori's bed. A warm, hard-muscled, naked man pressed snug against her back. She went from cozy and sleepy and—oh, yes—satisfied to panicked in 0.2 seconds.

OMG, the bed belonged to Garrett Black.

Okay, okay, she needed to calm down, to think beyond the roar of her pulse in her ears. Breathe, that's what she needed to do. She inhaled a slow, deep breath. And choked on her own air when the action rubbed her bare skin over the hair-roughened chest of the man behind her.

Big mistake. No more breathing.

She opened her eyes and looked directly at the shallow remains of a candle on the bedside table. She frowned and blinked. Then the events of the previous night came flooding back. The storm, the fear and loneliness, relief when Garrett arrived, heating stew and…dessert.

She swallowed back a moan. One minute she and Garrett had been chatting over leftovers, the flicker of candlelight adding to the intimate mood, the next they'd both lost their minds and the moment had gone beyond the boundaries of a professional relationship.

Lauren was going to kill her. Employee-client fraternization was much worse than taking her heels off at an event.

Tori had reasons of her own why last night should never have happened.

Unnerved by the storm and being caught in the dark in an unfamiliar house, she'd let the coziness in the kitchen go to her head. In an unexpected move he'd put business off-limits, which left her defenseless. She got swept away by the closeness of the moment and lowered her guard.

He'd sat across from her, relaxed and comfortable in sweatshirt and jeans, his hair disheveled from the rain and his recent shower. For such a strong, confident man, he'd looked…ruffled.

Sexy.

Vulnerable.

And entirely too approachable.

Everything after that took on a sensual haze: a tangled limbs, heated skin, breath-stealing, wonderful haze. She'd reached heights last night where she'd actually touched fireworks.

Her blood still hummed.

Behind her Garrett stirred, his hand burned a brand on her hip.

Tori froze, her heart pounding as she waited for him to wake, to speak, to regret what happened between them. And he would regret the night of passion. She knew how he felt about keeping the world at a distance. How fanatically he protected his heart.

He stirred again and rolled on to his back.

Sighing, she allowed herself to breathe again. After a few minutes, enough to figure he'd settled into sleep, she slowly began to inch away from the heat of his body. Immediately she missed the warmth and safety of being enveloped in his arms. Determinedly she pushed the illusion away.

Did she regret the passionate interlude?

Oh, yeah.

She liked her job, liked the challenge of it, the glamour, the satisfaction of keeping up with Garrett's fast-paced intelligence. By Arrangement still had several events to complete for the studio. She didn't want to put their reputation at risk because of a slip of judgment and a surge of hormones.

Especially when no chance of a future existed for her and Garrett. She'd experienced firsthand the pain and loss that came from loving someone emotionally injured, someone who lived in a perpetual cycle of angst. She'd sworn never to put herself in that situation again.

On her feet, she slipped into his shirt. No way was she taking the time to dress. Besides, there was no sign of her sweater, which meant it probably littered the floor of the kitchen.

She may never wear the sweater again. Too many memories.

Avoiding the sight of his large body sprawled under the sheets, she tiptoed about, gathering clothes, blushing when she found her lace thong buried under his black boxer briefs. Vivid memories of how the snug fabric clung to his muscular body assailed her. Swallowing back an urge to drool, she snatched up the thong.

She debated waking him to discuss the situation and how it affected their business relationship, but decided nothing could be gained by rushing the confrontation. Far better if time and distance separated them when they discussed the events of last night.

Thank God the work here was nearly finished. It was beyond time for her to return to her duplex. Hopefully she could pack and escape before she encountered Garrett.

Decision made, she headed for the door.

"Tori?"

She stilled, her hand wrapped around the knob as the husky voice reached her. Fingers flexing on the brass knob, she stared at the heavy oak door. "Yes."

Sleep thickened his next words. "It's best we forget this ever happened."

"Yes." Equal parts of relief and, surprisingly, disappointment rushed through her. "It's best forgotten."

With a sigh she quietly stepped outside and pulled the door closed behind her.

"Are you going to be seeing Ray tonight?" Tori asked to take her mind off Garrett and their mad night of passion.

If she stopped concentrating for two seconds, memories, regrets, wishes took her mind over in a flash. Little of it made sense, some was just irrational and none of it was productive. *Self-destructive* was the best word to describe her mental gymnastics. She just needed to stop.

She thought it would help them both to move beyond that night if she set him up with his next date. It hadn't. Not her, anyway.

Who knew how he was doing?

He hadn't talked to her since she'd left the house. She'd sent him the information about his date, which was for the opening reception of the film festival, through email. He'd simply responded he'd see her there. A none-too-subtle reminder for her to be available to rescue him if necessary.

She'd been looking forward to tonight. The reception was one of the few events she and Lauren were attending instead of working.

Now she had to spend the night watching Garrett with another woman. She accepted the two of them had no future together. Still, seeing him escorting someone else was not her idea of fun.

"He'll probably be there," Lauren answered her question about Ray. "But I told you there's nothing between us."

"No, you said what was between you was over. That it was just a flash in the pan." Tori watched her sister's profile as she drove. "I can't believe you did it in the laundry room with Mom and Dad in the house." Actually, she couldn't believe Lauren did it in the laundry room at all. She didn't normally do spontaneous.

Lauren flicked Tori a narrow-eyed glance. "You promised you'd never say anything to them."

"And I won't," Tori assured her. "That's not a conversation I want to have." But focusing on her sister's love life beat brooding on her own. "So you won't say hello?"

"Not unless we end up in the same group." From her tone, the likelihood seemed slim.

It appeared they were in the same boat tonight.

"Tell me about Garrett's date." Lauren changed the conversation.

Tori turned her gaze to the lights flashing by her window. She hadn't told Lauren about sleeping with Garrett and it ate at her. They were partners. Lauren had a right to know. More, they were sisters, twins. Tori couldn't know about the laundry room without being honest about the night of the storm.

"I slept with Garrett."

"What?" Lauren's head swung her way.

"Watch out!" Tori threw up a bracing hand as Lauren slammed on the brakes at a red light. "Sorry."

Lauren gave her a look, and when the light changed she pulled through the intersection and into a parking lot. She put the car in gear, turned off the ignition and faced Tori.

"Spill."

"It just happened." She tried for a careless shrug. "Like you and Ray."

"Try again. We have no open contracts with Ray."

"I know, okay." Tori stared at her hands to avoid the censure in her sister's expression. "It shouldn't have happened. I've been careful to keep things as professional as possible. But the storm..." Tori shook her head. "Don't worry, it won't happen again."

Lauren's warm grip settled over Tori's restless fingers. "Tell me about the storm."

Tori glanced over and swallowed hard when she saw it was her sister asking, not her partner. The words bubbled out of her then, about being caught in the dark and being spooked. How happy she was when Garrett got home and how sexy he looked all disheveled and ruffled. And oh, the way he looked at her, all hot and bothered.

"And?" Lauren prompted when she finished.

Tori hesitated for half a second. "And OMG, it was magical. I have seen the creative side of Garrett Black."

"Award worthy?" Lauren grinned.

Heat rushed to Tori's cheeks. "Oh, yeah."

"So why did you set him up with another date?"

She sighed. "Because he's a client, and emotionally constipated, and it would never work between us."

"Emotionally constipated?" Lauren about choked on the phrase. "Is that another way of calling him a shit?"

"It means he's blocked. He's been hurt so many times he protects his heart like it's made of gold." Tori bit her lower lip, already swollen from days of similar torture. "Oh, Lauren, sometimes I see the same look in Garrett's eyes I used to see in Shane's."

"God, Tori. Garrett has had a really tough year, but you can't possibly think he'd—"

"No, of course not," Tori quickly denied, not allowing Lauren to finish. The man had way too much ego to give up. But that didn't mean he was willing to live life to the fullest. "At least, I don't think so. But then, I never would have thought it of Shane, either."

"Shane was a boy, a selfish, immature child who felt the world owed him." Lauren didn't sugarcoat her opinion. "Garrett is a man who has suffered much and not only has he endured, he's a successful director and businessman."

"I know. Of course, I know." Lauren wasn't saying anything Tori hadn't told herself. "But he's blocked himself off, just as Shane withheld himself from me. No matter what I did I couldn't reach him. I can't go through that again."

Lauren squeezed her hand, asked softly, "Do you care for Garrett?"

"More than I should," Tori confessed. "Which makes it all the more imperative I put the brakes on now."

"So you never feel any vibe when you're with Garrett?" Lauren asked her. "Nothing to give you a clue that you belong together?"

Totally unprepared for the question, Tori blinked at her. "Like our matchmaking vibe? No. And I'm glad. It would be terrible to know we were meant for each other when he's so out of reach."

"Right." Lauren got them back on the road. "Do you want me to take Garrett duty tonight?"

Tori wished. "No. You may as well enjoy the party. I won't be able to keep from watching him anyway." She remembered Lauren's original question. "I went outside the industry for this date. Mari is a financial advisor. Stocks, retirement funds, that kind of thing. She's a brown-eyed brunette, striking rather than pretty."

"Good choice. He'll appreciate someone with brains."

"Some men preferred beauty to brains."

"Uh-huh."

Tori crossed her arms over her chest. "Just drive."

The film festival chose a rooftop ballroom in a beautiful old hotel on Sunset Boulevard for the opening reception. Garrett looked on the red carpet as a necessary evil. His strategy involved powering forward until a microphone got shoved in his face.

His date, Mari, carried herself well. Exotic brown eyes changed her average features from plain to interesting.

Her floor-length navy sheath dress clung to slim curves. When asked what she was wearing, she simply replied she'd picked it up at a boutique in Hollywood.

"And here we have Garrett Black, the new president of Obsidian Studios." A perky blonde from a prime-time entertainment show stepped into his path. He exchanged pleasantries. Then she asked, "What's it like being on the executive side of the industry? Does it mean you've given up directing?"

"I'm still evaluating my options," he responded vaguely, then added, "The studio is excited to celebrate its nineti-eth anniversary at the film festival."

"Yes, the party is being held at The Old Manor House from the classic horror film," the woman gushed. "I have to say it's one of the events I'm most looking forward to."

"I'm glad to hear it. I hope to see you there."

"I wouldn't miss it. Thanks, Garrett Black." The blonde nodded to them and moved to her next victim.

Garrett mixed up his comments to include some of the premieres planned for the film festival but by far the most enthusiastic reaction was anticipation of the anniversary party. He had to hand it to Tori, she'd made the right call there.

As if her name magically conjured her, the crowd parted and there she stood. He was used to seeing her in black or jeans. Tonight she wore a short dress in holly berry-red. The dress clung and shimmered with every move she made. The bodice angled up to ring her neck, leaving her beautiful shoulders bare.

When she turned, he nearly choked on a sip of cham-pagne. The back consisted of a single red strip from her neck to her waist. She'd bundled her long blond tresses into a loose bun on top of her head, leaving all her silky skin on display.

His fingers twitched with the need to touch.

She glowed bright as a flame and with her ready smile she brought light and warmth wherever she went. He felt it all the way across the crowded room.

"Garrett. Garrett?" A hand touched his arm and he glance down into Mari's slanted gaze.

"Did you want to mingle?" she asked.

"Yes, of course. Is there anyone in particular you'd like to meet?" He found there usually was.

She brightened. "Do you think Meryl Streep is here?"

How novel. It was usually George Clooney.

"Possibly, shall we see?" He offered her his arm and they made a turn around the room.

He tried, and failed, to keep his eyes off Tori. She drew him like an elf to Santa's workshop. She was a bright gift he longed to unwrap.

He'd been surprised to get her email informing him of his date for tonight. It just felt wrong. He'd even considered suggesting the two of them pretend to hook up to satisfy her need to please the starlets.

But once he thought about the situation, he realized it would be a mistake to let the feisty minx get any more entrenched in his life. He already had to deal with constant recollections of her passionate caring, of being wrapped in her arms. Any insecurity he felt about his leg vanished under her soft touch. She never flinched as she kissed each scar.

He still smelled her in his house, still heard the echo of her chatter.

Who knew he'd miss it?

Exactly why he needed to put her from his thoughts, why he needed to forget the memory of her sweet response. So the house felt empty. He could live with that. He couldn't live with losing anyone else. Except he'd never actually had anyone, had he? Mother, father, fiancée, they were all supposed to love you, but they'd all walked away from him.

He could only conclude he lacked whatever it took to attract love. Better to be alone than to continually be judged wanting.

He enjoyed talking to Mari. She had a sharp mind and a quick wit. He'd be happy to have her in his accounting department, but there was no spark. And that suited him just fine.

"Good evening, Garrett." Tori snuck up on him as he stood looking out at the spectacular view.

"Tori." He inclined his head. "You look lovely this evening."

"You, too. Where did you stash Mari?" She propped her hands on her curvy hips. "You didn't put her in a car home, did you?"

"No. I introduced her to my chief financial officer."

Her eyes widened. "You palmed her off on someone else?"

He lifted a dark eyebrow, a silent reprimand. "I left them talking. They really seemed to hit it off. Perhaps I have talent as a matchmaker."

She sent her eyes heavenward. "Oh, you're a hoot."

"Relax. I have no desire to be a marriage broker."

"You don't understand. It's not a matter of marriage but of soul mates."

"Come on." He mocked her. "We both know you and your sister dreamed up the matchmaking scheme to drum up business. If you introduce a couple, they're hardly likely to go to another event coordinator."

She paled. "That's not true. And it's a terrible thing to say."

"So you haven't handled any of the weddings?"

"Yes, but it wasn't some diabolical, preconceived plan like you're suggesting." He'd clearly insulted her. "We've matched up plenty of couples and got nothing out of it."

"Then why bother?" He wasn't being cynical. He could understand matchmaking as a good marketing plan. It was an effective gimmick. But as an altruistic act? That was beyond his comprehension.

"Why?" Her brow furrowed in bafflement. "How could we not? People search their whole lives for love. If we can help them find the special someone to grow old with, we feel it's our obligation to do so. If anything, it's complicated our work. As you can attest."

"So you do it out of the goodness of your hearts."

"Pretty much."

"And you don't care if they get married?" He would have taken her for a white-picket-fence gal.

She shifted, turning to look out the picture window. "How people choose to be together is their own business."

"That doesn't sound like a wedding planner," he pointed out.

"Just because I believe in marriage doesn't mean everyone does. Some people feel a marriage certificate is just a piece a paper. Some still get married, others don't. We assist the ones who do." She swung around, the action putting her between him and the window, mere inches away. Her chin went up and her hands landed on her hips. "Why the interrogation, Garrett? Are you thinking of getting married? Did you connect more with Mari than you let on? Because no matter how good I am at forgetting certain things ever happened, By Arrangement would have to respectfully decline planning your wedding."

"I'm not attracted to Mari, and I would never ask you to."

"Good."

Was it his imagination or did she relax a little? Her scent distracted him. She usually smelled of her cherry blossom lotion. Tonight he inhaled an intoxicating musk.

"So why all the questions?" she persisted.

"Just curious."

"About matchmaking and marriage?"

He understood her puzzlement. Truthfully, he was unsure what drove him. "I just made an offhand comment, you took it from there. Still, I'd like to know, what does marriage mean to you? Is it just a piece of paper?"

Her eyes delved into his, probably questioning his sanity. Finally she answered.

"No, when I get married, I hope it'll be forever. I want my vows to have meaning and value, and for my promises to be made before God because it matters."

She cocked her head. "Now I'm curious. You were engaged once. What does marriage mean to you?"

CHAPTER ELEVEN

GARRETT SCOWLED, TOOK a step back. Suddenly he'd had enough of this conversation. Tori's hand landed on his tux-covered arm, blocking his retreat.

"Oh, no, you don't. I answered all your questions."

What the hell? "I thought it meant committing ourselves to each other, being there through the tough times. I was wrong. I should have known better. That was one lesson I should have learned from good old Dad."

"So you gave up on relationships. But not sex."

His eyebrow shot up. She should know the answer to that. "I don't have to be in a relationship to have sex."

Her eyes flashed. Oh, yeah, she remembered. She shook her finger at him. "I'm talking about bad sex. You don't give up on sex because of a bad experience. You shouldn't give up on love, either."

He stared at her. "Are you saying the sex was bad for you?"

"No." Shock crossed her delicate features. "It was…" He saw the exact moment when her mind caught up with her emotions. "Adequate."

Ouch. But he was too gratified by her reaction to let her attempt at retaliation get to him. He bent over her ear, whispered, "Liar."

She pushed him back with a finger in the center of his chest. "You're missing the point."

He wrapped his hand around hers, swept his thumb over the skin at her wrist. So soft.

"The thing about bad sex is once it's over, you're done and gone. A bad relationship stays with you forever."

As if the admission jarred a nerve, something shifted in him. Feeling exposed, he lifted her hand to his mouth and kissed her palm. "Good night, Tori."

"W-wait." She cleared her throat. "What about our arrangement?"

He lifted one shoulder, let it drop in a gesture of unconcern. "Enjoy your evening. I think I'm safe with Mari. Now if you'll excuse me, there's Meryl Streep. I promised Mari an introduction."

Tori watched his broad shoulders disappear in the crowd. She rubbed a spot over her heart. What an odd conversation. And how dare he blame her? He'd been the one with all the questions.

Was it her fault he didn't care to have the tables turned on him? She thought for a moment he might really open up to her. Maybe he had. *A bad relationship stays with you forever.* Did that mean he still had feelings for his former fiancée? That wasn't the impression she'd gotten before tonight.

And she didn't like the thought of it now. One thing tonight revealed, she was in worse trouble than she wanted to admit. As of now, Garrett duty went to Lauren.

Because watching him walk away to be with another woman broke her heart more than a little.

Four days and three events later Tori did a final walk-through of The Old Manor House. Outside the house maintained the classic appearance the guests would expect to see; inside the beauty and warmth of the Christmas holiday invited the guests to come in and celebrate the season and Obsidian Studios' ninetieth anniversary.

When she walked through the foyer, she came across Garrett staring at the largest tree they'd bought together. It stood in the middle of the entry hall, a sentinel of the event.

"What do you think?" The decorations had just been completed this afternoon. She'd sweated the timing but she'd special ordered the ornaments and they hadn't arrived until this morning. It turned out better than she hoped.

"I have no words," Garrett said. "How did you do this?"

"Anything is available for a price. Time was our biggest factor, but it worked out." Decorated in silver bows, red crystal holly berries and gold statues, the tree sparkled from every direction. Each mini Academy Award–shaped statue bore the name and date of an award-winning movie, actor, director and so forth earned by Obsidian Studios films over the past ninety years.

"It's stunning."

He was pretty stunning himself in an Armani tuxedo. "There are actually more statues than the tree could hold. The rest are bunched in displays throughout the party area."

He stepped close. "I've been here through the whole process and I'm still amazed with what you've done."

"It's what we do," she said simply.

"No. This is all you." He tugged softly on the end of her sleek ponytail. "You went beyond the call of duty. Thank you."

"All part of the service." She played it cool. "Tomorrow is the end of the film festival. This is our last event together. I want to say it's been interesting working with you."

"Interesting?"

Surprisingly they'd managed to put personal matters aside the past few days and work very well together. Obsidian's events were the talk of the festival along with Ray's film and an independent production that was getting lots of good press. After tonight's party, no one would talk about the film festival without mentioning Obsidian Studios.

"How would you describe it?" she wondered.

"Parts of it were quite pleasurable."

Of course he had to go there. She'd spent the past four days pushing every hint of their sensuous interlude from her mind. Keeping up a professional facade had been the only way to see him daily and retain her sanity.

"We agreed to forget those parts."

"I haven't been as successful at forgetting as I'd like." His gaze ran over her, approval in the silver depths. "You look lovely tonight."

She wore a black cocktail dress with a V-neck, off-the-shoulder sleeves and a flowing skirt that showcased her legs. An ornate clip adorned a sleek side ponytail. The outfit was dressier than her usual garb when working, but tonight she considered herself a hostess.

"You set the rules, Garrett," she reminded him. "You can't change them now."

"But you're a rule breaker." He ran a finger down her cheek. "Don't think I've forgotten."

She caught his hand, pulled it down. "Not when it comes to my heart."

"The first car has arrived." The warning came through her headset from the valet station.

"Your first guest is here." She squeezed his hand and released it. "Have fun tonight. We'll take care of everything."

Garrett stood on the terrace with the film festival officials talking about the overall success of the festival when Ray joined the group.

"Well done," Ray addressed the officials. "This festival is the best I've been to this year. And Garrett Black, here, is the man of the hour." Ray clapped Garrett on the back. "You put Obsidian Studios in the hot spot."

"He did indeed," Martin, a portly gentleman, agreed. "We were just talking about the high energy of the festival this year, not least of which is due to Obsidian's events. Both premieres got a lot of buzz, but the open house is the talk of the festival."

Still stunning in her late sixties, the grand dame of the festival, Estelle, hooked her arm through Garrett's. "The Art Deco decor made you feel as if you were walking back in history to Old Hollywood. Dressing the waitstaff in fashions of the era was brilliant."

"My event coordinators are By Arrangement. They've done an outstanding job."

"Truly spectacular." Estelle waved her hand to encompass the terrace. "The decorations are lovely, well-placed and tasteful, but it's also comfortable and welcoming. I especially like the conversational area around the fire pit and the fact there are lap blankets if anyone gets chilled. Martin, make a note of By Arrangement."

"Of course. Garrett, you'll send me their information?"

"It would be my pleasure." Moving them along, Garrett suggested, "Estelle, why don't you try out the fire pit."

"I believe I will." She kissed Garrett's cheek and the pair wandered off.

"Thanks for coming tonight and agreeing to do the anniversary toast." Garrett led Ray inside to a pub table in the corner of the parlor.

"I'm happy to do it. Some of my best work has been with Obsidian."

"I heard your film got some good quotes."

"Yeah. We're getting some award buzz. Nothing resembling Obsidian, though. Congratulations, bro, you're already making your mark on the company." Ray took a sip of beer. "I was angry when you closed my set and messed with my schedule, but it was a smart move. The studio's reputation was suffering, but it's already turning around." He tapped his beer bottle against Garrett's Champagne glass. "I predict good things for Obsidian in the coming years."

"I'll drink to that." Garrett lifted his glass to his lips.

"Those two did a hell of a job." Ray nodded his head toward the hall where Tori and Lauren stood together surveying the scene.

"The Dynamic Duo," Garrett agreed. He caught the way his buddy eyed the women and his back went up. He turned a narrowed gaze on his friend, for some odd reason feeling proprietorial about the twins. "I saw the tabloid with you and Lauren. What's going on there?"

Ray lifted a sandy-colored brow. "What's your interest?"

"I've worked closely with the girls." He put the weight of his concern in his voice. "I'd hate to see either of them hurt."

Ray laughed. "Dude, you sound like their big brother."

"I'm serious, Ray."

"No need to worry about me and Lauren." Ray held up a pacifying hand. "It was a few moments out of time, not to be repeated. Seriously, dude, instead of me, you should look to yourself."

Garrett stilled. "There's nothing between me and Tori."

"I'm a director, Garrett. I have a trained eye. There's more sexual tension between the two of you than Brad and Angelina."

"You're imagining things," Garrett denied.

"If that's true, you need to stop gazing at her as if she's the last lollipop." Ray stepped between Garrett and Tori, breaking his line of sight. "Because she looks at you like most women covet chocolate, and if you're going to close her out the way you do most people, she will get hurt."

"Do you have a sudden candy fetish?" Garrett frowned his annoyance. "Who's sounding like their brother now?"

"You brought it up," Ray pointed out. He swung around so they both faced the twins. "I'm fond of them, too, but you saw their family. They have to believe in love, marriage and happily ever after, which puts them firmly out of our reach."

Garrett said nothing. Because there was no arguing with the truth.

"Woo-hoo!" Tori kicked her shoes off and wrapped her sister in a big hug. "The last guest is gone. We did it. The Obsidian contract is done. Once the cleaning is over, of course." Maria and her crew would be here first thing in the morning. The food service had already packed up and left.

Lauren gave her a squeeze. "Yep, and people are going to be talking about this party for years. You did a great job."

"We did a great job. We're a team."

Lauren framed Tori's face. "No, this one goes to you. It was your genius idea. You pushed Garrett. You put the time into the house and decorations. The victory on this party is yours. Congratulations."

"This party was just the crowning glory. Everyone was talking about Obsidian's events tonight. We were a hit."

"On that we agree." Lauren walked to the table and poured them each a glass of champagne. "To By Arrangement."

Tori clicked classes. "Only one more party, then we're off until New Year's Eve. I'm ready for a holiday."

"Amen." Lauren clinked glasses again.

Tori dropped into a chair. She propped her head on her hand, sighed deeply, then peeked at her sister. "Well, except for planning another date for Garrett. You're really okay with handling that?"

"About that." Lauren slid into the seat across from Tori. "We're off the hook."

"What do you mean?" Exhaustion must be catching up with her because that didn't make sense.

"I saw Jenna and Cindy during the party. We got to talking and get this, they decided that having closed sets wasn't such a bad thing."

"You're kidding."

"Nope. It turns out they can focus on their roles and concentrate better when they don't have loved ones on set distracting them."

"Hmm. Who knew?" Tori rolled her eyes. Now they saw the wisdom of Garrett's rules, after she'd turned cartwheels to meet their matchmaking demands. And turned her heart inside out.

"I know." Lauren covered her hand. "But at least we don't have to continue with it. Shall we tell Garrett?"

"He drove the film festival officials back to their hotel. I lent him the SUV."

"Why didn't he just call them a cab?"

"Estelle was insistent."

"Gotcha." Lauren smothered a yawn. "I'm beat. Do you want me to drop you off? We can pick up the SUV tomorrow."

Tori was tempted. The Lord knew it had been a long week. "I'll wait. I want to do a last sweep through."

"I'll go with you."

"No, you go ahead. It'll only take a few minutes, and then I'll put my feet up and wait for Garrett." She walked Lauren to the door, watched her take off and then she locked the door and grabbed a trash bag.

She started on the terrace, brought in the lap blankets and turned off the lights. She found a diamond earring in the upstairs bathroom—someone would be calling about that—and a shawl pooled behind a poinsettia on the stairs.

The items went next to her purse on the coffee table. She'd see if Garrett wanted the studio to take charge of them or for By Arrangement to hold on to them.

She fought off a yawn. Garrett should be along anytime. Anytime…

Garrett stepped in the back door and made his way through the house in search of Tori. He saw some cleanup had yet to be done, but Tori told him a crew would be there in the morning. He hoped she wasn't trying to do anything more tonight. Sometimes he thought of her as an energized bunny, all go, go, go.

The Lord knew she lived life to the beat of her own drum. A beat that used to drive him crazy, but with the last of their events wrapped, he had to admit—if only to himself—he might miss her just a little. The characteristics he originally found irritating, her cheerful chatter, her wry humor, had grown on him. He'd always respected her intelligence and the way she challenged him.

Which all meant it was a good thing their contract was at an end. Ray thought Garrett had the power to hurt Tori, but what he didn't realize was Tori had the power to decimate Garrett. He didn't have it in him to be rejected again. Better to go through life lonely than shattered.

He walked into the parlor and found her asleep on the couch. He half smiled. So much for go, go, go. No surprise really. She arrived just after seven that morning, worked her shapely butt off all day and had juggled both the front and back of the house during the party. All on top of a very hectic week.

She looked lovely in the soft glow of the fire. Her golden hair picked up the flickering light, bringing it to life. Thick lashes fanned her cheeks, the creamy skin almost translucent in the dimness. The movement of her chest drew his gaze. Her breasts lifted and fell with each breath she took.

He remembered the taste of her, the softness, the perfection of her sensual responsiveness. But he pushed all that from his mind. Time for her to go.

Except he hated to wake her after such a long day. She'd done so much for him. Tonight's party wouldn't have been as successful at any other location. Successful, yes, but not special. She'd pushed for The Old Manor House, turned her life upside down to get it ready and delivered on a unique experience for every attendee.

The awards tree drew everyone's attention, shouting Obsidian's accomplishments without saying a single word. It was brilliant and creative, a gift he'd never forget.

"Tori," he said softly. She sighed but didn't move. "Tori," he spoke her name louder. Her keys jingled in his hand as he leaned over her.

"Hmm." She shifted, repositioning her shoulders, but she didn't awaken.

Enough. She'd slept here before; he'd just tuck her into bed and let her sleep.

He swept her up in his arms, inhaled her sweet scent. It only took a moment to reach the study, but of course the bed was in sofa mode. He should have thought to check before moving her. No problem. He'd just put her in his bed and sleep here himself.

He eyed the stairs. He'd experienced some aching with the recent damp weather. He worried briefly that it might give him trouble with Tori's extra weight. Being careful, he made it to the top without incident. Triumph trumpeted through him. The personal accomplishment proved he was still a man, capable of taking care of his woman in her weakest moment. *His woman?* Of course he meant *a woman.*

In his room he shouldered the light on, made his way to the bed and, grabbing the edge of the spread, pulled it back. He carefully laid Tori on the crisp white sheets. Before standing, he released her hair from the jeweled clip, letting the lush tresses loose to flow over his pillow. He set the clip on the night table and stepped back.

Never had he seen anything more beautiful, sleeping beauty in his bed.

He reached to remove her shoes, but, of course, they were already gone, her pretty, pink-tipped feet were bare against the bedding. He fondly shook his head. The woman was forever kicking off her shoes.

Okay, time to go when he started thinking a woman's feet were sexy. He grasped the spread, only he couldn't bring himself to pull it over her.

No. That wasn't the problem. He didn't want to leave her. And why should he? They'd shared a bed once; they could do so again. He dropped the covers over her. Then he stepped back and reached for his tie.

CHAPTER TWELVE

TORI WOKE TO an odd sense of déjà vu. A man was in her bed. Only this time there was no doubt in her mind of whom. Garrett. She clung to him like ivy wrapped around a trellis, her head on his chest, arm over his waist, legs entwined. His body cushioned hers, while his heat warmed her, inside and out.

The fuzziness came from how she got there.

The last thing she remembered was waiting for Garrett to get home last night. She must have fallen asleep in front of the fire. Which didn't actually explain how she ended up in his bed.

She sighed, not really caring how she got there. It felt too good to be snuggled up to him. Her mind screamed at her to peel away, to make a stealthy exit, just like last time. But she hadn't escaped unscathed. And this time she had no pleasure to offset the upset.

So she shut her mind to sense. Instead she gave in to her senses and turned her head to press her lips to the hard plains of his chest. In the pale light of dawn she drew lazy patterns in the dusting of hair on his pecs as she slowly kissed a path up his side. Lifting her head, she lightly nipped the ball of his shoulder and met pale gray eyes searing her through half-lowered lids.

"Good morning." The words came out in a husky purr.

"A most excellent morning." A bit of gravel made his early morning voice a sexy rumble.

She ran a finger down his shadowed jaw. "Did you take advantage of me last night?"

"I wanted to—" he bit the tip of her finger "—but I was a gentleman."

"Good. I wouldn't have wanted to miss anything."

"Hmm." He rolled so she was under him. "I find it's better when both parties participate."

"Mmm." She savored his weight pushing her into the mattress. Nothing quite equaled the sense of security and excitement that came with being wrapped in the arms of a strong man. She looped her arms around his neck, threaded her fingers in his thick hair, loving the softness against her skin. "It does add to the experience."

He buried his mouth in the curve of her neck, licked the spot behind her ear that made her body shudder with want.

"I need to brush my teeth." It was the first sensible thought in her head since she woke up. Maybe it would spark more, and she'd find the resolve to stop this before it went too far.

"Me, too." His breath feathered over skin as he kissed a path down her neck to the edge of her dress.

Her dress. Now she thought of it, she felt the skirt bounced around her thighs. How sweet of him. He could have stripped her or even left her in her underwear, they had been lovers after all. Instead he allowed her the modesty of her dress. How chivalrous.

But not something he chose for himself, she discovered as she ran her hands down the length of his back to the treasure of his tight derriere. She savored the feel of skin and muscles on the return journey.

"And a shower." An imperative, now that she knew she'd slept in her clothes.

"Good idea." He kissed her softly on the lips and slipped from the bed to sweep her into his arms.

"Garrett," she gasped, "I'm too heavy."

"Hardly." He walked into the bathroom. "How do you think I got you upstairs?"

"Oh, my Lord, I didn't thing about it. You shouldn't have. What about your leg?"

"It's fine." He dismissed her concern and set her down. He opened a drawer and handed her a new toothbrush. Then he took a black shaving bag from a cabinet and went to the door. The look he shot her made her toes curl against the cool tile. "I'm going to use the other bathroom. You have five minutes."

Tori lost thirty seconds of her allotted time peeking around the door, admiring his magnificent backside as he left the room. Then she hopped to, taking care of business before he returned. All too soon a knock sounded at the door.

"Come in." She struck a sultry pose, but when the door began to open she felt foolish and quickly dropped it so she stood one bare foot over the other. Her hair fell free over bare shoulders and she clasped a towel around her with one hand. With the other she twirled a piece of hair around her finger.

He stepped inside, his eyes darkening as he stalked her. Up close he framed her face in warm hands and lifted her face for kiss after kiss. He tasted of man and temptation.

She lost her hold on the towel to grip his shoulders, her body melded to his, skin to skin, curves to plains, lip to lip. Blood surged through her veins, spreading heat to every part of her. Anticipation sent butterflies fluttering.

He pulled back. Breathing hard, he rested his forehead against hers.

"You are so beautiful."

Eyes closed, she smiled. "When you look at me, I feel beautiful."

"I was afraid you'd come to your senses."

"Seriously? I was naked except for a towel."

He traced her jaw. "I meant while I was gone."

"No." Suddenly uncertain, she struggled to engage her mind through the fog of lust. "I should have just left, huh? It would have been the sensible thing to do." She bent and gathered up the towel.

"Sensible is overrated." He pulled her against him, re-igniting her passion with a wild kiss. He lifted his head without releasing her and catching the edge of the door, he swung it closed. "You'll feel better after you shower."

Wrapped in a damp towel Tori used Garrett's hair dryer on her hair. Satisfaction lifted the corners of her mouth and hummed lightly through her body. She viewed Garrett from the corner of her eyes.

He leaned against the counter, arms crossed over his chest, watching her. A towel was draped low around his hips. Catching her scrutiny, he lifted one dark eyebrow.

She turned off the dryer. "You should dress," she urged, sweeping her hair into a knot and securing it with the jeweled clip. "The cleaning crew will be here soon."

"I like watching you."

She liked watching him, too, liked having his eyes on her. But as the buzz of his loving faded, common sense invaded. The wonder of being with him confirmed her worst fear. She loved him. But she could never be with him. He rejected love, preferred to live an isolated existence.

She needed people, family, a commitment that included open communication.

"I have to go." She edged past him into the bedroom, clutching her clothes to her chest.

He followed. "Why don't we give this a try?"

She stilled, blew at a loose piece of hair. Was he really suggesting a relationship? "Define *this*."

"Us. As lovers." He tucked the bothersome hair behind her ear. "It would have been awkward while By Arrangement was under contract, but the events are over now."

"True, but we hope the studio will want to rehire us for future events. If things end badly between us, that's not likely to happen." And his belief that isolation equaled safety guaranteed a bad ending.

"I can separate work and play."

She had no doubt. He'd been doing it for years. "Yeah, well, I'm not that sophisticated. You don't do relationships and, as good as this was, a random series of booty calls doesn't sound appealing."

He crowded her, leaned close to whisper in her ear. "I can change your mind. Let's go to breakfast, talk about it."

"I don't think that's a good idea." No, it was a very bad idea. She imagined he could all too easily change her mind. Just standing over her smelling of man and soap, he tempted her.

"Why not?"

"Because I'm already too emotionally involved for either of our comfort." No reason not to be honest. Nothing would get through to him faster. Her heart picked up speed, dread filling her as she contemplated leaving him.

And it did bring him to a stop. Hands on hips, he considered her.

She expected him to send her on her way, hoped for a gracious departure and the chance of a cordial future.

"Who is Shane?" he asked.

She blinked at him. That she hadn't expected. "What? Where did you hear the name?"

"From you. The night of the storm. You said his name just before you provoked me into making love to you."

"Really?" She didn't remember saying it, but she had

been thinking of Shane as she often did around Garrett. "He's not important." She backed toward the door. "A friend from high school."

"He must be important for you to mention him." Garrett advanced on her.

"Why do you care?" she wondered. She waved at the bed. "This is as far as we go. We have no future. There's no need to delve into our histories."

"Says the woman who searched for me online." He caught her hand, drew her to the bed to sit. "Tell me."

"It was a long time ago." Wanting space between them, she sat sideways, with her legs half off the bed. "I don't like to talk about it."

"If it's not important, why are you upset?"

"I'm not." She secured her towel. Really, she needed to get dressed. "It's ancient history."

"Not so ancient if you still think of him."

"I don't usually. Not for a long time, anyway."

"Then why now?" He pulled her foot into his lap, gently massaged the sole. "What does Shane have to do with us?"

There was that word again. *Us.* With all her heart she wished it were true, wished she could believe in it, in them. And for the first time she felt some of Shane's pain. She couldn't be what he wanted, couldn't feel what wasn't there. Just as Garrett couldn't give her the love and affection he'd cut from his life so long ago.

"Nothing. Everything." His touch, the muscle melting massage, vanquished her resistance. Maybe if she told him, he'd find his way back someday. "Shane lived across the street. We grew up together. Next to Lauren, he was my best friend. We really got close in middle school when his parents went through a divorce. He didn't like change and that was the mother of all changes. He hated having to split his time between his parents' houses. He told me I was the only sane thing in his life."

"Divorce is hard on kids. Most of us survive."

"Shane didn't. He committed suicide."

His fingers stilled and he raised his gaze to hers. She saw concern and compassion, all for her. "I'm sorry."

She knew in that moment he'd never take his own life. She'd always suspected his strength and self-discipline made it unlikely, but the way he focused his sympathy on her and away from Shane revealed his disdain for the act.

"His mother moved our sophomore year of high school and he had to change schools. He hated her for that. He was so upset and negative it was hard to be around him. His dad stopped trying. Shane felt rejected and betrayed by everyone.

"It was such a difficult time. He wanted to spend time with me and I wanted to help, but he wouldn't talk to me, he wouldn't open up. My mom said I helped just by being there for him. And I get that, but it's frustrating to be shut out. I felt helpless."

"The only place he felt safe was with you," he guessed.

"Pretty much. We talked every day but between different schools and work it seemed we saw less and less of each other. Then he learned I was dating a guy in my class. I didn't consciously keep it from him, but he could be jealous of me spending time with my own family so I just didn't mention it."

Those months had been the worst of her life, even more than after Shane passed. Seeing her friend suffering, not knowing what was in his head made her sad. And angry. Which was the reason she went out with the jock to begin with. It was so hard spending time with Shane, who was in turns sullen and withdrawn, that a carefree date seemed like heaven.

It took her a long time after Shane's passing to get over the guilt of that. She hadn't dated again until college.

"Did he hurt you?"

Again Garrett's concern was for her. She'd never heard his voice so hard, and she'd been the victim of its cutting edge a time or two.

"Not physically. He went ballistic. He loved me and we were meant to be together. He accused me of leading him on, of lying to him. I was a slut and I betrayed him. Just like everyone betrayed him. Nobody cared about him. Nobody understood him." Even after all this time, his accusations and contempt still hurt.

"I tried to explain I did love him, but as a brother, that I would always be his friend. But he wouldn't listen, not that day, and not in the weeks to follow. I tried to reach him. I left messages. I went to his house. His mom said he completely retreated into himself and he wasn't talking to her, either."

"And then he took his own life." Garrett said it for her, as if he understood how difficult it was for her to say.

"Yes. I did talk to him one last time. He sounded so despondent. I repeated what I'd said before, told him I missed him. He said he missed me, too, but it would be too hard to be around me knowing I didn't care for him the same way he cared about me. Two days later his mom called to tell me. He left a note saying he'd love me forever."

"Bastard." Surging to his feet, Garrett paced away.

"Garrett!"

"Sorry." He barked out the word, yet clearly felt no remorse. He went to his dresser, pulled out jeans and a T-shirt. "But he sounds like a self-absorbed punk who couldn't hack the reality of life and blamed you for his shortcomings while he took the easy way out." He dropped his towel and yanked the clothes on.

"Why are you so mad?"

"Because he hurt you and because you obviously associate me with this guy, and not in a good way."

Of course he caught the similarities and the significance of the story. "This is why I didn't want to have this conversation."

"You don't know me at all if you think I'd commit suicide."

"I don't believe you would, no. I haven't honestly thought so at any point. But did the notion occur to me, yes." She stood, hugged her dress to her chest. "Suicide is ugly. It's not something you just forget. I'm sorry if it offends you."

He stared at her with stark eyes, then turned away and raked his hands through his hair. "I'm not that weak."

"I know." Tired of clutching the towel, needing to be ready to leave when this grim discussion ended, she dropped the towel and quickly dressed. Stupidly a blush heated her cheeks when he spun and caught her in her underwear. Ignoring the irrational reaction, she pulled her dress over her head.

"If you didn't fear I'd kill myself—" he gritted through clenched teeth "—what's the deal?"

"I've seen the same look in your eyes as Shane used to get. A raw vulnerability immediately eclipsed by a chilling disconnect." Avoiding the accusation in his eyes, she tugged her skirt into place over her hips. "I understand it's a protective mechanism, cut off the need before it can hurt you."

"So Shane and I learned the same lesson. When life kicks you in the balls, you find a way to survive."

"Commendable." And so very sad. She made a move toward him, but he jerked back. She stopped, cleared the sudden lump from her throat. "But the problem with shutting out emotion is you close yourself off from any chance of getting past the hurt, of finding the happiness you secretly long for."

"Psychobabble," he dismissed. "I've heard it before. I don't need to hear it again."

"And that's why we can't have a bit of fun." She shrugged her right shoulder, trying for uncaring, though her heart was breaking. "You're dark and withdrawn, happy to bury your emotions and deny your loneliness.

"I need light and joy in my life. I like people and sharing my triumphs and struggles. You won't take a risk for love, and I'd risk everything." A glance around for her shoes and purse resulted in nothing. They must be in the parlor. "But I can't divorce my body and emotions, and I wouldn't want to. Even in a fling I can't be with someone who closes me out. I won't go through the pain of sitting on the sidelines again."

She blinked back tears, swallowed the lump in her throat.

"I don't believe you'll take your own life, but I never conceived of Shane doing so, either. As long as you bury your pain instead of dealing with it, the risk is there." Her heart pounded in her chest, it felt as if a fist were squeezing the organ, slowly crushing it. She backed to the door. No more. She had to end this. "Losing him nearly broke me. If I lost you, it would destroy me."

CHAPTER THIRTEEN

"I MADE YOU a cup of jasmine tea." Lauren came into the room carrying a tray with two mugs.

"Thanks." Tori sat up on the beige ultrasuede couch and pulled another tissue from the box on the huge ottoman Lauren used as a coffee table. Tori mopped her cheeks while Lauren set the tray down. Mom always served jasmine tea when they were upset. The smell comforted her, making her wish Mom were here.

Tori would have left for Palm Springs today if they didn't have an event Monday night.

"Are you sure Garrett has no feelings for you?" Lauren sipped her tea. "The fact he wanted to have a fling tells me there's something there."

Tori sent her an arch glance. "Good sex."

Lauren returned the look.

"Really good sex." Tori sighed and stared into her mug. "Fantastic, blow-your-mind good sex."

"Which makes me ask again, are you sure there's nothing more there? In my experience the more involved my heart the better the sex."

"It doesn't matter, because even if he felt something, he'd never admit it. Not to me, probably not to himself."

"I've seen the way he looks at you," Lauren said. "He's not indifferent. Ray noticed it, too."

"I don't deny the chemistry. I'm ashamed to say my

first reaction when he suggested being lovers was excitement. I was so tempted just to go with the moment and jump into his arms."

"Why didn't you?" Lauren asked softly. "You love him. There's no shame in wanting to be with him. If you went into the affair with your eyes open, maybe you could make it work."

Tori lifted teary eyes to her sister. "I can't be in someone's life and not be a part of it. Can you see me respecting those boundaries?"

"Considering you ask complete strangers personal questions, I suppose not."

"We'd both be miserable."

And Lauren was usually the first one to point that out. She hadn't been as close to Shane as Tori, but they'd been friends. Lauren had been the one to help Tori pick up the pieces of her life.

"I'm surprised you're in favor of it." A just-lovers relationship wouldn't offend Lauren, but the impetuosity of it would.

"Yes, well. I saw—" Lauren leaned forward to adjust her mug on the tea tray. "I mean, this is the first time I've seen you so gaga over someone. I would hate to see you lose out on something special."

More tears welled. Tori leaned her head on her twin's shoulder. "That's so sweet."

"So what are you going to do?"

"Move on." She willed the tears away. "Get through the holidays, then bury myself in work."

Lauren laid her head on top of Tori's. "Sounds like a plan."

"I can't talk to him again, Lauren. Will you handle the rest of the communications with Obsidian?"

"Of course."

"I sent a picture of the diamond earring to your email and put the original in the lockbox at the office."

Yes, focusing on work helped.

"I'll take care of it." Lauren took Tori's mug and set it on the tray. "Now, if I know you, you still have some Christmas shopping to do. How about some shopping therapy?"

A deep and familiar love welled in her shattered heart. "Now there's a plan."

"Mr. Black." Garrett's secretary hovered in his doorway. "Will we be getting off early tomorrow? Some of the others were wondering. It would be nice if I could put out an email."

He closed his eyes. Ah, damn. How had he forgotten Christmas? He should have arranged for gifts for the office staff. No doubt she would have reminded him except he'd been out of the office most of last week. He couldn't pass the chore off to her at this late date.

Tossing down his pen, he asked, "How many support staff do we have on this floor?"

"Eight, including myself."

"Right." The offices would be closed Wednesday through Friday for the holiday. The phones had barely rung. No reason to keep the support staff hanging around. "The staff can leave at one tomorrow."

"Thank you, Mr. Black. Have a nice evening."

He nodded and she left. Great, now he had to go shopping. He could let it go, but that just felt petty. His first thought was to call Tori and ask her advice. And that just pissed him off. He didn't need her to save him.

He didn't need to be saved at all. He wasn't about to off himself.

At his lowest point he may have wondered why he bothered, but his response had been to reach deeper, try harder. He never contemplated giving up.

The insult injured him to the depths of his soul.

How could she think him that weak?

Unable to concentrate on work, he closed up and headed out. Maybe he'd do better at gift shopping. The fact Tori interfered with his work irritated him all over again. Nothing outside the physical demands of recovery and therapy had ever had the power to distract him from his career be it director or executive.

He restrained the urge to put the Maserati through its paces on the surface streets. Later, after he finished his shopping, he'd take to the freeway and open it up. Perhaps he'd drive to his place in Santa Barbara. His leg was much better. He could manage the daily trip. There was no longer a need to stay so close to the studio.

His decision had nothing to do with the fact the old place was now haunted with Tori's ghost. Wherever he went in the house, memories of her assailed him.

She had a nerve accusing him of being closed off. He savagely shifted gears. Hell and damnation. He'd shared more with her than he had with his fiancée.

Which might explain why his fiancée found it so easy to walk away.

He flinched at the traitorous thought, blamed Tori for it, as well.

Pulling into the parking garage for the Hollywood and Highland mall, he avoided the valet service—he needed no additional reminders of the blasted woman—found a parking spot and stepped out of the elevator to a view of the Hollywood sign.

His momentum petered out at that point. He pulled out his phone and called Ray. When his friend answered, he explained his dilemma. "Any suggestions for gifts?"

"You're asking me?" Ray laughed. "Except for my grandmother and aunt, I haven't bought a woman a gift in years. My assistant handles all that."

"What's his number?"

"Forget it. He's out of the country. Why don't you call Tori?" Ray suggested. "She'll know the perfect thing."

"Tori's out of the picture." The words cut deeper than Garrett expected.

Ray didn't answer for a moment. "Your choice or hers?"

"Our contract was at an end," Garrett reminded him. "What makes you think there was any choice involved?"

"Your tone, for one thing." Ray's rueful response was a testament to how well he knew Garrett. "And Tori genuinely enjoys helping people. She wouldn't need to be under contract to answer your question."

"Her choice," Garrett confessed. "I proposed an affair. She wasn't interested. End of story."

"You mean you offered to be her lover and she refused your no strings, no emotion relationship. I'm not surprised. I told you she wasn't the type."

"Well that's all I have to offer," Garrett stated, pushing down the panic that rose up when he probed at the guards he held so firmly in place. Tori was right about one thing, he was dark and unfeeling, too damaged to risk the light. Loneliness was the price he paid for peace of mind.

"If you have no gift ideas for me, I've got to go." Garrett rubbed a hand over the back of his neck.

"Hey," Ray said before Garrett could disconnect.

"Yeah?"

"For what it's worth, I think you'd be safe with her."

Garrett didn't know what to say, so he said nothing. Ray got it.

"Merry Christmas, buddy." The call ended with a soft chime.

Bastard. He said that to mess with Garrett's head, worse, to mess with his heart.

He started walking, window-shopping, except he saw little. His mind replayed every memory of his time with

Tori, kind of like a near death experience, from the time she tripped barefoot down Ray's front steps to leave her toe prints in his car, to the professional who challenged him in his own office, negotiating dates, moving in, picking out then decorating Christmas trees, dancing poolside in the moonlight, throwing herself into his arms during a raging storm, making love in the candlelight, shining bright in a flame-red dress, playing hostess to his host, waking with her in his arms, making love in the shower, her walking away.

Each memory lashed at his soul bombarding him with emotions. Isolated for nearly a year going through surgeries, recuperation and physical therapy, he'd barely felt human when he went to Ray's party. From the first moment she'd brought him to life. He'd been intrigued, frustrated, attracted.

Good God, he'd convinced himself paw prints were her toe prints just so he could see her again.

He sank onto a bench, yanked at his tie and unbuttoned the top two buttons of his shirt so he could breathe. His phone rang. He pulled out his cell and his heart lurched. Tori.

"Hello," he rasped around a constriction in his throat.

"Garrett." It hurt to hear her saying his name. "Ray said you could use some help."

"He shouldn't have bothered you."

"It's no problem," she assured him. Now he was past his original shock, he heard the chill in her tone. "I needed to talk to you anyway. We heard from the woman who lost her earring."

"Yes, my secretary gave her your information."

"The studio is closer than our showroom, so she'd prefer to pick up the earring there if possible."

He didn't care about the frigging earring. "I'll have my secretary arrange it."

"Great. Now, where are you shopping?"

"Hollywood and Highland."

"There's a lovely day spa at the Loews Hotel adjacent to the mall. A gift certificate would be nice. They should be able to put together a basket of products to make it a delightful package."

"Excellent. Thanks for your help." He cleared his throat. "How are you?"

A pause. "Hurting."

He closed his eyes. "I'm sorry."

He wanted to say more, to see her again. But he couldn't. He might not have the strength to let her go again.

"Goodbye, Garrett." Tori ended the call and his last link with her was gone.

Garrett downshifted and within seconds the car shot to ninety-five miles an hour. He headed the car west, toward Santa Barbara and home. He'd feel more settled once he was back in his own space.

He couldn't get the last phone call out of his mind. During most of their contract he'd dealt with Tori, an unusual circumstance for By Arrangement. Lauren usually dealt with the client. But from the very beginning he'd gone straight to Tori. She'd always been warm and approachable.

Her cool tone hammered home the fact Tori didn't want to talk to him. From the way she said goodbye, he deduced By Arrangement wouldn't be accepting any more contracts with Obsidian Studios.

His chest clenched, making it hard to breathe.

Needing to get out of his head, he turned on the radio, flipped through the stations. He tried a sports station first, but couldn't find a spark of interest in who won the football play-offs, so he switched to hard rock. A few minutes later he turned the radio off with a savage twist of his wrist.

The music made his head hurt and provided no release from his revolving thoughts.

There would be no release until he successfully buried his feelings behind the armor he'd built to protect his heart.

But no matter how hard he tried, he couldn't bury the hurt this time. Tori cracked the shields with her quirky good cheer, quick creative mind and genuine caring, not just for him, who spurned most overtures, but everyone around her. She'd brought light into his life, made him feel again. He could choose to hide. Eventually shore up the shields until all feelings disappeared.

Or he could reach for the light and push the darkness out.

His heart pounded, a frantic beat, reminding him he was alive. He thought of the risk if she should reject him, and a strange sense of calm came over him. She loved him. He trusted her. Ray had said it. Garrett would be safe with her.

He checked the rearview mirror and began to make his way to the right-hand lane and the nearest off-ramp. He was turning around and going after the woman he loved.

He commanded his phone to place a call. He let out a held breath when it was answered.

"Lauren, about that third date, I need your help."

Tori pulled up to The Old Manor House with mixed feelings. She really didn't want to be here. Too many bittersweet memories. Lauren should be the one returning the earring. She'd agreed to handle the last of Obsidian Studios' business.

So of course this was the only time their client from last night could do their closing interview. Tori volunteered to meet with them, but Lauren was already on that side of town, and she assured Tori Garrett wouldn't be home while she was at the house. When they each completed their meetings, they'd get together and drive home to Palm Springs.

With any luck she wouldn't even have to get out of her car. She parked in front, in clear view of anyone coming up the drive. The temperatures had dropped overnight and the day was chilly. Heavy clouds speckled the sky. After a few minutes, the cold finally drove her inside.

This would give her a chance to return the key he'd given her while she stayed here. She'd planned to mail it to the studio. Her hand shook a little as she set it on the kitchen table. She paced the room, trying not to think of the meals she'd shared with Garrett.

She missed starting the day with him, talking to him, working with him. Him.

When her mind jumped to the night of the storm and she remembered how his body pressed hers to the sturdy table, she moved into the parlor.

She fingered the earring in her pocket. Where was the owner? The longer Tori lingered the more chance she'd run into Garrett. A glance at the mantel clock showed the woman was ten minutes late.

Nerves bristling, she walked through the downstairs rooms. In a professional capacity, of course. The cleaning crew had done a great job. Garrett had left the decorative lights lit and the place looked beautiful, festive. If she did say so herself. She turned away from the tree they'd decorated together, needing no reminders of his deprived childhood.

She heard a car pull up and breathed a sigh of relief until she saw the Maserati. Oh, no, this wasn't going to happen. She hiked her purse strap over her shoulder and went out the front door. She'd hand off the earring and be on her way.

He met her on the bottom step. Her higher position put them eye to eye. He looked more peaceful than she'd ever seen him. Great, her heart ached with the active pain of an abscessing tooth and he'd found the tranquility life had denied him.

She held up the earring. "The owner is running late. I'll be on my way now that you're here."

His hand wrapped around hers. "Can you stay for a few minutes? I'd like to talk to you."

She shook her head, pulled her hand free. Seeing him melted her insides. If she gave him half a chance, he'd change her mind. And that would not be a good thing.

"I have to go. Lauren and I are leaving town this afternoon." She tried to slide past him.

He shifted to block her, the movement bringing him closer, so his male scent reached her, setting her senses spinning.

"A few minutes won't delay you much."

"There's really nothing more to say." She retreated a step. Then sidestepped and went around him, making for her car.

"I love you."

She froze. Had she heard right?

Strong hands settled on her shoulders, and his warm breath brushed over her ear. "I love you."

She shook her head, turned to face him, arms crossed over her chest. "No. You don't get to say that to me. You don't believe in love."

"You showed me." He caught her hand, brought it to his mouth. "Come inside. Let's talk. I have a Christmas gift for you."

"No." She backed up a pace. A gift to remember him by was the last thing she wanted. Bad enough to have a broken heart to mark the holiday into the future. "Give it to someone else."

"It's just for you."

"Don't, Garrett." Confused, she tugged at her hand, pushing the rising hope aside. She didn't know why he was messing with her, but she couldn't let herself believe. Leaving had been hard enough when she thought he didn't care. How much worse would it be if she gave in to her love and lost him again? "I have to go."

He held on to her. "You love me, too."

"I loved you when I walked away. Nothing has changed."

"I've changed. Give me a chance to show you."

She chewed her lip. He sounded so sincere. "Five minutes."

His face lit up. "You won't regret it. Come with me." Grabbing her hand, he led her inside and out onto the terrace.

She shivered. "Maybe we should talk inside. It's cold out here."

"We have to watch for Mrs. Davis. We'll be able to see her car come up the drive."

Avoiding his gaze, she focused on the scenery. The Christmas tree lights were on out here, too. Shiny ornaments glimmered in the fading sunshine. She rubbed her hands together.

"I'll light the fire." He led her to the fire pit. A fire had been laid and he used a fireplace lighter to get it going. Then he sat down beside her on the bench seat. "I've missed you."

"Me, too." She stared down at her hands. "It's only been two days and it feels like forever."

"Too long for me. In all the time I've stayed at the Old Manor I've never seen or heard a ghost. Now it's haunted with images of you. I can't sleep, can't think of anything but you."

"It'll fade," she whispered, "just like every good memory you've buried."

"I deserve that." He took her hand, played with her fingers. "It was easier not to feel at all, so yeah, I buried the good with the bad. It became habit after a while to focus my feelings into my films."

"That's why story is so important to you."

He inclined his head. A soft wisp of wind blew a strand of hair across her face. He reached to brush it away and she ducked her head.

White fluff began to drift past her vision. She dismissed it as something in the air until some landed on her legs and melted into the fabric of her jeans. Her head jerked up. Snowflakes floated down on the terrace.

She looked with wonder at Garrett. "It's snowing."

"Merry Christmas."

"Oh, God. Oh, Garrett." Tears added to the snow drops on her cheeks. Somehow he'd tuned in to her childhood fantasy and arranged to give it to her. She threw her arms around his neck, hugging him with all her might. "Thank you."

How did she walk away from someone who saw so clearly into her heart?

"You turned my life upside down, Tori. My somber demeanor didn't deter you at all. You were irreverent and friendly, pushy and caring. You tried to deceive and fool me, but were horrendously bad at both."

She squirmed a little. "You never said how you knew I wasn't Lauren."

"I always know when it's you," he said simply.

Okay, that got to her, too. As a twin, knowing someone saw you as you touched something deep inside, filling a void she hadn't even known she had. He was racking up points left and right, but could she trust this turn in his feelings?

"I didn't want to deceive or fool you. It was your own fault."

"Please. You manipulated me to get your way. Then you moved in. And you were dragging me out to shop for Christmas trees and conning me into decorating one. Cooking and sharing coffee in the morning. You gave me a home, Tori. You can't just take it away again."

Every memory he dragged out meant something to her, too. The house had become a home, a dream she hadn't allowed herself to believe in. Did she dare take a chance?

"Garrett, you can't just flip a switch and suddenly change. I believe you want to, but a month from now you could find it all too much and long for your isolated existence again."

"You said I'd have to address the pain that caused my behavior or be buried under the weight of it. All I know is I can't change the past. And right or wrong, I lost a lot of my anger at my father when he left me the studio. But for me what really matters is my trust in you. If you never give up on me, I promise never to give up on us."

"That's beautiful." Oh, he shamed her. She'd chided him for being afraid to risk, boasted she'd risk everything for love, and yet she'd left when he'd been reaching out. Because she feared his power over her, feared love. She knew how much it hurt to lose someone. And her feelings for Garrett were so much stronger than what she'd felt for Shane. Looking deep into Garrett's gray eyes, something eased around her heart.

Gaze locked on hers, he leaned forward and kissed her, a soft meeting of lips as his gift of snow floated around them.

Love bloomed brighter, grew stronger as walls fell. She trusted him, too. With her heart, with her future, with her soul.

"I love you," she said against his mouth.

"And you'll marry me?"

She pulled back. "Marriage? Don't you think that's moving kind of fast?"

He cupped the back of her head, dragged her close for

a demanding melding of mouths and crush of bodies. "No reason not to move fast when you're certain of something. How does a Valentine's Day wedding sound to you?"

"A wedding in less than two months?" She found it sounded good. "Luckily I know a good event company. I think we could make that happen."

He grinned his beautiful smile and lowered his head again. "I'll take that as a yes."

* * * * *

a thundering melody and reduch, and crash of bodies. 'No one has ever [it's] her favourite tripping something.'

'How does Valentine's Day wedding sound to you?'

'A wedding? It has that two months?' She found it sounded good. 'I nobbly I know a good event company. I think we could make that happen.'

He smiled his breath of smile and looked her intend again. 'I'll make you my wife...'

...doing a work shift to have a game of cards in the house when the workers leave.' 'To sleeve more?'

This was what her life was like, he realized.

Everyone came to her when they needed something. She didn't expect Luke to be there for any other reason. Did no one seek her out just to talk during a work shift? To play a game of cards in the shade when they were off duty? To share a meal?

He didn't feel like smiling at the moment, but he did, anyway. She'd asked if he needed anything. "Nope. Nothing."

She tilted her head and looked at him, those eyes that had opened so wide now narrowing skeptically. "Then what are you doing here?"

I can't stop thinking about you. I want to feel you against me again.

* * *

Texas Rescue:
Rescuing hearts…one Texan at a time!

NOT JUST A COWBOY

BY
CARO CARSON

MILLS & BOON

Published in Great Britain 2014
by Mills & Boon, an imprint of Harlequin (UK) Limited,
Eton House, 18-24 Paradise Road, Richmond, Surrey, TW9 1SR

© 2014 Caro Carson

ISBN: 978-0-263-91316-3

23-0914

Harlequin (UK) Limited's policy is to use papers that are natural, renewable and recyclable products and made from wood grown in sustainable forests. The logging and manufacturing processes conform to the legal environmental regulations of the country of origin.

Printed and bound in Spain
by Blackprint CPI, Barcelona

Despite a no-nonsense background as a West Point graduate and US Army officer, **Caro Carson** has always treasured the happily-ever-after of a good romance novel. After reading romances no matter where in the world the army sent her, Caro began a career in the pharmaceutical industry. Little did she know the years she spent discussing science with physicians would provide excellent story material for her new career as a romance author. Now, Caro is delighted to be living her own happily-ever-after with her husband and two children in the great state of Florida, a location which has saved the coaster-loving theme-park fanatic a fortune on plane tickets.

For Barbara Tohm,
my very own fairy godmother

Chapter One

Patricia Cargill was not going to marry Quinn MacDowell, after all.

What a dreadful inconvenience.

She'd invested nearly a year of her life to cultivating their friendship, a pleasant relationship between a man and a woman evenly matched in temperament, in attractiveness, in income. Just when Patricia had thought the time was right for a smooth transition to the logical next step, Quinn had fallen head over heels in love with a woman he'd only known for a few weeks.

A year's planning, a year's investment of Patricia's time and effort, gone in a matter of days.

She tapped her pen impatiently against the clipboard in her hand. She didn't sigh, she didn't stoop her shoulders in defeat, and she most certainly didn't cry. Patricia was a Cargill, of the Austin Cargills, and she would weather her personal storm.

Later.

Right now, she was helping an entire town weather the aftermath of a different kind of storm, the kind that made national news as it made landfall on the coast of Texas. The kind of storm that could peel the roof off a hospital, leaving a town in need of the medical assistance that the Texas Rescue and Relief organization could provide. The kind of storm that let Patricia drop all the social niceties expected of an heiress while she assumed her role as the personnel director for a mobile hospital.

Her hospital was built of white tents, powered by generators, and staffed by all the physicians, nurses, and technicians Patricia had spent the past year recruiting. During Austin dinner parties and Lake Travis sailing weekends, over posh Longhorn football tailgates and stale hospital cafeteria buffets, Patricia had secured their promises to volunteer with Texas Rescue in time of disaster. That time was now.

"Patricia, there you are."

She turned to see one of her recruits hurrying toward her, a private-practice physician who'd never been in the field with Texas Rescue before. A rookie.

The woman was in her early thirties, a primary care physician named Mary Hodge. Her green scrubs could have been worn by anyone at the hospital, but she also wore a white doctor's coat, one she'd brought with her from Austin. She'd already wasted Patricia's time yesterday, tracking her down like this in order to insist that her coat be dry cleaned if she was expected to stay the week. Patricia had coolly informed her no laundry service would be pressing that white coat. This Texan beach town had been hit by a hurricane less than two days ago. It was difficult enough to have essential laundry, like scrubs and bed linens, cleaned in these conditions. Locating an operational dry-cleaning establishment would not become an item on Patricia's to-do list.

Dr. Hodge crossed the broiling black top of the parking lot where Texas Rescue had set up the mobile hospital. Whatever she wanted from Patricia, it was bound to be as inane as the dry cleaning. Patricia wasn't going to hustle over to hear it, but neither would she pretend she hadn't heard Hodge call her name. The rookie was her responsibility.

Patricia stayed standing, comfortable enough despite the late afternoon heat. Knowing she'd spend long days standing on hard blacktop, Patricia always wore her rubber-soled Docksides when Texas Rescue went on a mission. Between those and the navy polo shirt she wore that bore the Texas Rescue logo, she could have boarded a yacht as easily as run a field hospital, but no one ever mistook her for a lady of leisure. Not while she was with Texas Rescue.

As she waited in the June heat, Patricia checked her clipboard—her old-school, paper-powered clipboard. It was the only kind guaranteed to work when electric lines were down. If Texas Rescue was on the scene, it was a sure bet that electricity had been cut off by a hurricane or tornado, a fire or flood. Her clipboard had a waterproof, hard plastic cover that repelled the rain.

She flipped the cover open. First item: *X-ray needs admin clerk for night shift.*

There were only two shifts in this mobile hospital, days and nights. Patricia tended to work most of both, but she made sure her staff got the rest their volunteer contracts specified. She jotted her solution next to the problem: *assign Kim Wells.* Patricia had kept her personal assistant longer during this deployment than usual, but as always, Patricia would now work alone so that some other department wouldn't be shorthanded.

Second item: *Additional ECG machine in tent E4.*

That was for Quinn, the cardiologist she wouldn't be marrying. She'd make a call and have one brought down from Austin with the next incoming physician. She could have managed Quinn's personal life just as efficiently, making her an excellent choice for his wife, but that concept wouldn't appeal to the man now that he was in love.

If there was anything Patricia had learned as the daughter of the infamous Daddy Cargill, it was that men needed managing. Since Patricia genuinely liked Quinn, she hoped the woman he married would be a good manager, but she doubted it. Fortunately for Quinn, he didn't need much direction. Cool-headed and logical—at least around Patricia—he would have been a piece of cake for her to manage after living with Daddy Cargill.

Third: *Set up additional shade for waiting area.*

The head of Austin's Texas Rescue operations, Karen Weaver, was supposed to be responsible for the physical layout of the hospital as well as equipment like the ECG machine, but Karen wasn't the most efficient or knowledgeable director to have ever served at the helm of Texas Rescue. Waiting for Karen to figure out how to get things done was hard on the medical staff and the patients. Patricia would find someone to get another tent off the truck and pitch it outside the treatment tents.

"Patricia." Mary Hodge, sweating and frowning, stopped a few feet away and put her hands on her hips.

"Dr. Hodge." Patricia kept her eyes on her to-do list as she returned the curt greeting. The woman had earned her title; Patricia would use it no matter how little she thought of the doctor's lousy work ethic.

"Listen, I can't stay until Friday, after all. Something's come up."

"Is that right?" Patricia very deliberately tucked the

clipboard under her arm, then lifted her chin and gave Dr. Hodge her full attention. "Explain."

Dr. Hodge frowned immediately. Doctors, as a species, gave orders. They didn't take commands well. Patricia knew when to be gracious, and she knew how to persuade someone powerful that her idea was their idea. But Patricia was also a Cargill, a descendant of pioneers who'd made millions on deals sealed with handshakes, and that meant she didn't give a damn about tact when a person was about to welch on a deal. Dr. Hodge was trying to do just that.

The doctor raised her chin, as well, clearly unused to having her authority challenged. "I have a prior commitment." Unspoken, her tone said, *And that's all you need to know.*

Patricia kept her voice cool and her countenance cooler. "Your contract specifies ninety-six hours of service. I haven't got any extra physicians to take your place if you leave."

"I'm needed back at West Central."

Patricia had recruited as many physicians as she could from West Central Texas Hospital. The hospital had been founded by Quinn MacDowell's father, and his brother Braden served as CEO. She knew the hospital well. It had just been one more item on the list of reasons why Quinn had been her best candidate for marriage.

Her familiarity with West Central gave her an advantage right now. "West Central is perfectly aware that you are here until Friday. If you went back this evening, people might wonder why you returned ahead of schedule."

The woman started to object. Patricia held up a hand in a calming gesture. It was time to pretend to be tactful, at least. "You have a prior commitment, of course, but some people could jump to the conclusion that you just didn't like the inconvenience of working at a natural disaster site.

Wouldn't that be a terrible reputation to have in a hospital where so many doctors somehow find the time to volunteer with Texas Rescue? I do hope you'll be able to reschedule your commitment, just to avoid any damage to your professional reputation."

The threat was delivered in Patricia's most gracious tone of voice. Dr. Hodge bit out something about rescheduling her other commitment at great inconvenience to herself. "But I'm out of here Friday morning."

"After ten, yes." Patricia set Dr. Hodge's departure time as she unflinchingly met the woman's glare.

Dr. Hodge stalked away, back toward the high-tech, inflatable white surgical tent where she was supposed to be stitching the deep cuts and patching up the kinds of wounds that were common when locals started digging through rubble for their belongings. Patricia didn't care if Hodge was angry; that was Hodge's personal problem, not Patricia's.

No, her personal problem had nothing to do with this field hospital, and everything to do with her plans for the future. Every moment that Texas Rescue didn't demand her attention, she found her mind circling futilely around the central problem of her life: *How am I going to save the Cargill fortune from my own father?*

The radio in her hand squawked for her attention. Thankfully. Patricia raised it to her mouth and pressed the side button. "Go ahead."

"This is Mike in pharmacy. We're going through the sublingual nitro fast."

Of course they were. After any natural disaster, the number of chest pain cases reported in the population increased. It was one of the reasons she'd recruited Quinn to Texas Rescue; she'd needed a cardiologist to sort the everyday angina from the heart attacks. The initial treatment for both conditions was a nitroglycerin tablet. The pharmacists she'd recruited always kept their nitro well stocked, but a new pharmacy tech had freely dispensed a month's worth to each patient instead of a week's worth, and the hospital had nearly run out before anyone had noticed.

Patricia had recruited that pharmacy tech, too. She accepted that the shortage was therefore partly her fault. Even if it hadn't been, Patricia would've been the one to fix it.

She pressed the talk button on her radio again. "You'll need to make what you've got last for several more hours. I'm going to have to reach quite a bit farther out of town to source more."

She'd find more, though. *Failure is not an option* was the kind of cheesy line Patricia would never be caught saying, but it fit the mission of Texas Rescue.

Patricia started through the white tents toward the one that housed her administrative office. The Texas Rescue field hospital had been set up in the parking lot of the multi-story community hospital. The missing roof of the town's hospital had rendered it useless, and the building now stood empty. Its shadow was welcome, though, to offset the Gulf Coast's June heat. She noticed the Texas Rescue firefighters had moved their red truck into the shade, too, as they used their axes to clear debris from the town's toppled ambulances. The fire truck's powerful motor turned a winch, metal cables strained, and an ambulance was hauled back into its upright position.

There was a beauty to the simple solution. The ambulance had been on its side; the ambulance was now upright. If only her world could work that way…but Daddy Cargill had tangled the family fortune badly, and Patricia needed more than a simple winch to set her life back on track.

The shade of the damaged building couldn't be doing much to help the firefighters as they worked in their protective gear. Patricia barely tolerated the steamy heat by wearing knee-length linen shorts and by keeping her hair smoothed into a neat bun, off her neck and out of her face. There hadn't been a cloud in the sky all day, however, and the heat was winning. Thank goodness the administration's tent had a generator-run air cooler.

Unlike the surgical tents, her "office" was the more traditional type of structure, a large square tent of white fabric pitched so the parking lot served as the hard but mud-free floor. Before pushing through the weighted fabric flap that served as her tent's door, Patricia caught sight of Quinn at the far side of the parking lot. Tall, dark and familiar, her friend stood by a green Volkswagon Bug, very close to the redheaded woman who'd stolen his heart—an apparently romantic heart Patricia hadn't suspected Quinn possessed.

Her name was Diana. Patricia knew Diana's forty-eight hour volunteer commitment was over, and her career in Austin required her return. Quinn was committed to staying the week without her.

Patricia watched them say goodbye. Quinn cupped Diana's face in his hands, murmured words only she would ever hear and then he kissed her.

Like the worst voyeur, Patricia couldn't turn away. It wasn't the sensuality of the kiss that held her gaze, although Quinn was a handsome man, and the way he pulled Diana into him as he kissed her was undeniably physical. No, there was more than just sex in that kiss. There was an intensity in the kiss, a link between the man and woman, a connection Patricia could practically see even as Diana got behind the wheel of her tiny car and drove away.

The intensity in Quinn's gaze as he watched Diana leave made Patricia want to shiver in the June heat.

It was too much. She didn't want that. Ever.

Nitroglycerin.

With renewed focus, she pushed aside the fabric flap and entered her temporary office, grateful for the cooler air inside. The generator that powered their computers also ran the air cooler and a spare fan. The tent was spacious, housing neat rows of simple folding chairs and collapsible tables. It was the nerve center for the paperwork that made a hospital run, from patients' documents to volunteer's contracts.

Her administrative team, all wearing Texas Rescue shirts, kept working as Patricia headed for the card table that served as her desk. Only a few nodded at her. The rest seemed almost unnaturally busy.

She didn't take their lack of acknowledgment personally. She was the boss. They were trying to look too busy for her to question their workload.

She was grateful, actually, to slip into the metal folding chair without making any small talk. She placed her clipboard and radio to the right of her waiting laptop, opened its lid, and waited for the computer to boot up—none of which took her mind off that kiss between Quinn and Diana.

The kind of desire she'd just witnessed had been different than the kind she was generally exposed to. Her father was on his third wife and his millionth mistress. He was all about the pet names, the slap-and-tickle, the almost juvenile quest for sex. Quinn had been looking at the woman he loved in a totally different way. Like she was important—no, crucial. Like she was his world.

That kind of desire would be demanding. Unpleasantly so. Burdensome, to have a man need her so completely. It would only get in the way of what Patricia wanted in life.

She didn't want the perpetual adolescence of a man like her father, but neither did she want the intensity of a soul mate. No, she just wanted a husband who would be an asset, who would efficiently partner her as she achieved her goals in life. A man who would slide as seamlessly into her world as one of her beloved sailboats glided through water, barely disturbing the surface.

"Coming through!"

A fireman crashed through the tent's door, dragging another firefighter behind him. He pulled off his friend's helmet and tossed it on the ground as he yelled "Water!"

No one moved. Lined up in their matching polo shirts, Patricia's entire workforce froze with their fingers over their keyboards.

The next second, Patricia was on her feet, coming around her table toward the men. Clearly, the second guy was overheated and on the verge of passing out.

"There's cool air here," she said, stepping out of the way as she pointed toward the side of the tent where the blower was located.

The first man, a giant in his helmet and bulky uniform, hauled his stumbling buddy past her. He dropped to one knee as he lowered the man to the asphalt in front of the cooler, then took his own helmet off and set it lightly on the ground. He let his head drop as he took one long, deep breath. His black hair was soaked through and his own skin was flushed from heat, but then his one-second break was apparently over, and he was back in motion.

To Patricia, the two men were a heap of reflective tape, canvas straps, rubber boots, and flashlights tucked into more straps and pockets on their bulky, beige uniforms. It took her a moment to make out what the first man was doing. He'd zeroed in on the toggles that held his friend's coat shut.

His friend fumbled at his own chest with clunky, gloved hands. "S'my coat." His words were slurred. "I get it."

"Yeah, sure." The black-haired fireman pushed his buddy's hands out of the way and kept unfastening.

Patricia knelt beside him, ignoring the rough asphalt on her bare knees, and tugged off the overheated man's gloves. "Do you want me to radio the ER? We've got a back board in here that we could use as a stretcher." She turned to speak over her shoulder to the nearest person. "Bring me my walkie-talkie."

"He'll be fine once he's cooled off." The black-haired man tugged the heavy coat all the way off his friend, then let the man lie flat on his back in front of the cooler. "You're feeling better already, Zach, right? Zach?"

He slapped the man's cheek lightly with the back of his gloved hand. By now, Patricia's team had gathered around. She took her walkie-talkie from her staff member, and the black-haired firefighter took one of the bottles of water that were being held out. He dumped it over Zach's hair. The water puddled onto the asphalt beneath him.

Zach pushed his arm away, still clumsy in his movements. "Stop it, jackass." His words were less slurred, a good sign, even if he spoke less like an admin clerk and more like a…well, like a fireman.

The black-haired man turned to Patricia. Their eyes met, and after a second's pause, he winked. "Told you. He's feeling better already."

Patricia kept looking at his impossibly handsome, cheerfully confident face and forgot whatever it was she'd been about to say. He had blue eyes—not just any blue, but the exact shade that reminded her of sailing on blue water, under blue sky.

He shook off his own gloves in one sharp movement, then shrugged out of his own coat. As he bent to stuff his coat under his friend's head, Patricia bent, too, but there was nothing for her to do as he efficiently lifted his friend's head with one hand and shoved his coat in place. She straightened up, sitting back on her heels and brushing the grit off her knees, but she stayed next to him, ready to help, watching as he worked.

As the muscles in his shoulders moved, his red suspenders crisscrossed over the black T-shirt he wore. A brief glance down the man's back showed that those suspenders were necessary; his torso was lean and trim, while the canvas firefighter pants were loose and baggy. The stereotypical red straps weren't just designed to make women swoon....

She looked away quickly when he finished his makeshift pillow and straightened, too.

Propping his left forearm on his bended knee, he extended his right toward her in a handshake.

"Thank you for your help, ma'am." His voice was as deep as he was large. Deep, with a Texas twang. "My name's Luke Waterson. Pleased to meet you."

He had cowboy manners even when he was under stress, introducing himself like this. She had to hand that to him as she placed her hand in his. His skin was warm and dry as she returned his handshake in a businesslike manner. He was still a giant of a man without his fireman's coat, broad-chested with shoulder and arm muscles that were clearly defined under his T-shirt, but he returned her shake without a trace of the bone-crushing grip many men used.

Patricia knew some men just weren't aware how strong their grip was, but others—including her father's cronies— used the too-hard handshake as a form of intimidation. If this fireman had wanted to play that game, Patricia would have been ready.

But he didn't hold her hand too long or too tightly. He let her go, but that grin deepened, lifting one corner of his mouth higher than the other as he kept those sailing-blue eyes on her.

Patricia looked away first. Not very Cargill of her, but then again, men didn't often look at her the way this young fireman did. A bone-crushing handshake? No problem. She could handle that. But to be winked at and grinned at like she was…was…a college coed…

As if.

She'd never been that flirtatious and carefree, not even when she'd *been* a college co-ed. In college, she'd come home on weekends to make sure her father's latest bed partner wasn't robbing them blind. She'd gone over every expense and co-signed every one of her father's checks before they were cashed.

Lord, college had been a decade ago. What was it about this fireman—this Luke Waterson—that made her think of being twenty-two instead of thirty-two?

He used his heavy helmet to fan Zach's face, a move that made his well-defined bicep flex. Frankly, the man looked like a male stripper in a fireman's costume. Maybe that explained her sudden coed feeling. When she'd been twenty-two, she'd been to enough bachelorette parties to last her a lifetime. If she'd seen one male review with imitation firemen dancing for money, then she'd seen them all.

Those brides had been divorced and planning their second weddings as everyone in her social circle approached their thirtieth birthdays together. Patricia had declined the second round of bachelorette weekends. Always the bridesmaid, happy to have escaped being the bride.

Until this year.

The real fireman used his forearm to swipe his forehead, the bulge of his bicep exactly at her eye level. Oh, this Luke was eye candy for women, all right. Muscular, physical—

There's no reason to be so distracted. This is absurd.

She was head of personnel, and this man was wiping his brow because he was nearly as overheated as the unfortunate Zach-on-the-asphalt. If Patricia didn't take care of Luke, she'd soon be short two firemen on her personnel roster.

She plucked one of the water bottles out of her nearest staff member's hand. The young lady didn't move, her gaze fastened upon Luke.

Annoyed with her staff for being as distracted as she'd let herself be, Patricia stood and looked around the circle of people. "Thank you. You can go back to work now."

Her team scattered. Patricia felt more herself. It was good to be in charge. Good to have a job to do.

She handed Luke the bottle. "Drink this."

He obeyed her, but that grin never quite left his face as he knelt on one knee before her, keeping his gaze on her face as he tilted his head back and let the cool water flow down his throat.

Look away, Patricia. Use your radio. Contact the fire chief and let him know where his men are. Look away.

But she didn't. She watched the man drink his water, watched him pitch it effortlessly, accurately, into the nearest trash can, and watched him resume his casual position, one forearm on his knee. He reached down to press his fingers against his friend's wrist once more.

"He's fine," Luke announced after a few seconds of counting heartbeats. "It's easy to get light-headed out there. Nothing some shade and some water couldn't fix."

"Is there anything else I can get you?"

He touched the brim of an imaginary hat in a two-fingered salute. "Thank you for the water, ma'am. You never told me your name."

"Patricia," she said. She had to clear her throat delicately, for the briefest moment, and then, instead of describing herself the way she always did, as Patricia *Cargill,* she said something different. "I'm the personnel director."

"Well, Patricia," he said, and then he smiled, a flash of white teeth and an expression of genuine pleasure in his tanned face. His grin had only been a tease compared to this stunning smile. "It's a pleasure to meet you."

He meant it, she could tell. He'd checked her out, he found her attractive, and that smile was inviting her in, inviting her to smile, too, inviting her to enjoy a little getting-to-know you flirtation.

Patricia couldn't smile back. She wasn't like that. Flirting for fun was a luxury for people who didn't have obligations. She'd never learned how to do it. She'd known only responsibility, even when she'd been twenty-two and men had been interested in her for more than her bank account and Cargill connections.

It almost hurt to look at Luke Waterson's open smile, at the clear expression of approval and interest on his handsome face.

She preferred not to waste energy on useless emotions. And so, she nodded politely and she turned away.

Chapter Two

So, the princess doesn't want to play.

He'd given her the smile, the one that had kept the woman of his choice by his side for as long as he could remember, whether at a bonfire after a high school football game or at a bar after a livestock show in Austin. Patricia-the-personnel-director, apparently, was immune.

That was a real shame. He couldn't remember the last time he'd been around a woman who was so…smooth. Smooth hair, smooth skin, a woman who handled everything and everyone smoothly. She spoke in a smooth, neutral voice, yet everyone ran to do her bidding as if she were a drill sergeant barking out threats. This Patricia was the real deal, a Texas beauty who looked like a princess but had a spine of steel.

It was a shame she wasn't interested. He watched her walk away, headed for the chair she'd been in when he'd first hauled Zach in here. He liked the way she moved, brisk and businesslike.

Businesslike. He should have thought of that. She was clearly the boss in here. The boss couldn't flirt in front of her staff. If they weren't in her office space, would he be able to get her to smile?

Luke switched his helmet to his other hand and kept fanning Zach. Maybe it wasn't that she wasn't interested. She'd been a little flustered when they'd shaken hands, not knowing quite where to look. Maybe she wasn't interested in *being* interested. That was a whole different ballgame.

She wore diamonds in her ears, discreet little studs, but none on her fingers. If she wasn't married or engaged, why not give him a smile?

When he reached for Zach's wrist to check his pulse, Zach shook him off. "I'll live," he said, managing to sound tired and pissed off at the same time.

Patricia picked up a clipboard and turned their way.

Luke ducked a bit closer to Zach and spoke under his breath. "Be a pal and lay still a while longer."

Patricia returned to his side of the tent. She didn't crack a smile, but she crouched beside him once more. Her arm brushed his, and she jerked a tiny bit, as if she'd touched something she shouldn't. It was the smallest of breaks in an otherwise excellent poker face, but Luke was certain: she wasn't totally immune to him.

He sure as hell wasn't immune to her.

"You can stop fanning him," she said. "Rest. I'll take over. You need to cool down, too."

Aw, yeah. Talk to me some more. Her voice fit her looks, sophisticated, assured. She had the faintest accent, enough to identify her as a Texan, but she was no cowgirl. She had the voice of a woman raised with Big Money, the kind of woman who'd gone to college and majored in art history, he'd bet.

She started fanning Zach with her clipboard, so Luke

put his helmet down and studied her profile until she glanced at him. She had eyes as dark brown as her hair was pale blond. She didn't drop her gaze this time. Luke was torn between admiring her self-control and wishing she'd act flustered once more.

She kept fanning Zach with her clipboard in one hand. With her other hand, she handed Luke another bottle of water. "Here, drink this. You're as hot as he is."

He nearly laughed at that. Maybe she wouldn't flirt back with him in front of her staff, but he couldn't resist such an easy opening. "Well, ma'am, I'd say thank you for the compliment, but only being as hot as Zach isn't truly that flattering. He's just your average-looking slacker, laying down on the job."

Zach grunted, but didn't bother opening his eyes. Zach had always been a good wing man.

Luke gestured toward him with the bottle of water. "That eloquent grunt means Zach agrees."

Patricia looked away again, but not in a flustered way. Nope, now she just raised one brow in faint disgust and turned away, the princess not lowering herself to comment on the peasants' looks.

Luke chuckled, enjoying this brush with a Texas beauty queen, even if it led nowhere. It was something else to be in the presence of royalty.

She pointed toward the unopened bottle in his hand, but before she could repeat her order, he raised his hand in surrender.

"I'm drinking. I'm drinking." He had to stop chuckling in order to down the second bottle of water.

Princess Patricia stood abruptly, but she only stepped a foot away to grab a metal folding chair and then place it next to him. "Here, you'll be more comfortable."

Not quite royalty, then. Or at least, she was hard-working and considerate royalty.

"Thank you, ma'am." Before rising, he clapped Zach on the shoulder. "How 'bout you sit up and drink some water now?"

"I'll get another chair," Patricia said.

Then it happened. She turned away for a chair. He turned away to extend his hand to Zach. He hauled his friend to his feet; she set a folding chair next to the first. They finished at the same second, turning back toward each other, and collided. He steadied her with two hands. Her elegant fingers grasped the edge of his red suspender for balance. The rubber edge of her boat shoe caught on the rubber of his fireman's boot, tripping her, and she clung a little tighter. She was tall, but he was taller, and into the side of his neck she exhaled a single, awkward, warm and breathy "oh."

In that moment, as he stood solidly on his own two feet and held Patricia in his hands, Luke knew that a slender, soft woman had just knocked all two hundred pounds of him flat on his back.

She looked away, then down on the ground, flustered again. The diamond stud in her delicate ear lobe grazed his chin. She let go of his suspender and pushed back a half step, turning to collect her clipboard off the chair she'd placed for him. "Stay as long as you need to," she said without making eye contact. "I'll let the fire chief know where you are."

She left, pushing the tent flap out of her way as impatiently as Luke had when he'd been coming in.

Luke sat heavily where her clipboard had been, frowning as Zach guzzled his water next to him. Patricia had felt every bit of electricity he had, he'd bet the ranch on it. He'd never had a woman who was so attracted to him be so eager to get away from him. There had to be a reason, but damn if he could guess what it might be.

Zach finished his water and started a second bottle. Halfway through, he stopped for a breath. He jerked his head toward the door flap. "Give it up now, rookie. You aren't getting a piece of that action. Ever."

"Not here," Luke silenced him tersely. There were too many people listening to the firemen who'd landed themselves in the middle of a bunch of paper pushers. Luke sat back against the cold metal of the chair and crossed his arms over his chest.

So, Patricia didn't want to flirt. He could understand that on one level, but he felt instinctively that it went beyond being on duty or in charge. She'd hightailed it out of there, if such an elegant woman could be said to move so hastily, yet they'd just experienced chemistry with a capital *C*. Chemistry that couldn't be denied. Chemistry that Luke wanted to explore.

"You ready?" he asked Zach. Without waiting for Zach's grunt of agreement, Luke stood, then started picking up coats, gloves, and his helmet. As the men headed toward the exit, they passed Patricia's table. Luke dropped one glove, kicking it mid-stride to land precisely under a chair. Her chair.

Zach noticed. "You gonna get that now or later?"

"Neither," Luke said under his breath. When they reached the door, he bent to scoop up Zach's helmet. They stepped outside, into the blinding Texas sun.

Luke handed Zach his coat and helmet. "I'm gonna let her bring that glove to me when she's ready."

"You never leave your equipment behind, rookie."

"True enough." Luke wasn't going to argue that point. He was a rookie for the fire department, but he was a twenty-eight-year-old man who'd been running a cattle ranch for seven years. No cowboy worked without gloves, so he'd known to bring more than one pair. He could leave that one for Patricia to find. To find, and to decide what to do with.

Zach smacked dirt and grit off the polished black surface of his helmet. "For future reference, rookie, throwing a helmet on asphalt scratches it all to hell."

"Battle scars, Zach. We've all got 'em."

Luke didn't mind his engine's tradition of calling the newest member "rookie" for the first few months of service, but Zach was laying it on a bit thick, considering they'd gone to school together. They'd played football, suffered through reading Melville and handfed goats in 4-H together.

Zach shook his head. "You may have a way with the fillies on your ranch, but that woman isn't a skittish horse. She runs this whole place, whether it's official or not. I worked with her last summer after those twisters in Oklahoma. If you think she just needs patience and a soft touch and then she'll follow you around like a pet, you're wrong."

"We'll see." Both men started walking toward their fire engine, taking wide strides out of necessity in their bulky turnout pants and rubber boots.

"You're too cocky, Waterson. Go ahead and ignore my advice. It'll be good for you when she shuts you down before you even make it to first base."

"First base? A kiss? High school was a long time ago, Zach."

"You won't get that much, I promise you. You aren't her type."

Luke remembered that moment of impact. Chemistry with a capital *C*, all right. He smiled.

Zach shook his head. "I know that smile. Tell you what.

You manage to kiss that woman, and I won't make you re-paint my helmet."

Luke's smile dimmed. On the surface, Zach's casual dare seemed harmless enough. They'd been through plenty of dares before. *You buy the beer if I can sweet talk that waitress onto the dance floor while she's still on the clock.* But this was different. Somehow.

"You're forgetting two things," Luke said. "One, my mama raised me better than to kiss a girl for a dare. Two, my daddy raised me that if I broke it, I had to fix it. I'll paint your damned helmet when we get back to Austin."

"Two more things," Zach said, laying a heavy hand on Luke's shoulder. "One, thanks for getting me out of the sun when I was too dazed to do it myself. Forget about the helmet. I owe you more than that."

"Don't worry about it."

Zach let go of his shoulder after a hard squeeze. "And two, that was my glove you left behind, Romeo. If your filly shies away from you, you're gonna have to go back and get it. Today."

Chapter Three

Darkness came, and Luke was glad that a strong breeze from the ocean came with it. Cutting vehicles loose from downed trees had been grueling in the motionless air the storm had left behind. When the order came to stand down, Luke was glad for that, too. He considered himself to be in good shape, working on the ranch day in and day out, but wielding an ax for hour after hour had been back-breaking, plain and simple.

The one thing he would have been most glad of, however, never came. Patricia never appeared, not in a flustered way, not in a collected way, not in any way. Whatever the beautiful personnel director was up to, she wasn't up to it in his part of the relief center. But since impatient Zach wanted his damned glove back, Luke was going to have to go and get it.

Determined to make the best of it, Luke had hit the portable showers when the fire crew had their allotted time. He'd dug a clean T-shirt out of his gym bag and run a comb through his hair while it was still damp. Shaving was conveniently required of the firemen, since beards could interfere with the way a respirator mask sealed to the face. He'd been able to shave without drawing any attention to himself.

All he had to do was tell the guys to head off for chow without him, and then he could take a convenient detour that would lead him past Patricia's tent on his way to supper in the mess tent. He'd listen for her voice, and if she was in, he'd go in to retrieve his glove. Damn, but he was looking forward to seeing her again.

He was so intent on reaching her tent that he nearly missed her voice when he heard it in a place he hadn't expected. He stopped short outside the door marked "pharmacy," a proper door with a lock, set into a wooden frame that was sealed to an inflatable tent, similar to the kind he knew were used for surgeries and such.

"The rules exist for a reason." Smooth but unyielding, that was Patricia's voice.

"I thought we were here to help these people," another female voice answered, but this voice sounded more shrill and impatient. "These people have lost their houses. They've lost everything. If I can give them some free medicine, why shouldn't I? When I went to Haiti, we gave everyone months' worth of the drugs they needed."

There was a beat of silence, then Patricia's tone changed subtly to one of almost motherly concern. "It might help if you keep in mind that this isn't Haiti. Half of the homes in this town were vacant vacation homes, second homes for people who can well afford their own medicine. You don't need to give them a month's worth, just a few days until the town's regular pharmacies re-open."

"Then I don't see what the big deal is." The other

woman, in response to Patricia's gentle concern, sounded like a pouting teenager. "Nitroglycerin is cheap, anyway."

"It's not the cost, it's the scarcity. I had to send someone almost all the way to Victoria to get more. He was gone for nearly four hours. He used gallons of gasoline that can't be replaced because the pumps aren't running yet because the electricity isn't running yet."

Luke nearly grinned when he heard that steel slip back into Patricia's voice. He crossed his arms over his chest and tilted his head back to look up at the stars. She was right about the electricity being out, of course. When an entire town's streetlights were doused, the stars became brilliant. When all traffic stopped, the crash of the ocean surf could be heard blocks away.

It should be easy to set the right mood to explore a little physical chemistry, and he realized now he'd been hoping to find Patricia—and Zach's glove—alone. It would have been better if he could have waited until she'd had the time and the desire, or at least the curiosity, to come and find him. But since he needed to get that glove, he'd half hoped she'd be happy to see him walk back into her tent tonight. He'd forgotten something important: Patricia was still working. Still working and still the boss.

He should get to the mess tent. He could stop by the admin tent an hour from now, or three, and he knew she'd be there, working. There was no need to wait for her right now.

Yet he lingered, and listened, and admired the way she stayed cool, alternating between logical and sympathetic until the other woman was apologizing for the trouble she hadn't realized she'd caused, and Patricia was granting her a second—or what sounded more like a third—opportunity to prove she could be part of the Texas Rescue team.

The door opened and Patricia stepped out. As she turned

back to listen to the other person, the generator-powered lights inside the tent illuminated Patricia's flawless face, her cheekbones and elegant neck exposed with her pale hair still twisted up in that smooth style.

"The regular pharmacies will re-open, don't forget. This isn't Haiti. The buildings are damaged, but they didn't disappear into a pile of rubble. If they had, I promise you, we'd be working under a different policy entirely."

Luke hadn't thought of Patricia as a high-strung filly, and damn Zach for putting the thought into his head, but now he could imagine a similarity. Patricia was no ranch workhorse, though. Once, after a livestock show in Dallas, Luke had been invited by a trainer to spend time in the Grand Prairie racetrack stables. He'd found the Thoroughbreds to be suspicious and nervous around strangers, requiring a lot of careful handling. But once they were brought out to the track, once that starting gate sprang open and they raced down their lanes, doing what they were born to do, those Thoroughbreds had been a sight to behold. Unforgettable.

He'd just listened to Patricia doing what she was born to do. She kept people at their jobs, working hard in hard conditions, serving a community. Whether it required her to revive a pair of unexpected firemen or turn around a pharmacy tech's attitude, that's what Patricia did to make her hospital run, and she did it well.

The unseen pharmacy girl was still apologizing. In the glow of the lights, Luke watched Patricia smile benevolently. "There's no need to apologize further. I'm sure you'll have no problems at all complying with the policy tomorrow, and I look forward to having you here on the team for the rest of the week. Good night."

Patricia shut the door with a firm click. With his eyes already adjusted to the dark, Luke watched her polite, pleasant expression fade away, replaced by a frown and a shake of her head. She was angry. Perhaps disgusted with a worker who'd taken so much of her time. Without a glance at the brilliant stars, she headed down the row of tents toward her office space.

After a moment, Luke followed. He told himself he wasn't spying on her. He had to pass her tent to get to the mess tent, anyway. But when she stopped, he stopped.

She didn't go into her tent. She clutched her clipboard to her chest with one arm, looking for a moment like an insecure schoolgirl. Then she headed away from the tent complex, into the dark.

Luke followed, keeping his distance. When she stopped at a picnic table near a cluster of palm trees in the rear of the town hospital building, he hesitated. She obviously wanted to be alone. She sat on the bench, crossed her arms on the table, then rested her head on them.

The woman was not angry or disgusted. She was tired. Luke felt foolish for not realizing it sooner.

While she apparently caught a cat nap, he stood silently a short distance away. He didn't want to wake her. He'd look like an idiot for having followed her away from the tents. On the other hand, he couldn't leave her here, asleep and unprotected. Except for the starlight, it was pitch black. There'd been no looting in the storm-damaged town, but there were packs of displaced dogs forming among the wrecked homes, and—

Hell. He didn't need wandering pets for an excuse. He wasn't going to leave Patricia out here alone. Period.

He cleared his throat as he walked up behind her, not wanting to startle her, but she was dead to the world. He sat down beside her. She was sitting properly, knees together, facing the table like she'd fallen asleep saying grace over her dinner plate. He sat facing the opposite way, leaning back against the table and stretching his legs out. The wooden bench gave a little under his weight, disturbing her.

"Good evening, Miss Patricia."

That startled her awake the rest of the way. Her head snapped up, and she blinked and glanced around, looking adorably disoriented for a woman who carried a clipboard everywhere she went. When she recognized him, her eyes opened wide.

"Oh."

"It's me. Luke Waterson. The firefighter who barged in on you today."

"Yes, I remember you." She looked at the watch on her wrist and frowned.

Luke figured she couldn't read it in the faint light. "You've only been out a minute or two."

She hit a button on her watch and it lit up. Of course. He should have known she'd be prepared. She touched her hair, using her fingertips to smooth one wayward strand back into place. She touched the corner of each eye with her pinky finger, then put both hands in her lap and took a deep breath. "Okay, I'm awake. Did you need something?"

This was what her life was like, he realized. Everyone came to her when they needed something. She didn't expect Luke to be there for any other reason. Did no one seek her out just to talk during a work shift? To play a game of cards in the shade when they were off duty? To share a meal?

He didn't feel like smiling at the moment, but he did, anyway. She'd asked if he needed anything. "Nope. Nothing."

She tilted her head and looked at him, those eyes that had opened so wide now narrowing skeptically. "Then what are you doing here?"

I can't stop thinking about you. I want to feel you fall against me again.

His mother had always told him when in doubt, tell the truth, but he wasn't going to tell Patricia that particular truth. He settled for a more boring—but true—explanation. "I left a work glove in your tent. I was coming to get it when I saw you walking off into the dark. I was worried about you, so I followed."

"You were worried about me?" She gave a surprised bit of a chuckle, as if the idea were so outlandish it struck her funny. She got up from the table, then picked up her walkie-talkie and her clipboard, and held them to her chest.

Luke stood, too. As if he were handling a nervous Thoroughbred, he moved slowly. He stood a little too close, but unlike this afternoon, she didn't back away.

He hadn't imagined that chemistry. It was still there, in spades. Looking into her face by the light of the stars, he wanted to hold her again, deliberately this time. To kiss her lips, to satisfy a curiosity to know how she tasted.

But he wouldn't. Standing this close, he could also see how tired she was, a woman who'd undoubtedly been handling one issue after another since the first storm warnings had put Texas Rescue on alert. A woman so tired, she'd fallen asleep while sitting at a wooden table.

"Let's go back to the hospital," he said, when he would rather have said a dozen different things.

He took the clipboard and the radio out of her hand, then offered her his arm. She slipped her hand into the crook of his elbow immediately, and he suspected she did it without thinking. Her debutante ways and his cowboy etiquette meshed with ease for a second. Then she seemed to realize what she'd done and started to drop her hand.

He pressed her hand to his side with his arm. "It's dark. This way you can catch me if I trip."

"This way you can drag me down with you, more likely." But she left her hand where it was as they walked in silence.

When he started to pass her office tent, she pulled him to a stop. "You need to get your glove."

He turned to face her, and now it was easy to see every detail of her face in the light that glowed through the white walls of the hospital's tents. She was so very beautiful, and so very tired.

"I thought that was what I needed when I first followed you out into the dark, but now I know I need something else much, much more."

He moved an inch closer to her, and he felt her catch her breath as she held her ground. "What is that?" she whispered.

"I need to get you into bed. Now."

Chapter Four

He wants to take me to bed?

What a stupid, stupid suggestion. They were in the middle of a mission, in the middle of a storm-damaged town, not to mention that Patricia felt gritty and hungry and so very damned tired. How could any man think of sex when all she could think of was—

Bed.

Oh.

"You're trying to be funny, aren't you?" she accused.

That lopsided grin on his face should have been infuriating instead of charming. She drew herself up a bit straighter. It *was* infuriating. It was.

Luke had the nerve to give her hand a squeeze before she pulled it away. "There, for a few seconds, the look on your face was priceless."

"I hope you enjoyed yourself. Now, if you'll excuse me—"

He didn't let go of her clipboard when she reached for it.

"Nope," he said. "You go where this clipboard goes, so you'll just have to follow me if you want it back." He took off walking.

She was so stunned, he was several yards away before she realized he really expected her to follow. He turned at the corner of her tent and disappeared—but not before he looked over his shoulder and waved her own damned walkie-talkie at her.

Shock gave way to anger. Anger gave her energy. She caught up to him within a few seconds, her angry strides matching his slower but longer ones as they headed down the aisle between tents.

She snatched her walkie-talkie out of his hand. "You're being childish."

"I am." He nodded, and kept walking.

"This isn't summer camp. People are relying on me. On all of us. They rely on you, too."

"And yet, I can still respond to a fire if I hear the signal while I'm enjoying this romantic walk with you. It's okay, Patricia."

She yanked her clipboard out of his hand and turned back toward the admin tent. He blocked her way just by standing in her path, being the ridiculous, giant mass of muscle that he was. She felt twenty-two again. Less. Make that nineteen, handing a slightly altered ID to a bouncer who was no fool.

"It's not okay," she said, and her jaw hurt from clenching her teeth so hard. "I cannot do my job if I can't get to my headquarters. Now move."

Instead, Luke gestured toward the tent they'd stopped next to. "This is the women's sleeping quarters. Recognize it? I didn't think so. You were first on scene, weren't you? You decided where the first tent spike should be driven into the ground, I'll bet. So, you've been here forty-eight hours, at least. You were supposed to have gotten sixteen hours of sleep, then, at a minimum. You've taken how many?"

Patricia spoke through clenched teeth. "You're being patronizing."

The last bit of a grin left his face, and he suddenly looked very serious. "I just watched you fall asleep sitting up on a piece of wood. Forty-eight hours is a long time to keep running. Take your break, Patricia."

Patronizing, and giving her orders. She didn't know him from Adam, but like every other man in her life, he seemed to think he knew best. She was so mad she could have spit. She wanted to shove him out of her way. She wanted to tell him to kiss off. But she was Patricia Cargill, and she knew from a lifetime of experience that if she wanted to get her way, she couldn't do that.

She'd learned her lessons at her father's knee, and she'd seen the truth over and over as stepmamas and aunties had come and gone. If a woman got spitting mad, Daddy Cargill would chuckle and hold up his hands and proclaim a soap opera was in progress. His cronies would declare that women were too emotional to be reliable business partners. The bankers would mutter among themselves about whose turn it was to deal with the harpy this time.

No one ever said those things about Patricia Cargill, because she never let them see her real feelings, even if, like her father's discarded women, those emotions were justified now and again.

Luke was standing over her like a self-appointed bodyguard. He'd decided she needed protecting. That was probably some kind of psychological complex firefighters were prone to. She could use that to her advantage.

She placed her hand oh-so-lightly on his muscular arm, so very feminine, so very grateful. "I've gotten more sleep than you think. That power nap was very refreshing. It's so very thoughtful of you to be concerned, and I'm sorry to have worried you, but I'm fine." She took a step in the direction of the admin tent.

"Where are you going?"

"Let's get your glove. It will only take a minute." She smiled at him, friendly and unoffended, neither of which she felt. She didn't give a damn about his stupid glove, but it gave her an easy way to get back to her office.

"Forget it. You're very charming, Patricia, but you're very tired."

For a fraction of a second, she felt fear. She'd failed in an area where she usually excelled. She'd failed to manage this man effectively.

Luke lectured on. "The rules exist for a reason. You've been working nonstop, and you're going to get sick or hurt."

The rules exist for a reason. She wasn't sure why, but that sounded so familiar.

"Who takes your place when it's your turn for downtime?" Luke tapped her clipboard. "I bet you've got a whole organizational chart on there. I'm curious who you answer to, because you seem to think the rules don't apply to you."

"Karen Weaver is the head of the Austin branch of Texas Rescue," Patricia said. She sounded stiff. That was an accomplishment, considering she felt furious.

"I bet you make sure every single hospital volunteer from the most prestigious surgeon to the lowliest rookie gets their breaks, but Karen Weaver doesn't make sure you get yours?" Luke used her own trick on her, running the tips of his fingers lightly down her arm, all solicitous concern.

"Karen is…new," Patricia said.

Luke laughed. The man laughed, damn him. "She's new

and she doesn't know half of what you do, does she? You don't trust her to take care of your baby."

Bingo. But Patricia wouldn't say that out loud, not for a million dollars.

Luke's hand closed on her arm, warm and firm. "Karen isn't you, but she's good enough to handle the hospital while everyone's sleeping." He turned her toward the sleeping quarters and pulled back the tent flap, then let her go. "Please, take your break."

She wanted to object. She made all the decisions. She was in charge. But even her anger at his high-handedness wasn't sustaining her against her exhaustion. He'd brought her to the very threshold of the sleeping quarters. To be only a few feet away from where her inflatable mattress lay, empty and waiting…it was enough to make the most adamant woman waffle.

Luke's voice, that big, deep voice, spoke very quietly, because he was very close to her ear. "I'm not your boss, and you aren't mine. You answer to Karen, and I answer to the fire chief. But this afternoon, you gave me orders, and I obeyed them because they were smart. You told me to drink; I did. You told me to sit; I did. So it's my turn. I'm telling you to get ready for bed. I'm going to bring you a sandwich from the mess tent and place it inside the door, because it's a sure thing that you haven't taken time to eat. You'll eat it and you'll get some rest when you turn off that walkie-talkie, because you know it's the smart thing to do. You've worked enough."

Patricia had never had a man speak to her like that. Telling her to stop working. Telling her she'd done enough. It made her melt the way poets believed flowers and verse should make women melt. It made her so weak in the knees, she couldn't take a step for fear of stumbling.

Weakness was bad.

"You can't give me orders," she said, but her voice was husky and tired.

"I just did." With a firm hand in her lower back, an inch above the curve of her backside, Luke Waterson pushed her gently into the tent, dropped the flap and walked away.

Patricia felt strange the next day.

It should have been easier to focus on the relief operation after a full meal and a good night's sleep. Instead, it was harder. That sleep and that meal had come at the hands—the very strong hands—of a fireman who looked like—

Damn it. There she went again, losing her train of thought.

She checked the to-do list on her clipboard. The items that had been done and crossed off were irrelevant. Being at the helm of Texas Rescue's mobile hospital was like being at the helm of one of her sailboats. Congratulating herself on having handled a gust of wind two minutes ago wouldn't prevent her boat from capsizing on the next gust. Whether on a lake or at a relief center, Patricia looked ahead, planned ahead, kept an eye on the horizon—or in this case, on her checklist. One unfinished item from yesterday jumped out: *Set up additional shade for waiting area.*

Patricia tapped her mechanical pencil against her lips. She had the additional tent in the trailer. She just didn't have the manpower to get it set up. According to the tent's manual, it would take three people twenty minutes. That meant it would require forty minutes, of course, but she didn't have three people, anyway. She could serve as one, although she wasn't good with the sledgehammer when it came to driving the spikes in the ground. At this site, the spikes had been driven right through the asphalt in many cases, and she knew her limits. Driving iron spikes through asphalt, even crumbling, sunbaked asphalt, wasn't her skill set.

An image of Luke Waterson, never far from her mind this morning, appeared once more. Appeared, and zoomed in on his arms. Those muscles. The way they'd flexed under her fingertips as he'd escorted her back to the tents in the dark...

Luke could drive a spike through asphalt.

Patricia went to her tent and fetched his glove.

Chapter Five

Being a rookie was everything Luke had expected it to be. He'd volunteered for Zach's fire department just for the chance to be the rookie. For the chance to shed some responsibility. For the chance to have a little adventure without having to do any decision-making. For a change, any damned change, from the endless routine on the James Hill Ranch.

He'd gotten that change on Sunday night. Their fire engine had driven through the still-powerful remains of the hurricane as it had moved inland toward Austin. They'd arrived at the coast only hours after the hurricane had passed through, and they'd had rescues to perform the moment they'd rolled into town.

The repetitive ladder drills they'd practiced for months had finally proven useful as they'd reached a family who'd been stranded on a roof by rising water. Then they'd laid that ladder flat to make a bridge to a man who was clinging to the remains of a boat on an inland waterway. In the predawn hours, Luke had waded through waist-deep brackish water with a kindergartner clinging to his neck.

That experience had been humbling. He'd been seeking adventure for its own sake, but that rescue made him rethink his purpose as a part-time volunteer fireman. He'd been blessed with health, and strength, and in that case, the sheer size to be able to stay on his feet and not be swept away by a rush of moving water. Being able to carry a child who could not have crossed that flood herself had made him grateful for things he normally didn't give a second thought.

But it was Wednesday now, the water had receded substantially, and they'd "rescued" only empty, toppled ambulances yesterday. Today, they'd cleaned their fire engine. And cleaned it. And cleaned it some more.

He shoved the long-handled broom into the fire engine's ladder compartment, a stainless steel box that ran the length of the entire fire engine, then swept out dried mud that had clung to the ladder the last time they'd slid it into its storage hold. *Yeah, big change from mucking stalls.* At least this dirt smelled better.

Luke had looked forward to following someone else's orders, but being a rookie gave him too much time to think. He wasn't required to use his brain at all, not even to decide what to clean next. This gave him way too much time to relive the mistakes he'd made with Patricia last night. He'd been childish, she'd said, refusing to return her clipboard. He'd shoved her into a tent, like giving an unwilling filly a push into her stall. He'd slid a sandwich and a bag of chips and a Gatorade bottle under the edge of the tent door like he was feeding a prisoner.

Yeah, he'd been a regular Casanova.

He pushed the broom into the ladder compartment

again, and hoisted himself halfway into the compartment after it, head and one shoulder wedged in the rectangular opening so he could reach farther.

Zach's whistle echoed in the metal box. Luke felt Zach's elbow in his waist. "Don't look now, but I think a certain filly is finally curious about the man who has been standing by the corral fence. You patient son of a bitch, she's coming over to give you a sniff, just like you predicted."

Luke backed out of the compartment, cracking his head on the steel edge in his haste.

Zach was leaning against the engine, one boot on the rear chrome platform that Luke would be sweeping next. Zach shook his head as Luke rubbed his.

"I just said 'don't look now' and what did you do? Jumped out of there like a kid to get a peek. You're losing it bad around this woman, Waterson. Don't look."

Luke looked, anyway. Patricia was walking straight toward them, no doubt about it. Her hair was piled a little higher on her head today and her polo shirt was white instead of navy, and God, did she look gorgeous in the sunlight, all that blue sky behind her blond hair.

Luke took a step toward her. "She's got my glove."

Zach put a hand in his chest. "I wasn't in a condition yesterday to fully appreciate the view. Now I am. That's my glove. I'll get it. You keep sweeping, rookie."

He took no more than two steps before Chief Rouhotas appeared from around the side of the engine. The chief was looking in Patricia's direction even as he stuck his hand out to block Zach. "I've got this, Lieutenant Bishop. Back to work."

Luke crossed his arms over his chest as he watched Chief Rouhotas walk up to Patricia and greet her with his head bobbing and bowing as if she really were the princess she looked like she was. Patricia nodded graciously.

They spoke for a minute, then she offered him her hand. He shook it as if it were an honor.

The important detail, however, was in Patricia's other hand. When the chief had greeted her, she'd casually moved her left hand behind her back, keeping the glove out of sight. She could have given it to Rouhotas, of course. She could have asked for it to be returned to Luke—which would have earned Luke another round of hazing, he was certain, for leaving a piece of equipment behind—but she kept it out of sight as she concluded whatever business deal she was making with the chief. No mistake about it, an agreement about something had been reached. Luke recognized a deal-sealing handshake when he saw it.

He didn't have to wait long to have that mystery solved. Patricia walked away—without a backwards glance for as long as Luke watched her—and the chief started bellowing orders.

"Waterson. Bishop. Murphy. Report to the hospital's storage trailer. Bring your sledgehammers. Looks like they need help setting up a tent to make an extra waiting room for the walk-ups."

Zach and Luke exchanged a look, but Murphy complained. Out loud. At nineteen, he still had moments of teenaged attitude. "Seriously, chief? It's already a hundred degrees."

"That's why they need the shade, genius."

Murphy opened the cab door and retrieved his own work gloves, muttering the whole time. "We're not even part of the hospital—"

"They're feeding us and giving us billets, so you don't have to sleep in this engine," Chief cut in.

Murphy ought to know the chief heard everything his men uttered. Luke had figured that out real quick.

"So quit your whining and moaning," Chief said, "or

I'll let Miss Cargill be your boss for the whole day instead of an hour. You'll find out what work is."

Miss Cargill, was it? Patricia Cargill. He liked the sound of it. They couldn't get to Patricia's job soon enough to suit Luke. He had no doubt that more back-breaking labor would be involved, but given the choice between sweeping mud here or getting an eyeful of Patricia, he'd take the hard-earned eyeful.

First, of course, they had to pack the engine's gear back in place. The engine had to be ready to roll at all times. Luke took one end of the heavy, twenty-eight-foot extension ladder as Zach gave the commands to hoist and return it to the partially swept compartment.

It was more grunt work, leaving Luke's mind free to wander, but there was only one place his mind wanted to go: Patricia. She'd kept the glove. She still wanted to talk to him later, then, maybe to chew him out for last night. That was all right with him. That gave him a second chance.

She was waiting by the trailer, no glove in sight, when he and his crew walked up in the non-flammable black T-shirts and slacks they always wore on duty, even under their bulky turnout coats and pants. They were big men, all of them, and they carried sledgehammers, so they were stared at openly as they hauled the several-hundred pound tent out of the trailer and carried it on their shoulders, following Patricia down the row of hospital tents.

When a nurse wolf-whistled at them, Luke grinned back. Whether working on the engine or on the ranch, a little female appreciation never hurt his spirits.

He wasn't getting any of that appreciation from Patricia, unfortunately. Or maybe he was, but her calm, neutral expression certainly gave none of it away.

They dropped the tent where she indicated, and Murphy

and Zach started freeing the straps. That was a two-person job, so Luke kept himself busy by taking their sledgehammers and setting them aside with his, right at the feet of the woman who was pretending he didn't exist.

"I've been officially informed that you are my boss today," Luke said, giving her the smile she was so good at ignoring, but which he liked to believe she wasn't entirely immune to. "What do you want to do with me? Tell me to go to hell, maybe?"

She didn't say anything, but held a cell phone up in the air and squinted at its sun-washed screen. "The cell towers are still down."

"I think it's only fair that we reverse positions after last night. I was a bit overbearing, so now it's your turn. You should order me to get in bed. I'll be very obedient."

She lowered the phone with a sigh and gave him a look that could only be described as long-suffering martyrdom. "I assume you are, once more, enjoying yourself ever so much."

He smiled bigger. "Around you? Always."

She shook her head, but he caught the quirk of her lips. He wasn't in the dog house, after all. Her next words confirmed it.

"Thank you for the sandwich last night." Before he could say anything, she smoothly changed the subject. "There's no cell phone service. The towers are usually fairly high priority after a disaster. Phones have really become essential to daily function—"

"You're welcome. What are you doing for dinner tonight?"

"Absolutely nothing. I'm your boss. I can't go on a dinner date with a subordinate."

"You're only my boss until this tent goes up. Twenty minutes, tops."

"It'll take forty," she countered.

"Twenty, and you have to eat dinner with me."

"You've made yourself a bad deal." But she held out her hand, and they shook on it.

After unpacking the tent, Luke drove the first spike into the earth around the remains of the town hospital building's shrubbery in a single, satisfying stroke. He glanced in Patricia's direction, ready to deliver some smack-talk that twenty minutes was all they'd need at his pace. But her back was to him, the walkie-talkie pressed between her shoulder and ear as she signed a form for one of her staff members who'd appeared from nowhere. She'd missed his fine display of manliness.

The heat was already broiling. Murphy and Zach shed their shirts to a few appreciative female whistles, but Luke, too aware of Patricia, kept his on. Call it instinct, but behind that neutral expression, he thought the wolf whistles from the women bothered Patricia.

Maybe she just thought others were being lazy. Actions spoke louder than words or whistles. While passers-by slowed down to watch the men at work, Patricia helped. She didn't just give verbal directions, although she did plenty of that to get them started, but she also held poles, spread canvas, untangled ropes. She cast a critical eye at Murphy's first guy line, then crouched down, undid his knot, and proceeded to pull the line beautifully taut while tying an adjustable knot that would have impressed any lasso-throwing cowboy.

Since Luke threw lassos in his day job, he was impressed. "Where'd you learn to tie knots? Do you work the rodeo circuit when there aren't any natural disasters to keep you busy?"

"You're quite amusing." She didn't answer his question

as she moved to the next line. "Once it's up, I want to be able to pull the roof taut. There's more rain in the forecast."

And since she wanted it taut, she did the work. Patricia Cargill, with diamonds in her ears, didn't stand on the side-lines and giggle and point at shirtless men. She worked. Luke thought he might be a little bit in love. He'd have the chance to explore that over dinner. They had half the tent up already, and only ten minutes had passed.

The spikes on the other side of the tent, however, had to be driven into asphalt. Although they adjusted the lines to take advantage of any existing crack or divot in the as-phalt, their progress slowed painfully as every spike took a dozen hard strikes or more to be seated in the ground. The sun cooked them from overhead, the asphalt resisted their efforts, and then Patricia's walkie-talkie squawked.

"I'm sorry, gentlemen, but I'm needed elsewhere. You're free to leave when you're done. I'll come back to check on things later."

"Doesn't trust us to put up a tent," Murphy grumbled.

Patricia was a perfectionist, Luke supposed, a usually negative personality trait, but if she wanted a job done just right, it seemed to him she had good reason for it. When she'd told him rain was in the forecast, she hadn't needed to say anything else. A tent that sagged could hold water and then collapse, injuring those it was supposed to shel-ter. Luke understood that kind of perfectionism.

He stepped closer to her. "Just take care of your other business. Don't worry about this shelter. That roof will be stretched as tight as a drum. I'll check all the guy lines before we go."

She looked at him, perhaps a bit surprised.

"In other words," he said, "I'll fix Murphy's knots."

She almost smiled. Luke decided it counted as a smile, because it started at her eyes, the corners crinkling at their shared joke, even if it didn't quite reach her perfect, passive lips.

"Thank you," she murmured, and she started to walk away.

"I know it's been more than twenty minutes," Luke called after her, "but you could still eat dinner with me."

She kept walking, but tossed him a look over her shoulder that included—*hallelujah*—a full smile, complete with a flash of her pearly whites. "A deal is a deal. No welching, no cheating, no changing the terms."

Zach interrupted Luke's appreciation of the view as Patricia walked away. "Hey, Romeo. It's not getting any cooler out here. How about we finish this up?"

Luke peeled his shirt off to appreciative cheers from the almost entirely female crowd that had gathered, then spread it on the ground to dry. Without cell phones, TVs or radios, Luke supposed he and Zach and Murphy were the best entertainment around.

For all his talk about hurrying, Zach was going all out for the onlookers, striking body-builder poses and hamming it up for the ladies for the next quarter hour as they finished the job.

Luke double-checked the last line, then bent to swipe his shirt off the ground. The sun had dried it completely. He stuck his fists through the sleeves, then raised his arms overhead to pull the shirt on. Some sixth sense made him look a little distance away. Patricia was leaning against a tree, eyes on him, watching him dress, not even trying to pretend she was looking at anything else.

She was caught in the act, but long, gratifying seconds ticked by before she realized it. She was so busy looking at his abs and his chest, she didn't realize he was looking back until her eyes traveled up to his face.

Bam. Busted.

She ducked her head and stuck her nose in her clipboard instantly, as if the papers there had become absolutely fascinating.

Luke pulled on his shirt, tucked it into his waistband, picked up his sledgehammer and walked toward Patricia, who was conveniently standing in the path he needed to take to get back to the fire engine. Her paperwork was so incredibly absorbing, she apparently didn't notice that a two-hundred pound man had come close enough to practically whisper in her ear.

"That's all right, darlin'," Luke said, giving her a casual pat on the arm as he continued past her. "I enjoy looking at you, too."

Patricia could not look up from her clipboard. She was simply incapable of it. A coward of the first degree, humiliated by her own weakness. She was so grateful she could have wept when Luke kept walking after telling her it was all right.

It wasn't all right.

He'd caught her looking. Caught her, and loved it, no doubt, as much as he'd undoubtedly loved that crowd of women feasting their eyes on him with his shirt off. Was every man on earth a show-off, so eager to be adored that they had to flash their cash or their fame or their looks—whatever they had that foolish women might want?

She forced herself to look up from the clipboard. The other two firemen had their shirts on now, too. Their little audience had dispersed and the men were headed her way, following Luke. She smiled thinly at them and said her thanks as they passed her.

Every man in her world certainly was after as much female attention as he could get, even her father, who'd long ago let himself go to flab once he'd realized his money would keep women hanging around. He wore tacky jewelry encrusted with diamonds as he drove a classic Cadillac convertible with a set of longhorns, actual longhorns, attached to the front. The sweet young things of Austin fell all over themselves to hitch a ride around town in that infamous Cadillac. It was revolting.

Now Patricia had been just as bad as Daddy's bimbos. She hadn't feigned a giggling interest in a fat tycoon, but she'd been ready to drool as a man showed off his body. And dear Lord, what a body Luke had. Not the lumpy muscles developed out of vanity at a gym, but an athlete's body, real working muscles for swinging a hammer or an ax with force. She couldn't imagine what it would be like, having that kind of strength, that kind of physical power, to be able to push an obstacle out of the way at will.

And yet, he shook hands like a gentleman.

What an irrelevant thing to think about.

The distinctive sound of an emergency vehicle's horn sounded in the near distance, three distinct tones that were repeated almost immediately. It must have been a signal from their particular fire engine, because Luke and the other two men broke into a jog. Luke slowed enough to look over his shoulder at her, catching her staring, again. He tipped the brim of an imaginary cowboy hat, then turned away to run with his crew, answering the emergency call.

Patricia had to admit it was all so appealing on a ridiculously primitive level. It was too bad she needed a husband, and soon, but a deal was a deal, and her father would never let her change the terms now. She couldn't attract the right kind of husband while she kept a pool boy, so to speak, which was her loss. Luke Waterson would have made one hell of a pool boy.

Her last lover, a Frenchman who'd sold yachts, had been less than satisfactory. Easy enough on the eyes, somewhat knowledgeable about sailing and a fair escort in a tuxedo, he'd nevertheless been easy to dismiss once she'd needed to set her sights on a suitable husband. She hadn't missed Marcel for a moment.

But Luke…

Luke, she had a feeling, would not be a lover one took lightly.

And so, physique and handshake aside, she couldn't afford to take him at all.

Chapter Six

Less than a minute after Luke's chief had used his engine's siren to call his crew back, another fire engine sounded three notes in a different sequence. Patricia guessed it was the larger ladder truck from Houston that was also stationed by her mobile hospital. Somewhere in town, a situation required urgent attention.

Patricia scanned the horizon, turning in a slow circle, but saw nothing out of the ordinary. Three days after the storm, floodwaters were subsiding. People had settled into shelters where necessary and repairs were underway, so Patricia doubted it was any kind of storm rescue. They still had a huge line of patients waiting to be seen at the hospital, but the life-threatening injuries of the first twenty-four hours had given way to more conventional complaints.

She heard the massive engine of the ladder truck as the Houston firefighters pulled out of their parking spot by the hospital building. Perhaps a car accident required a fire truck's Jaws of Life tool to get an occupant out of a car.

Patricia's staff were lining up folding chairs in the new tent, so more of the waiting line could be moved out of the sun. All the fabric walls had been rolled up so that any passing breeze could come through. Patricia walked around the outer edge, inspecting the set up. She ran her fingers over the ropes, testing their tension. They were all correct, each and every one.

She paused on the last guy line, envisioning Luke's hand on the rope she held. She'd been watching him long before he'd caught her, mesmerized as he'd tightened this very rope. For once, his nonchalant grin had been replaced by concentration as he'd kept his eye on the roof, hauling hard on the rope until the fabric had been stretched perfectly taut. The muscles in his shoulders and arms had been taut, too, as he'd secured the line to its spike without losing the tension.

Then, shirtless in the Texas sun, he'd walked exactly as she just had, touching each line, checking every knot while she'd watched from a distance. He'd understood why it mattered to her. She'd known he was doing it because he'd given her his word that he would.

It was the sexiest sight she'd ever seen.

She let go of the rope. It was stupid, really, to take a volunteer fireman's attention to detail so personally, but an odd sort of emotion clogged her throat, like she'd been given a gift.

More sirens, the kind on a speeding emergency vehicle, sounded in the distance. Patricia started scanning the horizon again as she turned her walkie-talkie's dial to the town's police frequency.

Chatter came over the speaker immediately. She couldn't follow all the codes and unit numbers, but she heard enough to know a large-scale emergency was in progress. *All vehicles please respond....*

She'd almost completed her slow circle when she spotted the smoke, an ugly mass of brown and black just now rising high enough to be seen over the trees and buildings. Last summer, as she'd volunteered near the Oklahoma border after some terrible tornados, the dry conditions had caused brush fires all around them. That smoke had been white and beige, a hazy, spreading fog. This smoke was different. Concentrated. The black mass looked almost like a tornado itself, rising higher into the sky with alarming speed.

Patricia's stomach twisted. It was a building fire, and a big one. She'd seen building fires before, too. The variety of burning materials, from drywall to shingles to insulation, each contributed their own toxic colors of brown and yellow and black to the smoke. It looked almost evil.

Charming, carefree Luke was heading into it.

Clogged throat, twisting stomach—all were signs of emotions she'd prefer not to feel. All of it made Patricia impatient with herself. She had a hospital to run. If the structure that was burning in the distance was an occupied building, then her mobile hospital's emergency room might be put to use very soon.

And if it is an abandoned building, firemen could still be hurt.

A useless thought. Regardless of who might be hurt, the emergency department needed to be put on alert. Patricia started walking toward that high-tech tent, ready to find out if they needed extra personnel or supplies. She'd be sure they got it.

"Oh, Patricia, there you are." Karen Weaver stopped her several tents away from emergency. "I couldn't reach you on the radio."

"I'm on the police frequency."

"Oh." For whatever reason, Karen seemed inclined to stand still and talk.

Annoyed, Patricia gestured toward the emergency facility. "Let's walk and talk. What do you need from me?"

"Well, I was hoping you could tell me where I could find—"

"Wait." Patricia held the walkie-talkie up, concentrating on making out the plain English amid the cop codes. "Seaside Elementary. Isn't that the school that was turned into the pet-friendly shelter?"

"I don't know," Karen said, frowning. "Is there a problem with it?"

Patricia stopped short. "Have you not heard all the sirens?"

The question popped out without the proper forethought. Fortunately, they'd reached the entrance to the emergency room, so her abrupt halt could be smoothed over. "I'm here to be sure the ER knows there's a fire. Their tent is sealed, so they may not have heard the emergency vehicles, either."

There, she'd given Karen an easy excuse for failing to notice blaring sirens in an otherwise silent town.

"You think there's a fire?" Karen asked.

Silently, Patricia pointed to the north, to the dark funnel of smoke.

"Oh, I see."

Patricia waited, but Karen didn't seem inclined to say anything else.

So Patricia did. "This will impact us. We may have injured people arriving with pets in tow. We just put up a new shade tent outside the primary care. That could be a designated pet area. You could assign someone to be there with extra rope in case a pet arrives without a leash. We'll need water bowls of some sort."

"Yes, but we can't keep pets here."

"Of course not." Patricia tempered her words with a nod of agreement. "The Red Cross has responsibility for relocating the shelter, but expect them to call you for support. Transportation, probably. We could loan the van, but let's keep our own driver with it. Food, definitely. You may want to head over to the mess tent now for a quick inventory. Better yet, see if there's anyone in that hospital building at the moment. They've been pretty good about letting us raid their pharmacy. There should be usable stores in their cafeteria."

As soon as she said it, Patricia thought of a better idea: put the town hospital CEO and the Red Cross directly in touch with each other, leaving Texas Rescue out of the food supply business altogether. She didn't suggest it, because Karen was looking overwhelmed already, and Patricia had a feeling Karen hadn't made contact with the hospital they were temporarily replacing. In Austin, Karen had seemed adequate, pushing paper and calling meetings, but here in the field, it was obvious that she was in over her head.

"I'll get you the van driver and someone to act as unofficial pet-sitter," Patricia said. "I need to take care of the ER now. You get rope and water bowls."

"Okay, that sounds good." Karen turned her walkie-talkie to the police frequency and left to start her assigned task.

Patricia entered the multiroomed ER tent, stopping in its foyer to pull paper booties over her Docksides.

Rope and water bowls. Pitiful that a simple task like that would keep a grown woman busy. Patricia couldn't coach incompetence. It was easier just to handle everything herself.

She took a breath and composed herself before entering the treatment area that she hoped would not see heavy use this day. At least she could be grateful to her supervisor for one thing: she'd managed to prevent Patricia from thinking about Firefighter Luke Waterson for two whole minutes.

Patricia no longer thought Luke or any fireman had any sex appeal whatsoever. It had been a moment of temporary insanity when she'd had the crazy idea that Luke Waterson could have made a memorable lover.

Hours had passed. Darkness had settled in. Information was scarce, and the reports they received were inconsistent and sporadic as sooty and smoky patients arrived at her hospital, telling conflicting tales. The school had burnt to the ground; only a small part of the school was damaged; the top story had collapsed into the ground floor. Everyone had evacuated the building on their own; firemen had gone in to carry out injured people; a fireman had died while saving a pet—that one had made Patricia's heart stop—but no, a pet had died but a firefighter had brought its body out of the building.

Patricia heard enough. Luke with the sailing-blue eyes and the unfunny wisecracks was fighting a fire that could cost him his life. And Patricia cared, damn him.

She told herself the knot in her stomach wasn't unusual. She always cared for the people who were her responsibility, and although the fire crews were not technically part of her hospital, they'd made her relief center their home base, and she'd gotten used to seeing them around. Heck, she'd used them to get her extra waiting room erected today. But when she heard a firefighter was injured, she didn't think of Zach or the Chief or the other guy—was the name Murphy?

No, she thought of too-handsome, too-carefree Luke.

She kept her walkie-talkie set to the police frequency nearly the entire time. The fire was burning itself out.

Austin Rescue, *Luke,* was still on the scene, along with the Houston ladder truck, something from San Antonio and the town's own fire department. Patricia's emergency room hadn't treated any life-threatening injuries, thankfully.

The Red Cross had opened a new shelter—also thankfully, because the patients were starting to hurl accusations at each other about who had been burning forbidden candles. Patricia didn't want to break up any fights tonight. She just kept loading people in the van, round after round, smiling reassuringly and ignoring her growing ulcer as they were driven away to their new shelter.

Food might have helped settle her stomach, but she wanted to be sure her staff got to eat first. All of her staff, including the temporarily assigned fire crews. Still, she could get coffee. She refused to have so weak a stomach that she couldn't tolerate coffee.

She entered the mess tent just as Karen was scooping mashed potatoes from the steam tray into a portable plastic container. "The Red Cross called, just like you said they would. We're giving them our leftover food."

"These aren't leftovers. We need this food."

Karen stopped in mid-scoop, surprised. "Dinner hours are over. Everyone's eaten."

"No, they haven't. The fire crews are still out there." Patricia wanted to yank the giant spoon out of Karen's hand. She clenched her clipboard tighter instead.

"Oh, that fire might go until dawn. You never know." With a plop, Karen dumped more mashed potatoes into the plastic container.

"Don't do that." Patricia's tone of voice made Karen and the cook both look at her oddly. She realized she'd stretched out her hand to physically stop Karen.

She snatched her hand back. "I haven't eaten yet. How about emergency? Has anyone checked with them to be sure they've all had their break?" Feeling clumsy, she switched her radio back to the hospital channel, ready to call the ER.

She had to wait. Others were talking on the channel, but she shot Karen a look that made her wait, too. *Don't you dare give away one more scoop of those mashed potatoes.* What kind of supervisor gave away her own people's food?

Patricia was being a little irrational, and she knew it. The rules of safe food handling wouldn't allow them to keep food warm until dawn, but Patricia couldn't let go of this idea that she had to have dinner with Luke. He'd wanted to eat a meal with her, and she'd made a big deal out of saying no, although he'd been thoughtful enough to bring her a sandwich the night before.

The radio traffic caught her attention. The ER had definitely been too busy to eat. A firefighter had fallen from a ladder. Too many bones broken to treat here; no MRI facility on site to be certain organs weren't perforated. A med-evac helicopter was on its way to transport him to San Antonio. Patricia had been listening to the town's police radio when the real news had been right here in her own hospital.

"Don't touch that food," Patricia ordered, and she threw open the door and left the tent. Her neat and orderly complex seemed like a maze in the dark, and she nearly tripped on a tent's spike as she tried to take a shortcut to the emergency room.

A fireman fell from a ladder. His arms must have been tired. Luke's arms were tired. I made him swing a sledgehammer. A sledgehammer! After he'd come into my tent exhausted from cutting down trees with an ax the day before. He fell from the ladder. His arms were tired.

She didn't know which firefighter it was, of course. There were firefighters in town from all over Texas. She just wanted desperately to get to the ER to find out, because she was being irrational and weak and she hated herself for it.

The helicopter sounded close. Patricia started running.

Chapter Seven

She was too late.

The lights over the emergency room's door were bright enough for Patricia to see a stretcher being rolled to the waiting helicopter by personnel in scrubs. They had a distance to go, because the helicopter had landed as far from the tent city as possible. Wind from the blades still beat rhythmically at the complex. Strands of Patricia's hair came loose from her bun and whipped painfully at her eyes.

She cleared them away and blinked twice at the group of firemen who were walking past her. They were absolutely filthy, their heads uncovered, their coats undone. Underneath, they wore polo shirts instead of black Ts. *Houston,* their coats read.

Patricia, breathing a bit hard from her short run, counted them silently. Six. Were there usually six people manning a ladder truck? Was there a seventh being wheeled into a helicopter? She felt like an awful person for half hoping so.

She stopped an exhausted-looking female firefighter. "Have you seen the Austin truck?" she asked, trying to control her panting.

The woman, probably too tired to talk, as well, stuck her thumb over her shoulder and kept walking with her crew. Patricia looked, but didn't see another truck, just the stretcher being loaded onto the helicopter. Did the woman mean someone from Austin was on the stretcher? Patricia stood helplessly, staring at the little hum of activity around the distant helicopter. In mere minutes, the nurses in scrubs ducked as they ran with the empty gurney back toward the ER from under the helicopter's downdraft.

His arms must have been so tired....

She was responsible. If the injured firefighter was Zach or Murphy, she was to blame, as well. But Luke—if it was her fault Luke had been hurt—her mind kept focusing on Luke.

Stop it. This was useless conjecture. She needed to find out the patient's name, now. Determined, she spun toward the ER's door, and crashed right into a man. A very solid man in a black T-shirt.

"Luke!"

He steadied her with a hand on each of her upper arms. One of his cheeks was black with soot, his hair was a crazy mess and he reeked of smoke.

"Oh, it's not you," she sighed, then took in a gulp of air.

Even tired and dirty, he looked a little amused. "Actually, this is me."

The helicopter was taking off behind her. She gestured in its general vicinity and raised her voice a bit. "I mean, that's not you. I thought, you know, with your arms being tired and all...I thought..."

He said nothing at all, but stood there with a ghost of a grin on his face, watching her intently. Even in the glow of the ER's artificial light, she could see how blue his eyes were.

"They said a fireman fell off a ladder," she explained. "His arms must have been tired, and I thought…"

Realizing it still could be an Austin crew member on that flight, she glanced up at the rapidly receding helicopter. "That's not one of your friends?"

"No. We're all present and accounted for."

Luke was here. He was fine. The wave of relief was a palpable thing, as physically painful as the worry had been. She was unprepared for it and the uneven emotions crashing inside her.

She shook one arm free of him and poked him in the chest. "That could've been you. You realize that, don't you? You shouldn't have let me boss you around. You shouldn't have done all that work for me today. I mean, sledgehammers are not easy—"

"Patricia." He gave her arms a friendly squeeze as he chuckled.

Her poke became a fist. She gave him one good thump on his uninjured, healthy chest. "You can't let someone wear you out like that. It's dangerous. I shouldn't have made you do it."

He caught her fist to his chest and held it there, pressing her hand flat against his cotton T-shirt and the muscle underneath. "You didn't make me. You can say Chief Rouhotas made me, if it makes you feel better. And that guy in the helicopter got hurt because his ladder collapsed, not because his arms were tired. It was their mistake, a bad one. They didn't secure their ladder properly. I'm okay."

"You're okay this time." The relief was coursing through her, an adrenaline rush she didn't welcome. "But let me tell you something. I do not ever want to do this again. It is sickening and awful. I don't even like you anymore, if I ever did."

"I can tell." He was smiling openly at her now.

"I'm serious." She jerked her hand out from under his and took a step back. "But I saved you some dinner. There's mashed potatoes in the mess tent for you. Go eat."

"So we're on for dinner after all?"

"I would never, ever date a fireman. Especially not you."

"Patricia, come here." He tugged her with him out of the light, around the side of the tent. In the darkness, he stood very close, too close, the way he always did. Then he took it further, and put his arms around her.

She shuddered. All her muscles shook with that relief, and she put her arms around his chest, needing to hold something solid, just for a second, until that shudder passed. She rested her head against him a little bit, her cheek on the top of his shoulder.

"You were worried about me," he said.

"You smell like smoke," she said, an accusation spoken into the side of his neck.

She felt his ribcage expand, felt his breath in her hair. "And you, thank God, do not."

"I didn't know what your call sign was. They kept calling for squad this and unit that, but I couldn't remember what number was painted on your truck." She picked her head up and glared at him. "I could hardly understand anything on that police radio. How can that be efficient communication in a situation that involves so many different agencies?"

"Patricia," he said, and he kissed her forehead. The bridge of her nose. Her cheek. "You were worried about me, and it's about the sweetest damned thing I've ever heard. Now quit yelling at me."

He kissed her mouth, fully, gently, his lips covering

hers as if he had all the time in the world. She felt his hand smooth up the nape of her neck to cradle the back of her head just below her pinned-up hair. His other arm stayed around her waist, holding her firmly against his body—as if she weren't holding him tightly enough herself. Then his mouth lifted away for a breathy whisper of a second, and came back a little harder, at a different angle, nudging her mouth open to kiss her more intimately.

Her knees gave way. Truly weak, she fell in a tiny dip of a curtsy, but his arm must not have been tired at all, because he kept her secure against his body. Still in no rush, he tasted her, tested the way their tongues could slide, teased her by lifting away again, just far enough to toy with her lower lip. He planted small kisses at the corners of her mouth.

She wanted him to kiss her deeply again, to take all her weight against his body. It was beyond reason. She'd never needed a kiss before, but she had this terrible want. When he didn't kiss her right away, she opened his mouth with hers and took the kiss she wanted.

She could have cried at his perfect response, and she could have cried again when he broke off the kiss, the best kiss of her life.

"Patricia, Patricia." He murmured her name and lifted her against him so only her toes touched the ground. He hugged her, hard, then set her down again and stepped back, looking her over and reaching out to tug the hem of her shirt into place and brush some dust or dirt off her sleeve.

She missed his kiss already, sorry it was over, because it could not be repeated. There was no place for this kind of helplessness in her life. There never would be. It served no purpose. She felt a little fuzzy about the exact reasons why, but she knew she had things to do, responsibilities to other people. Business entanglements. Family obligations.

She gestured between the two of them. "This can't be a thing between us."

He quirked one eyebrow at her. "A thing? Sweetheart, this is most definitely a thing."

"I mean, I can't...I can't be kissing you. I'm working. I've got things..."

Luke stepped closer again, but he only rested his forehead to hers. "I know I'm filthy dirty, and I know you're worn out from worry, so we're going to call it a night. I know you're always working. You are the boss around here, and you don't want to be caught sneaking away to kiss a boy like this is summer camp. I respect that, but darlin', do not kid yourself that I'm never going to kiss you again.

"Now, take off while I'm being good and keeping my hands to myself. I'll see you in the mess tent in a few minutes, because I could eat about a hundred pounds of mashed potatoes right now, and we'll pretend we're just pals and this never happened. For now." He kissed her once more, a firm press of his mouth. "You're beautiful. Now go."

Patricia went, looking back just to catch another glimpse of him, wanting to see him standing safe and sound in the middle of her hospital, but he'd already disappeared in the shadows, leaving her faster than she could leave him.

There was good, and then there was good enough. When it came to preparing the fire engine for another run, good enough was all Luke had patience for tonight. They'd been on the fire scene almost six hours. He wanted to get cleaned up himself, and he wanted to sleep, but mostly, he thought as he mindlessly executed the chores that came with a fire engine, he wanted to leave good enough and get back to what was great: Patricia Cargill. More specifically, kissing Patricia Cargill. He wanted to do it again, for far longer, until he lost himself completely in her cool beauty and forgot the black destruction he'd just lived through.

Luke gave the pry bar a cursory swipe with a towel before returning it to its assigned place on the engine.

"Heads up." Zach sounded impatient.

Luke turned and caught the pike pole Zach threw his way. Tempers were short because they were all tired. Even with full stomachs, they were snapping at each other. That hot meal was probably the only reason they hadn't killed each other yet. Thank God Patricia had done that smooth-talking thing she was so good at, persuading Chief that the men needed to eat immediately so the rest of the food could be sent on to the new shelter.

Patricia had eaten dinner with him, after all. In a way. She'd stood just a few feet from his table, eating precise forkfuls as Karen asked her questions about handling requests from sister agencies. Patricia had dished out instructions in a way that had Karen nodding and agreeing as if she'd always planned to do things Patricia's way. Luke had been content to listen to his Thoroughbred race down her lane, but as the Houston and Austin fire crews rested and ate, they'd gotten louder and more raucous and ruined his ability to eavesdrop. Patricia had slipped away before Luke could invite her to sit down and get off her feet, too.

He didn't know when he'd see her again.

Luke unpacked hose as Zach ran it to the overfull pond on the edge of the hospital parking lot. While the engine sucked in hundreds of gallons to refill its tank, Luke lifted the pike pole and slid it into its place along the ladder. Every muscle in his body protested.

The pole wasn't that heavy. Its fiberglass handle was the lightest in the industry, the best available, like everything else on this brand new engine, but Patricia had been right. His arms were tired. Damned tired. He'd ended days on the ranch with his body aching like this, but not many.

His head wasn't in the best place, either. No lives had been lost in the fire, but it had been harrowing to enter the building repeatedly, first to get all the people out, then again to retrieve pet carriers with terrified animals in them. Each trip in had gotten darker, smokier, hotter.

The chief had been about to call it off, but a child's high-pitched voice had carried right over the roar of fire and the growl of the vehicle engines. "Is it our cat's turn? The firemen get our cat now, right?"

Luke had heard the question, and all the faith in it, loud and clear. The bullhorn was in the chief's hand, but he hadn't given the command to stay clear yet. Luke had headed back in, tank on his back, pulling his mask on as he went. It had been bad, though. He'd lumbered in upright, but he'd ended up crawling out on his hands and knees, shoving the last two cat carriers in front of him as he went.

Zach had met him at the egress point and grabbed the carriers. As Luke had struggled to his feet, the chief had practically lifted him by his coat collar and given him a hard shake by the scruff of the neck, the only condemnation Luke had received. He'd skated a fine line, but he hadn't technically disobeyed an order, because chief hadn't spoken the words yet.

The families had stayed behind the yellow tape the cops had put up. They'd peered in their pet carriers and wept tears of gratitude and called out to Luke and the rest, thanking them and calling them heroes.

Luke hadn't felt like a hero. The only normal emotion in that situation was fear, and he'd felt it. He'd used that fear to keep himself going in the growing inferno, crawling as fast as he could while trying to control his breathing in the mask. He'd managed to keep the correct wall to his right and not lose his bearings, and he'd made it out. But hell, he was no hero. He was lucky.

He wasn't a man to stake his life on the whim of luck, not if he could help it. Just when he'd been feeling darkest, watching another fireman who was less lucky being wheeled away to a waiting helicopter, he'd run into Patricia. Her feelings for him had been transparent, all of her unflappable cool stripped away by worry. For him. And her kiss…

Well, that had soothed his soul. Whatever it took, Luke planned on running into her again. Soon.

Chief's handheld radio squawked as they packed the last hose away. The voice that came over the air was feminine and cultured, extending an invitation as graciously as if she were inviting them to tea. "Chief, I'm re-opening the shower facility for you and the Houston crew. The generators would wake our in-patients, but if you could bring flashlights and tolerate the inconvenience of unheated water, I think the noise will be minimal."

Chief keyed his mike to answer. "As long as the water's wet, ma'am, we'll be there."

Luke felt his mood lift. He wasn't going to have to wait until morning to scheme for a chance to see the woman he couldn't stop thinking about. It looked like his very near future included soap and water and Patricia.

How lucky could a man get?

Patricia knew he'd be here any moment.

She was sitting on a plastic chair at the entrance to the field showers, waiting with the female firefighter for the men to finish so the women could take their turn. Still, when Patricia saw Luke's large frame emerging from the shadows, striding toward her with a towel slung over his shoulder, she felt a little flutter, like she wasn't ready for something.

The shower facility was, of course, a specialized tent, with a locking wood door set into a wood frame at each end. Six vinyl shower stalls and a common area of tub sinks and benches were inside. Water from an external tank could be pumped in by hand, but lights and heated water were provided by generators. The showers were available to men and women in alternating hours during the day, but they closed every night at nine. There was a reason for that rule: in order to reduce noise when the majority of the staff and patients were sleeping, the mobile hospital ran only vital generators at this hour of the night.

Patricia hadn't bothered consulting her supervisor for permission to break the nine o'clock rule tonight. These showers weren't a luxury for the firefighters. They wouldn't wake the sleeping staff as long as they didn't run the generators, so Patricia had made the decision and retrieved the keys from the admin tent. Besides, Karen was already in bed. Why wake her up only to tell her what she was going to agree to?

Chief Rouhotas hurried ahead of Luke to greet her first. He was very appreciative. So much so, it confirmed Patricia's earlier suspicion that he knew exactly who she was. The daughters of Texas millionaires were spoken to in a different way than non-profit personnel directors. Judging from his men's antics while putting up the tent this morning, however, Luke and Zach and Murphy had no idea that Patricia Cargill was *that* Cargill.

Her eyes strayed to Luke. He was watching Rouhotas kowtow to her as if the chief had lost his mind. The chief was starting his second round of thanks. Patricia held up the keys in her hand and gave them a jangle. "I did nothing daring. The keys were already in my office. I'd appreciate it if you and your men keep it quiet, that's all. No locker room antics, please."

The chief chuckled, but that didn't mean she'd actually said anything amusing, of course. It only meant she was a Cargill.

"Got that, guys?" the chief said, turning back toward Luke and the guys. "No towel snapping."

If he said anything after that, Patricia paid no attention. The sudden image of a nude Luke having a towel snapped at what was undoubtedly a muscular backside made that fluttery feeling return in force.

Luke lingered as the rest of his crew entered the facility, but Patricia didn't get out of her chair for a private word. It would be too obvious that she knew him better than the others. She stayed next to the woman from Houston, knowing—hoping—Luke wouldn't say anything inappropriate in front of his peer.

"So we have you to thank for providing the cold shower," he said.

"It is June, and this is Texas, so I don't think the water will be that cold." She tried to make her voice cold, though. He couldn't expect her to fall to pieces like she had earlier.

"Cold is fine with me," Luke said, sounding perfectly sincere. "After the heat we dealt with earlier, a cold shower is just what I need."

As he walked away, he took the towel off his shoulder and started spinning it into a loose whip, which he cracked at the handle just before he opened the door and walked into the showers.

"Men," said the woman beside her.

Patricia closed her eyes, willing herself not to envision Luke stark naked, just a few feet away.

"Men," she agreed.

Chapter Eight

Patricia was the first woman to finish her shower. She combed out her wet hair and twisted it up with a clam-shell clip. The Houston firefighter and the cook who'd made the late night run to the new pet-friendly shelter were still showering, as well as an ER nurse. How the cook and the nurse had found out the showers were open was a mystery, but Patricia knew from previous missions that word traveled fast when everyone worked together in a confined community like the mobile hospital.

The exit from the showers was at the opposite side of the facility from the entrance. Patricia gathered up her toiletries bag, her towel and her deck shoes. She'd wear her shower flip-flops back to the women's sleeping quarters. Although she'd have to wait for the others to finish so that she could lock up, she'd rather wait in the open air. The forecasted rain was threatening, but Patricia knew she'd be able to hear the ocean in the quiet of the night. She could listen, and dream of something that had nothing to do with Texas Rescue and hospitals and firemen.

She could dream of sailboats. Large, oceanic ones. The kind that went somewhere. The kind she would own some-day soon, when her money was her own.

The exit door had just shut behind her when a man's voice quietly said, "First one out. I knew that high-maintenance look was just an act."

Patricia squealed in surprise and whirled to face Luke.

"Shh," he said, and he took her shoes out of her hand and pulled her deeper into the dark.

"What are you doing?" she hissed.

"Making sure no one sees you running off to kiss a boy, remember? You wanted to keep this a secret."

Luke stopped when they reached a tree, a multi-branched oak that had survived the hurricane. There was enough light to see his smile. There was enough night to make it feel like they were alone.

Patricia kept her voice to a near-whisper as she set the record straight. "That's not what I said. I said kissing you wasn't going to be an ongoing thing."

"Why not? It's fun." Luke dropped her shoes and looped his arms around her waist, then leaned back against the tree and pulled her to stand between his legs.

"Because...but...*fun?* What does fun have to do with anything?"

He was wearing a T-shirt again, but his uniform slacks had been replaced by some kind of athletic track pants after his shower. They were probably what he slept in. Their nylon fabric slipped over her freshly-shaved legs when she shifted her weight, restless in the loose circle of his arms. Her own cotton T-shirt and drawstring shorts were meant for sleeping, too. They felt too flimsy for staying outdoors like this.

"You told me this wasn't summer camp," Luke said, "but you're sure making it as fun as one. The one year I actually went to a summer camp, I didn't have the courage to stand outside the showers to steal a girl. I wish I had. Right now, I need a little bit of courage again, because you are looking mad as a hornet, but I want to kiss you pretty badly. I don't want to look back on this moment and say I wish I had."

Patricia held her breath in the moonlight. The coming storm clouds sent a gust of wind through the branches above them. Luke's grin faded, and the look in his eyes was intense as he pushed off the tree and stood over her. He moved his hands to hold her waist securely, one warm palm above each hip. She had all the time in the world to back away.

But she didn't.

She held on to her towel and her toiletries, but she lifted her chin, making it easy for him to dip his, and for their mouths to meet. It was the sweetest thing, almost tentative, two kids learning how to kiss at summer camp.

Except, this was the man she'd been worried about all day. It was scary to be so concerned for one person. It was achingly good to have him here now.

Then his hands were sliding up her ribcage, and she recalled watching them tying knots, just for her. Hands so strong and sure then, hands so strong and sure now. She wanted those hands on her, everywhere, but he kept moving slowly.

And still, their lips touched lightly, closed and soft, the kiss almost chaste.

She let her arm relax, extending it toward the ground and dropping her towel and the zippered bag. Luke's hands traveled just a little higher, and his thumbs grazed the sides of her breasts. She was wearing an athletic bra, the stretchy one-piece kind that pressed a woman's breasts flat against her body. She felt suddenly self-conscious, like the teenager she'd once been, afraid she wouldn't measure up to a boy's expectations.

But Luke's warm hands slid around to her back, not her front, and began a slow descent. He didn't stop at the curve of her lower back, but slid farther down, warm palms smoothing over the curves of her backside, until he cupped her to him. With strength.

Summer camp was over. As one, their mouths opened hungrily and the kiss became adult. Patricia pressed against him, pushing him back against the tree. He took her with him, lifting her to her toes, her soft body sliding up his hard body. She raised her arms to circle his strong shoulders, burying one of her hands in his thick hair, which was clean and still damp from his shower.

She kissed him with abandon. It was just the two of them in the dark. There was no one to see, no one to judge her, no one to remind her of who she was and what she needed to do.

When the first pattering of rain came, she didn't care. Neither did Luke. But when the first lightning strike cracked the sky, they let go of each other.

Everyone at summer camp knew not to stand under a tree in a lightning storm.

Luke bent to scoop her belongings up from the ground, then took her hand and ran with her through the rain, which was falling harder by the moment. They reached the exit door of the showers quickly. Patricia opened the door and leaned in. "Ladies? Are you dressed?"

The inside was dark.

She stepped inside and held the door open for Luke. "There's no one here."

He stepped inside and the door banged shut in its

wooden frame just as the skies opened and the rain came down, full force. The sound of it was like a roar against the tent. She couldn't see in the dark, so the sound was all she had to focus on. That, and Luke.

"It's lucky you hadn't locked the door yet," Luke said. "If you'd spent one second finding the key, we'd be soaked through."

It was unnerving, not being able to see to move away. The moment under the tree had passed, and she needed space. "If you'll hand me my bag, I've got a flashlight in it."

Immediately, a flashlight lit the night. Luke had it aimed at the floor so she wouldn't be blinded, but now she could see his face. He looked friendly, not as hungry as she felt. She cleared her throat. She should be friendly, too.

"You had a flashlight in your pocket this whole time?" she asked. "I thought you were just happy to see me."

The rain thundered down for a second more, and then Luke laughed. "Why, Miss Cargill, you find yourself ever so amusing, don't you?"

Patricia took her shoes and towel from him, unable to stop her own smile. She'd just told what was quite possibly her first crude joke. Luke had laughed, and not because she was a wealthy benefactor. He just thought she was funny.

What does fun have to do with it?

She slid the deadbolt on the back door and walked away from him. The tent was only about twenty feet long, so the glow of his flashlight gave her enough light as she went to the front door and opened it an inch. There was nothing to see outside except a deluge of falling water.

"Looks like we'll be here a while," Luke said. "We might as well be comfortable."

The light careened around the space as he moved to the long bench that ran the length of the common area.

He rubbed the towel over his arms, then spread it on the double-wide bench.

Patricia shut the door and hung her towel on the hook by the nearest shower stall. "Maybe you should turn that light off. Anyone walking by will wonder why there are people in the shower at this time of night."

Instantly, the tent was plunged into darkness. "Wouldn't want the camp counselors to walk by and see us in here," Luke said.

Patricia couldn't take a step, the darkness was so absolute. "Okay, point taken. Turn it back on."

He did, and then he reached to set it on the edge of one of the tub sinks, pointed away from the bench so it gave the space an ambient glow. "No one in their right mind is walking outside right now, Patricia. You aren't about to get caught doing anything. In fact, you *aren't* doing anything. Come sit down."

She did, sitting next to him on the wooden bench, knees together, facing forward, prepared to wait for the storm to die down.

After a moment, Luke leaned forward and stuck his face in her line of vision. "Seriously? You're killing me. We might as well be comfortable. Come here."

He kicked off his flip-flop and swung one leg onto the bench, sitting sideways, knee bent. With an arm around her waist, he slid her closer, turning her so that her backside securely fit in between his thighs and the warmth of his chest was at her back. Trying not to sigh at the futility of resisting him, Patricia kicked off her flip-flops and put her feet on the bench, then hugged her bent knees.

"You could lean back against me," Luke said into the nape of her neck.

She reached forward to brush leaves off her feet. "It's been a horribly long day. You must be exhausted by now."

"The day that I'm so exhausted that I can't stay upright when a beautiful woman leans against me is the day that I turn in my spurs and hat and walk off into the sunset without a horse."

Patricia laughed a little. "You're too much, Luke Waterson."

"Am I?" He slipped his fingers under the short sleeve of her cotton sleep shirt. With agonizing patience, he slid his fingers and her sleeve up over her shoulder. He bent forward and kissed her bared shoulder. "Funny, but it seems to me that you can handle anything I dish out."

As if they'd choreographed it, he released the clip in her hair, and she leaned back to rest her head on his shoulder. He set her clip on the bench, then smoothed his hand down her arm. He kissed her temple. The shell of her ear.

She drew her knees in a little closer, afraid of the spell he was casting, afraid she wouldn't say no.

Afraid she wouldn't say yes.

Afraid he wouldn't ask her at all.

Luke was a patient man. Any good cowboy had to be. Horses weren't trained in an hour. Grass didn't grow overnight and steer didn't fatten in a day.

But, like any good cowboy, Luke stayed alert for the signs that things were about to change. He looked for steer that drifted farther to forage. Trees that started to bud. Horses that twitched their ears in confusion before they got spooked and tried to bolt.

Patricia, who'd been open and bold outside in the rain, was on the verge of being spooked right now. Luke wasn't sure what had caused the change. He was fairly certain she didn't know, either, so he didn't ask her. He just touched her, starting with another kiss on her bare, rounded shoulder.

She responded with a small shudder, reminding him

of her reaction when he'd touched her for the first time, after she'd learned he was not the injured man leaving in a helicopter. Was that shudder a sign of relief? A release of tension?

She held a lot of tension in her body, her posture always perfect, her arm always flexed with a clipboard or handheld radio in her grip. She shouldered a lot of responsibility with Texas Rescue, just as he shouldered responsibility for the James Hill Ranch. He knew bosses were people, too. Patricia wasn't just a director; she was a woman. He wanted to know what made this woman relax. What made her tension disappear. And, perhaps selfishly, what made her aroused.

Luke ran his hand down her arm again, going slowly, putting gentle pressure on her muscles even as he savored the perfection of her skin. Her hand was resting on her knee, curled up as she was in front of him. He passed his hand over hers, then slid his palm down her impossibly smooth shin to hold her ankle in his hand.

She leaned back, turning her face to cuddle into the area between his shoulder and neck, making herself more comfortable. Relaxing. She liked this slow, thorough touch.

Luke's body was already hard as hell, but there was nothing he could do about that, and no way to hide it. He didn't have to act on it, though, and he didn't intend to, not with a woman who couldn't decide whether to kiss him or sit a foot away from him. He was a patient man, he reminded himself. He enjoyed simply touching her.

"What are you doing?" she whispered after long moments of silent caresses.

"I'm learning you. You like this." Luke ran his thumb down the front of her shin. "But you love this."

He slid his cupped hand up the underside of her bent leg. She breathed in on a little moan of pleasure. It felt incredibly intimate to him. The curve of her calf and the bend of her knee were his to know.

"But I was very sincere," she said, "that I didn't want to date a fireman."

He kissed her jaw near her ear. "Luckily for us, I'm just a cowboy."

She shivered as she laughed. Laughter was good. Luke caressed her from her thigh to her waist to her breast, kissing her neck again as he kept his hand still on her breast, letting the heat from his skin penetrate her damp shirt.

"I'm wearing a sports bra." Her words came out in a rush as she placed her hand over his. Luke thought she sounded almost defensive. She couldn't be insecure about her gorgeous body. She just couldn't be.

"I don't want to boast or anything," he said, "but I do know the difference between a sports bra and the other kind. I'm grateful this job calls for you to wear athletic gear and polo shirts. You'd kill me with cleavage."

In the soft light, he saw her smile. She tilted her head so he could nuzzle her neck more easily. "I do have a little black dress that could possibly knock you out."

"You could send me straight to my grave, I'm sure."

Her leg was warm where it settled against him, her body heat reaching him through the thin nylon he wore. Relaxed by their nonsense talk, languid under his caresses, she let her other leg fall open to the side.

The feast wasn't only one of touch. It was visual, as well. The sight of her thighs, parted before him in the dim light, was so arousing Luke stopped talking. He could only breathe for long, painful seconds. He'd already been hard, but there was aroused, and then there was *ready*. Ready could get damned uncomfortable.

He tore his gaze from her thighs, but looking at her foot resting delicately next to his was no help. Her foot was incredibly feminine compared to his, so yin to his yang with her polished, pedicured toes. The sight only drove home the fact that she was his opposite in the best, most feminine way.

The storm outside was relentless. He spoke beneath the low rumble of thunder. "Even your damned toes are sexy."

He hadn't meant to curse, or make it sound like an accusation, but inside his body, pleasure was losing to pain.

Patricia stretched her leg out and flexed her foot in response. "Do you know what that color of polish is called? Fire-engine red."

She was killing him, no cleavage required, reclining against him trustingly, head resting on his shoulder as she spoke against his neck. She smelled clean, like she'd used shampoo and soap in girly scents. Her body looked ready and waiting, her open thighs forming a triangle. He was going to have to get up and walk away to regain some command of himself, yet he didn't want to move.

His hand wrapped around her upper arm. "You're strong. I noticed that today when we were putting up the tent. What do you do when you're not running a mobile hospital?" It was a pretty blatant attempt to change the subject. Clumsy, but necessary.

If their bodies hadn't been so close, he would have missed the way she stiffened almost imperceptibly. She'd been tempting him intentionally, then, wanting him to want her.

I'm not rejecting you, I'm just slowing things down.

He stroked her arm again, so that she'd see that he loved touching her. "I can't picture you doing something as mundane as lifting weights at the gym scene. My guess is that you play tennis."

"When I must."

That was an unusual answer. He tucked his chin to

kiss her temple, then smoothed her hair with his hand. He twisted one long, damp strand around his finger. Watched it unwind as he let go.

Into the intimate quiet, she said, "I sail."

"Boats?" he asked, surprised. Then immediately, "Never mind, stupid question."

"Do you sail?" she asked.

"I never have."

She sat up a little higher and turned toward him. For the first time since they'd run in here, they made eye contact as she talked.

"You should try it sometime. Out on the water, speed is a beautiful thing. When you've caught the wind just right, you slice through the water without disturbing it. It's quiet. Fast and quiet. I think you'd love it."

"I think I would." He rested his hand on his bent knee, ready to listen all night, because she settled back into him and started explaining more about what was clearly her life's passion. He looked down at her body. Her bare feet and bare legs were no longer artfully arranged, yet they were all the sexier for being casually nestled against his.

She made little boat gestures with one hand as she talked, slicing this way and that through imaginary water. Her other hand rested on his.

"You can't control the wind," she said. "You have to work around it, tacking at different angles. Even if the wind doesn't cooperate, you can use it to get where you want to go. You just have to be clever about it."

He turned his palm up, and she slid her fingers between his. "Have you been sailing your whole life?" he asked.

"Since I was a very young teen. I first learned how at…" She twisted toward him once more. "At summer camp."

For a moment, they laughed. Then she kissed him as she had by the ER and as she had under the tree, full on, burying both her hands in his hair. It was a relief to meet her need, to plunge into her warm, wet mouth. To hold her with hands that weren't steady or slow or particularly gentle.

Greed ignited greed. She turned toward him fully, climbing into his lap and straddling him as best she could, but the bench was too wide and their position too awkward.

Luke's thoughts were reduced to two-word bullets that tore through his mind. *God, yes. Too soon. Not here.*

"Please," she said, straining against him, frustrated. Patricia was begging him. All he could think was, *She shouldn't have to beg me for anything.*

She took his wrist and moved his hand from where he cupped her cheek, dragging his hand over her collarbone, down her breasts, until his palm was spread on the impossible softness of her stomach. "Please," she repeated, "you've touched me everywhere else."

He was a patient man, but if she wanted to set the pace faster than he did, then maybe he didn't know best. Her belly button was an erogenous indentation. He ran his fingertips over it, lightly, then slipped his fingers so easily under the drawstring of her loose cotton pants. She inhaled in anticipation. Luke realized he was controlling his breathing like he was wearing a mask in a fire.

The angle was wrong for his hand to do what she wanted. They were chest to chest, breathing heavily, able to kiss one another, but...

"Stand up," he said quietly, "and turn around."

They stood together, Luke behind her, and Patricia reached for the flashlight on the edge of the sink and turned it off. With her back to his chest, he pinned her in place against him with one arm across her middle. With his free hand, he lifted the edge of her shirt and let his fingertips find the smooth skin of her stomach once more. He slid his hand lower, under the drawstring of her shorts.

A few inches under the drawstring was the elastic of her panties, and underneath that, his fingers slid into curls.

She groaned, and he hushed her gently. His fingers explored, wanting to find what made her feel best, but it was difficult to tell when his every stroke brought a response. He pressed in small circles, and she put her hand out to the edge of the sink to steady herself, tension building until her body gave in to sweet waves of shudders, one after the other. Then she sagged against him and he held her, savoring every after shock and the little tremors that shimmied through her.

The rain had stopped. Their breathing was loud in the new silence. The words in Luke's mind were crazy and intense, *only you* and *perfect,* but again he heard *too soon, not here,* so he and Patricia panted into the silence until their breathing slowed.

The distinctive sound of wood on wood sounded nearby, a door opening and swinging shut on a tent across the way. There were voices outside.

The change in Patricia was immediate. All the tension returned to her body as she whirled to face him. "Security," she breathed, nearly silent but completely petrified.

"They won't come in here," he assured her, speaking low.

"Yes, they will. They make rounds."

She was so nervous, Luke swiped his towel off the bench and pulled her with him into one of the shower stalls. If the main door opened, they would be hidden from sight. They were both dressed but damp from the earlier rain, so he wrapped the towel around them for warmth and an extra layer of modesty that she seemed to need.

She clung to him under the towel as they listened. Several people were talking, murmuring as they walked to wherever they needed to go. The mess tent wasn't far away;

Luke was certain the night shift was taking advantage of the break in the weather to get one of the cold sandwiches that were available twenty-four hours a day.

Gradually, he felt Patricia relax.

"The camp counselors didn't catch us," she said.

He smiled, but he cupped her cheek in the dark, tilting her face up to his and resting his forehead on hers. He wished he could see her eyes. "We weren't doing anything wrong. There's no law against two adults kissing."

Patricia was silent.

"Is there some Texas Rescue regulation I don't know about?" Luke asked.

"Not that I know of," she said, but only after a pause so long, he was willing to bet she'd mentally reviewed the rulebook first. "We should get to our sleeping quarters while the rain's stopped. I'm, uh, I'm sorry I didn't… you know."

An insecure Patricia was an adorable Patricia. "No, I don't know."

"I didn't reciprocate."

"I love the way you talk dirty."

That made her gasp, a tiny, indignant sound. She was so fun to tease, it almost took Luke's mind off the pleasure-pain of his body.

"If you'd reciprocated, I'm pretty sure I wouldn't be able to stand right now, let alone walk you to your quarters," he lied. "Tonight has been plenty of fun. Have breakfast with me tomorrow."

"I can't. I can't be doing this."

"I've got no intention of doing this to you over breakfast, darlin'. Some things should be private. I'm just asking you to share a table and some soggy scrambled eggs."

"It's not that easy. People will wonder how I've come to know you so well, don't you see? Murphy and Zach would wonder what's happened between putting up the tent this morning and us having breakfast tomorrow morning."

Luke didn't like it. A little romance between adults should be no big deal, but Patricia was acting like it would be the end of the world. "You just trusted me completely, but being seen with me would destroy your reputation?"

In the dark, she reached for him, her palm cool against his jaw. "Don't you see? It's nearly impossible to be a female boss without being labeled as a bitch, but I think it would be even more difficult to be labeled a bimbo who chases after a cute fireman when she should be working. I'm trusting you to be discreet. Please."

The "please" undid him. A woman like Patricia shouldn't have to beg, not for completion, not for discretion. She was so very serious, and that bothered him, too. He wanted her to be happy, so he kept his answer light. "Well, since you pointed out how cute I am, I can see the potential problem. Your reputation is safe with me. Sneaking around will be fun, anyway."

The rain started falling again, pelting the tent sporadically. She stepped out of the shower stall. "I'm not going to lock up. The other women think I left with the keys, so it would look odd if it were locked now. There's nothing to steal here, anyway."

Luke had to admire her attention to detail. He was also going to have to be truly creative when it came to hiding places, if he expected her to relax enough to kiss him again. They left together, but when they reached the main aisle, she stopped him a full tent away from the women's sleeping quarters.

"You're beautiful," Luke said. "Sleep tight."

He thought she'd leave him easily, but to his surprise, she reached for his hand. "I'll only sleep well if I don't hear any fire engines going out. Be safe."

Then she squeezed his hand, let go and walked quickly and gracefully to the women's tent, head held high. She could have been in high heels instead of flip flops.

She was a rare kind of woman, and she cared about him. Luke decided not to question his luck.

Chapter Nine

Patricia woke feeling strange once more. She'd slept like a baby on her air mattress with her sleep mask over her eyes.

Not like a baby. Like a satisfied adult.

Because of Luke Waterson. It had been vain to try to push him out of her mind yesterday morning. Today, it was impossible. He was so vivid to her now. No longer a handsome man viewed from a distance or a person with whom to match wits at an arm's length. Now he was strong hands and warm skin. They'd been so close, she'd felt the bass of his voice through her body while they talked.

Luke was the reason she'd had another night of sound sleep. At this rate, she was going to finish this Texas Rescue mission more rested than she'd begun. The thought made her smile to herself. That would be a first.

Rain was falling. She listened to its steady patter on the fabric roof of the sleeping quarters. Last night, it had thundered and poured. Today, it was gentle, constant, almost comforting in a way, like the difference between sex and cuddling. She'd never been much for cuddling. King-size beds were her preference if she anticipated spending an entire night with a man.

But this morning, she could imagine Luke beside her, and she felt a little pang of longing for the way she envisioned him. She didn't have a word for it. Close? Almost... welcoming? Or comforting, like the sound of this morning's rain.

Rain. Patricia yanked her sleep mask off. Rain wasn't comforting on a Texas Rescue assignment. Rain meant floods. Rain meant mud and the challenges of keeping patients and equipment both clean and dry. Lord, she needed to snap out of it. A firefighter's warm hands were making her brains turn to mush.

She blinked as light hit her eyes, impatiently squinting at the watch on her wrist without waiting for her eyes to adjust. Good lord. She'd slept so long, all the other cots and air mattresses that stretched the length of the tent were empty. The mess tent would soon end its hot breakfast hours. She'd miss her chance to see Luke, even if they were only going to nod politely at one another like distant acquaintances.

She pulled her navy polo shirt on over her stretchy sports bra and swiftly started brushing her hair. With an elastic band and a dozen bobby pins, she began twisting it up, rushing against the clock.

Why rush?

Missing Luke at breakfast would be for the best. She'd dismissed Marcel so easily when she'd needed to focus on securing Quinn MacDowell as a husband. Now that Quinn had fallen through as the man who could defeat Daddy Cargill's demands, she needed to find a new candidate for a husband as soon as possible. She shouldn't be rushing into a relationship with another Marcel.

Luke is nothing like Marcel.

True, and that made it worse. If she couldn't dismiss Luke easily, then he was a liability. He'd distract her from her husband hunt, and she'd fail to win her fight against her father. She let her hands fall to her lap, bobby pins resting in one palm like a child's game of pick-up sticks.

Little girl. Her father's voice grated even in memory. He'd always called her "little girl," and he still did. It had taken her years to realize it wasn't a term of endearment.

Little girl, you can't expect me to release millions of dollars to a spinster. You've got no one to take care of. You don't need the money.

Father, you know perfectly well the reason we have money in our trust fund is because I invest it wisely. I'm not a spinster. I'm single by choice.

Prove it. Land yourself a suitable husband within the year, and half the trust fund is yours. I'll co-sign a money transfer to your personal account. You won't have to wait for me to kick the bucket.

She'd stood, prepared to leave the bank president's private office, insulted beyond the high tolerance she usually had for Daddy's nastiness.

Daddy Cargill had stood, too, blocking her path to the door. It was an old trick and one of his favorites: negotiating while standing up. His height, a fluke of DNA he'd done nothing to deserve, gave him a psychological advantage over nearly every opponent. She'd had no choice but to stand there and wait as he dared her to disagree with his description of a suitable husband for a Cargill heiress.

Patricia had been seething inside. His games would never end. Cargill men had lived well into their eighties generation after generation. She had decades of this ahead of her, an entire life that was going to be spent cajoling and bargaining, dealing with him and his mistresses and enduring his whims.

I could call his bluff and marry a man like he's describing. It wouldn't be hard.

None of his fanciful ideas had ever offered her an out before. She could taste the freedom.

You have yourself a deal, Father. The look on his face when she'd held out her hand had been priceless. It hadn't lasted for a full second, but she'd seen it. He'd been forced to shake on his own deal, because their bankers had been avidly watching, eager to witness a living example of Texas lore. Everyone knew once a Cargill shook on a deal, there would be no welching, no cheating, no changing the terms. For two Cargills to shake hands was a once in a generation event.

The deal was set. All she needed was the husband.

Luke Waterson, young and sexy and unpaid as a volunteer fireman, did not meet the criteria. He was, in other words, a waste of Patricia's time. Daddy Cargill himself might as well have put him in her path to distract her from gaining her financial independence.

Patricia stopped rushing. Very carefully, she placed each pin in her hair. A French twist took a few minutes longer than a chignon, but it was just as practical. In the end, underneath the elegant veneer expected of a Cargill heiress, Patricia was a practical woman.

She never ate breakfast, anyway. Coffee would do.

The mess tent was not empty. Patricia had donned her yellow boating slicker and taken the time to stop at administration. She needed her clipboard and a fresh battery for her walkie-talkie. Even so, when she walked through the wood-framed door, Luke and his two buddies were still sitting at one of the tables. A deck of cards were being dealt.

Patricia experienced another annoying clash of emotions. Irritation, that her plans to avoid him had failed. Pleasure, because the man was beautiful to look at, and he was looking at her. A quick wink, and his attention returned to his hand of cards.

It was raining, and she realized the fire crew had no assigned place to be except the cab of their engine—or at a fire. At another table, a cluster of women in nursing scrubs were chatting over coffee. They didn't look guilty or jump from their chairs when Patricia entered, which was how Patricia knew they must have finished the night shift, and were unwinding before going to sleep for the day.

Unwinding apparently entailed gazing at the firemen quite a bit. Murphy seemed equal parts interested and embarrassed, making eye contact and then ducking his head to fiddle with the radio attached to his belt. Zach was eating it up, stretching his arms over his head and flexing as the women looked his way. And Luke, well, every time Patricia glanced his way, their eyes met. Either they had perfectly synchronized timing, or he was staring at her.

Please don't be too obvious.

The day shift cook was pulling empty metal bins out of the steam table's compartments. He seemed to enjoy making a terrific clatter. "Miss Cargill, you missed breakfast."

"Good morning, Louis. Coffee's fine." Patricia started to pour herself a cup from the army-size container that held coffee for her team, twenty-four hours a day.

"I'll get you a biscuit with some gravy."

"Please don't go to any trouble. I'll grab a sandwich if I get hungry later."

Please don't make me stay here longer than I have to.

"You know the biscuits and gravy are the only tasty

thing we get out of these prepackaged rations." He began his usual tirade against the food that kept for years in plastic bags while he opened a warming drawer and produced a plateful of white cream gravy. "Lunch will be tasteless. Eat while you can."

Patricia was unable to refuse. When someone was being gracious, she was too well trained to be anything but gracious back. "Thank you, Louis. I'll see if I can get access to the hospital building's cafeteria for you. They might have some produce that didn't go bad with the power outage."

She sat alone. She kept her back to the fire crew and her profile to the nurses. It was, she had to admit, exceedingly uncomfortable. She didn't belong. It was like being in the sixth grade all over again, the new girl at Fayette Preparatory Boarding School.

Unwelcome childhood memories killed her appetite. Still, she ate, bite after bite, at an unhurried but steady pace. She'd risen to the challenge at Fayette, keeping her chin high the way her mother did when she returned home from one of her equestrian events to find a party of bathing beauties in her swimming pool...with her husband.

At eleven, Patricia had sat at the marble-topped table in the refined prep school dining hall, frightened and lonely, and imitated her mother. She'd raised one brow at anyone who dared to approach her. At breakfast, girls had scoffed at her and loudly asked each other who she thought she was. By lunch, they'd whispered that she was Daddy Cargill's one and only child. By dinner, Patricia had been holding court, requesting her fellow students' surnames before granting them permission to sit at her table.

It was nothing to sit alone this morning. Truly nothing a grown woman couldn't handle.

"Patricia!" Luke called. "Come be our fourth, so we can play hearts."

So vividly had she been reliving her Fayette Prep School awkwardness, Patricia felt shocked that someone had dared to speak to her. She turned to face Luke while keeping her chin high and one brow raised.

He raised one brow right back as he shuffled the cards. "Hurry up. I'm dealing."

He was serious. She was the director. She didn't play cards on duty. "I'm sorry, but I was just leaving to check on something."

"This will be over fast. First one to a hundred points. Ten minutes, tops." He pushed a metal folding chair out from the table for her with the toe of his boot.

Zach twisted in his seat to face her. "You know how to play hearts, don't you?"

She nodded, surprised he was seconding Luke's invitation, such as it was.

"Then you know it sucks with three people. Help us out. We helped you out yesterday."

The nurses were silent, watching her. Louis was whistling, rain was falling, and Patricia couldn't see a way out without appearing churlish. She sat at their table, Luke to her right, Zach to her left, and Murphy, who failed to make eye contact with anything but his cards, seated directly across.

She started enjoying herself, especially after she stuck Luke with the queen of spades, the card that caused the most damage in the game.

"Ouch," Luke said, scooping the cards toward him with the same hand that had trailed its way up her bare leg last night.

Patricia pressed her lips together to cover her smile.

"Glad you're so amused," Luke said.

Apparently her attempt to hide her triumph hadn't been totally successful.

The radio on his belt sounded an alarm. The volume was multiplied as all the men's radios sounded the same three tones. She remembered that sound. Her heart jumped into her throat as the men around her came to their feet.

"Oh, no." The words escaped her in genuine dismay. Murphy was practically out the door already, but Zach and Luke both turned to her. "I didn't think you could have a fire in the middle of a long rain like this one."

"Lightning," Zach said. "It can set stuff on fire even when it's wet." He shrugged into the bulky beige overcoat they wore to fight fires. All three men had been using them as raincoats, she guessed.

Patricia set her cards down and put her hands in her lap. "Be safe, gentlemen."

Luke stood with his coat slung over his shoulder. "Don't let Zach here impress you too much. It's probably nothing. A cat in a tree. A false alarm, like ninety percent of our calls are."

Zach started toward the door, stopping to bid a flirtatious farewell to the nurses on his way out.

"Engine thirty-seven," Luke said quietly. "But it's probably nothing."

"Thirty-seven. Thank you."

Then he turned away, gave Zach a push toward the door and left.

Patricia gathered the cards up. She supposed she could keep them with the glove at her desk, all to be returned as soon as possible.

"Could we borrow those cards?" a nurse asked. "We'll give them back to the guys."

"Certainly." Patricia gave them the cards, knowing full well the nurses were less interested in playing cards now and more interested in having a reason to seek out the fire crew later.

Zach seemed like the kind of guy who'd like to keep them all entertained. Murphy might overcome his shyness. And Luke, well, Patricia could imagine him turning on that lazy grin as the nurses suggested they have a little game of cards. But what Patricia wanted to imagine was a Luke who was too interested in her to notice a table full of nurses.

The way he treated me this morning.

Patricia stood and snatched up her walkie-talkie. She knew better. Men were men. For her to even begin to wish for something different with one man in particular was a sure sign that she was losing focus. She had long-range goals, short-term plans and an immediate job to do. Nothing in her life required the devotion of a cowboy.

It was time to get to work. She refilled her coffee as she thanked Louis again for the breakfast, then she headed back to her admin tent, pulling the hood of her yellow raincoat up as she walked. As she passed the new waiting room tent, her hand itched to trail itself along the guy lines. She kept it in her raincoat pocket.

The door to the admin tent had been zipped shut against the rain. She opened it, then kept her chin raised as she entered the admin tent. A few people nodded at her. Most just kept themselves looking very busy.

Patricia sat at her laptop after setting down her clipboard and walkie-talkie neatly to the right. No one dared to approach her table. She told herself she liked it that way.

Discretion sucked.

Luke wanted to stop by admin to let Patricia know he was fine. The call had been to a traffic accident that hadn't required the use of any of their tools. They'd basically shown up, met the local police, hung around for half an hour and returned. Luke had joined the fire department to find adventure, but this was the most common kind of call they responded to. He wanted Patricia to know it, because she worried about him.

She was concerned for the other guys, too. Hell, she worried about every aspect of this hospital. But mostly, Luke knew she was worried for him, and he'd gotten the kiss to prove it. It seemed like the least he could do, to let a woman who'd kissed him know he was okay.

Right now, Luke couldn't spare Patricia from any worries, however, because he was supposed to be sparing her from…hell, he wasn't sure. In the light of day, it seemed hard to recall just why she'd been so adamant in the dark that their new relationship be a secret. He'd made a promise, though. He'd keep it.

It was painful to watch Patricia at lunch time. The moment she got herself a lousy salad, she had to set it down to write something on her always-present clipboard that the cook had asked about. When she picked her food up and turned toward the tables, Luke knew she wouldn't sit with him, but he willed her to sit with someone else. Anyone else. She'd been such a lonely princess this morning, sitting with her perfect posture at a table meant for ten.

"Ah, Patricia, there you are." A woman in a white lab coat approached her.

Good. Someone was seeking her out. Luke relaxed a little and took another bite of the brown meat patty that passed as a preserved hamburger. He'd been concerned that Patricia wasn't eating enough when she'd taken that salad, but now he had to acknowledge her greater experience with Texas Rescue food. She'd probably known the salad would taste better than the hamburger puck.

"Dr. Hodge," Patricia greeted the woman. "Did you need something else?"

"Yes."

Not a friend, then.

Patricia put her salad down once more to consult her clipboard and answer a question. Apparently satisfied, Dr. Hodge stepped away. Patricia stopped to speak to another physician, chucked her coffee in the trash can by the door, and left the mess tent alone, carrying her Styrofoam bowl of lettuce leaves.

Luke managed two more bites of the hamburger before he tossed it onto his plate and stood up. "I'll see you back at the engine," he said to Murphy.

Zach checked his radio. "Did I miss a call? Where are you going?"

"It's time for me to get your glove."

Chapter Ten

The rain had stopped, so Patricia had walked slowly enough that Luke caught up to her easily. Maybe too quickly. He only had a half-formed plan. He wanted to talk to her about how dangerous his job usually *wasn't*. He also hated seeing her eat alone, and he thought it had something to do with her assumption that everyone resented the boss. She'd said something along those lines last night. And speaking of last night, he wanted to change this agreement that they'd pretend they barely knew one another.

Luke wasn't sure how he was going to say all that, but he was within a step of her already. "Hey, beautiful."

She stopped to let him join her, but he watched her brown eyes dart left and right, looking for eavesdroppers. "Just call me Patricia, please."

"I've been thinking." He paused, weighing his next words, wondering where to begin.

"I assume that's not an unusual activity," Patricia said after a moment.

Luke smiled. "No, but it's more fun when I've got you to think about. I've had a lot of time to think this morning because we've only been on one call, and that call was a boring one."

She started walking again, and he fell into step beside her.

"Every time you hear the engine go out, I don't want you to worry. You've said a couple of times that you don't want to date a fireman, but it's really not that big of a deal. Most calls are very boring."

They were walking a little distance apart, but he felt her sincerity when she said, "I hope you have many boring mornings like that."

"It is pretty nice to know a pretty woman cares, and you sure are pretty."

"Of course I care."

Yes, she did. After her passionate kiss when she'd learned he wasn't the injured firefighter, after their intimacy as they'd waited out the rain—

"I care about all the Texas Rescue personnel," she added.

He felt the sting of her words. She was trying to say she cared no more for him than for the cook or that Dr. Hodge. That was bull, and Luke couldn't let that statement stand.

He stopped in front of her and crossed his arms, if only to prevent himself from reaching for her. With a kiss, he could remind her just how much they meant to each other. *Not now, not here.*

He strove for outward calm, aware that they weren't the only people outside. "Why would you say that? We practically made love last night, Patricia. I would hope you'd spare me a little more concern than the average person on your roster."

She looked very controlled. Too controlled, like all the muscles in her face were very carefully being held in a neutral expression. Her words, however, were fierce. "I do not like when you do that."

"Do what?"

"Block my way. You are forcing me to stop walking by blocking my way. Physically."

"I'm what?" Luke was baffled. They were talking about attraction, or lying about attraction, or something like that, and her change of subject made no sense. "I'm not blocking you."

She said nothing but stepped around him. Like one of the sailboats she'd described last night, she stepped diagonally to pass him, then diagonally back to her original path, marching on with her clipboard in one hand and her salad in the other.

Luke turned in place to watch her continue walking in a straight line. By God, he had been standing directly in her way. He uncrossed his arms and caught up to her in a few strides.

"I didn't realize I did that." And he wasn't sure what the significance was, but it obviously meant something to Patricia. "I'm sorry."

They were at the entrance to her tent. He was careful not to stop between her and the door.

"I can't stand here and talk to you." Patricia hitched her clipboard under one arm and placed her hand on the zipper of the tent door. "People will start to wonder."

Two of those people happened to pass by them at that moment, a man in jeans and a woman in scrubs. They barely glanced at Luke and Patricia.

Luke began to cross his arms again, then stopped himself. He didn't want to do anything to spook Patricia further. She was already dying to bolt into her tent.

He nodded toward the couple that had just passed them. "What do you think those people thought of you just now?"

Judging by the confusion in her expression, it was Patricia's turn to be thrown by the turn of the conversation.

"Last night," he continued, "you said they'd think less of you as a boss if you were seen flirting with a fireman. Do they think you are a bimbo for having a normal conversation with me in broad daylight?"

"No, of course not."

"I'm glad to hear that. Then we can be friends during the day."

"I have friends," she said.

It was a lie. She couldn't meet his gaze as she said it, and he wanted to call her out on it. *Name them, tell me.* She'd have no answer, because she hadn't made any friends here. With her head bent, avoiding his gaze, she looked just lost enough that his heart wanted to break for her.

"Darlin', haven't you noticed that every day, people are becoming friends around here? Playing cards, lingering over delicious meals. People talk. They make friends. We can act like that, too."

She let go of the zipper to reposition her clipboard. "That always happens, on every mission. Wait until the cell towers are up and running. People will be absorbed in their phones so fast, your head will spin."

"In the meantime, Patricia, I want to be your friend, not your secret."

She looked up at him quickly. "That's very sweet of you, but we made a deal. I didn't think you were the kind of man who'd try to change the terms. It will be my misfortune if you do. Now, if you'll excuse me, I need to get back to my desk. This salad is wilting in all this humidity."

She unzipped the door, and slipped inside. The sound of the zipper going up again infuriated him. It wasn't raining any longer. She wasn't shutting the weather out. She was shutting him out.

He scrubbed a hand over his face. This woman had him tied up like one of her nautical knots. He felt sorry for her. He was furious with her. Through the tangle of feelings, he grasped onto the one thing that seemed black and white: she was accusing him of trying to welch on a deal. That was an assault on his manhood if he'd ever heard one.

It was absurd. He'd proposed being friendly. Talking to each other, not gossiping to other people about what had transpired in the dark.

On that point, at least, he wanted to be perfectly clear. He'd get that glove back in front of her little platoon of clerks, and he'd give nothing of his feelings for her away. Actions spoke louder than words.

He unzipped the tent. The air inside was almost cool, and the light was considerably less bright, but his eyes adjusted quickly. He saw the panic on Patricia's face as she looked up from her desk in midbite and saw him.

"Afternoon, Patricia. I came to see if I might have left a glove in here from the other day."

"Oh." She set her plastic fork down. "Yes, you did. I have it right here."

As she unzipped a briefcase bag at her feet, Luke looked around and realized there was only one other volunteer in the tent, a young woman who was typing furiously fast on her computer. One clerk was witness enough as he demonstrated that he was keeping Patricia's secrets.

Patricia stood and walked around her table, glove in her hand, keeping up appearances herself. "Here you go. Is there anything else you need?"

His poor princess. What a normal question for her to ask any of the personnel she claimed to be so concerned about. Of course she had no friends here; they were too busy bringing her all their needs, their shortages and their problems. He'd thought it was sad that she didn't sit with friends to eat her meals, but he'd rather eat alone if he were in her shoes, too. If she'd stayed in the mess tent, her to-do list would have grown longer than it already was.

"No, we're doing fine on engine thirty-seven."

He couldn't think of any way to say he understood. He could only wait until dark, and hope she gave him a second chance to explain.

"Finished." The young woman stood as if she'd just won a race. "I'm going to take my break now before lunch closes, if you'll be here for a while, Miss Cargill?"

"Go right ahead, and please call me Patricia," she said, but the young girl was already heading through the door. The sound of the zipper going up after she left was music to Luke's ears.

He didn't have to wait until dark to steal her away. They could speak privately right now. He just didn't know what to say.

"Patricia," Luke said. He got no further.

"Thank you for not making a scene." She tossed the glove on the table and then turned to perch in a half-sit on the table herself. "I thought you were charging in here to make some kind of point."

"I was. I just can't remember what that point was. Something to do with showing you that you can count on my discretion."

"Why did you follow me out of the mess tent in the first place? You wanted to tell me I had no friends?"

She was direct, his Patricia. Luke scrubbed his jaw for a moment. "I think I wanted to tell you the opposite. Last night, you said that it was easy to be labeled as a bitch when you're the boss. I'm guessing you sat alone at breakfast and you didn't sit at all at lunch because you assume that everyone thinks of you that way."

"I don't put that much thought into it, I assure you."

"It's just a reflex with you, an automatic assumption. But I don't think it's true."

"You don't?"

Those two words gave so much away. Luke realized his intuition had been right. Patricia, deep down, assumed no one liked her.

"What I see is that everyone has a great deal of respect for you. They bring you all kinds of problems, and you never roll your eyes or act like they've wasted your time. I've watched you, Patricia. Not once have you made someone feel foolish for asking for your help."

"And yet, plenty of their requests are absurd." She crossed her arms over her chest as if his words didn't particularly interest her, but she was listening. She stayed exactly as she was, waiting for him to go on.

"You may think that when you take charge, people resent your abilities or your assertiveness. I think the truth is, they're glad you're on their team. You know what you're doing, and you don't let anyone fail. That is not a bitch. People are glad you're part of this hospital, more than you know."

He moved to take a spot next to her, leaning against the table like she was, hip to hip. She glanced at the door immediately.

"It's zipped," he said. "You'll have plenty of notice before anyone barges in. Even a couple of firemen would have to stop for a second to undo that zipper."

She smiled a bit, then she moved her arm toward him an inch or two, just enough to pretend she was digging her elbow into his ribs. "I do have friends, by the way."

"I'm sure you do. You also have me now." If he'd hoped to see her smile at that, he could only be disappointed at her small frown.

"You are hard to be friends with," she said. "I couldn't stand it while you were at the fire. I couldn't...not care."

He kept his arms folded like hers, wondering why a woman would be so set against caring for a man. *What happened to someone you cared for?* There would be time for questions like that, as long as he was patient and didn't push too soon.

Job safety was a simple issue to address. "It's not as dangerous as you think."

In a flash, the memory returned. *Keep the wall to my right. Trust the mask. Get out of the building.*

He wasn't lying to her, really. He'd made it out without a scratch.

"You should come and check out engine thirty-seven. We've got the best equipment available, and I know we might not seem that impressive, but we are well trained. Come and see, and then maybe you'll have a little more confidence."

"That will seem just a tad suspicious, don't you think? Me, coming to inspect a piece of equipment that isn't technically part of the hospital? Chief Rouhotas would have a fit."

"People love fire engines. They look all the time. Come and see it for fun, on a break. Talk to Murphy the whole time. No one will suspect a thing."

That did get her to smile a bit, if only at the idea of Murphy being sociable.

Luke pressed his luck. "This being discreet thing has its limits, you know. You're right that it would seem odd if we were suddenly close today, but our public relationship has to evolve. A week from now, if we still aren't speaking and you're still avoiding me like I've got mange, that will set people talking. It's not natural in this situation. We've only been here a few days, and I can see bonds forming all over this relief center."

"They don't last." She stood and walked away a step. "This is an unreal situation. People get close too fast, and then when the situation is over, the relationship is over. Friendship or otherwise."

He stood, too, close but trying not to crowd her. The need to touch her was strong, so he placed his hands on her upper arms and tried not to hold very tightly.

Her breathing was unsettled, her arms flexed and still crossed over her chest. "It really is like a summer camp. Friendships seem so real, but they don't last after everyone goes back to their regular lives."

Luke rested his forehead to hers. A minute ticked by, but their silence made it feel like a long and lazy time. Patricia uncrossed her arms and placed her hands on him, palms against his chest. He drew her in close, and she slid her hands up his chest to wrap her arms around his neck.

"It's nothing but a summer romance," she whispered against his lips.

"If that's what you believe—"

"It's what I know. It will only last a week."

"If that's what you believe, then I believe we should make it the best week of our lives."

The zipper was loud. And fast. Luke only had time to drop his arms as Patricia whirled to the desk to snatch up the glove.

One male clerk came in, followed by another.

"Here it is," Patricia said, sticking the glove nearly into Luke's stomach, because he was standing a shade too close.

"Thank you." Luke took the glove and turned to the two men. "Don't bother zipping it. I'm leaving."

He had one foot out the door, literally, before he realized that he wasn't certain if he'd see Patricia at dinner—and if she'd sit with him or anyone else. If she'd come by to see the engine. If she was committed to a week of romance or an indefinite relationship. Anything.

"Do you happen to know what's for dinner?" he asked.

She shook her head the way he'd seen her do when she'd so graciously, so regretfully, been unable to help someone. "I'm sorry, I'm really not sure."

"Then I guess I'll have to wait to find out. Good afternoon."

He stepped out of the tent just as three distinct tones sounded on the radio at his waist. He hoped Patricia hadn't heard them.

Chapter Eleven

It's not that dangerous.

Right. Easy for Luke to say, hard for Patricia to believe. She'd turned her handheld radio to the town's emergency frequency and deciphered enough to know there was no fire. The rain had caused some already-damaged buildings to collapse. Power lines that weren't downed by the hurricane were down now. It sounded like Luke and the rest of the crew were being called upon to use those axes and sledgehammers. Not that dangerous.

Patricia sat at her desk, resolved to put firefighters out of her mind. She had a hospital to run—or rather, to help Karen to run. Updating her records for Texas Rescue hadn't taken very long, so Patricia didn't mind reviewing the areas Karen was supposed to manage, too.

The hurricane had come through Sunday night. It was now Thursday, and the hospital was running nicely on autopilot. Outpatient, inpatient, emergency: all shifts were covered, all equipment functional. Supply lines had been established. Personnel were departing and arriving as scheduled.

In other words, she had nothing to do. There were no Texas Rescue problems to solve at the moment. There was no firefighter to distract her.

Patricia had time to work on her personal problems, then. She'd left Austin with a banking issue unresolved. Specifically, money was disappearing from the trust fund she shared with her father. Since neither one could withdraw money without the other one's signature, it had to be a banking error, one she'd caught and reported on Friday. It should have been resolved when the banks opened on Monday, Patricia had been running a hospital in a town with no cell-phone service, so she had no way to verify it.

Out of habit, she checked her cell phone again. Nothing.

She looked over to Karen Weaver's desk. The hospital had one phone that could make outgoing calls by a special satellite uplink. It was not for personal use. Patricia repeated that rule to others regularly.

Still, it was tempting. Patricia couldn't have a conversation with the bank, not with clerks coming and going, but she could dial the automatic teller and check the balance on her account. That would tell her if the problem had been rectified. One quick call. Karen would never know, because she never asked for itemized bills. She'd never see the number that had been dialed.

Disgusted with herself for even thinking of misusing Texas Rescue resources, Patricia left the tent. The Cargill fortune had survived through one hundred and fifty years of Texas history. It would survive this week.

The original Cargill millionaire, her several-greats grandfather, had made sure of that. Cliff Cargill had set up all kinds of rules to protect his money, and generations later, most of those rules still held.

The entire fortune was tied up in trust funds. Perhaps he'd done it to keep his children together, but Cliff had set up the trust fund so that no one family member could spend a dime. Three legal signatures were required to disperse any funds. His descendants had to sink or swim together.

Decades after his death, Cliff's grandchildren had spread across Texas in what Patricia thought of as clusters of legal-signature siblings. There were now three branches of the family. The Dallas, the Houston and the Austin Cargills each held their own trust fund, but each fortune still required multiple signatures.

For generations, the Austin Cargills had been the richest, because they'd been the stingiest. Not with their money, but with their *seed,* for lack of a better word. Having few children meant fewer people among whom to share the money, of course. Fewer combinations of siblings and cousins existed, so the Austin Cargills didn't experience episodes where one group would gang up and sign money away from other cousins who didn't want it spent or invested the same way. Those episodes were part of a saga that had provided fodder for Texas lore for generations.

Daddy Cargill had continued the Austin tradition, fathering only one child, and that one only because Patricia's mother was no fool. Patricia had been born exactly nine months after her parents' wedding. If her father had paid more attention to his inheritance before his young marriage, he would have realized he had to share his money with his progeny. Patricia doubted she ever would have been conceived.

Afterward, he'd certainly taken steps to ensure he'd never have any more children. There were only two living

Austin Cargills, Patricia and Daddy. Only two possible signatures on every check. Lord, how she envied those Dallas Cargills. There were so many of them, they probably ran into a co-signer every time they went to the grocery store.

Not her. She had to persuade the same obstinate man to agree to every investment, every expenditure, every time.

Patricia sat at her picnic table, the one that was just far enough away from the mobile hospital to prevent people from passing by. The one where Luke Waterson had found her sleeping. He said he'd been coming to get his glove. In retrospect, it had been much simpler. Boy had met girl. Boy had wanted to get to know girl.

I'm that girl.

She felt the most sublime shiver of satisfaction. Luke Waterson had found her at this table because he'd come looking for *her,* not a glove.

If she sat at one particular corner and perhaps craned her neck in an unladylike way that would never have passed muster at Fayette Prep, Patricia could see two fire engines from her picnic table. The Houston ladder truck was parked in its usual spot. Engine thirty-seven was still gone.

Her pleasure dimmed.

She didn't want to sit alone at this table any longer.

I have friends, she'd assured Luke.

Not many. She'd recently damaged the one friendship she'd relied on the most: Quinn's.

She couldn't fix any other problems right now. The bank was unreachable. She couldn't snap her fingers and produce a qualified husband. With engine thirty-seven out on a call, she couldn't even enjoy a summer romance that wouldn't last a week.

But she could apologize to Quinn MacDowell. Then,

when Luke asked her if she had any friends, she could look him in the eye the next time and say yes.

Patricia found Dr. Quinn MacDowell in the mess tent at a crowded table, eating his supper. She paused behind the chair across from him, summoning her poise. It took a lot of summoning. Not only might Quinn reject her overture of friendship, but so might everyone else at the table. *I was saving this seat for someone else* was polite-speak for *I don't want you to sit with me.*

Luke thought people were glad she ran the hospital. She didn't believe him, but she was going to risk that he was right. Right now.

"May I sit here?"

There, she'd said it.

Quinn hesitated for the briefest moment. "Of course."

She sat down, but he said nothing else. They ate in silence for a few minutes, until the two people next to them got up and left. Patricia told herself not to take it personally. Besides, now she could talk to Quinn in relative privacy.

He didn't seem inclined to talk. He didn't even glance up from his plate.

She'd been hard on his girlfriend, she knew. Cold, shutting her out of their social circle, hoping that Quinn would see Diana didn't belong. Diana had nothing to do with the medical world. She volunteered at dog shelters, of all things.

Patricia started there. "Did you see the dogs I had to corral yesterday because of the pet-shelter fire?"

Quinn didn't answer, but he did meet her gaze. He was gauging her, she knew, wondering where the conversation was headed. He no longer trusted her. He no longer found her conversation amusing.

Her heart sank. He'd been her closest friend every other time they'd served together with Texas Rescue. He'd never been intimidated by her, and there were very few people in her world who treated her like she was normal, not like her DNA came from a Texas legend. She wanted her friend back.

"Your girlfriend would have been a real asset in that situation," Patricia said. She had to call on a considerable reserve of Cargill confidence to keep chatting as if he weren't staring her down.

Quinn stopped eating and sat back, watching her warily.

"Dogs are her specialty, right?" Patricia asked. "If your girlfriend is interested, she could come back. I could get her—*Diana*—in touch with the pet-friendly shelter. Diana would be a huge help with them."

It could have been her imagination, but Quinn's expression seemed to soften. "Patricia Cargill, are you trying to apologize for something?"

She looked around a little, making sure their conversation was private. "How much humble pie would you like me to eat? I can do it. I hate having you not speaking to me."

Quinn picked up his fork, digging back into his meal casually. "What, exactly, made you so set against the idea of me dating Diana?"

"I wanted to get married."

"To me?" He looked very concerned, like she was telling him she was experiencing some terrible medical symptom.

"I still need to get married." She sighed, wishing she didn't need to explain anything at all. "It's a long story, but Daddy Cargill's involved, so it's no joke. You were the man I thought would be the least horrible to be married to."

"Least horrible. I was supposed to jump at the chance to be your least horrible option?"

She felt defensive. "I would have made you an excellent wife."

"In a terrifying way, you probably would."

"I couldn't get you to see me as a potential wife as long as Diana was in the picture."

"That's true. Although you've made it clear your heart isn't exactly broken over me, I'd like you to hear something from me before you hear it from the grapevine. I intend to ask Diana to marry me as soon as I get back to Austin."

So soon? Patricia stopped herself from saying it out loud. She wanted to be Quinn's friend again. He knew his own mind—or rather, his own heart. If he wanted to marry a woman he'd known a month, she could support him.

"You know," she said, "I heard the power is back on at a McDonald's on the other side of town. Karen Weaver came back from an errand with a milkshake today. You know what that means."

Quinn set his fork on his plate with a bit of a smile. "It's the surest sign we won't be needed much longer. Once a town gets their McDonald's up and running, our days are numbered."

"We've seen it before, haven't we?" She consulted her clipboard, flipping through her rosters. "I don't see why I should keep you past Saturday morning, if you had something in Austin you'd rather do."

Quinn started to smile.

"Congratulations in advance," she added, and then forgot the rest of her friendly, no-hard-feelings sentence, because Luke walked into the dining area. He spotted her immediately and winked, but rather than pretend he barely knew her, he started to walk straight toward her.

Patricia felt her heart beat a little harder. She directed

her attention back to Quinn, summoning a smile while she wondered what on earth Luke was doing, coming right up to her table. They had an agreement. They were discreet. He couldn't just walk up and say hello like this.

"How's it going?" Luke clapped Quinn on the shoulder.

Quinn looked up at him. "Hey, Luke. Long time, no see. How's it going with you?" He extended his hand and they shook hands like old friends.

"Same old, same old," Luke said. "How's your mom?"

"Better. Thanks for fixing that light for her."

"No problem." Luke nodded politely at Patricia as if she were an acquaintance with whom he played cards, then left to get in line for the food.

Quinn resumed eating, like nothing was out of the ordinary.

It took Patricia a moment to find her voice. "Do you know that fireman?"

"Who? Luke? He's a good kid. I used to ref his Pee Wee football games. Why do you ask?"

She and Quinn were the same age. Thirty-two. Quinn had been a referee while Luke was in Pee Wee football. How old were children in Pee Wee football? Six years old? Luke's boyish charm suddenly took on more significance.

Good lord, I'm a cougar.

Patricia studied Luke's back as he waited in line. She'd been lusting after a man far too young for her, following in her father's footsteps, chasing an outrageously young piece of eye candy. It was so unfair, though, to be expected to resist those blue eyes and those kisses. The man could kiss.

Quinn squeezed her hand. "Why Patricia Cargill, you think he's cute, don't you?"

She jerked her gaze back to Quinn. Alarm made her stiffen her spine. She couldn't give herself away. She couldn't stand for everyone to make fun of her for being just like her father.

"Who?" She raised her chin, prepared to brazen it out. Patricia Cargill was never teased, not about anything.

"Luke. You think he's cute."

"Cute?" She flicked her fingers dismissively. "That word isn't in my vocabulary. I wouldn't describe a puppy that way, let alone a man."

"No? How do you describe puppies, then?"

"Très charmant."

Quinn laughed, but he wasn't deterred. "You think Luke Waterson is cute. You can't take your eyes off him."

Caught staring at Luke again, Patricia cut her gaze back to Quinn and leveled her most condemning look on him, the one where she didn't so much as blink. It made bankers and businessmen squirm.

Quinn didn't squirm. "What is this, a staring contest? I was great at this in fourth grade."

She only narrowed her eyes at him, boring a hole right through his eyeballs into his tiny, man-size brain.

Quinn leaned in to speak conspiratorially. "Can you see what he's doing? Is he coming this way, or is he going to sit with another girl? Aren't you dying to take just a quick peek? Maybe he's checking you out right this second."

Patricia gave up and sat back, disgusted that Quinn was laughing at her. "Oh, do be quiet."

"Well, you have my blessing. Have some fun for once in your life. Those sharks you call your girlfriends are blessedly scarce around here, so I'll have to fill the role." Quinn affected a high-pitched voice. *"He's a total hunk. No, wait. He's a total hottie.* I think that's the going term."

"I'm leaving. Honestly, I thought we could be friends, but you're just a pest."

"Like a brother."

"Yes, a pesky brother."

She tossed her napkin on the table and stood, ready to make good on her threat to leave, but Quinn caught her hand. "But even pesky brothers are still brothers. Remember that."

She paused and looked down at him. Patricia had no brother, of course. Her father had made sure she had no siblings, unless she counted Wife Number Two's daughter from a previous marriage. Yet Quinn was telling her she had him.

Just when she softened, just when she wasn't sure how to handle the lump in her throat, Quinn smiled devilishly and very softly started chanting, "Tricia and Lukey, sittin' in a tree, k-i-s-s-i-n-g."

"Oh, for the love of God. I can't believe I ever wanted to marry you."

"Is this seat taken?" Luke said, standing right beside her.

Oh, the timing.

Quinn stood immediately, grinning like a fool. "Have a seat. This is my friend, Tricia. Keep her company for me, would you? I was just leaving." Before he left, he made a big deal out of raising Patricia's hand and kissing the back. "*Au revoir,* Tricia dear. *Très charmant.*"

"Go away."

He did.

Luke skipped Quinn's chair and sat next to Patricia instead, shoulder to shoulder. He began eating his prepackaged, reheated meatloaf with gusto.

Patricia knew her cheeks were burning. She picked up her fork and spun a cherry tomato around her plate for a moment. The suspense of waiting for Luke to say something was too much, so she decided to go first. "I gather you know Dr. MacDowell?"

"Apparently not as well as you do, Tricia dear."

She stabbed the tomato and watched the juice drain out around her fork.

He tore a ketchup packet open with his teeth and squirted it directly onto his meatloaf. "Were you two engaged?"

She hadn't wanted to give Quinn a hint about her deal with Daddy Cargill. She didn't want to tell Luke that she knew Daddy Cargill, period. Luke didn't know she was an oil baron's daughter. He liked her just for being Patricia, the personnel director who had no friends in the dining hall.

Luke pressed her for an answer. "I'm asking because that was a mighty interesting comment I heard as I walked up. You wanted to marry him?"

"Does it matter? He's madly in love with someone else. Or is there some guy code, and you can't date his sloppy seconds?" She stared straight ahead, looking at the door.

"Since Quinn was nice enough to introduce us, I believe you can look at me without anyone thinking twice about it. Look at me, so I can casually smile at you and pretend I'm not about to say something important."

She looked at him.

He smiled, but his eyes didn't quite crinkle at the corners as they usually did. "If you told me that you'd married and divorced Quinn MacDowell, it wouldn't change the fact that I can't get enough of you. You're in my thoughts all day. I can't wait for night to come, so I can touch you again. Just so you know, of all the women I've ever met, you are the least likely to ever be sloppy, and no man could ever look at you and think 'seconds.' You are first quality, Patricia. The finest."

She ignored his smile for the public and looked into his serious eyes. He meant what he said. She didn't think she'd ever heard a more sincere compliment. She doubted she'd hear one like it again. It had taken her thirty-two years to receive this one.

"Since we are supposed to be making small talk," Luke said, "why don't you smile politely and say something?"

"I'm the same age as Quinn," she blurted. "Thirty-two."

"Okay." He shrugged. "Why are you looking like you just confessed a murder to me?"

Patricia stole a look around the tent. Most people had cleared out, thankfully, because she was having a hard time pretending this conversation wasn't engrossing. "How old are you? Quinn said he refereed your Pee Wee football games."

"I don't remember that, but it's not hard to believe that he did."

"So, how old are you?"

"Afraid you're robbing the cradle? I'm twenty-eight. Twenty-nine come November, if you'd like to throw me a party."

She was four years older. A woman in her thirties befriending a man in his twenties sounded a little desperate, maybe, but a four-year age difference wasn't so bad.

No daughter of mine will get a dime for marrying a man who's not of the right age. You want to prove you're not a spinster, then don't marry a doddering old man with one foot in the grave, and no college boy, either. Believe you me, it's a piece of cake to get a sweet young thing half your age to marry you for money. And you're getting old enough for a man to be half your age, aren't you?

Her father had failed to set a specific age. Twenty-eight wasn't all that young.

Patricia stopped herself short. Luke didn't meet any other criteria, anyway.

She stabbed another tomato. "I'll kill Quinn for lying to me about that. When he said Pee Wee football…"

"Pee Wee isn't as young as it sounds. I played when I was twelve, so he was probably fifteen or sixteen. I reffed a few times in high school myself. Got twenty dollars on a Saturday morning to spend on a girl Saturday night. Please pass the salt."

Patricia reached for the plastic shaker and slid it down the table, feeling stiff and self-conscious.

Luke salted his green beans like this was just any old dinner. "Do you like me more or less, now that you know I'm younger than you? I think I like you more. The idea of dating an older woman is hot. When we're done being discreet, can I tell everyone you're much, much older? It'll make me seem like a gigolo."

"You just keep amusing yourself, Waterson." She didn't have any fresh tomatoes to stab, so she pricked the first one again. "So, if you don't remember Quinn from being a Pee Wee—" she paused to cast a skeptical look at the man who looked like he couldn't possibly have ever been a Pee Wee anything "—then how do you know him?"

"Ranching, mostly. We spent school vacations rounding up steer. Branding calves."

"Really? But he's…he's a cardiologist. And you're…"

"Still branding calves."

He didn't sound happy about it.

How could he be? Cowboys weren't any more glamorous than firemen, and probably were paid less. "A cowboy paycheck" was a daily wage, paid in cash. The last time Patricia had fancied herself in love with a cowboy, the standard rate had been one hundred dollars a day.

She'd just turned eighteen and didn't think her father could control her anymore. Daddy had found out about the cowboy, who'd worked on the ranch of a girl from Fayette.

Daddy had offered him ten times his pay to leave her. One thousand dollars, spread like a fan in his hand. The cowboy had turned him down, and Patricia had felt the thrill of being valued.

She was better than the dollars that had made her family so famous.

Then her father had offered the cowboy one hundred times his pay. Ten thousand dollars. The cowboy had taken it and left. Proof that at the age of eighteen, Patricia had been worth ten thousand dollars.

She supposed she ought to be pleased with this year's upgrade. A suitable husband for the Cargill heiress would hold at least a million dollars in liquid assets, in addition to owning land in the great state of Texas. Her father now thought she was worth a million. How fast would a cowboy leave her if Daddy Cargill offered him a million dollars?

Patricia knew, suddenly, that was exactly what her father planned to do when she produced a prospective husband. She was the real Cargill, the one who had the Midas touch. She could turn money into more money. Daddy Cargill was just the front man in his white suit and his longhorn Cadillac. She hadn't thought he realized that—but he knew. Daddy wouldn't let her go. She was worth too much.

Still, they'd made a deal. They'd shaken hands, with witnesses. He couldn't welch on the deal. He couldn't cheat. He couldn't change the terms—but he would surely try to offer a millionaire of the right age a better deal to leave her. And he'd surely never offer her another chance to escape again.

Luke patted her on the arm as he got up, a friendly, "nice seeing you" type of gesture for the dining public. "I don't know what has you looking so sad, but hang in there. It will be dark soon, and I'll help you chase away the day's worries."

He threw his paper plate in the industrial garbage can and walked out the door.

Chapter Twelve

She did not need a handsome fireman to make her forget her worries.

She needed to focus on them. If it hadn't been for this hurricane, she'd be making the rounds to all the right events in Austin, perhaps branching out to Dallas, putting herself in the path of the right type of men, inquiring discreetly into their financial and marital backgrounds.

Instead, she was at a hurricane relief center where the only man who kept crossing her path wore a close-fitting black T-shirt and called her *darlin'.* The only thing she had to do discreetly was purely physical and involved sneaking around after dark.

She wondered if it was dark yet. One of her clerks left the tent, and Patricia watched the door as he unzipped it. It was still only dusk outside.

She returned her attention to her laptop. Local medical personnel had been walking up to the relief center and volunteering to work with Texas Rescue, a typical occurrence in this kind of situation. Patricia appreciated their willingness to help, but she still required them to fill out the application forms. Just because people introduced themselves as nurses or doctors didn't mean they were. Her clerks had been verifying licenses and running background checks all day.

Another Dr. MacDowell could have been entered into the system. Patricia slid a glance to the satellite phone. Reviewing personnel files wasn't really abusing Texas Rescue resources, not like making a call to check her bank balance would be. Personnel files were at her fingertips, right here in her laptop. It was her job to verify physician's applications. And if she found a man who fit certain criteria while she did it…

She scowled at her fingers and the way they just rested on the keys, refusing to type. The average family doctor was almost never a millionaire, she knew. Having a medical degree did not mean one owned land, either. The doctors who had the time to volunteer tended to be the older ones, retired or semiretired.

Still, she should look. It was possible the right man was right here, right now.

Or, I could take a week off from the husband hunt. Quinn even said I ought to have a little fun for once.

She could be blowing a golden opportunity here. All she had to do was open the first file of a local volunteer and check the date of birth. Just take that one, tiny step.

Her fingers wouldn't move. Disgusted with herself and afraid the two night-shift clerks would notice her lack of activity, she opened a game of hearts on her laptop.

This did not take her mind off Luke in the least.

"I've never heard of a horse named Pickles."

Patricia froze, finger poised over her touchpad, as Luke's voice carried through the fabric wall of the tent.

Feminine giggles followed. "'Pickles' was my idea. He's my horse, so I got to name him."

"I could've guessed that. You don't think any man would ride the open range on a horse named Pickles, do you?"

More giggles. "If you're a cowboy, what's your horse's name?"

"Only manly names are allowed on the ranch. We've got Killer, T-Rex, and his son, Ice-T."

"You do not."

"We do have a horse named Ice-T. That's the honest truth, and he looks like a badass, too, just like the actor. Ice-T glares at a cow and it's too afraid to move. That's why he's my favorite mount. Cows are much easier to rope when they're not moving."

The peal of feminine giggles snapped Patricia into action. She killed her game and closed her laptop's lid. Like a fool, she'd started listening to Luke's tall tale as if she was one of the girls he was telling it to, but the sound of a real horse snuffling and chewing on a bit was unmistakable. The girl or girls Luke was wasting his time charming were on horses in Patricia's hospital.

"If the cattle heard me call a horse Pickles, I'd lose their respect as fast as that."

The answering giggles were like fingernails on a chalkboard.

Patricia headed out of the tent. The door, naturally, was on the opposite wall of the tent from where she was hearing Luke's voice. She had to go out the front and then walk around to the back side, where the tents backed into one another.

When she rounded the corner, she saw the rear of a

large, brown horse. Luke was standing at its head, stroking its muzzle as he kept entertaining the young ladies who were sitting on the horse's bare back. No wonder Patricia had been able to hear him so clearly through the fabric walls. The horse's flank was practically touching the tent.

Two young women, riding double and riding bareback, had attracted the attention of a cowboy. Had Patricia seen it anywhere else, she would've turned to an acquaintance and made a cutting quip about the predictability of such a thing. She was at her hospital, though, and the cowboy was Luke. It was hard to deny that there was something distinctly unpleasant about it all.

Lord, it was jealousy she was feeling. The young women, despite being on a horse, wore denim cut-offs and no shoes. Their legs looked long, but their feet were filthy, Patricia noted with a sniff. She doubted Luke or any other man would notice such a thing, because the girls were also wearing bikini tops. They were as tanned as only girls who lived in a beach town could be.

And they were definitely girls. Perhaps they were teetering on the edge of adulthood, but they were still teenagers. Surely Luke could see how painfully young they were.

Patricia was accustomed to seeing older men with much younger women, but generally that didn't occur until the men of her acquaintance were on their second wives, and then those women were generally no more than two decades their husband's junior. Only men like her father pushed the boundaries further. It went without saying that he'd slept with women younger than Patricia while Patricia was in college.

Are you quite sure she's eighteen, Father? Think of the negative press. The cost of a good legal team. Yes, twenty-one is a much safer age.

Patricia would have bet a million dollars that Luke was

nothing like her father, and yet before her eyes, he was enjoying a long and silly chat with pretty young girls on a horse. She shouldn't have been surprised. Men were so predictable.

The real issue here was that there was a horse in the hospital. Once more, she'd lost her focus around Luke.

From a good five yards away, she broke into their party of giggles. "Good afternoon, ladies. I'm sorry, but you need to take your horse out of the tent area immediately. It may not look like it, but this is a hospital. The horse presents sanitation and safety issues."

At the sound of her voice, the horse stepped in place, dangerously close to the guy lines. The girls on its back twisted around to glare at Patricia, causing the horse to shift more nervously.

Luke kept his hand on the horse's muzzle. "Don't walk up behind the horse, Patricia. You'll get kicked." He sounded perfectly calm.

"I know that," she said. Basic equestrian skills had been a mandatory part of her schooling. Besides, she'd once been in love with a cowboy, back when she'd been young like these riders.

"Then stop doing it." Luke sounded quite firm, although his posture was very relaxed, and all his attention was on the horse. Patricia had thought she was walking toward them at an adequate angle for the horse to see her coming, but she stepped farther to the side at the tone of Luke's voice.

"We're not hurting anything," one girl said, clearly feeling her oats. "You can't make us leave."

"Actually, she can," Luke said. "This is a restricted area, and she's the boss lady."

The girls, who moments ago had seemed on the verge of womanhood as they'd practiced their feminine wiles on

Luke, became petulant children. "Fine, we'll leave. What a bitch."

The horse whinnied, bobbing its nose under Luke's hand.

"Now look there," Luke said. "Pickles doesn't want to hear such an ugly word coming from his owner's mouth. I know you love this horse, but look at his feet. You've got him ready to trip over a tent spike, and he's going to have to step around a half-dozen more to get back out to the main walkway. There's a difference between someone being bitchy and someone enforcing a rule to save your horse, isn't there? Hand me the reins, and I'll walk you out."

And that, Patricia realized in a flash, was why Luke had been talking to those girls in the first place. He must have spotted the horse and had stepped in to prevent it from getting hurt. How easily it could have tripped on a rope and torn down part of the hospital, possibly hurting itself or others. Luke had been talking to the girls in order to keep the horse in place, giving the horse time to smell him, then more time to adjust to his touch as he petted it.

The horse, relaxed and trusting Luke, willingly followed him out of the tangled danger into which its young owners had placed it. Patricia drifted along at a little distance, watching Luke as he coaxed the giant horse to take delicate steps over and around the guy lines. Luke needed nothing more than his calm voice and a gentle tap of the reins on a foreleg that needed to be lifted higher before he would let the horse proceed.

Patricia didn't want to feel the emotions he was stirring in her. Her fireman clearly had the horse sense of a cowboy, for example. It was easy enough to fool herself that her admiration wasn't really lust for a man who tamed a beast.

It was easy to admit that she felt gratitude, too. He'd stepped in to take care of a potential problem for her, after all. But it was the relief that worried her most, because she clearly felt relief, damn it, that Luke wasn't the kind of man who chased anything female in a bikini.

It shouldn't matter so much to her. After this week, she wouldn't care what he did with girls who wore bikinis or anything else. Patricia needed to stay detached, but he was making it so very difficult.

In the morning, Patricia woke feeling wonderful.

Luke Waterson was an excellent kisser. He'd come for her after dark, taking her back to the picnic table near the hospital building. He'd made her lay on top of the table with him. She'd felt silly, a grown woman reclining on wood planks, but he'd said he wanted her to look at the stars. They were brilliant in the black sky, undiluted by civilization's usual glow of street signs and restaurant marquees.

Even in June, the night air had felt a bit cool, and Patricia had stayed warm by keeping herself tucked by his side, her head on his chest, leg along leg. They'd kicked off their shoes and let their bare feet tangle, and they'd talked about stars they could see from horseback and stars they could see from boat decks.

Then, they'd kissed. Long and lazy, knowing the whole night stretched before them. She'd enjoyed the slow build-up. When he hadn't pushed for more, she'd enjoyed it a while longer, but eventually, she'd been confused. They'd taken things pretty far in the shower facility. Surely, he'd expect things to go further this time.

Men wanted sex. That was a fact of life. They wanted it, they appreciated the woman who gave it to them for a short while, and then they moved on, wanting it again from the next woman. Patricia excelled at keeping sexual relationships civilized, as did her friends. It was the height of bad taste to weep after a lover or to be enraged over a divorce.

Yet last night on the picnic table, Luke had kept things surprisingly PG. Maybe he'd lifted the elastic of her sports bra and let his thumb slide over her full breast. Maybe she'd let her hand slip over the nylon of his track pants, just to get a hint of the size and the shape of him. But mostly, it had been a starry night of kisses and whispers.

Surely, that meant he was enjoying her company, if he was delaying the sex. He was in no rush to be done with her and then move on to another woman. She felt dangerously pleased about that.

He won't be easy to leave.

She wouldn't think about that now. Fortunes and husbands and fathers could wait. She would work through this day, and live for another precious night.

Not touching a man was an aphrodisiac.

There could be no other explanation for it. Patricia was dying as she ate lunch sitting to the left of Luke. Others surrounded them, eating and talking, oblivious to the way Patricia tried not to stare at the man with the blue eyes and lazy grin. A nurse sat down to debate sci-fi movies with Murphy. Some of the Houston fire crew sat there, too, eating quickly and leaving. Quinn stopped in for a bite and stayed awhile.

Patricia found that being polite to an acquaintance so no one would guess he was really a man who'd caressed every inch of her body required concentration. She couldn't be too aloof, but she also had to be careful she didn't laugh any louder at Luke's jokes than Quinn's. When Murphy asked if anyone else had noticed how many more stars

there seemed to be in this part of Texas, she turned her
face away from Luke and brushed imaginary crumbs from
her lap, not daring to meet his eyes and share a memory.

Lunch could have been horrible hot dogs or heavenly
foie gras, so little did Patricia pay attention to her food. Instead, she was exquisitely aware of every move Luke made.
She deliberately didn't watch the muscles in his shoulders
move when he turned to toss a bottle of ketchup to Zach's
table. She was aware when he casually placed his left hand
on the table, perhaps four inches away from her right, and
kept it there. She didn't move her hand away, either. They
talked to other people while they didn't hold hands.

When his radio sounded its alert tones, though, she
forgot not to look into his blue eyes. He didn't look away,
either.

"Guess lunch is over," Luke said. *Don't worry about
me, darlin'.*

"I hope your crew gets back before dark this time," she
answered. *Because I'm dying to touch you tonight.*

And then he was on his feet and out the door, and she
was looking at her plate, vaguely surprised to see lunch
had been neither hot dogs nor foie gras. She'd apparently
chosen mashed potatoes and vanilla pudding, a gourmet
combination the elegant Cargill heiress would never have
touched before a hurricane had put her plans on hold.

She looked at the silly lunch on her disposable plate and
started to smile to herself. She wouldn't let herself laugh.
She had her limits. But then Quinn began whispering his
chant about kissing in a tree, and Patricia got a bad case
of the giggles.

Laughing must have been an aphrodisiac, too, because
when she left the mess tent and saw engine thirty-seven
pulling out of its parking space, she forgot to worry. She

was too busy imagining a certain fireman touching her tonight.

She checked her watch to see how many hours it would be before the world went dark and the fun would begin.

Chapter Thirteen

Patricia hid behind a tree, listening to the locker room sounds of men taking showers. The world was wonderfully, gloriously pitch black, and Luke would soon emerge, damp and clean. Then finally, finally, he'd come find her.

Patricia planned to make that the easiest of tasks. He hadn't come to find her when his truck had returned from its call. She'd monitored the police radio, so she knew engine thirty-seven had been called to yet another car accident. Luke hadn't been kidding when he said they rarely were called to fires.

This time, a car had rolled over on the main road out of town, triggering a series of smaller accidents with minor injuries her ER could handle. Only one person had been taken straight from the scene to San Antonio by helicopter, and that person had been a car driver, not an emergency responder.

She hadn't had to worry about Luke's safety. With nothing to dampen her spirits, she'd waited to catch another glimpse of him before darkness fell. He must not have been able to detour past her office after he'd grabbed a sandwich from the mess tent, although she'd managed to linger by the unzipped door flap. When Karen had stopped in the middle of the main thoroughfare to let Patricia know the permanent hospital's roof repairs had begun, Patricia had not kept walking as her supervisor talked. She'd stood still and listened, hoping Luke would pass by and send her a covert smile.

He hadn't. People or duties were keeping him from her. Since he couldn't get clear to come see her, she was going to come to him. Any moment now. It was late and the showers were closing.

The bark of the tree felt hard and intricate under her palm. Her whole body felt sensitive, every summer breeze making itself felt as it passed over her exposed arms and legs. She was even aware of the strands of hair that had come loose from her chignon to tickle the nape of her neck. With her drawstring sleep shorts, she'd worn an oversize shirt, easy for a man's hands to push out of the way. She intended to entice him to do just that.

It wouldn't take much doing. He wanted to touch her as much as she wanted to be touched. *What a perfect pair we make.*

The wooden door opened, light poured out. Luke stepped out, hair damp, towel around his shoulders, and Patricia stepped from behind the tree, ready to dart forward and snag his hand. Then Zach stepped out, and Patricia could have stamped her foot in frustration. In fact, she did.

Zach nodded at something Luke said and walked away. Patricia feared Luke would follow, but he paused to lift the towel from around his neck to give his hair another rub. Patricia seized her moment, stepping lightly over the ground to grab a corner of his towel and give it a tug.

"Shh," she whispered. "It's me."

In the half-light, he half smiled. "It *is* you."

She took his hand and pulled him into the darkness. She found the tree where they'd first kissed within a minute. Funny how it had seemed farther away that first night.

She turned and stepped into Luke, body fitting against body effortlessly. Her leg stepped in between his and her back arched as she raised her arms to wrap around his neck. The movement was smooth, as if she'd done it so often, it was part of her muscle memory. She tilted her face up, just so. Luke gave his head a little shake and closed his eyes before his mouth came down on hers.

Lord, he tasted good. He felt good. After a day of discipline and denial, it was like melting, a release of everything strict and straight. He ended the kiss, but he didn't let go. For a long moment, he just breathed in the dark with her, his mouth an inch away from hers.

Luke didn't want the kiss to be too sexual yet, perhaps. But he wasn't letting go of her, either.

She let one hand drift from his neck up to his wet hair. "What was that head shake for? What were you thinking?"

"Nothing," he murmured. "I'm just a lucky man."

And then he kissed her again, and this time there was less restraint. Less control. More hunger. More tongue, more heat, more strength in his hold.

This time, when he ended the kiss, they were both panting. His hand had messed up her chignon as he'd cupped the back of her head, keeping her where he wanted her as he kissed her. He'd controlled her during that kiss, deciding what angle, how deep, when to stop. Patricia felt a little thrill of discovery. *So this is what it's really like to belong to a man.*

That had been a taste. She wanted more. She wanted to lose herself, to let go and let Luke lead her somewhere she'd never been. She trusted him. She could turn her mind off and focus only on this craving that every touch satisfied and stoked simultaneously.

She felt the tension in his arms as he let go, almost like he was forcing himself to step back. "Not here. I don't think I should—it's not the right—not here."

Patricia was drunk on her taste of desire. If this wasn't private enough, she could fix that. She took his hand once more and pulled him deeper into the darkness. Silently, she led him out of the trees toward the hospital. She'd found this shortcut earlier. In moments, they stopped beside their picnic table.

He'd found her sleeping here that first day he'd crashed into her tent. He'd talked to her here last night for hours. Tonight...

Patricia didn't try to hide her smile. She pointed at the sky. "Stars."

She pointed at the table. "Talk."

Then, smiling and sure, loving the way his eyes were eating her up, she stepped into him again, thigh between his, arms around his neck. "Let's fast forward past all that tonight."

He didn't smile back. For a moment, her confidence faltered. She'd misread something. Could a kiss like that be one-sided? He didn't want her. Then he had a fistful of her shirt and his hand cupped under her thigh to lift her body so he could press against her intimately.

She read that message loud and clear.

The hospital building loomed over them, offering protection, offering privacy. Luke took it, lifting her off her feet as he leaned her back against the building, looming over her.

She wrapped her legs around his waist. He said, "I'm not going to make love to you up against this wall, out in the open," and then he kissed her as if he was making love to her.

He kept her secure with one arm around her waist. He pressed the palm of his other hand into the wall by her head, keeping their balance as he rocked his hips into hers. She closed her eyes, loving the way he would move when they didn't have a paltry few pieces of clothing between them.

Her chignon caught in the stucco, tugging strands free a little painfully, but she didn't care. She pressed her head back as he kissed his way down her throat, giving him easy access.

She couldn't have been more willing, more open, more wanting.

Abruptly, Luke stopped. He froze in place, holding her against his waist, head bent into her neck, breathing like he'd just run five miles.

She felt, once more, like she'd made a terrible miscalculation. It was a very cold feeling.

"Patricia, Patricia." Luke pushed off from the building, holding her tightly to his chest, as she kept her legs wrapped around his waist, but then he found her knee with his free hand. He pressed gently, until she lowered her leg to the ground.

"I can't make love to you like this."

"You can't?"

She disentangled herself the rest of the way and stood on her own two feet. Aching with physical need, shaky with confusion, she held her chin high, long years of practice not failing her, even now. "It seemed like you wanted to."

"I want to, darlin'. I want to. But this would be a lousy first time." Luke didn't let her take another step back, but reached for her and pulled her into his chest. He pressed her cheek against the side of his neck and stayed like that, one hand cradling her head, pushing pins into her scalp, for long moments.

Patricia had no idea what Luke was objecting to. Being out of doors? Standing up? Those details were trivial. It was the desire that had been key.

"My head's not in the right place," he said, answering her unspoken questions. "The call we went on today was bad, and I can't forget it."

"You stopped because you were thinking about a traffic accident?"

"I stopped because I was using you to forget it, and that's a lousy reason to make love for the first time." He stopped squashing her, letting go of her head and holding her more loosely around the waist, so they could face each other.

Patricia felt so raw inside. She'd never had a man turn her down cold before. She'd never had a man with whom her desire had burned so hot.

"Isn't that what sex is for?" she asked. "To blot everything out for a moment?"

Luke frowned, so very unlike him that it helped Patricia refocus. Her head was clearing from its descent into passion.

Luke cupped her cheek with a warm palm. "I suppose people have sex for a million different reasons. I can only speak for myself, and the way I feel about you. There's a difference between wanting to make a new memory and trying to blot out an old one. When I have sex with you, I'm not going to want to forget a thing."

"But not tonight." Patricia said it calmly, confirming his timeline, feeling like a child being told her mother would come to visit her, but not this week. "I didn't realize you were bothered by anything. The accident didn't sound bad over the radio."

This time he was the one who took her by the hand, tugging her to the picnic table. They sat down on it, side by side.

"Do you know why they call fire engines out to car accidents?" he asked.

"In case the car catches on fire?"

"It's to free trapped people. Our engine carries the hydraulic Jaws of Life tool to cut through metal."

"Did you have to operate that today?"

"I'm just a volunteer fireman. I don't have certification on that yet. Rouhotas and Zach handle that piece of equipment." After a moment of silence, Luke leaned against Patricia's side. She put her arm around his back. Drew soft circles on his shoulder blade.

"The driver was a young mother. Unconscious. Helicopter standing by while they worked."

"That sounds awful. If you didn't operate the power tools, what did you do?"

"We know she was a mother because she had a little daughter in the back seat. She's this many years old." Luke held up three fingers, like a child would. "Thank God she was in a child safety seat, because that car was upside down, and she was upside down, too, but safely strapped in that five-point harness. While Rouhotas and Zach cut the car apart, my job was to keep the little girl from looking at her mom. You didn't like when I blocked your way the other day, but I crawled in the backseat and blocked her view."

"Oh, Luke." Patricia turned toward him and tried to hold him in her arms, pulling him to her chest, a little like the way he'd held her on the bench when they'd hidden from the rain.

"Three-year-olds don't understand why their moms won't answer them, you know. I kept telling her everything was okay, even the noise of the metal was okay. We don't carry ear plugs small enough for a kid that tiny, so I had to cover her ears with my hands."

"Oh, Luke," she repeated helplessly. Patricia couldn't remember the last time she'd cried. She honestly couldn't remember. A decade? Twenty years? Had she been eleven years old the last time she'd dashed a cheek against her shirt sleeve like this, aware that boarding school was her new life, aware that she'd never live with her mother again? There'd been no point in crying after that.

"It was a piece of cake to get the little girl out once her mother was removed. She had no injuries at all. When I have a kid, she's going to be buckled into a seat like that before I put my key in the ignition. Every single damned time."

He was going to have kids someday. It was a certainty, the way he said it. Those kids would have a daddy who protected them. Patricia didn't want to identify the emotions that thought stirred up.

"I just hope her mother made it. That woman never came to, never even moaned."

The mother had been the one patient airlifted to San Antonio, of course.

"Come with me." Patricia wiped her cheeks with the heel of her hand. She took Luke by the hand and started for the admin tent. "You know that phrase 'better than sex'? I think I've got something better than sex right now. I've got access to a satellite phone, and I can call San Antonio."

"You don't have to do that. Rouhotas will get on the radio tomorrow. Firemen relay info like that."

Patricia sniffed. "That's rumor. I'm going to get you the facts, so you can sleep tonight."

She stuttered to a stop. Luke nearly crashed into her. "If that would help you. Maybe you'd rather wait until morning? The facts might not be good. I can't stand not knowing, but maybe that's just me."

He rubbed his jaw, and it took her a moment to realize he was exaggerating the indecisive move. "Let's see. I could hope for info tomorrow and have Murphy to talk it out with, or I could find out tonight while I've got a beautiful blonde by my side who's being very kind. She's very soft, too, I might add, and a thousand times more fun to kiss than Murphy. Gee, this is a tough one."

"You are just a barrel of laughs, Waterson." Patricia couldn't quite hit her usual acerbic tone. Everything seemed more hopeful now that Luke was teasing her.

They continued walking to the admin tent. "This may not be a great idea, Patricia. Your hair is a mess. People will definitely talk."

Without stopping, she pulled a few pins out, held them in her teeth, made a quick twist of her hair, and stuck them back in.

"Okay, that's distracting. You know men are amazed at how women do that stuff, right?"

Luke stayed outside the tent while Patricia nodded coolly to the night clerks, used her laptop database to find the hospitals in San Antonio that had major trauma centers, and started dialing. No one questioned her right to pull the satellite phone from its orange case.

She'd refused to abuse Texas Rescue resources for her personal benefit, but when it came to Luke, she found it easy. Should Karen ask, Patricia could explain that Texas Rescue personnel had made the rescue, and she'd needed the patient's status for the follow up report. Or, the emergency responders needed to know if their efforts had been successful in order to refine their training. Or—oh, hell.

Patricia would just buy her own satellite phone and bring it next time.

She left the tent to find Luke and tell him the good news. The mother was already out of surgery and had awakened from anesthesia. She was under observation because she'd lost consciousness at the scene, but it was only a routine precaution. She was expected to be moved to a regular bed after twenty-four hours.

"The charge nurse was in a chatty mood, so I got her chatting about how patients fared better when family members were present. I asked her what kind of accommodations her hospital had for out of town families."

Luke pulled her into the shadow between the tents. "I heard some of that. You are one smooth talker, Patricia Cargill. What did the nurse tell you?"

"The husband is there, and the nurse says it's the sweetest thing, how he won't let his daughter out of his sight. The nurse was very proud to tell me how she'd arranged a room for them in the hotel next door. They're going to be okay."

Luke didn't say anything. In the dark, Patricia couldn't read his expression.

"Are you going to be okay?"

He answered her with a kiss that made her go weak in the knees. Patricia didn't worry that she'd fall. She didn't worry about anything at all. Luke was happy, and so was she.

Chapter Fourteen

Patricia couldn't wait for night to come again, but first, she had to face the day. She took her sleeping mask off and rolled onto her back, raising her wrist to squint at her watch out of habit. It took a moment for her mind to register the sounds coming from a few cots away. The distinctive *whoosh* sound that meant a text message had been sent. The chime of an email coming in.

Phones were working. The cell towers had been fixed.

As eager as everyone else, Patricia grabbed her cell phone and turned it on, then laid back on her air mattress to wait for the miracle of technology to begin.

It began slowly. Images of circles spun slowly, loading, loading, as Patricia's phone competed with every other phone in the city to claim space on the network. Thousands of people were undoubtedly trying to download four or five days' worth of information and updates.

Impatient, Patricia sat up and started brushing out her

hair, keeping one eye on her phone screen. This mission had pulled her out of her normal life in the middle of so many issues. There'd been that unauthorized withdrawal from her bank account, which should have been fixed. Patricia pressed the app for her bank account. Its circle started spinning.

She waited for it to open, hoping against hope to find that her father had finally signed the last series of checks she'd written. He'd been sitting on them, doing nothing, as usual. She hadn't had time to cajole him into signing before Texas Rescue had been activated.

She knew her father was busy with his new mistress, but the old one was pouting and getting in his way. Patricia could use that to her advantage. She'd handle the old mistress, if he'd sign her checks. It was a deal she'd made with him a dozen times.

From the cot across from Patricia's, Karen made a little squeal of excitement. Patricia closed her eyes briefly, her only outward show of her inward disgust. Her supervisor shouldn't have already been in bed if Patricia wasn't up and on duty.

Karen smiled at her and waved her phone. "Level eighty-nine, and I got an extra sprinkle ball, too."

"How lovely."

Honestly, what was the polite rejoinder to nonsense like that? *Get the hell off the network. I'm trying to verify that the Cargill donation to Texas Rescue went through. Your paycheck depends on it.*

That would be so satisfying to say. Her father would have said it in a heartbeat, and loudly, which is why Patricia did not. She'd been trained to be twice as classy to make up for his bluster.

Patricia glanced at her own phone. Half the screen had loaded, so she could see the trust fund's balance. Her father must have signed those checks, because the balance was considerably lower than she expected. Millimeter by millimeter, her bank statement appeared, but it froze before loading more than half the screen.

She read the two entries that appeared. The first was Wife Number Three's quarterly allowance, a hefty seven figures. Number Three and Daddy had never legally divorced, and the seven figures hurt less than alimony might have, so Patricia was relieved to see she'd been paid. *Keep her happy with her polo ponies in Argentina, where I don't have to deal with her.*

The second entry was an electronic funds transfer to a jewelry store, the one from which Daddy Cargill liked to buy baubles for his "girls." Patricia had long ago agreed to a standing order that pre-authorized a certain amount every month, so that her father could practice his largesse without consulting his daughter in public.

The two expenditures blurred before her eyes. Money for women, so he could have more women. A family fortune, a Texas legacy, squandered to appease one man's appetites. Patricia had to negotiate for every donation to Texas Rescue. He'd made her crawl before they'd donated an MRI machine to West Central, and then he'd shown up to cut the ribbon and flash his diamonds.

The humiliation would be over soon. She'd been foolish to place all her hopes on Quinn, but she'd find the right husband, and she'd find him before her year was up. She'd win his bet, take her inheritance and start her own branch of the Cargill family. Things would be different.

The first step in winning her freedom was simple: give up Luke Waterson.

The phone screen stayed stuck, half loaded. The jeweler's amount taunted her. Daddy had hit the spending limit already, and it was only early June. She supposed she'd have to call him, but a more unpleasant chore didn't exist.

Someone else in the tent didn't feel the same. Patricia heard a chipper "Hi, Daddy" spoken with such delight, it was startling. The new pharmacy tech was sitting cross-legged on her inflatable mattress, speaking happily into her phone. "Daddy, it's so good to hear your voice. I'm doing great. How are you?"

Patricia closed her eyes, blindsided by a sudden wave of emotion. She had no idea what it would be like to want to hear her father's voice. The joy in the young woman's words speared right past every defense Patricia had, painfully showing her what her life might have been like, had she been born to a different kind of man.

"Oh, Daddy, this has been the best week of my life."

The best week of her life. Patricia knew it was almost over. The cell towers were up. The McDonald's had reopened. The best week of her life would soon end, and her crucial hunt for the right husband would resume.

Patricia let the cell phone slip from her fingers. There was no contact in her directory, no family member, no friend that she wanted to call. The only person she wanted to see right now was a fireman named Luke. She wanted to see him right away, because soon, she wouldn't be able to see him ever again.

Her dearest Daddy—every Texan's favorite Daddy—had made sure of that.

"The rain was good for the grass, but it was bad for the dirt. The herd can't eat the green stuff without getting stuck in the mud."

Luke had been dreading this phone call, with good reason. He'd left the James Hill Ranch in the competent hands of his foreman, Gus, but he'd known Gus wasn't going to have any rosy news for him when Luke called. This morning, when everyone's cell phones had started to work, Luke had known he had to check in, anyway.

"How much feed have you laid out?" Luke asked.

"Hay every day."

Luke saw dollar signs going down the figurative drain. His herd ought to be grazing from pasture to pasture right now, but the mud was making him buy them dinner. The year's profits were literally being eaten up by the day.

"No way around it," Gus said apologetically. "That was a lot of damn rain."

"Yep. We drove through it on the way down here." Luke opened the door to the fire engine's cab and climbed in. He might as well sit while Gus hit him with bad news. "Move as much of the herd to the high hundred as you can. I know they ate it low already, but there should be enough left that you can put out less hay."

"Will do. And boss, I know this is a sore subject for you, but those free-range chickens are running out of dry places to do their free-range thing."

The damned chickens. Luke called them something else out loud, and Gus echoed it heartily.

Luke's mother had fallen in love with the idea of organic chicken-raising the last time she and his father had decided to come home from their endless travels and play ranchers for a while. They'd stayed a month longer than usual, all the way through Christmas. Then his father, one of the generations of James Watersons for whom the James Hill Ranch had been named, had suddenly realized that if he was going to the southernmost tip of South America to see penguins, he needed to do it in the winter. "Because when it's winter in Texas, it's summer near the South Pole."

Thanks for the tip, Dad. When it's winter in Texas, you

*work every day. How about we talk about penguins while
we drive some hay out to the dogleg pasture?*

He hadn't said anything out loud, of course. He loved
his parents, and they'd raised him to be respectful at all
times. But as they'd been doing since he'd turned twenty-
one, they'd packed their suitcases and left him to care for
the cattle, and a bunch of chickens to boot.

Luke had been born on the JH Ranch, because his
mother had been in love with the idea of organic home-
birth at the time. He'd been raised on the ranch. He was
trapped on it.

His older brother, another James Waterson, owned a
third of the JHR. He hadn't been home to the ranch he was
named after in years. Their parents owned a third, which
funded their world travels. Luke owned a third, but ran
the whole damned thing, of course. By default, because
everybody else was older and had left first, Luke was a
rancher, tied to the land for better or worse.

The fence line penned him in as surely as it did his
cattle. He felt it keenly enough that he'd joined Zach as
a volunteer fireman. A man had to be stir-crazy for certain, working natural disasters just for the change of pace.

Still, when this job was over, Luke would return to the
JHR. He knew every square mile. He'd touched every new
calf this spring. He was a cattleman.

But he wasn't dealing with someone else's left-behind
chickens any longer.

"I'll tell you what we're going to do with those chickens, Gus. Sell them."

As Gus agreed heartily over the phone, Luke looked
toward the tent hospital and saw a sight that wiped all his
thoughts of mud and hay and obligations clean out of his
mind. Patricia Cargill was walking toward him, looking

the same as always in polo shirt and knee-length shorts and boat shoes, yet looking completely, utterly different.

Her hair was down.

Luke knew it was long. He'd twisted it around his finger in the dark shower tent, when the strands had been wet and straight. But he couldn't have known how it would look in the sun, full and golden, framing her face and tumbling over her shoulders with every step. Patricia wasn't a princess. She was a movie star.

Luke had never before felt a woman was so incredibly out of his league. He could only stare for a moment. Then his brain began to work again, and he realized that for Patricia to come to him like this, something must be wrong.

"Boss, you there? Which way do you want to get it done?"

"Sure, Gus, that's fine."

Luke hung up and jumped out of the cab. He started walking toward Patricia, since she was clearly heading straight for him, discretion be damned. Luke might have to play it cool for both of them right now.

"What's up?" he asked, stopping a decent foot away from her. They were only a few yards from the engine, and Luke didn't know exactly where his crew were and who was watching.

"Cell phones are working now," she said.

"Tell me about it."

She looked like she had more to say, but she only clasped her hands together. And unclasped them.

Luke realized she wasn't carrying her clipboard or her radio. "Patricia, what's up?"

The sound of air compressors and nail guns filled the air. A construction crew had been on the hospital building's roof since yesterday.

"They're fixing the roof," Patricia said, stating the obvious, and she almost wrung her hands together. "It's only a matter of time now. Our work here is through."

Since she seemed to be sad about that, Luke tried to offer her some hope. "The power's still out."

"That hospital has generators. They only shut the place down because of the roof. If they hadn't lost their roof, we never would have been called down here." She didn't sound like herself. Her voice was shaky. "Your fire engine might have been called down, but they wouldn't have needed my mobile hospital. We're just temporary, you know."

"I know. Would you like to take a walk with me?"

"No, I might cry."

It was the most surprising thing Luke had heard in a long, long time.

"I just wanted to see you," she said, and she unclenched her hands and stuffed them in the front pockets of her crisply-creased long shorts.

"Because the cell phones came on?"

"It's silly, isn't it?"

Luke had a hunch that, like him, she wasn't eager to return to her normal routine. He was also pretty certain that whatever she was returning to was far worse than what he faced.

"Chief Rouhotas is coming," she said, looking over his shoulder. She started speaking quickly. "Tonight could be our last night. We could start breaking down as early as tomorrow."

"Then we'll make the most of it."

And I'll find out what you're afraid to go back to.

"Good morning, Chief," she said, and the smile on her face was almost as politely pleasant as usual. "I wanted to see the fire truck while I still could. Breaking the hospital down will be a twenty-four hour operation like setting it up was. I better play hooky while I can."

The chief was as dazzled by the waves of blond hair as Luke, but he managed to speak with his usual *un*usual courtesy, offering to show her the engine personally.

"Thank you, Chief, but Luke has already promised me a tour," she said, using her perfect manners to neatly force the chief to bow out. Whatever had upset her so badly this morning was a mystery, but Luke was glad to see she was back on her game, at least verbally.

He led her over to the red engine. "Here she is, engine thirty-seven."

Zach and Murphy paused in the middle of wiping down the smooth red side of the vehicle. After they grunted their "good mornings," Luke walked Patricia around the vehicle, opening doors and sliding open compartments, showing her the array of tools and ladders. She seemed impressed at how compactly they stored two thousand feet of hose, so Luke kept talking as the other guys kept cleaning, giving her the same spiel he'd give an elementary school class.

"What are you going to do today?" she asked.

"Murphy's already doing it. We clean. We clean every day."

"Can I help?"

Murphy and Zach didn't hide their surprise any better than Luke did. "It's grunt work."

Patricia picked up a polishing cloth from Murphy's stack and started wiping down the bottom row of gauges on the side of the trunk. They measured hose pressure, foam pressure, even air pressure to the horns. She began wiping down their cases and lenses as if it were routine. She did it well.

All three of the guys shrugged at each other. Zach announced that he was going to clean the other side, since the two of them had this. "C'mon, Murphy."

"Do you call this brightwork?" Patricia's demeanor

didn't change although they were relatively alone. "That's what we call it on a boat. You have to polish all the brass, all the time. Of course, on a boat it's not really made of brass anymore, but everyone still calls it that." She kept polishing, methodically moving from lens to ring, from left to right. She obviously found "brightwork" soothing.

Luke kept one eye on her as he picked up a rag and started polishing a higher row. "I hope you'll get some sailing in, when you get back to whatever you're dreading going back to. I assume 'dread' is the right word."

"Is it that obvious?" she asked quietly.

"Can I help?"

She shook her head slowly. He'd never seen her look so sad. They kept polishing gauges, wiping away every trace of sea salt left by the coastal air.

"Why don't you want this mission to end?" he asked, when they came to the end of their rows.

She folded and refolded the cloth in her hands. "Do you know what the problem is with sailing? The lakes in Texas are huge. I can run full sail for miles, outsmarting the wind, using it for speed. But at the end of the day, I'm still stuck on a lake in the middle of Texas. I haven't gone anywhere."

He took the neat square of cloth out of her hands. "Do you know what the problem is with being a cowboy? On a good horse, you can ride for miles without seeing another soul as far as the eye can see. But at the end of the day, you're still stuck on a ranch in the middle of Texas."

"Come see me tonight."

"Leave your hair down."

Without looking around to see if anyone was watching, she kissed him on the lips, and then she was gone.

Chapter Fifteen

Luke heard Zach's whistle, but he didn't take his gaze off Patricia's receding figure.

"I guess you don't have to paint my helmet when we get back," Zach said.

"I wasn't painting your helmet because I saved your sorry hide from heat stroke."

"That, too. But damn. You got her to kiss you."

Patricia disappeared among the tents. Luke chucked the polishing cloth she'd folded into the bin where they kept the rest.

Zach gave a swipe to an already-shining gauge. "You're not as happy as I would be about getting kissed by a woman with some sexy friggin' hair."

"She's from Austin, right? She must be. We're all part of the Austin branch of Texas Rescue. So answer me this. Why does she act like she'll never see me again?"

Zach was silent, which meant he was actually giving

it some thought. "I can't help you there. Be careful these last few days. I wouldn't want to see it go bad on you."

Murphy came around the side of the truck. "Are you guys going to talk all day? You got time to lean, then you got time to clean."

Zach deliberately leaned against the engine. "No one says that in real life, Murph."

Chief Rouhotas walked up, too. Luke thought they might as well be livestock. A beautiful female had scattered them, and now the men were huddling up, ready to regroup. Luke would've found that amusing, if he'd felt better about the whole situation.

Chief spoke first. "I didn't expect to see Miss Cargill cleaning a fire engine, I'll tell you that."

Murphy's laugh sounded suspiciously like a snort of disgust. "I guess it's fun when it's not your real job. Right, Luke?"

Luke was in no mood for surly remarks. He felt too surly himself. "Your panties are in a wad because I'm an unpaid volunteer? Feel free to share your paycheck."

"I'm just saying it must be nice to stop and chat when you feel like it. No one can tell you to get to work, since no one is paying you. Miss Cargill shows up and wants to flirt, then you get to stop and flirt."

Zach made a great show of banging his forehead on the red metal of the engine. "Murphy, Murphy, Murphy."

The chief just shook his head at Murphy. "I've got a life lesson for you, son. Be nice to money."

"Whose money? Hers, or Luke's?" Murphy jerked his chin at Luke. "At least you work on your ranch. She just sits around and gets her nails done."

The unfairness of his assumption hit Luke in the gut. Sure, Patricia had money. She looked like money, from her yacht-club clothes to the way she carried herself. Murphy had noticed that much, but he didn't recognize the work Patricia did. That required a correction. Luke was in the mood to give it.

He stepped forward. "Did you like your warm, dry bed last night? She's the reason you had a place to sleep. You enjoyed having a hot meal and a shower after that fire, didn't you? Guess who you have to thank. Before you get pissed off that she's got diamonds in her ears, you better be thankful she's got a mind as sharp as a diamond, too. Are we clear on that?"

"All right, okay, enough." The chief backed Luke up a step with a hand on his shoulder.

Zach tried for a joke as he backed Murphy up. "You can't get mad every time a woman likes Luke better than you. It happens for no good reason, now and then."

But Murphy shook Zach off. "Of course she likes him. He owns a goddamn cattle ranch."

Luke didn't like the way this whole morning was going. He tried to follow Zach's lead and laugh it off. "She must just think I'm pretty. She doesn't know I own a ranch."

"Sure, she doesn't."

Back off. Luke rested his hands on his hips. No fists. No fighting stance. But aggressive enough that thick-headed Murphy ought to get the point. "Unlike some men, I don't go around bragging to women about the size of my acreage."

"You got oil wells on your ranch, don't you?"

Obviously, Murphy didn't know when to stop. Equally obviously, he had a chip on his shoulder when it came to money from some past slight. Luke wasn't going to knock that chip off since he hadn't been the one to put it there. He turned away.

"You think a Cargill doesn't know about an oil well?" Murphy said to his back. "Hell, they smell it miles underground. Maybe she's not after your body. Maybe she's after your land."

Luke opened the cab door, prepared to climb up to get the phone he'd left on the seat. Chief's next words gave him pause.

"The kind of oil the Cargills go after is too big for them to concern themselves with a few wells on ranches. If you're going to talk out of your backside, at least know your facts."

Luke turned back around. "She's related to those Cargills?"

Chief was just getting warmed up as he laid into Murphy. "You like this engine, son? Her father bought it. That's right. For years, we struggled to find enough in the budget to maintain the old engine. Then one day, out of the blue, Daddy Cargill himself just writes us a check. Six hundred thousand dollars. And while he was at it, threw in a hundred thousand more so we'd have all new equipment on the shiny new truck."

"Daddy Cargill?" Luke asked. He'd seen him once in Dallas, showboating at an NFL game. He'd walked down the sideline, a rhinestone cowboy, filling his arms with cheerleaders as the crowd took photos.

He was nothing like Patricia.

"This engine was a gift from the oil baron himself. He was wearing a white suit when he came by the station in his Cadillac. Why did he throw nearly a million our way? It's because his daughter works for Texas Rescue, that's why. So you're not going to piss her off, understand me, Murphy? If Miss Cargill likes the fire department, then the fire department gets money. She wants you to put up a tent in hundred degree heat, then you put up a tent, and you smile at her while you do it, understand?"

"Chief." Luke spoke his name firmly, but the chief was on a roll.

"She can come by as often as she wants, and she can touch anything or anyone she wants."

"Chief, that's enough."

"If she wants to talk to Luke, hell, if she wants to sleep with Luke, you get them a bed and you plump the god-damned pillows for them."

"*Chief.*" Now it was Luke backing the chief up a step. "That's out of line."

The chief shut his mouth abruptly. He ducked his head. "Sorry. No offense."

"For God's sake, you have a daughter yourself."

"You're right. Forget I said that, Murphy."

There was nothing else Luke could do. Nothing to say. He could barely think straight.

Patricia was the daughter of Daddy Cargill.

Luke repeated that to himself a few times, but it didn't sound real. To hell with waiting until dark. He wanted to talk to Patricia now.

"I'm going to get coffee." He slammed the cab door shut as he passed it.

"Me, too." Zach ruined his show of solidarity by turning around to holler at the chief. "If any Rockefeller ladies are looking for someone to bat their eyelashes at, let me know. I'm happy to help out the department."

"Hello, Daddy."

There was a long pause. Patricia waited patiently, sitting at her out-of-the-way picnic table, staring at the nearby stucco wall of the hospital that would soon put hers out of business. She'd waited for a break in the construction on its roof to place her call. The smell of hot tar was wafting down, pungent enough to make her consider moving, but while the workers were applying it, the construction noises were minimal.

She listened to the quieter sounds of fumbling on the other end of the phone line. Rustling sheets made such a distinctive noise. Her father had grown so heavy in the past twenty years, he grunted when he tried to sit higher on his satin pillows. Patricia closed her eyes, but it didn't help erase the visual image.

"Hello, sugar. Give me just a moment—don't go anywhere—"

There was no caller ID on the phone by his bed. Last time Patricia had been in that house, the phones throughout had been oversize Victorian abominations of gold and ivory. In what Daddy thought was true Texas fashion, the old-fashioned ivory handsets were made from the horns of steer. Patricia never used them. She didn't have to; she and Daddy had a deal. The tacky palace was his. The lake house was hers.

"All right, sugar, tell Daddy what you need that couldn't wait until tonight, but make it quick. I've got company, but I just sent her to fetch me a snack."

Wait until tonight? Good Lord. Her father thought she was one of his women. He must have already lined up an even newer mistress while he was seeing the new mistress, and the old mistress hadn't been paid off and put out to pasture yet.

"Daddy, it's me. Patricia."

The change of tone was immediate, and defensive. "How am I supposed to know it's you if you call me 'Daddy'?"

"I'm your daughter. Who else would I call 'Daddy'?"

"You're not cute. Get down to business, little girl."

"You haven't signed the checks I left. Only Melissa's." Melissa was Wife Number Three in Argentina. Patricia had checked her banking app once more and gotten a full screen this time. Only Melissa's check and the pre-authorized withdrawals like the jewelry store were listed.

Her father's chuckle was transparently forced. "That's the most important one. Keep the women happy, that's what I always say."

"I'm a woman. It would make me happy to be able to pay for maintenance on the lake house. The staff deserve their paychecks on time. One of the boats needs a new furler and they are all due for bottom jobs—"

"You know I don't like all those fancy boating terms."

"Paint, Daddy. The bottoms of the boats need painted every year. It will cost less than a tennis bracelet, and you give those out like candy."

"No one sees the bottom of a boat, sugar. You should spend the money on yourself. Get your own topside spiffed up. That's the way to get a man."

The insult stung like a slap. Patricia was tallish, and slender, but she had breasts. She just wasn't an inflated stripper. Her father's view of women was distorted after decades of keeping the company he did. He didn't know what a good figure was, and that was all there was to it.

It shouldn't have mattered. Yet, after shedding tears over Luke's experience at the car accident last night, her eyes watered now. How rotten, to have remembered how to cry.

"Your year is almost up." Daddy's reminder was malicious.

Patricia couldn't stand it a minute longer. "I'm sorry, the connection is really bad here on the coast. You're breaking up. I'm going to have to go."

"The coast? What are you doing there?"

"The hurricane. There was a hurricane last Sunday, remember? Never mind. Sign the checks. Please."

She ended the call. Very carefully, she placed the phone on the picnic table, face down. She'd slept so well last night, feeling good because she'd made Luke feel better after a tough accident scene. It was still morning, but already Patricia felt as tired as she'd ever been in her life. She folded her arms on the table and put her head down.

I cannot live my life this way. I will do anything. I will marry anyone I have to.

She felt the bench give next to her.

She only knew one man who was big enough to rock her like that.

An arm brushed her arm. A hip pressed against her hip.

She only knew one man who was confident enough to sit so close to her.

She picked up her head and blinked at the sunny day until her vision cleared.

I will say goodbye to anyone I have to.

"Hello, Luke."

He had no idea what to say.

Nail guns fired high above them on the hospital roof. Patricia was sitting properly at the table, of course, with her hair pinned up properly, too. Luke was facing the other way. He stretched his legs out and leaned back against the table. He knew he ought to say something, but his mind was drawing a blank.

This was getting to be a bad habit of his, chasing after Patricia with no more than a half-baked plan in mind. He'd done it the first day he'd laid eyes on her, when he'd come back for the glove at night. He'd found her right here, and he'd cared enough to make her eat and sleep. In return, she'd cared about him so much that when he'd fought a fire, she'd worried herself nearly sick.

Ah, but that had made for a great night, hiding out from the thunderstorm. Not a bad outcome for a man with no plan.

He'd chased after her again after that, after watching

her work alone through lunch, on some half-baked hunch that she might need a friend during the day as well as a secret lover during the night. She never ate alone now, and it was a helluva lot of fun to tease her in broad daylight. That chase had turned out all right.

Here he was without knowing what he wanted from her. Again.

"Since I said 'hello, Luke' and you haven't said anything, I can only assume you are about to tell me you've had a thought. Perhaps two, given this long silence."

The words were right, a classic Patricia zinger that should have made him grin, but she seemed fragile today.

"I'd say it's less like I'm thinking and more like I'm wondering. For one thing, I'm wondering what it is you're dreading going back to. For another thing, I'm wondering why you didn't tell me you were Daddy Cargill's daughter."

He was watching her closely, but she gave no indication that he'd surprised her at all. Not the smallest flinch.

"Chief Rouhotas told you?" She immediately answered her own question. "It wouldn't have occurred to Quinn to tell you. It had to have been Rouhotas. I could tell that he knew, although he's never said so."

"If he's never said so, then how do you know he knows?"

She laughed, but it sounded as brittle as she appeared. "It's obvious in the way he looks at me." She turned her chin, not her shoulders, just her face, and looked him in the eyes. "Look at how you're looking at me now. Money changes everything."

"I'm not looking at you like Rouhotas."

"No, not quite. It hasn't occurred to you yet to ask me to buy you something."

That shocked him. He was already edgy and frankly angry that he'd been blindsided by Rouhotas. "I don't ask women for gifts. Cash has nothing to do with what I need from you."

"Then what do you need from me, Luke?"

From the roof above them, more nail guns fired away. Their private place had been invaded. Their summer romance was ending.

Not like this. Not here. Not now.

"What I need is more time with you. Have Karen take over at supper, like she's supposed to. Eat dinner early. I'm not waiting until dark to see you again."

Chapter Sixteen

Luke barged into Patricia's admin tent, hauling his bulky, beige turnout coat and pants with him. "Ready, Patricia? It's quitting time."

Patricia froze right along with her clerks. He'd been serious about not waiting for dark. She hoped she looked less surprised than she felt as she stood up from her desk. She grabbed a bottle of water, said good-night to everyone in general and no one in particular, and left. Even with his arms full of his uniform, Luke held the tent flap open for her as if it were a proper door and he was the perfect gentleman.

"Where are we going?" she asked, when Luke headed away from both the permanent and mobile hospitals. He walked with energy, a man who knew where he was going. Gone was the scowl from this morning.

She wished she didn't have to bring that scowl back.

"I borrowed a ride from one of the firefighters in town.

It's part of the code. If your fellow firefighter has a beautiful woman and no way to take her to the beach, then you must loan him your pickup truck. We're going to go gaze at the waves and think deep thoughts—"

"Oh, dear. More thinking?" Her soft-spoken barb came automatically.

Luke grinned, as she'd known he would.

Immediately, she felt guilty, like she'd led him on, letting him believe this would be a fun evening and not a hard goodbye.

"And we're going to watch the sunset," Luke finished.

Tomorrow, Texas Rescue would begin breaking down the less essential tents at eight in the morning. The town hospital was anxious to have them leave. Every day that the mobile hospital operated was a day the town's hospital lost its usual income. It was another sure sign that a town was recovering, when their gratitude for the emergency help turned into calculations of lost revenue.

Money changed everything—except the compass points on the earth.

"There's a small problem with your plan," Patricia said. "If we're watching the waves, we're facing east. I do believe the sun sets in the west."

"Annoying, isn't it? There's an obvious solution. We'll turn our backs on the shore and watch the sunset over the town."

That was exactly what they did. It wasn't as romantic as either of them might have hoped. The buildings on the beach had been hit the hardest. The pink and orange sky was beautiful, but it was viewed over a tattered skyline. They had the apocalyptic scene all to themselves.

"You know, I didn't plan to go riding off into the sunset any time soon, anyway," Luke said. "Let's look at the waves."

As easily as that, Luke turned his back on the negative, and changed their plans. Patricia wished she could be as carefree.

He'd brought his uniform and radio in case there was a fire call. He'd have to drop her off and then meet the engine at the site, but Patricia soon learned that the thick fire uniform also made a good cushion for the bed of the borrowed pickup truck.

Luke made an even better cushion. She hadn't objected when he'd pulled her into his lap. He lounged against the metal wall of the truck bed, facing the gentle waves of the ocean. She felt so safe, curled against his chest, head on his shoulder. It felt like nothing could hurt her when arms as strong as his were wrapped around her.

It was a lovely fantasy. The whole week had been a lovely fantasy. But just as the placid waves of the Gulf of Mexico could turn into the crashing danger of a hurricane, this was only the calm before her personal storm. She couldn't delay it any longer. She had to say goodbye.

"We start breaking down tomorrow," she said.

But Luke had spoken at the same moment. "I let you down today. I'm sorry for it."

"You did?" She looked up at his face, his short hair tousled by the strong ocean breeze, his eyes a beautiful gray in the dwindling light. But his gaze was narrowed as he looked over the abandoned beach, and there was a serious set to his jaw.

"You were upset this morning, so upset that you came to find me. Then I found out that you were related to Daddy Cargill, and I came to find you for the wrong reasons. I asked you the wrong questions."

Patricia tried to think back to exactly what had been said. "I don't remember."

Luke bent to kiss her lightly on the lips. "I asked you

why you didn't tell me you were a famous heiress. What I should have asked you is why don't you want this week to end?"

It was just the opening she needed. *I don't want this week to end, because I'll miss you forever.* It seemed so strange to her that she should end it in his arms, feeling cared for, feeling safe. It would have been better to say goodbye this morning amid the noise of construction and the horrid smell of hot tar, to walk away as he scowled at her.

She had to say it now. "I'm going to miss you. Terribly. You're a good man, in every way. You are very hard to say goodbye to."

"Luckily for us, we don't have to say goodbye."

"This is our last night. We live in different worlds."

"Patricia, we live in Austin. My ranch is about an hour out of town. I mean, sure, that's a little inconvenient, but it's hardly—"

"I can't have you!" Her voice was loud in the metal truck bed. The fact that she'd nearly shouted at him made her feel disoriented. And then, once more, the cursed tears were blurring her vision.

There was no need to shout. Ever. She lowered her voice, but then it came out a whisper, which wasn't right, either. "I can't have you. We had our week, and I loved it. I loved it. But this is our last night, and that's the way it has to be."

"Or else…what will happen?"

"Daddy Cargill will make my life a living hell."

If he'd been serious before, he was ten times that now. "What do you mean? Are you in danger?"

His entire body went on alert. The muscles holding her were suddenly charged, ready to take action.

"Not physically in danger, no. It's being a Cargill. He makes it hell to be a Cargill. It's hard to explain."

"I want to hear it. Please."

"You mean, what's it like to be the daughter of Daddy Cargill?"

"No. What's it like to be *you?*"

The facts were the facts. Whether she told Luke or not, it wouldn't change anything. But just once, Patricia wanted somebody to know the truth. And so, safely tucked in Luke's arms, she started talking. She told him about the money and the signatures, and how they weren't a Cargill myth. She told him about the begging and the negotiating, day in and day out.

"When did you start dealing with this?"

"I was eighteen when I co-signed the first alimony check for my mother. She's Wife Number One. Then I had to sign a check for Wife Number Two. I didn't mind too much, because she'd brought a little girl from a previous marriage into the mix, and I'd kind of liked having another kid in the house. I figured little Becky deserved to go to college and have nice things, since my dad had cheated on her mom. It seemed fair."

Patricia fell silent. She'd forgotten how painful it had been when Number Two and Becky had suddenly disappeared from her life. They'd gone from being part of her life to a check she signed quarterly.

Luke began rubbing her arm with slow, deep strokes. "Go on. I'm listening."

"Fair or not, there was a lot of money going out, and nothing coming in. I started moving our investments around, changing the balance of high-risk stocks and low-yield securities. Daddy didn't care, and the money started growing. Once I started managing the portfolio, though, it became apparent that if I was going to protect my inheritance, I needed to manage the mistresses, as well.

"Daddy was always buying his girlfriends a bracelet or a necklace or what have you. When he was ready to move on, I'd hear him say, 'Take the bracelet with you, honey. It's so you.' It never made a woman happy. Not a single one, and the drama would start. But at this point, I was getting to be around the same age as the mistresses, so I asked myself—"

"How old were you for this?"

"This was when I was about twenty."

Luke stopped his caress and held her tightly for a moment, like a reflex had made him squeeze her a bit. She stole a look at his profile again. He was still alert. Tense.

"I asked myself, what do girls my age really want?" Patricia tried for some levity. "Do you want to guess? Test your knowledge of young bimbos?"

He looked at her, and his eyes, for the first time that she could remember, looked sad. "I probably would get it wrong. There aren't many twenty-year-old girls hanging around the JHR."

Patricia knew that ranches were sometimes referred to by their brands. As cute as names like "the Rocking C" sounded, most ranch brands were a rancher's initials.

"The JHR? Is that that ranch you work on?"

"Every day, unless Texas Rescue calls."

"What does JHR stand for?"

"The James Hill Ranch." He watched her as he said it.

"I don't know if I've heard that one in particular." Patricia rolled the name over in her mind. "Is there a man named James Hill, or is it a corporate holding?"

"There's a James or two, but the Hill is because the main buildings are built on a hill. It's mostly a cattle operation, but there are two oil rigs on the property."

"And as I'm a Cargill, you expect me to know all the ranches that have oil rigs." Her family's lore was common knowledge in Texas. Luke's assumption shouldn't have tasted so bitter.

"Wasn't Daddy Cargill born on an oil rig?" She heard the amusement in his voice. The bitterness grew.

Luke rubbed her arm briskly. "There's no insult intended. Just the opposite. You're so sharp, Patricia. If Daddy Cargill can smell oil a mile away, then I expect you can smell it two miles away."

That was the story, all right. That was the reputation her father worked so hard to maintain. Lifestyle came with being a legend. He was welcomed everywhere, from horse races to the governor's inaugural ball. He was the kind of man everyone wanted to believe had made Texas the great state it was, a self-made millionaire who could smell oil under the ground.

"He's never discovered a drop of oil. He spent one day working on an oil rig because his grandfather made him. Then he threatened to never sign a check for his grandfather, and he never had to work another day in his life."

She probably sounded like an awful person, trashing her own father like this. "The right answer is 'cars,' by the way. Twenty-year-old girls like cars. Not very expensive ones, either, which is lucky. A Mustang will do the trick."

"Lucky. That's what you call lucky? Where was your mother for all of this?"

"Oh, she stuck it out until I was old enough to go to boarding school. Then she moved to Argentina. She loves the polo ponies. Ironically, she and Wife Number Three move in the same circles."

"At what age does an heiress go off to boarding school?"

"I was eleven. It's hard when you are a pimply preteen and you know darned well that you sure as heck can't smell oil. But when everyone thinks being near you gives them a certain *cachet,* you learn to play along. You pretend your life is charmed. You pretend you are an American princess."

"And the next thing you know, you really are?"

"Something like that."

He'd been caressing her arm and dropping kisses on her temple or her cheek, but now he shifted, setting her next to him and turning to look at her fully, face-to-face. "You really are an American princess, Patricia, but it doesn't sound like a good life. If you are tired of it, you can decide to be something else now."

He looked so confident. He sounded so certain.

"Like what else?"

"Like the well-loved woman of a cowboy like me."

If only that were possible, because right now, in the bed of a truck parked on the edge of a dark ocean, she wanted nothing more in life than to be loved by a man like Luke. His words made her heart hurt. She could feel the contraction in her chest.

I still have tonight.

The strong, salty breeze made her eyes sting. Strands of her hair were pulled loose from their pins, whipping her cheeks.

You could be the well-loved woman...

Calmly, Luke tucked the strands of her hair behind her ear. "This wind is too much for that twisty thing you do with your hair."

"It's a chignon," she said, sitting up straighter when she wanted to melt under his touch.

Luke raised an eyebrow at her term, or perhaps at her posture. One corner of his mouth lifted in a bit of a grin, as if she were still amusing despite the ugly tales she'd just told about her own family.

"When you go to school at Fayette," she said severely, to counter his mockery, "it's a chignon."

"Take it down for me."

She shivered.

Luke kissed her, gently, his mouth covering hers for a warm, summery moment. "Take it down for me."

She moved to her knees. With trembling fingers, she lifted her hands and started pulling out pins. Each one fell to the truck bed with a metal ping, a little noise that sounded clearly over the sweep of the waves. When all the pins were gone, she shook her hair out, then turned her face into the wind.

"You are so very, very beautiful."

Luke laid her down, the beige uniform thick and dry beneath her, and then he stretched out beside her. He propped himself on one elbow and smoothed her hair outward, fingertips touching the skin of her forehead and chin as he pushed her loose hair away. The sides of the truck bed shielded them from the wind, so her hair stayed where he smoothed it.

"I enjoy looking at you, too," she said.

He laughed, and she tried to laugh with him, but it might have sounded a bit like a sob. He kissed her, lightly, playfully, like it wasn't the last day of summer camp, and they still had time.

But they didn't.

Patricia reached for him, trying to tell him with her kiss and with her hands in his hair that she wanted him, all of him, before time ran out. Hands and mouths were not enough. She wanted to touch him, everywhere, anywhere she pleased.

She grabbed a fistful of his black T-shirt and pulled, jerking it free from his pants. When she tried to yank it over his head, he helped, sitting up to grab the hem and pulling it off over his head in one beautiful, masculine movement of muscle.

She exhaled at the sight, then sat up, eager to press herself against his bared skin. Her polo shirt was coarse and covered too much of her body, so she imitated him, grabbing the hem and pulling it over her head, leaving her bared except for her sports bra. She barely had time to shake the hair back from her face before he was on her, spreading his hands flat on her back and pressing her body into his. The sensation of skin meeting skin overrode her thoughts, making her melt.

They lay down again, together. Horizontal was where they both wanted to be, pressed together, kissing, kissing. Luke broke the kiss as he rolled to his back. Patricia rolled with him, lifting herself on one arm over him. Before she could start kissing him again, he pulled her bra's shoulder strap down, the firm elastic pinning her arm against her side but freeing her breast.

His mouth was hot and moist, a sure sweep of tongue, a greedy taste of her body. Patricia knew she would not stop this. She wanted to make this memory, like he'd said they should. She'd take the passion now; she could have regrets in the morning.

Oh, she would have regrets.

Just a few days ago, when she'd been so happy to see him after the terrible fire, she'd been afraid he would stop. She'd hugged her knees as she sat on that bench, so afraid he wouldn't touch her as she'd longed to be touched.

She wasn't afraid anymore, because now he knew who she was. If she decided *yes, you may,* then men did not say no to Daddy Cargill's daughter.

Luke shifted positions again as he laid her back and pulled her bra down further, freeing both breasts, sliding her arm out of the strap. He ran his hand gently over her body, making her arch her back, seeking more.

"Did you bring protection?" she whispered.

He hesitated, and she knew he had, just in case. *Daddy Cargill's daughter, what a prize.* But he would be discreet, just like Marcel and the rest she'd so carefully chosen over the years. He wouldn't brag after they'd gone their separate ways.

Luke held himself over her, studying her face in the starlight. "In a truck?" he asked. "On a beach?"

She knew what he was really asking. *Are you sure?*

She smiled at him. *Yes, you may.*

But as his mouth came down over hers, she said, "I won't want to forget a thing."

And then, she started to cry.

Chapter Seventeen

"I can't make love to a woman who's crying. Talk to me, darlin'."

Luke watched Patricia's expression closely. Her poker face was gone. Her hair was a pale blond tumble around her face, her throat tan in contrast, her eyes dark and huge as she stared up at him. She was exposed to him for once, her cool and haughty veneer gone as she lay beneath him, her naked breasts pressed beneath his chest.

She wiped her tears with a single swipe of her hand. "It's nothing. The wind."

Incredibly, she seemed to think she could hide from him, still, but he could read her like he'd never been able to read any other woman. She was aroused, but she was feeling desperate about more than just his body.

"It's something. Tell me."

"We've talked enough. I don't want to talk. I want to make love to you."

"That makes two of us."

As she blinked up at him, more tears trickled from the corners of her eyes, rolling into her hair.

Sexual frustration combined with true concern. He shifted to the side, but her body, bare from the waist up, was too hard to ignore. He grabbed his T-shirt and bundled it over her. Maybe she'd feel more secure if she was less exposed. He didn't know. She was complicated, but by God, he was into her. This was so much more than sex.

She pulled his shirt aside and pulled his head down for a kiss. "This will still be great," she said, and then kissed him again, rebuilding their passion to where it had been a minute before. "It will still be great."

"Even though...fill in the blank for me, Patricia." The physical demands of his body clamored for him to forget it. Take what she offered. He commanded himself to control the need. "This will be great, even though what?"

She blinked up at him, perhaps surprised he wasn't giving in to her seduction. "It's just..."

Then she closed her eyes, and he looked at her dark lashes on her smooth skin as she whispered what sounded like a fervent wish. "It would have been so nice if you hadn't known. Just once, to have a lover who didn't know."

He could feel her heartbreak. What must it be like to live as she did, always with her father's legend over her head? Never knowing at age eleven or twenty or thirty-two if someone wanted to be with you because they liked you, or because they wanted a taste of that Cargill *cachet*.

He wished he had a blanket to cover her for this conversation, but since he didn't, he interlocked his fingers with hers, and brought their joined hands to rest between their hearts, hiding her nudity with their arms. *Cuddling*. It wasn't a word he ever used, but he sure didn't mind having Patricia close.

"How soon you forget," he said. "When I asked you if

you'd known Quinn, didn't I make it clear that nothing in your past mattered to me? Nothing changes the fact that I can't stop thinking about you, every minute of the day."

"Now that you know I have money, I bet that's about a million times more true."

Her words were tough, but she looked so vulnerable beneath him, her words only made him more aware of the lifelong depth of her pain. "Patricia, Patricia. Money has hurt you so badly. I don't want to talk about money. Let's talk about love."

"Love?"

That cooled her ardor. Luke was sad to feel it, the little recoil in her body.

"Love me, love my money, it's all the same," she said. "You can't separate one from the other."

"But I did. Until this morning, I had no idea whose daughter you were. So all week, I've been kissing you, not your money."

He kissed her again. "Does that feel like I'm kissing money? You must know what it feels like when a man kisses the Cargill heiress. Go ahead. Close your eyes. Remember some other man for a moment."

"You want me to think about another man?"

"Yes."

"You're crazy. Men don't like to be compared."

"It's for a good cause. Close your eyes. Remember him. Remember the guy before him."

He studied her closed eyelids once more, waiting until it looked like she was concentrating as he'd asked.

The jealousy was worse than he'd thought. He controlled his breathing, like he was wearing a mask. Waited another moment, and then he kissed her. He kissed her to make her forget. He kissed her as if he could draw all that pain and uncertainty from her.

He kissed her as if she were his one and only. She was the only woman in his world, the only woman who really touched his heart.

My God, that's who she is.

She began kissing him back, passion for passion, until she made a little whimper of need that nearly sent him over the edge.

He tore his mouth away, ending the kiss abruptly and panting as he concentrated on controlling this lust that was more than lust.

"Do you see it?" he said into the warm space filled by their mingled breaths. "Do you see the difference? This is a man who is kissing Patricia, only Patricia, not an heiress. I kissed you in the rain under a tree, do you remember? The night when I came back from the fire, we kissed in the rain. Close your eyes and remember that. Then lightning struck, and we hid in the showers, and we kissed some more. Remember those kisses."

He kissed her again, remembering the rain himself, and the surprising, soothing sweetness of knowing she cared about him. This kiss, he ended gently.

"It felt like that," he said. "It doesn't matter if you have a billion dollars, I'm kissing my beautiful, mysterious Patricia when I kiss you."

She opened her eyes, humbling him by looking at him as if he'd hung the stars above them. Another tear ran down from the corner of her eye, but this time, Luke understood. This tear was different. He could kiss it away.

They began removing their remaining clothes, anticipation tempered by a near reverence at what they were about to do. Luke lowered himself over her, pausing one last time to whisper in her ear.

"And when we make love, you'll remember the night of the fire and the rain, and you'll know that the first time I brought you release, you were Patricia to me. You are Patricia to me still. Always."

The next meeting of the Texas Rescue and Relief leadership team was uneventful for everyone except the daughter of Daddy Cargill.

The meeting started inauspiciously in one of the conference rooms at West Central Texas Hospital. Karen Weaver droned on, attempting to disguise her incompetence with long-winded explanations. Impatient with Karen's nonsense, Patricia opened her email on her phone. The message from the bank stopped her heart.

Please be advised that there will be a maintenance fee assessed this month due to a low account balance.

Impossible. The daily interest on the trust fund was enough to keep the account above the minimum balance. This insanity had to stop. The balance hadn't been stable since the hurricane. As soon as Patricia challenged one expenditure, another unauthorized one would appear.

She preferred to call on the bank by appointment. Appearances were everything with her father's cronies, so she usually ensured they were assembled and waiting for her entrance. Then she would arrive wearing the appropriate attire for negotiation, a severe suit with the length of the skirt tailored precisely to midknee.

This email was the last straw. She was done with their games. The bank wasn't far from the hospital. She could use the element of surprise to her advantage. Besides, although her tailored slacks were grey and her silk blouse was pink, their pastel colors were icy, not to be mistaken as weak. She would remove the string of pearls, though. They might be seen as feminine. Weak.

She felt weak.

Darlin', you do not look like a woman who was well-loved last night. You're more worried this morning than I've ever seen you. I have to ask you again, when you return home, are you going to be in any danger?

The mobile hospital had broken down and packed up in a record fast forty-six-hour stretch, but engine thirty-seven had been sent home early in the process. Luke had had no choice but to go. The engine had to carry its full crew. Patricia had used those regulations to prevent Luke from persuading her to extend their romance beyond its week's limit.

I told you the truth last night, Luke. I'm going to miss you. This was a week of summer-camp romance. So very real, but unable to last. I just can't see you anymore.

Karen droned on. Patricia stole a look around the conference room at her fellow directors. She apparently was no longer the only one who could see through Karen's act. Things were going to change, and soon.

I remember the day after our first kiss. You tried to deny that we meant something then, too. This is no summer romance, darlin'. You're going to have to get used to being loved for more than a day or a week.

Don't be so kind, the daughter of Daddy Cargill had said, chin in the air, spine straight.

Give me your number. We have the rest of our lives to sort this out.

She'd pronounced each digit precisely. He'd typed them in his phone. Looking her square in the eye, he'd held his phone up and hit the green call button. Her phone hadn't rung.

He'd taken her phone from her hand, dialed his own number, and let his phone ring twice before silencing it. In equal silence, he'd kissed her on the cheek, then just as chastely on the lips, and he'd climbed into the cab of engine thirty-seven.

"I'm sure the operational expenditures will be counterset by the financial expenditures of the host city," Karen said.

Patricia jerked her attention back to the issue at hand. Karen was speaking accounting gibberish. If she stayed at the helm of Texas Rescue, she'd run its finances into the ground as surely as Daddy would if he didn't get her approval on every move.

She studied the phone in her lap again, refreshing the screen for the banking app. The door to the conference room opened. Out of the corner of her eye, she saw the polished leather of a cowboy's boots stop by her chair. Dark blue jeans. Slowly she lifted her head. Pale blue Western shirt.

Sailing blue eyes.

"I'm sorry I'm late," Luke said. "Is this seat taken?"

Chapter Eighteen

The meeting was adjourned.

Luke stood and got Patricia's chair. She looked so achingly familiar, yet different. Her boat shoes had been replaced by high-heeled silver sandals, impractical but sexy. He'd gotten used to seeing her trim calf muscles at the mobile hospital, but now her legs were hidden by immaculate creased slacks. She looked more like a beautiful, off-limits princess than ever.

He spoke to her as if she wore shorts and ate in mess tents. "I thought that would never end. You actually volunteer to sit in these meetings?"

She didn't quite look at him. "You actually volunteer to go into burning buildings?"

"Ah, that's the Patricia I know and love. It's good to see you."

"Thank you." She snuck a peek at him. He noticed, studying her as he was. She wasn't immune to him, but she sure didn't want to be attracted to him.

It made no sense. They should be openly in love, holding hands and making goo-goo eyes at each other until everyone was sick of them.

She picked up a purse with leather that was dyed so close to the shade of gray of her pants, it nearly disappeared. It was hard to imagine this woman living on his ranch. He had to remember the hard worker who'd tied knots in tent ropes. *That* Patricia would be at home on the JHR.

Which Patricia did Patricia prefer to be?

For once, he hadn't pursued her with a half-baked plan. He'd come determined to bring her to her senses. She hadn't called him, and he'd been certain that meant her life was miserable. He'd come to save her. They belonged together.

Seeing her in this environment gave him pause, he had to admit. She looked incredibly affluent in her pearls and silk clothing, a woman of leisure who chose to volunteer her time. She didn't look like someone whose life was a living hell.

Her cell phone vibrated, still on mute from the meeting. She glanced at the screen. "Excuse me, I need to take this. It was lovely seeing you again."

She walked briskly toward the door as she answered the phone in her cool and cultured voice, leaving him behind.

The pain of being dismissed was sharp. It simply wasn't *normal* for her to act that way toward a man she'd shared so much with. Was this some high-society game, a test to see if he'd come to heel?

Luke wasn't in the mood to play games. If she wanted to know if he'd follow her like a puppy dog, then she'd find out. He'd follow her, all right. But when he caught up, they were going to talk.

In the hospital hallway, she turned right, walking at a

steady clip as she spoke. "No, I will not pay for an after-market paint job. I'm sure the Mustang is available in at least one color that she will find acceptable. The sunroof option is fine. Randolph, I would appreciate it if you could limit any further requests from this one. Perhaps tell her everything else is standard, or that the order has to be placed by noon. Whatever it takes. Please."

The please was Luke's undoing, as always. Patricia should not have to beg him for anything, and she sure as hell shouldn't have to beg a car dealership to run interference between herself and one of her father's cast-offs. His irritation toward her softened; his disgust with her father grew.

"Patricia."

She was startled by the sound of his voice, jerking her hand a bit as she dropped her cell phone into her purse. Not normal behavior for the confident personnel director, again, and Luke hated to see her this way. He slowed his steps, taking his time to cover the polished linoleum between them. He stopped just a little bit too close to her. She didn't move away.

He'd missed her so much. *I love you* would have been so easy to say. It was close to frightening, the way he had to consciously not speak the words.

"You shouldn't have come," she said, and then the chemistry took over, and she was kissing him at least as hungrily as he was kissing her.

"You two should get a room." Quinn's voice boomed in the sterile hospital corridor.

Patricia pushed away from Luke as if she'd been caught doing something forbidden, darting looks down the hall like a nervous bird. Something was wrong, and Luke needed to find out what it was.

"Do you have a room we could use?" Luke turned to

Quinn. The look on his own face must have been intense, because Quinn's expression turned sober.

"Most of the conference center should be unlocked. Help yourself." Quinn stepped back as Luke took Patricia by the hand and led her back the way they'd come.

The second door Luke tried was unlocked. He pulled Patricia in with him, then turned and shut the door. Neither one of them hit the lights. A week without contact had left them starving for one another. It wasn't just him. She felt the same, her need obvious in the dark as she wrapped her arms around his neck and pressed her body to his.

The high heels changed the angle that their mouths met. The silk of her shirt was nothing like the cotton of her Texas Rescue polo. She was new, she was familiar, she was his.

After long moments of physical communion that filled Luke's soul, Patricia backed away. Her voice was less than steady in the artificial darkness, like she was on the verge of bolting. "I've got to get to the bank."

Luke tried for humor. "It's a sad thing when a woman would rather go to a bank than keep kissing."

"You make it so hard."

"Well, thank y—"

"Damn you, why do you have to make everything so hard for me? I have to go to the bank. I have to do a lot of things, and I have to do them quickly, and you are making it so hard."

Luke fumbled for the lights. In the sudden brightness, Patricia looked just as upset as she sounded.

"Then we'll go to the bank," he said. "Together."

"No, we will not. I have a life that cannot include you. I told you that."

"Or else Daddy Cargill will make yours a living hell.

I remember. It's apparently already a living hell. Let me help."

She put her hand out to stop him when he tried to step closer. With distance between them, she took a deep breath. She stood taller, graceful in her high heels. "I explained that incorrectly. I should have said that my life is a living hell now, but if I leave you and keep my focus on what I have to do next, I can be free of Daddy Cargill forever. I will have my own life. I want, more than anything, to stop living his."

"I want that for you, too. I'll do anything I can to help. I'm all yours, all my time, all my energy."

"Oh, Luke." She looked at him, finally, with an expression more like the one she'd had in the pickup truck, under the stars. A tightness in his chest eased. She was still his Patricia.

"You cannot help me at all, my darling."

He put his hands in his jean pockets, because she so clearly didn't want his touch. "What is it you have to do that I can't help with?"

"I have to marry another man."

The hit was hard, like hitting the ground after being bucked off a stallion.

He saw red. "Who?"

"I don't know yet. I have to find him. There's a set of criteria that must be met for the terms of the deal. My time is running out to find someone suitable."

"Terms of the deal? No one can make you marry anybody. You know that. You must know that."

"It's a personal bet between Daddy and me. We shook hands on it. You've heard of Cargill handshakes. If there's one thing he has, it's pride in his own legend. He started offering me a deal, my financial freedom if I could prove that I was single by choice, not because I couldn't land a man. He was running off at the mouth in front of his friends, but I saw my chance. He was forced to shake when I agreed to his terms."

"You don't really think the man is going to honor this deal, do you? I assume you're talking about serious money. A million dollars? More? Your deal is unenforceable by law. He won't follow through."

"He loves his own legend. A Cargill deal must stand. No welching, no cheating, no changing the terms."

She was actually excited about this. As she spoke, she looked more animated. She looked like a woman who could run the world, so confident was she that she could win this bet.

It was a sick bet, made with a sick man. Luke had to find a way to show her that, before it was too late.

She actually placed her palm on his arm, a soothing gesture, as if so little could fix this mess. "You can see why you are a terrible distraction. I only agreed to a week's romance with you. I need you to stick to that deal, so that I can stick to mine. Please."

A week's romance? He ought to throw her over his shoulder and take her back to his ranch. That week hadn't been long enough. Not nearly long enough.

She was begging him, *please,* but it hadn't been long enough, because it hadn't been a full week. Zach had passed out while they'd been flipping those ambulances on a Tuesday. Engine thirty-seven had been sent home on Sunday. Six days.

"You expected me to take that week literally?"

"Yes, of course. Please, Luke."

"You can stop begging me. First, I hate to hear you beg for anything. But second, you owe me one more day."

"But…"

He could practically see her counting the days on a

calendar in her head. "You owe me one more day," he repeated. "No welching, no cheating, no changing the terms of the deal."

She was all offended dignity, the princess drawing herself up to stare down her peasant.

Luke could finally find it in himself to laugh. "Forget the bank. Today is my day. Don't bother glaring at me." He kissed her lightly on the lips. "I'm going to show you a good time, princess, and it starts right now."

He hit the lights, and took her in his arms, and let chemistry do the rest.

Patricia couldn't deny it. She'd never been happier to be forced to obey a man. Luke wanted to remind her of what the truly good things in life were, he said. So far, they'd involved kissing her senseless in a hospital conference room and feeding her Mexican vanilla ice cream with candy crushed in it.

He handed her up into his truck, for she'd needed a boost to climb into the pickup's cab. It seemed to be a ranch vehicle, meant for pulling horse trailers, because it had a significant hitch on the back. It was hardly her style, but when Luke swung into the cab and settled behind the wheel in his denim and boots, he looked almost as sexy as he had in his red suspenders. A fireman cowboy. Lucky her.

For one day.

Then she'd get back to the real world.

They didn't drive far, just from the hospital to Lady Bird Lake, the wide part of the Colorado River which Austin's downtown was centered around. Luke parked in front of a humble chain hotel, the kind found at interstate exits across the country.

"Really?" she asked him.

They were going to spend the rest of the afternoon in a hotel room. Her body said *yes*. Heck, her mind said *yes*, too. But her heart knew that passion was fleeting, even destructive. She'd seen three marriages die passionate deaths, and her childhood die with them. If Luke thought she'd give up her chance at lifelong freedom from Daddy Cargill because he'd shown her that an afternoon of sex was fun, then Luke didn't know her as well as he thought. Maybe not as well as she'd hoped.

Have I been hoping for him to change my mind?

He paused to kiss her in the lobby. He paused to kiss her by the elevators, and then he pushed through the glass doors to go out the other side of the hotel, and Patricia realized he knew her very well. Oh, so very well.

The park between the hotel and Lady Bird Lake was littered with sailboats on trailers. Little two-man boats with colorful sails were just waiting to be rolled into the water. They were nothing like her sailboats, her twenty- and thirty-five-foot beauties moored at her house on Canyon Lake, but they were sailboats all the same, designed to catch the wind and race across water.

Patricia looked to the sky, automatically checking the sunny weather. The lake was perfectly calm. Luke came up behind her and pulled her to his chest.

She sighed. "We're not dressed for this."

He kissed her ear. "I only have a day. No time for wardrobe changes. If you feel a wardrobe malfunction is imminent, though, be sure to get my attention first."

"You're really not as funny as you think you are, Waterson."

She wanted to smile as she said it, but she suddenly felt very, terribly sad. Sad enough to cry, and there was something about Luke that seemed to make her want to cry. It was a weakness around him.

"Are we going to go sailing?" she asked. Weakness made her impatient.

Luke spread one arm wide, gesturing toward the variety of sailboats before them. His voice was strangely serious when he spoke.

"Choose your destiny."

Chapter Nineteen

The two-man sailboat skimmed with surprising speed along the water. Luke recognized that there were expert hands on the reins, to put it in cowboy terms, so he reclined next to Patricia as she perched at the rear of the boat and handled everything with ease. He practically had his head in her lap, so he could look up at her and enjoy her pretty face. She looked completely and utterly at home, focused and yet relaxed. His Thoroughbred was doing what she'd been born to do.

"He has to be the right age," Patricia said quietly.

Luke almost asked *who?* because he'd been so content to watch her blond hair in the sunlight. The pins had lost their battle as soon as Patricia had captured the wind.

"Not too young, not too old," she said. "At least average-looking, although my father and his cronies are strange people to judge male beauty."

"So far, so good."

She looked down at him and smiled, but she didn't seem happy. Maybe resigned was the right word for her expression.

"I think you're too good-looking. Daddy wouldn't like that."

Luke thought back to the NFL game where he'd seen Daddy Cargill. He was an imposing figure. Patricia shared his bone structure. It bothered Luke to be reminded that the bastard was truly her father.

"He must own land. Texas land, of course, and not just a little suburban house plat. Oil fields would be best, but Daddy didn't technically say there had to be oil on the land. He must have a million in liquid assets. Cash he can get his hands on, not something like a vacation home that's appraised at a million."

Luke recognized himself. He felt unnaturally calm. His emotions were neither hot nor cold. He just existed for a moment, letting Patricia's words sink in.

He was the perfect candidate for her husband hunt. The liquid assets were high, and he thought only a fool would keep that much ready cash or stocks on hand, but Luke could sell off his cattle early in the season, if a man really needed a bank balance to read a certain number on his wedding day.

He thought this all through in a detached way. Then one clear emotion broke through his neutral review of facts: outrage.

There was no way on God's green earth that he was going to play any game by Daddy Cargill's rules. If Patricia realized he was not just a cowboy—and God, he hadn't meant to deceive her so thoroughly, but now he was glad he had—then he'd end up with a wife who'd married him for his money. He'd marry Patricia Cargill if she asked, but only when she realized how much she loved him, not how much land he owned.

My God, I would marry Patricia Cargill.

The truth of it was obvious, now that he'd thought the words. He rubbed his jaw, wanting to file away these sudden revelations before they showed on his face. From now on, he was a cowboy, and nothing more as far as Patricia Cargill could know. A cowboy who loved her.

"The last requirement is fairly easy. He has to have a job. How many men would meet the other requirements without working? People who just slip into an inheritance are very rare."

"Present company excluded." He congratulated himself for coming up with a rejoinder when his mind was still reeling.

"I am very rare."

"But you do work, and hard, for Texas Rescue."

"Thank you. It's a pretty unfair parameter for my father to place, though, considering Daddy's never worked a day in his life. His cronies probably believe the oil-rig story. Everyone does."

"Except me."

"And my mother. I wonder if she always saw through him, or if her first year of marriage was a crushing disappointment."

"You could ask her."

"That would imply that we have some kind of regular communication."

His poor princess. Such a hard life she'd been handed on her silver platter. But she didn't have to keep living it. This day was meant for him to show her a better option.

"This is the good life," Luke said. "Is there really anything more that you need?"

The sail began to deflate. Patricia loosened a rope and

wind pulled the nylon taut immediately. "Why do I think this is a loaded question?"

"Can you sail and kiss me at the same time?"

"That's definitely a loaded question."

She made him wait for it, but she finally bent over and kissed him. She even slipped him a little tongue, shy and quick. Funny how she could be shy after they'd made love out in the open, under the stars.

"You're making the sailing tricky by lying on my side of the boat," she said. "I have to compensate for the uneven weight."

"You like the challenge."

She quirked her lips a bit. "You could just move over to the other side and lay down there."

"That would put the rudder between us. I don't want a rudder in my face. I like what's in my face right now just fine." He settled his head more firmly in her lap and looked up at her face. Of course, he had to look past her boobs to get to her face.

When she looked down at him, he wiggled his eyebrows and was rewarded with a laughing roll of her eyes. She was so beautiful when she laughed. She was beautiful when she didn't laugh, too. And she was most beautiful when...

"Can you make the boat stop?" he asked.

"Stop? We're cruising perfectly."

"Yes, we are. Make the boat stop, darlin', and then lay down here with me. We haven't had enough chances to make memories."

She made him wait again, an eternity this time as she tacked the boat, but when she had them in an uncrowded spot, the sails went slack and she started tying things off.

"When I wonder if there is anything more I really need in life," he said, as she settled beside him, "my answer will always be more of you."

She didn't answer him in words, but her responsive body gave him the answer he wanted to hear.

They turned the boat in as the sun was setting. Luke didn't want Patricia to see the color of his American Express card as he paid for the extra time they'd kept the boat. He'd be damned if she chose him now for being rich.

He just wanted her to choose him.

So before he gave the rental attendant his card, he gave Patricia the keys to his truck, knowing full well she'd go dig out the cell phones he'd left in the glove box. What he hadn't expected to find when he joined her in the truck cab was a white-faced, shell-shocked Patricia.

"What's wrong? What happened?"

"My mother called. She never calls." Patricia held out her phone and played a voice mail.

Hello, Patricia. I hope you're well. I did hear the most interesting news today, and I wondered if you'd heard it, as well.

The voice sounded distinctly like Patricia's. Bone structure from her father, vocal cords from her mother—he wondered if Patricia realized she shared more than a famous name with her family.

The Houston Cargills got a ruling on their trust fund. It seems the court decided that Cargills by marriage can sign the name as legitimately as Cargills by birth. Of course, it doesn't matter to me, but I did wonder if dear Melissa's divorce had ever gotten filed. She's been missing from the club for the last few days. You might want to check into it, dear. Everything's fine here, give your father my love. Or better yet, don't. Ciao.

Luke looked at Patricia's white face, and he knew someone named Melissa had a legal marriage to Daddy Cargill.

Patricia tapped one particular app on her phone. "I noticed a strange charge the Friday before the hurricane."

He wasn't sure what a man was supposed to do in this situation. Commiserate with the heiress? He tried. "And then you were at the disaster site without any way to check."

Her phone screen changed color, and she looked into it like she was looking into a crystal ball.

What the heck. He might as well ask. "How bad is it?"

"About a million so far."

He was struck silent. The one aspect of the Cargill legend that was apparently true was the income.

Her crystal ball must have shown her something awful. She literally backed her face away from what she saw on the phone. "Half a million dollars just cleared today. Today."

Her gaze locked on his, her eyes extra dark in her unnaturally pale face. "I was on my way to the bank. You stopped me."

He said the first thing that came into his mind. "I'm sorry."

She was chillingly calm. She even leaned back into the seat as she gazed out the windshield at the humble cars of the hotel patrons. "Half a million dollars today, while I was sailing. We had half-a-million-dollar sex. I am my father's daughter, after all."

The truck cab seemed huge. Patricia was too far away physically. He was afraid she was growing unreachable, mentally, but he tried. "If this Melissa is a legal second signature, then they could have authorized that half-million right in front of you. You would have watched it happen, and you wouldn't have been able to stop it. Are you listening to me? I'm glad you were sailing. You couldn't have stopped it."

"You're right, of course. The sailing was very nice."

Yeah, she was not in a good place mentally. Luke walked around the truck to her side, yanked open her door, and bodily lifted her out of the cab. It was enough to snap her out of her daze.

"What are you doing?"

"Are those sandals comfortable? Good, because we're going for a walk."

They hadn't gone far when Patricia suddenly snapped her fingers and stopped on the hotel's sidewalk. "It's not legal. In Dallas and Houston, you need three signatures for every expenditure. The only reason Austin requires two is because there are only two Cargills in Austin. If Melissa is now the third, then all three of us needed to sign. I'll phone the bank first thing in the morning. It's going to be a mess, but it can be undone."

Luke looked her over. Her color was returning to normal. "Honestly, I don't know whether to be appalled or impressed."

But she was still rolling with her train of thought, dollars and legalities on her mind. "I need to make this marriage happen more than ever. Every time Daddy gets married, I'm going to have to convince both him and his wife to sign for every expense. That will be a nightmare. I've got to get out while I can."

The woman he'd just made love to was planning to marry a stranger as soon as she could. It made Luke's stomach turn.

"Listen to me, Patricia. Walk away from the money. It's making you miserable."

"My inheritance is not making me miserable. Daddy Cargill is."

"That's the problem. If this marriage takes place, and if your father honors his deal, you still won't be free of

Daddy Cargill. His share of the money will still require your approval."

"I'll have to sign his checks, but I won't care how he spends his half."

Luke laughed, because otherwise he'd break down. He knew she didn't see the absurdity of her claim. "You will care. You can't stand to see Cargill money wasted. You say he has pride in the Cargill legend, but you're the same."

She stepped back. "Don't say that. Don't say I'm like him."

"How long do you think it will take him to lose his last penny?"

She pressed her lips together.

"You've already calculated it, haven't you? You know exactly how fast he'll lose it. You're looking forward to proving that you can handle your half better. It's poison, don't you see? That money has owned you for thirty-two years."

"Do you think I don't know that?" She looked so fierce, standing there with her arms crossed over her chest and her hair hanging wild. Fierce, and all alone.

"Choose to walk away."

"The law won't let me."

"The law can't force you to be rich, Patricia. You're choosing the money, and you're choosing it over me, damn it."

They'd raised their voices at each other. They were facing off like fighters, not lovers.

"Don't tell me what to do. *Don't tell me what to do.* You cannot possibly imagine what it's like to be me. Money hasn't destroyed my family. Passion has. Passion like this. I never raise my voice. I never cry. This is what rips marriages apart. This is what destroys families. Don't tell me to choose this."

"You can't decide not to feel passion." Luke remembered, suddenly and too late, how she'd been so distressed when she couldn't *not* care about a firefighter. About him.

"Darlin', passion can be a bond, too. It can hold two people together."

She looked away from him, impatient. "It does not. Sex is fine. People get together, they have a few laughs, someone moves on. But passion is different. People yell, and they cry, and they leave without letting you say goodbye.

"You think I'm crazy to choose a marriage without passion, but I'm not going to be like my father. He loves the drama and the ups and downs, and he forgets what's important. He'll remember now. For the rest of his life, he'll remember that the spinster he laughed at for not knowing passion turned out to be the best Cargill of them all."

Luke let her words sink in, trying to imagine the little girl she'd once been. "Your father has done a lot of damage to you. I can see why you want your revenge."

"Revenge?" She frowned as she repeated the word.

"I imagine that after thirty-two years, it would be very hard to be this close and then deny yourself your revenge."

"That's such an ugly word."

"I can't tell you what to do. I'm hoping you decide to forgo it, though, because I love you."

She looked up at him then, eyes wide. Alarmed, perhaps.

"It's not a crazy kind of love. It feels very solid in here." Luke pressed his fist to his chest. "I know I came into the game at the last minute, but I want to offer you a choice. You can finish your game, and be Patricia Cargill, the heiress who saved the family fortune from Daddy Cargill's ruin, or you can be Luke Waterson's woman. Loved and valued and cherished."

"I can't be that and Patricia Cargill, too?"

"You can. You are. But it seems to me that Patricia Cargill doesn't particularly enjoy her life. You could be Luke Waterson's girl, and you could relax your guard, and you could—"

"Lose my inheritance." She said the words adamantly. "I had no childhood because of it. I've spent my entire adult life fighting my father to keep it. It's not revenge, Luke. It's justice. I deserve to have the life I want. I want to spend money on what is important to me. To me, do you understand? Without sweet-talking and wheedling and begging any man for permission to do what I want to do. I'm thirty-two. I will have my own life, and I will stop enabling his. I will."

She was so angry, she was crying.

Luke held open his arms. It was her choice. If she wanted his comfort she had only to walk forward.

She did. Luke closed his arms around her, and she clung to him while she tried so pitifully to not cry.

"I know Patricia Cargill is unhappy," she said, not sobbing, "but I am her, and I will get free of my father no matter what it takes."

Luke stroked her hair. "Then you be her, and this cowboy will love you, anyway. I just pray you choose to let go of the poison. The money is poison. The revenge is poison. I don't want to lose you."

Chapter Twenty

The night of the annual Cattleman's Association black-tie gala would be the night Patricia Cargill found the right man to marry. It was her last chance. She could not fail.

It had been two weeks since she'd gone sailing with Luke, two weeks of using cold logic to choose the course of her life. She'd spent a sleepless night imagining marriage to Luke. As Mrs. Waterson, she would remain in her current financial situation. She'd be no worse off than she'd been for the past thirty-two years, with the positive addition of living with a man who loved her.

Daddy, Melissa, I need an allowance established at the feed store. No, more than that. Luke needs a new saddle. Yes, I know he got new bridles, but these things wear out when you're a cowboy.

Luke would not have taken a dime of her money. She could not have bought him a gift, because her money was always half Daddy's. Children would be an issue. One child would bring the amount of Austin Cargills to four, depending on Daddy's marital status. Two children would mean five Cargills. When they turned eighteen, her two children could help her overrule Daddy and his wife *du jour*.

That possibility, more than any other, decided Patricia against marrying Luke. She would not curse his children with the Cargill fortune.

She did not return his calls. He left her messages several nights a week when he could get away from the JHR. He'd wait in the Driskill Hotel's famous bar, knowing she'd be comfortable in that elegant atmosphere, in case she wanted to talk. In case she needed a friend. She did not show up, not the first time he did this. Not any of the nights he did this.

She cried a lot, but she made her list of eligible men. There were only three. Unsurprisingly, they all owned ranches. They would be at the Cattleman's ball.

How perfectly convenient.

Her limousine entered the last set of gates at the breathtaking estate that was owned by one of the members of the board of directors of the Cattleman's Association. She'd timed her arrival so that she could make an entrance. The candidates should all have arrived. In a sea of black tuxedos, her brilliant blue dress would stand out without being tacky or showy. She was looking to be chosen as a wife, not a one-night stand, after all.

Get your own topside spiffed up. That's the way to get a man.

She hated that there was truth in her father's words. She had a black dress that showed her cleavage to perfection. It would have been the smart choice this evening, a way to short circuit a man's brain and skip ahead a few levels of intimacy. But she'd mentioned the black dress to Luke, just once, and he'd said it would probably kill him to see her in it. That was enough to make her not want other men to see it first.

Foolish.

The blue dress was elegant, a single column of cloth that fell from a collar around her neck, but its sex appeal was more subtle. Feeling desperate in the limousine, she'd carefully picked out the stitches in the long skirt's side seam, extending the slit from mid-thigh to upper thigh. She couldn't take chances. Tonight was the night.

Her entrance went brilliantly. The main entertainment area was on a flagstone terrace that had sweeping views of the sunset. Patricia passed through the house and paused on the steps that led down to the terrace. The pause had been no more than a few seconds, carefully timed to not be obvious. Carefully timed to let one man after another nudge each other and nod her way. Then she'd descended the stairs, the conservative dress revealing nearly the entirety of her leg—but only one leg, and only every other step.

By the time she reached the bottom, she didn't have to look for her three candidates. They'd already clustered around her.

She hadn't known Daddy Cargill would be in attendance, but when his white suit caught her eye, she had a moment of sweet revenge. *Yes, Father. It's me. Look how easy it is to catch a man.*

The moment was brief, because she heard Luke's voice in her head. *The revenge is poison. I don't want to lose you.*

She accepted a glass of champagne from an admiring candidate. He proposed a toast, and she laughed appropriately, doing her best to sparkle like the elegant, golden bubbles as she clicked her flute gently against one man's, then another's.

Then she looked directly into a pair of sailing blue eyes.

Luke Waterson turned his back on her and walked off the terrace, into the sunset.

Patricia hid in the bathroom.

She tugged on her dress, but the damage had been done. Because she'd snipped the first thread, the seam kept unraveling. The slit was so high, she was going to have to remove her underwear.

Then I really will be the kind of girl Daddy Cargill approves of.

Too late, she realized this hadn't been about Luke. It hadn't been about independence. It hadn't even been about revenge. It had been about Daddy, and trying to win his approval. Finally, after thirty-two years, she realized that he only approved of one type of woman, and she was not and never would be that type.

Her father would never love her.

The real tragedy was that Luke would never love her now, either. He'd witnessed her triumph, which had come at the cost of lowering herself to her father's standards.

She'd have time to regret this for years to come. She couldn't cry about it in her host's bathroom much longer. She pulled her compact from her purse and leaned forward to powder her nose in the mirror. The seam opened another notch higher.

There was a tap at the door. "Occupied," Patricia called, her voice sounding shockingly normal.

"Patricia? It's Diana. Quinn sent me to check on you."

Quinn. He was present as one of the owners of the Mac-Dowell's River Mack Ranch, of course. He was one of her least favorite people right now, because he must have brought Luke as a guest.

"I'm fine, Diana. Thank you. I'll be out in a minute."

Another tap. "Would you let me in?"

Patricia looked at herself in the mirror. She deserved this. She really did. Why not let Diana have her moment of triumph? Patricia had tried to marry her man, after all, and had been rather nasty about it.

She unlocked the door. Diana stuck her head in, all cheerful smiles. Immediately, her eye dropped to Patricia's dress. "Oh, I see the problem. Here, I've got a safety pin. It will be tricky but if you turn the dress a little, you know, like this, you can pin it from the inside and no one will see it. Do you want me to do it for you?"

"No, thank you."

Lord, how did Quinn stand so much sunshine?

In a flash, she realized Luke had been her sunshine, too. Patricia and Quinn needed that balance in their lives. They would have stifled one another in a perfectly proper marriage.

"Okay," Diana said, setting the safety pin down on the counter and stepping back. "Well, if you need anything else, just come find me."

She put an extra safety pin on the counter and turned to go.

"Diana? Is Luke looking for me?"

She wrinkled her nose in a way Patricia imagined Quinn found adorable. "Luke who?"

"Luke Waterson. Didn't he come with you and Quinn?"

"I don't know the name. Do you want me to ask around?"

"No. Please, no. It's nothing. Thank you again for the safety pins. And…I just wanted to say, I think you and Quinn make the perfect couple. He's very happy now that he has you."

Diana's smile was radiant. "Thanks. Pin your dress and come on out to the party."

* * *

Luke waited on the edge of the terrace, wearing a tuxedo but having nothing to celebrate. He placed one polished black boot on a planter. He idly repositioned his formal black Stetson on the table beside him. He'd kept his hat handy. He wouldn't be staying much longer. Patricia would find him soon.

He'd chosen a spot that was quiet and shadowed, appropriate for a private conversation. He would spare Patricia from a public humiliation, if he could, but that was the kindest thought he had for her right now.

Only a few hours ago, he'd still believed there was nothing he wouldn't do for her. He would offer his friendship. He would sit alone at a bar, holding vigil, just in case she needed him. But now he knew there was one thing he wouldn't do.

He would not watch her sacrifice herself to please her father.

She walked up to him, a vision of elegance and sensuality in one. His body tightened in response, but then again, so had every other man's, earlier tonight. She'd made sure of that. *I'm available,* she'd announced with every sultry step down the staircase. *Let the bidding begin.*

Nausea could kill desire, Luke now knew. Nausea at seeing such a worthy woman still trying to earn her father's approval. That's what it had come down to. Her father would never love her, but Patricia would never stop trying to earn affection he didn't have in him to give.

"Hello, Luke. You look so very handsome."

He wore black tie, of course. In Texas, however, the bow tie was often replaced by a Western bolo, something Luke felt more comfortable wearing. The silver slide on his string tie had been in his family for generations.

Patricia noticed it, with her eye for quality. She adjusted it for him, moving it an imaginary centimeter to the left. She was using it as an excuse to touch him, obviously, but whether she hoped to entice him or she just missed him, he didn't know.

He didn't care.

"Are you representing the James Hill tonight?" she asked.

"Yes."

He watched her dark eyes drop to the silver slider at his neck once more. She touched his family's crest. He could tell the moment she made the right guess.

"Do you own the James Hill?"

"One third."

"Do you still love me?"

That one was harder to answer. But he looked at her, so beautiful, so vulnerable, so stubborn, and he told the truth. "I imagine I always will in one way or another."

"But not enough to marry me and help me defeat this Cargill curse?"

Her question was the answer he'd been looking for tonight. It was not the answer he'd wanted to hear. Resigned, he picked up his formal black Stetson and set it on his head.

"Don't try to defeat poison by swallowing more poison. Good night, beautiful."

He didn't allow himself to touch her, and he didn't allow himself a backward glance. Sometimes, a man had to know when to walk away.

August was a helluva time to have a practice runthrough, but Texas Rescue ran on a strict schedule. Although they'd run a real, full operation in June, they still had to do their annual practice scenario every August.

It was scheduled for a Saturday, and it would be hot.

They'd pitch a third of the tents in the parking lot next to the new Texas Rescue headquarters building, and they'd run a few mock scenarios. All personnel were supposed to report to the admin tent to check in, verify their contact information and receive fake orders.

The physicians were routinely sent home immediately after verifying their information, so Luke was surprised when Quinn MacDowell called early on Saturday to ask for a ride. He was at the River Mack, next to the JHR. They were miles apart, but in ranching terms, he lived just around the corner.

Luke couldn't refuse to pick him up.

"I wasn't planning on attending," Luke said, as they pulled into the parking lot.

"She's no longer the personnel director."

"Ah." Luke told himself he was relieved.

"I'm heading to the hospital after this, so I don't need a return ride. Diana will pick me up."

Luke pulled his firefighter's uniform out of the back of his truck and headed for the admin tent. It took him one second to realize Quinn was a liar.

Patricia Cargill was checking in the personnel.

He had way too long to stare as she checked in each person ahead of him in line. She was beautiful. She always had been. In his memories, she was beautiful. But now, to see her again, he was bowled over by her beauty.

"Name, please."

She couldn't be serious. "Luke Waterson."

"You are assigned to engine thirty-seven."

"No kidding."

"And the director of Texas Rescue would like to see you in her office as soon as you're available. The fire crews are dismissed for the day, so I can walk you over now. Have you seen the new headquarters building?"

"I can't say that I have."

She stood and came around the table that served as her desk. "I'll show you where her office is."

"I'm sure that's not necessary."

"Please?"

It was the please that did him in.

Patricia thought she might faint, she was so nervous. Her plan was working so far, but the early stages had been all logistics. Now came the hard part.

Now she would try to win Luke Waterson back.

He was here, big and real, carrying his heavy helmet and overcoat, so close she could have reached out to touch him. He might have offered her his arm, if they were walking in the dark. They might have held hands, if they were dashing through a thunderstorm. But they were simply crossing a parking lot on a routine Saturday morning, and he was no longer her friend.

He'd said he'd always love her, though. She was counting on that.

The building was nearly empty. She led him down the air conditioned hall to the office of the director of all of Texas Rescue. There was a little outer office for the secretary, but it was empty on a Saturday morning.

"Wait here," Patricia told him. "Let me go tell the director you're here. You can set your uniform down on that chair."

She went into the inner office and shut the door. Her hands were shaking as she took a seat behind her new desk.

"Come in," she called.

Luke walked in and stopped short when he saw her sitting there, alone.

She waited.

"I don't get it," he said, in a voice so flat her heart sank.

"I'm the new director. Karen Weaver was fired, and I applied for her position. I beat out three other candidates."

Seconds ticked by. "Congratulations."

She leaned forward and clasped her shaking hands on the desk top. "It's a paying position. I'm drawing a salary."

"And this makes you happy?"

Patricia hoped Luke was just thick-headed. She prayed he hadn't changed his mind about all the things he'd told her on a rented sailboat in the month of June.

"It makes me happy, because I need to pay my bills. I walked away from the trust fund. It wasn't as easy as you made it sound. The law does want you to do something with your money, but I filed a formal declaration that I would not authorize any expenditures for the indefinite future. Any attempt by the bank to get me to do so is considered harassment."

He put his hands on his hips as he loomed over her desk, but otherwise, he gave no indication that he was anything but a giant hunk of a firefighter statue.

"Do you know what happens to the money? Nothing. It just sits there, earning interest indefinitely."

"Where does this leave your father?"

"He couldn't win a job like this if he tried. He doesn't want to work, anyway. I believe he's moved to Houston, to mooch off some cousins there. I really don't care. He's never loved me."

Luke stared down at her.

"But you did."

Luke did not confirm this in any way.

So much for Plan A. He was supposed to be so amazed by her new independence that he'd sweep her into his arms, tell her that he loved her, and then quite possibly have sex with her in her new office.

Patricia stood and took a set of papers from her drawer. She set them on the edge closest to Luke. Plan B.

"I really do have an issue to discuss with you." It was so easy to slip into her role as the boss. She needed to function on autopilot like this, because her heart was breaking with disappointment. "I must transfer you to the Dallas branch of Texas Rescue. As a paid employee of Texas Rescue, I can be sued for sexual harassment if I attempt to seduce any volunteer. If you'll kindly sign these transfer papers, your reassignment will take effect immediately."

She held out a pen. It trembled in her fingers, but there was nothing she could do about that. No way to hide it.

She looked into Luke's blue eyes. "After you sign, I can seduce you. I'm quite determined, and I've planned a very long campaign. I intend to remind you of all the reasons we should be together, and none of them has anything to do with money and everything to do with—"

She finished her sentence in a yelp as Luke lunged for the pen. He dashed his name across the bottom of the paper, and practically vaulted over the desk to sweep her into his arms. He held her like she was a bride being carried over a threshold.

She was crying and laughing, both at the same time, which made it very hard to kiss. "I love you, Luke Waterson, with all the passion I have. It's the kind that keeps a couple together, if you'll let me prove it to you." When she said the words, her laughter faded at their importance.

Luke took advantage of her more serious demeanor to kiss her properly. She loved every taste of him, but she finally broke off the kiss. She was the boss, and she was a Cargill, so she wanted to be sure everything was handled properly.

"I have a deal for you," she said. "You love me for the

rest of my life, and in return, I'll love you until the day I die." She held out her hand.

He had to set her down to shake her hand properly. "Mrs. Luke Waterson, you've got yourself a deal."

* * * * *

MILLS & BOON®

Want to get more from Mills & Boon?

Here's what's available to you if you join the exclusive **Mills & Boon eBook Club** today:

✦ *Convenience – choose your books each month*

✦ *Exclusive – receive your books a month before anywhere else*

✦ *Flexibility – change your subscription at any time*

✦ *Variety – gain access to eBook-only series*

✦ *Value – subscriptions from just £1.99 a month*

So visit **www.millsandboon.co.uk/esubs** today to be a part of this exclusive eBook Club!

MILLS & BOON®

The Little Shop of Hopes & Dreams

* cover in development

Much loved author Fiona Harper brings you the story of Nicole, a born organiser and true romantic, whose life is spent making the dream proposals of others come true. All is well until she is enlisted to plan the proposal of gorgeous photographer Alex Black—the same Alex Black with whom Nicole shared a New Year's kiss that she is unable to forget…

Get your copy today at
www.millsandboon.co.uk/dreams